# THE GREAT HEARTS II

*A Game of Gods*

## David Oliver

# CONTENTS

# RECAP

The Great Hearts follows the story of Calidan Darkheart, Imperator of the Empire, both as a kind hearted but scarred youth, struggling to achieve the strength required to exact revenge on a horrific monster that slaughtered his village, and as a fully-fledged Imperator, his innocence long since lost in the wake of difficult missions and horrible tasks.

Together with his best friend, Cassius, he fled the massacre of the village, injured a man who he would come to be friends with, and bonded with Seylantha, a gigantic black panther who was one of what was known as a Great Heart. Intelligent, powerful and seemingly capable of providing Calidan with enhanced abilities, meeting Seya changed Calidan's life forever.

Along with the Tracker, the man who had hunted them from the village only to be crippled by a great boar and soon became a firm friend, the group arrived at Forgoth, met with Major General Kyle who became their surrogate father and trained in the ancient art of Kaschan with Tyrgan, ex-bodyguard for the Emperor.

The Imperators are a secretive order within the Andurran Empire that answers only to the Emperor. Assassins, spies, warriors, leaders - Imperator training is brutal and unyielding with the survivors forged into efficient tools for their Emperor to wield. Whilst in Forgoth, Calidan and Cassius met

Simone and Merowyn, two such Imperators, during their hunt for a dangerous and seemingly unstable Imperator-in-training called Rya.

Injured during a climactic fight with Rya, Cassius and Calidan were treated by none other than the Emperor himself, a man of huge proportions and untold power, and they eagerly joined the ranks of the Imperator Academy. Together with Ella, Sophia, Scythe, Rikol and Damien, the rest of their dorm, they overcame any obstacles in their way and progressed into the second year where they left to investigate a location described in a journal that ancient librarian Korthan passed to Calidan.

Deep in an ancient cavern in the desert they met with Ash, an artificial intelligence who revealed the origins of the mysterious magic known as seraph, along with the knowledge that an ancient demonic lizard called a skyren resided within the cave before turning hostile and refusing to allow them to leave.

Alongside Merowyn, Simone, Kane and Sarrenai, all fully fledged Imperators in their own right, the group managed to defeat both Ash and the rampaging skyren, but not before losing one of their own.

Present day Calidan was heading far into the barren north with a very different Cassius, one who was far larger than the average human and defined by Calidan as being completely and utterly insane. Together they encountered a group of thyrkan, a strange race of lizard-like beings that had struck from the north in the past decade to crush everything they had encountered. The fight enraged Cassius to the extent that he couldn't suppress his demonic side anymore and he transformed into a skyren, slaughtering everything that stood in his path.

Attempting to stop the transformed Cassius from slaughtering human slaves, Calidan sprinted into a mine shaft and quickly learnt why running shouldn't be done in an unstable mine.

# IMPORTANT PEOPLE TO REMEMBER

**Calidan**   Protagonist, Imperator in training (Imp), cold hearted killer in present day.

**Cassius**   Calidan's best friend. Insane and gigantic in the present day. Imp.

**Ella**   Ex street rat from Forgoth, Cassius's partner, Imp.

**Sophia**   Talented archer from nomadic tribe, Imp.

**Scythe**   Skilled warrior from nomadic tribe of the desert plains, Imp.

**Rikol**   Ex street rat, Imp.

**Seya**   Seylantha, Great Heart (gigantic panther), bonded to Calidan.

**Emperor**   Larger than life, charismatic with hints of a darker soul.

**Rya**   Corrupted Imp who Calidan, Cassius and Ella fought and killed.

**Simone**   Imperator who began the hunt for Rya.

**Merowyn**   Imperator who began the hunt for Rya,

appears to have a bound creature fighting for control within her.

**Kane**          Primary instructor at the Academy for the Imps.

**Adronicus**     Weapon master at the Academy.

**Korthan**       Wizened historian at the Academy. Calidan's friend and boorish instructor.

**Charles**       Ancient enemy of mankind, revealed as having bonded with a demonic spirit. Master of shadow seraph and revels in using it to control others.

**ASH**           Artificial Intelligence discovered in the desert

**Tracker**       Meredothian hunter who was forced to join in the attack against Calidan's village. Trained the boys in woodcraft.

**Damien**        Imp. Killed by a robotic scorpion at the whim of ASH

**Kirok**         Ex-Imp. Forced himself on Sophia and was brutally broken by Calidan in retaliation. Removed by Academy staff and not seen again.

# PART I

*A Winter to Remember*

# PRESENT DAY

*Glowing red eyes,*
*Blood-soaked claws,*
*The shadow of a friend.*

It turned out that running into a mine whilst being chased by the large, scary, demonic version of your large, scary, insane friend was not a good plan. I had plenty of time to reflect on this and the error of my judgement as the tunnel floor collapsed beneath me. At least that's what I decided to tell anyone who cared to listen, if I made it out of this dark hellhole. In reality my reaction was much more of a base instinct. It involved more of a high-pitched scream followed by a loud thud and a lot of groaning. Again, not something I planned to tell my fanbase of one, Cassius, when he wasn't trying to eat me. I'll pretend that I athletically bounced from wall to wall before landing like the graceful and deadly Imperator that I was. It wouldn't even be that much of a lie. I certainly bounced.

With another groan I managed to find my feet. Thankfully I had had some common sense to imbue some of my limited seraph into myself before I hit the ground, limiting the damage the fall had done. Nothing as spectacular as the mighty entrance I had made into the mine whilst attacking the thyrkan - the scaled beasts that had conquered many of the northern territories, coming out of nowhere in the last decade to become a major threat to humanity's survival. Now though I kind of regretted that flashy entrance. It had seemed like a good idea at the time and really caught the thyrkans' attention, but I could really have done with some more seraph right about now.

That's the problem with the stuff. Seraph, magic, call it what you will, you never have enough of it and it takes a good while for your reserves to refill. I can totally see why the old civilisations of this world created the Great Hearts. A much larger pool of seraph to draw from? Count me in. And for a time I had been one of those lucky few but-

No Calidan. Stay on track. Survive first, reminisce later.

I patted down my body checking for broken bones, finding none but discovering a plethora of cuts and bruises in their place. Satisfied that I was, technically speaking at least, in 'one piece', I picked up my blades and inspected them in the pitch darkness of the mine. Most mere mortals would have struggled with this act, but my eyes see more clearly than most, peeling back the layers of darkness with ease. Thankfully the two swords, Asp and Forsaken, the most priceless items I owned, were as good as ever. Not chipped, scraped or damaged in any way. Even after having fought trolls, demons, countless thyrkan and no small number of people, the blades' ability to look brand new still amazed me.

Sheathing my weapons, I turned my gaze to the walls. Smooth, cut rock on the immediate walls around me turned to a seemingly extensive natural formation that disappeared into the gloom. A look up confirmed that the top of the pit was barely visible, and thankfully Cassius must have got stuck before falling into the pit with me. Hopefully he would forget for a time and allow me to figure a way out of this place and so with a heavy sigh I leant against the wall and considered my options. They were few.

*Could I climb out?* I gazed at my hands; I potentially had the strength to climb up...though bringing more of the mine down on myself was definitely a possibility. Plus, chances were that upon reaching the top I would be food for a certain demonic man-beast. Of all the ways that I had imagined myself dying - a frighteningly long list at this stage in my life - being eaten was probably my least favourite. Silly really, considering that my speciality was ending beasts that like the taste of human flesh.

*So, to climb or to explore?*

After a few more moments of lamenting my situation I wearily dusted myself off and strode into the cavern, reasoning that whatever I might find couldn't be worse than an angry Cassius.

Hopefully I wasn't wrong.

# CHAPTER 1

### *Decompression*

Five weeks and six days after departing the hole in the desert that had claimed our friend and close to four months since we had initially set out, we arrived back in Anderal and the Academy. Little seemed to have changed in our absence and yet it felt like a much smaller place. I had expected to feel happy at the return to the Academy, eager to return to the relative safety of its walls, but memories of Damien haunted our every step as we trudged down the cobbled paths we knew so well.

Still covered with the dust of our travels Kane, Merowyn and Simone led the way to a small complex of buildings that had so far stood closed to us Imps. Inside were baths, steam rooms, a fully equipped gymnasium complete with a multitude of punch bags as well as a number of rooms that appeared to hold nothing but fresh plants and gentle incense.

"What is this place?" Ella asked as we walked up to the door. Simone and Merowyn had already gone inside without a word to the rest of us.

Kane started, as though he hadn't even considered that we didn't know where we were. "Apologies young ones," he said gruffly, "I forgot that you hadn't been in here before. This is known by Imperators as the Decompression Chambers."

He raised an eye at our confused expressions and let out a sigh. "Missions are hard. Some in different ways. We've had small attempts at talking about what happened in the desert during the return trip but it is really only when you get, for want of a better word, *home,* that you find that your mind begins to really wander. And believe me, it can take you down some strange and dangerous paths."

I eyed Rikol as Kane spoke. The loss of Damien had hit us all hard but Rikol by far the hardest. The usually talkative troublemaker had barely said a word during the entire trip back.

"This place is designed to be whatever you need it to be. A place to relax, a place to let out your rage and hate or a place to meditate and come to terms with events. There are bed chambers further down and clothes and food will be provided whenever needed. We will all be here for a week at the minimum. Do what you need to do and use this time however you choose." He turned to go before stopping and swivelling back around. "A word of advice. Don't ignore your emotions. Imperators become desensitised to a great many things over time, but that is not necessarily a good thing. Bottling everything up is not a wise approach and may make things worse down the line. Help each other, and find me if you want to talk or just to have an ear to listen." With a final nod to us all he walked inside and left us to our own ends.

On the second day of our stay in the decompression chambers I found Rikol hammering at the punch bags like a man possessed. There was no attempt at technique, just hurting himself and the bag for the sheer sake of it. Rikol's attitude had changed the most since Damien's death. Once his sarcastic nature had been underlined with good humour and his quick wit had ensured that everyone laughed. Now he brooded alone, his wit fashioning itself into barbed comments. The journey back across the sands had earned a stinging lash from his tongue for almost everyone in the party, with the only one he had held back for being Merowyn, perhaps in acknowledgement of her actions regarding Damien. Simone, Kane and Merowyn had said nothing about the changes in his personality and just suggested to give him some space to grieve.

Personally, I believed a month was enough.

"Hey Rikol," I said stepping into the room. "Want some company?"

He ignored me and punched the bag harder, the skin on his knuckles bloody and torn.

I took another step. "Rikol?"

He paused with his shoulders hunched and eyes on the bag. "Leave me alone Cal."

"Want to talk?" I asked with another step.

"Take another step and the bag won't be the one getting hit," he snarled, eyes wild. "Leave. Me. Alone."

I did what he asked.

The others of the dorm spent a lot of their time together, making use of the gyms and baths in a much less destructive way than Rikol. I knew that they, like me, were hurting in the wake of Damien's death, but the pain was becoming less intense. We had all extended olive branches to Rikol whenever and wherever we could but his replies ranged from mild civility to pure hostility. We could only continue to be there for him and to offer our support whenever he required it.

On the fifth day of our stay I found him in one of the meditation rooms, his gaze staring at nothing at all. Slipping inside I sat down against the far wall without a word, content to wait next to my silent friend. He acknowledged my presence with a slight tip of his head, but returned to contemplating whatever his thoughts were revolving around. After nearly an hour I began to stand, ready to go and join the others for the evening meal.

"Did we succeed Calidan?"

Inwardly startled it took me a second to reply. "What do you mean?"

"Did we succeed in our mission in the desert? Was it worth our time and effort? Was it worth Damien's death?"

"I don't think anything was worth Damien's death, Rikol" I replied.

"Then what was the point of it all?" he exclaimed angrily. "What was the point in him dying?"

I thought for a minute before responding. "I might not have thought Damien's death worthwhile Rikol, but that is because I am a selfish bastard like you," my slight smirk softening the words. "For someone like Damien or Cassius do you think that they believe it wasn't worth it? Finding buildings from before the Cataclysm, recovering information about seraph, skyren and Great Hearts from a person that wasn't real in the same way as you and I are and confirming the existence of and removing a threat to the surrounding tribes of the desert - a feral skyren. They would think that their mission made the world a better place. And they would probably be right."

In truth they were wrong. It was some time until I realised it, but these days my opinion is that we made the world much, much worse.

Rikol was silent for a few minutes. When he finally spoke it was barely above a whisper.

"He didn't deserve to die."

I stayed quiet, recognising that Rikol was more talking to himself than to me.

"Out of all of us, Damien should have lived," Rikol continued after a moment. "He was a better person than most, kind, considerate and above all else, my friend."

I pulled out the hip flask of whisky that I had purchased in Abador with Kane's expert advice on the subject and opened it.

"To Damien," I said, taking a swig before passing it to Rikol who accepted it slowly.

"To Damien," he echoed before taking a drink. Together we shared the hip flask, savouring the golden, peaty taste before finally, when empty, I clapped a hand on his shoulder and stood up, leaving to join the others for food.

To my surprise and delight, Rikol followed.

I would like to say that we were all fine after that, that everything went back to the way it was before. Unfortunately that was not the case. We were all different and all faced the difficulties of our mission in differing ways and on the whole we came through it relatively unscathed. As far as personalities went however Rikol never fully returned to the fun-loving trickster he once was. At times echoes of that version of him shone through but inevitably the clouds would draw in once again. Looking back, he was perhaps the first of us to truly start to embody the personality of an Imperator.

Seya visited every day. The decompression chambers were secluded away in a corner of the Academy compound, away from the training grounds, dorms and cafeteria, and were not remotely designed to accommodate a giant panther but nevertheless she was there, making sure to torment us all with a raspy tongue, each day getting more bold with her antics.

She caught me unprepared the first day, a pounce from the top of the building as I stepped outside to get some fresh air sending me tumbling to the floor in a bundle of fur and to the mercy of a thorough licking. The second day she caught Sophia and Ella as they went for a morning jog, stalking them through the compound whilst avoiding the eyes of the many Imps and Imperators around the area, laughing uproariously in my mind as she closed the distance before bounding over their heads and causing them both to scream in shock. On the third day I thought we had made it, as there were no reported attacks from any of the dorm, only to find her sitting in the bed chambers when we retreated for the night, her gigantic form somehow having managed to squeeze in through the ground floor window and cementing in my mind that cats were fluid.

The fourth day I opened the door to Rikol's preferred meditation chamber to find Seya sitting wrapped around him, his hand softly stroking her fur. She acknowledged me with a flick of her ear and spoke softly in my mind.

*Nothing fixes hurt like time. Leave him for today.*
"Are you sure?"
A swish of her tail. *Of course I'm sure. You're a long way from being the first humans I've helped in this manner. And you know what I have learnt time and time again over the course of history?*
"What?"
*That worshipping me with your hands helps you heal. As is only right of course.* Her voice trembled with a note of pride. *Nothing has fur as luscious as mine.*
Smirking, I softly shut the door and left them to it.
The fifth day the sniggering from Seya and muted shouts for help from the gym led me to find Scythe pinned under a paw the size of his torso. His every attempt to slip out of the clutches of the panther easily countered by adept use of her prodigious strength and sandpaper tongue. When I finally stopped laughing long enough to get him out from under her his face had a raw look like it had been freshly scrubbed.
Ella came to me on the sixth day with the idea that we turn the tables and show our feline overlord who was really the boss. Unfortunately whilst we were outside attempting to track her for a surprise attack of our own, she was inside the complex happily having an impromptu wrestling match with Cassius. By the time we arrived to help Seya had vanished, her giggles and a dazed Cassius the only evidence that she had ever been there.
On the seventh day of our stay we were summoned to the senior council chambers to discuss the expedition and debrief. I walked cautiously, expecting an attack from an indomitable feline at any moment, but made it to the chambers without incident. To our surprise upon opening the oak panelled doors to the chamber, the Emperor himself reclined behind one of the desks, dwarfing the chair upon which he sat.
As we filed in I noticed that the chamber was filled with roughly twenty Imperators - more than I had ever seen in one place. Most of the attendees were completely unknown to myself, and from the looks on my companions' faces, to them

as well, though I did notice with delight an aged Korthan half asleep on a desk.

Once we were in the room and the doors had shut with a resounding boom, a warm voice drifted musically through the air, "Thank you everyone for coming. This chamber is now sealed, nothing of what is spoken of is permitted to leave this room. Let the session begin."

The speaker was a tall, thin woman of perhaps fifty years, dressed in a long black Imperator coat, with long black hair, sharp green eyes and a long scar that extended from her ear to throat. The woman caught my gaze and smiled, "To those of you who don't know me I am Imperator Wyckan, or if you prefer my full title, High Imperator Wyckan."

High Imperator, the highest position in the Imperator circle and responsible for running the Academy. Imps rarely, if ever, saw the High Imperator until graduation. My mouth felt suddenly dry. In this chamber were the two most important people in the entire Empire.

"And for anyone who hasn't met him, seated to my right is the ruler of the Empire," she winked at our group, "so no pressure."

At this the Emperor guffawed and slapped a hand on the table, causing it to tremble ominously, whilst chuckling deeply.

"Ignore Acana, my young Imps, she just seeks to have some fun at your expense! We have already had a report from Kane and Merowyn and just wanted to hear from your own lips everything that happened so as to better understand the whole situation. Does that help?"

Everyone nodded in the group. Scythe, Sophia and Rikol looked awestruck at the prospect of being spoken to by the godlike figure before them. Having been in the Emperor's presence before, Cassius, Ella and myself felt a little more at ease.

"Excellent!" the Emperor retorted, slapping the table again. "So let's begin. Calidan, can you recount the entire trip as best as you can, from the beginning please."

Scythe, Sophia and Rikol turned to me, amazement in their eyes that the Emperor knew my name. Stepping forward I opened my mouth.

And thus began one of the longest evenings of my life.

Recounting my version of the expedition took a good hour, interrupted on several occasions by the Emperor and High Imperator to clarify a few points. Once I was done Ella and Cassius were then called forward by the Emperor to do the same thing and once again earning them jealous glares from the other three at the Emperor knowing their names. Eventually everyone had come forward and told their version of events. Thankfully after Cassius's rendition the Emperor had deemed it acceptable to start the recounting at the point of entry to the rift and thus saving a good chunk of time. Even so, it took at least three hours before Scythe, as the last, finally finished his story.

"Thank you all for bearing with us and for your actions whilst on this expedition," said High Imperator Wyckan, her smile warm. "I'm sure that you are all hungry and thirsty. Food and drink have been set aside in the adjoining room, please relax and refresh yourselves whilst the Emperor, Imperators and I converse."

Just like that we were sent from the room, unable to listen in to the facts and truths as they were disassembled and interrogated piece by piece. In hindsight this was not surprising; Imperators are by nature close mouthed and generally unwilling to reveal secrets even to those who uncovered them. I tried to use my senses to listen in on the conversation but the room was, as High Imperator Wyckan had stated, completely sealed - whether magically or just through brilliant engineering I wasn't sure, but either way we were out of the loop.

After an interminable length of time the door opened and the massive frame of the Emperor squeezed through, followed by the comparatively diminutive form of the High Imperator, who, at nearing six foot tall was not a small woman. The Emperor just seemed to soak up the space around him, overshadowing anyone nearby both physically, with his more than imposing stature, and subconsciously. One's eyes could not stay away from the man, finding them irrevocably drawn towards him to the extent that it almost physically hurt to try to move your gaze away. Together they entered the room and shut the door behind. The Emperor walked along to the food trestle and seized an apple, crunching into it joyously as he walked to a free chair at the end of the room.

"Mmmmm, you always know how to put on a good spread Acana," he said, winking at the blushing woman. His eyes turned to include us. "And your Academy certainly knows how to make good recruits. Excellent work out there everyone, I know the mission was hard and that you lost a good friend," Rikol's eyes gleamed wetly at this, "but you have achieved much and for that I am proud to know you. You've done the Empire a great service."

His beaming smile brought out a joyous response in all of us. Even the High Imperator broke out into a hearty grin and clapped as the giant of an Emperor showed us the full might of his charismatic smile. A more cynical mind might imagine that there was some odd trick at play to ensure a response such as this but to us in that room, the Emperor's pleasure at our achievement was an almost orgasmic feeling.

Once our celebratory antics had subsided the Emperor spoke more seriously. "Down to some important matters. As you know, one of the reasons that your dorm was allowed to go on this expedition was not just because of Calidan and old Korthan's incessant badgering of my Imperator staff, but because we deemed it could be an early assessment of your prowess."

Nods all round.

"Acana and I have been thoroughly briefed by the Imperators who went with you on your performance, involving aspects such as your ability to cope under pressure, leadership, adaptability and actions becoming of an Imperator - and I have to say, we were both very impressed with what we heard."

More smiles and nods.

"Furthermore all three Imperators highlighted your dorm's

skills and suggested that you were all performing at an above average level for second year Imps - both in areas of problem solving and fighting prowess. Defeating both an armoured scorpion and a fully-fledged skyren highlight this. Consequently the High Imperator and I have thus decided that you are ready to take the fourth-year test."

The fourth-year test. Much was unknown about this as it varied from year to year, and many of the fourth-year students did not want to or couldn't talk about it. Indeed it was only through our close relationship with the fourth-year students developed through our evening fighting practice that we knew such a test existed. So far our testing had been relatively minimal - if extreme physical and mental tests were deemed minimal. But this was suggested to be something completely different.

The Emperor carried on. "The fourth-year test is a major barrier to development in the Academy. The first three years are seen much as ensuring our new Imps are somewhat capable. The fourth year and above is where you learn to become Imperators. As such, think of the test as an entrance exam to the real Academy. It is designed to be physically and mentally tough, obviously. More than that however, it is designed to expose Imps to harsh environments and perilous situations. Believe me when I say that each year some Imps do not return from the test. It is dangerous, demanding and will require each of you to perform at your best for an extended period of time. Survive and you will return as fourth years and the secrets of the Academy will be that much more open to you." The Emperor nodded to the High Imperator who stepped forward.

"The test will take place in three months. You have this time to prepare yourselves as you see fit. The only advice that I will give you is to practice your survival skills - in any and all conditions. That is all." She motioned for us to leave. "Head back now, the Emperor and I have some more things to discuss, and remember - nothing we have spoken about is to leave this room and that includes your expedition."

Slowly we filed out of the room, minds afire with the information that the Emperor had revealed. The fact that they deemed everyone in the dorm able enough to skip a year of Academy training was high praise indeed. However the lack of information surrounding the forthcoming test certainly made it seem daunting. As we walked back to the decompression chambers for our final night I resolved to speak to my flaming haired muse Rinoa and the other fourth years as soon as possible. The others quickly went their separate ways, taking advantage of whatever method of coping they thought best for the last night of our stay and I headed to the steam rooms to ruminate on the findings of the day. I sat there alone in the swirling mist, completely lost in thought and oblivious to the outside world. At one point I thought I heard the door open and shut, but as no one came in I assumed that they had decided against joining. Closing my eyes I took a deep breath and forced my muscles to relax.

*Tough day?* Seya asked, her voice sliding its way into my mind.

"*Long and difficult,*" I replied, "*but with some interesting outcomes. They reckon we are ready for the fourth-year exam.*"

*The one that is meant to be life or death and that no-one talks about?*

"*The very same.*"

She scoffed. *With me by your side there will be nothing we can't overcome.*

I grinned, of course she was right, Seya and I could handle anything that the Academy could throw at us.

*Though if it is a test then you will really need to work on your awareness,* Seya said with an amused purr.

"*What do you mean?*"

*That just because you thought the day was over, doesn't mean I did.*

My eyes shot open but met nothing but swirling steam.

"S... Seya?" I murmured, casting my awareness as acutely as I possibly could but she had clamped down on the bond, reducing me to my own tools.

A low growl thrummed through the room, the force of it causing the steam to scatter.

"Now Seya, let's talk about this," I pleaded, walking in what I hoped was the direction of the door.

*You got off too lightly the first time Calidan. The others all had their just desserts. You will too.*

Slowly the steam parted and the majestic face of my Great Heart emerged, her orange eyes glistening with amusement. She licked her massive canines with a long raspy tongue.

*Time for your bath.*

# CHAPTER 2

## *Worries*

"T he fourth-year test?" puzzled Rinoa. "You know we aren't allowed to speak of it, Calidan. So stop asking."

I sighed. This was the third attempt I had made to prise some information out of Rinoa during the evening sparring sessions, so far to no avail. It turned out that successful fourth year students and above were banned from explaining anything about the test, a vow that they took very seriously indeed. I deflected a slash to my torso and raised instantly upward into standing guard to block an incoming overhead blow, Rinoa's sabre sliding off my own curved blade. As I made to riposte at her sword hand I spoke,

"So there is nothing that you can tell me about the test? No hints or tips?"

Rinoa swept away my blade and her left hand darted forward to catch my wrist. A quick twist and I landed heavily on the floor, her sword at my throat.

"You're not good enough to not be concentrating on fighting me Calidan," she said, a glorious smile softening the (truthful) blow of her words, "and I suspect that this will continue to be the case unless I answer what I can...then perhaps I can have a real challenge."

She extended her hand and pulled me up from the mud. The weather had been distinctly unseasonal, a far cry from the cloudless desert skies that I had been experiencing up until lately, with almost constant rain for the past week. As I brushed off what mud I could - I already looked like a man made of clay - Rinoa spoke softly.

"The reason that no one can tell you about the test is that it changes completely each year. And when I mean completely, I don't just mean a slight change of location. Rumour has it that one year's test was a two-month survival challenge in the frozen wastes of the north, whilst another was to infiltrate a large-scale smuggling operation. It seems entirely up to whoever organises the test." She smiled sadly. "Aside from the ban on talking about our tests the other reason most people will not talk about it is because they will have lost friends...I know that you know how that feels, with Damien not being here, and most do not want to relive that." She paused, as if weighing her choice of words carefully. "What I will say is this, the test is an individual assessment, each of you will be out there on your own. Even if you meet up and work together one of you could theoretically pass and the other fail, so make sure that you do your best at all times because, rest assured, someone will be watching. Be prepared for anything, your greatest threat could range from weather and animals to bandits or slavers to even something as simple as disease. Without knowing what you are going into I recommend what everyone recommends - ensure you know how to survive with nothing but your own hands."

I felt inwardly confident at this. Months of living on the mountain, surviving with only Seya, the Tracker and Cassius for company, had better prepared us for survival-based exercises than any amount of Academy training. My confidence must have shown on my face because Rinoa frowned and spoke again, "The only other thing I would say is that if the test is down to whichever Imperator is setting it then I would assume that the Imperator knows everything about you. In that case expect that the test will not play to your strengths, but to your weaknesses." Again her eyes clouded, as though remembering something distant and painful. I nodded and thanked her profusely.

"No need for thanks," she replied as she threw me my sword, "just fight better!"

Whilst I would like to say that concentrating on the fight made me thoroughly and comprehensively victorious I cannot. Now a fifth year, Rinoa's skill with her blade made mine look positively shabby in comparison. Cassius, as usual, was the only one among the dorm who could remotely match the higher-level students. Cassius aside, the rest of us were good, but we were not yet near the weapon mastery professed by a fully-fledged Imperator. So it was that a relatively bruised and muddy group trudged back to the dorm whilst I parted ways, going to check in on Seya who had been very excited to see me on the night of my return from overseas. My cheek still felt raw from the licking I received. I spent the night pondering Rinoa's words whilst curled up in Seya's paws and wondered who would set the test, and how it would change if the Imperator knew that I was bonded to a Great Heart.

The reality was something I could never have envisioned.

* * *

Seven weeks. For seven weeks Cassius and I put the rest of the dorm through rigorous survival practice, gaining leave from Kane for several multiple day trips. Sophia and Scythe already had a fair knowledge of survival training, having grown up in a tribal environment, however they had always had tools with them and the suggestion was that tools would not be an option. As a consequence we practiced making basic shelters, fires and - by drawing on the Tracker's training whilst on the mountain - weapons. Ella and Rikol struggled with some of these elements. Whilst we had all received some level of survival training during our time at the Academy, neither Ella or Rikol seemed to have an affinity for the subject, struggling to light fires or make traps. This was purely a matter of experience and so on several occasions we forced the two to be responsible for lighting the fire and catching the morning breakfast. The displeasure of having their comrades go hungry soon made fire starting second nature, although often accompanied by a hefty dose of grumbling.

One area in which everyone excelled was hunting. Training with Seya had massively increased our understanding of the natural world. Even Rikol and Ella, city slickers through and through, moved as one with their environment, relatively easily being able to sneak up on unsuspecting prey. This led to Rikol questioning my decision to force him to practice trap making, complaining that if he was hunting then why did he need traps? It took some considerable time before he was convinced that having back up snares for small game was a useful endeavour. It was hard to simulate just how difficult it could be to catch food, especially in an area with a dearth of prey, as the forest surrounding the Academy was teeming with abundant life. Granted, there were probably a few less deer now that Seya was in residence, but I had no doubt that if survival was to be involved in the test then it would be in an area very dissimilar to the Academy surrounds.

When we weren't outside the Academy practicing our survival skills we were inside fighting each other and the now fifth years at every available opportunity. As usual they often put us to shame, all except Cassius, but we were all skilled enough to more than hold our own in a real fight - if that is what the test held in store - and by this point had more than proved it. To my mind it was doubtful that fighting would be a core component of the test as we had theoretically already shown our skills in this area...but who knew?

The answer to that is no one. I spent every moment of spare time racking my brain trying to predict what might happen so that we could better prepare for it, and in the process drove everyone to distraction.

"Relax Calidan!" said Cassius for the fiftieth time as we played chess late into the evening. "You're too wound up, it's easy to see."

"Yeah, I know," I replied, sighing. "I can't help thinking about it. Is it that obvious?"

Cassius reached across the board and deftly knocked away my queen with a bishop. "Usually you wouldn't let me take anywhere near this many pieces. So yes, I would say that it is obvious. Breathe Calidan - the test will happen and you can't change it. Each of us will face what we have to, and what's more each of us will overcome it. Worrying is only going to cloud your judgement. Make you easier to predict." He grinned as I moved my knight to counter his bishop, falling into his trap and allowing his own knight to move to check my king. "See?"

I sighed and tried to relax. "You're right. I need to stress less. Thanks Cassius."

He winked at me as he watched my hands move across the board. Inwardly I smiled in amusement as his face opened in surprise when my trap was sprung. I always did like chess.

Smiling I got up, clapped Cassius on the shoulder and grabbed my coat.

"Going out?" asked Cassius absentmindedly, still trying to decipher how I had so completely rebutted his attack.

"Yeah," I replied, "not tired, so I think I will go and see if Seya is awake, if not her then Korthan. Don't wait up."

"Fair enough, see you later," he grunted and I sidled out the door.

I made my way to Seya's abode but it was empty, the entrance into the woods open. I tried contacting her but got no response, which wasn't unusual, especially if she was out hunting. With a shrug I set off to see if Korthan was around.

I had been making trips to see Korthan pretty regularly on my return from the expedition. We had had many long chats into the early hours of the morning as he avidly digested everything I had to say about the journey. I had no doubt that soon enough there would be a fresh treatise written on the subjects of skyren, seraphim and ASH. Furthermore I felt protective towards the old man, he was a friend and an enjoyably foul-mouthed rascal towards practically everyone in the Academy - no one, aside from the Emperor, was beyond the scathing wit of his tongue.

Feeling cheerful I wandered into the torch lit corridor, some-what excited at the prospect of drinking whiskey whilst learning what fresh piece of history Korthan had managed to dig up since I saw him last. I reached his door and knocked.

"Korthan?" I called. "Korthan, you awake?" No response.

"Korthan?" Still nothing. *Sleeping,* I surmised. But just to be sure I quested out with my senses, my ears twitching at a drip-ping sound. *What was that?* Korthan would skin someone alive if they spilt a drink in his library. The droplets seemed to be falling a long way however before hitting the floor.

Perturbed, I tried the door and finding it unlocked I stepped through into a dark room.

"Korthan?"

I stepped around a bookcase and stopped dead. Knees buck-ling and gorge rising I shut my eyes - willing my enhanced vi-sion to be wrong. But when I opened them again the scene was the same.

Hanging from the ceiling, bleeding from multiple wounds and face frozen in a grimace of agony was my old friend and men-tor. I didn't need my senses to know immediately; Korthan was dead.

As my soul cried out in despair I rose unsteadily and made to move to cut down my friend, to remove him from this depraved scene. As I tottered forward, teetering like a blind drunk, I slowly became aware of a presence behind me. Before I could move the room seemed to flash.

And everything went black.

# CHAPTER 3

## *Horrors*

*Drip*
*Drip, sway*
*Drip, sway, drip*

I awoke groggily with my head spinning and eyes feeling like they were weighted down, aware only of a constant dripping noise and the fact that I was swaying in a cool breeze.

Bit by agonising bit my mental faculties came back online. *Korthan dead. Light then darkness. Attacked?* I realised that I couldn't move my arms or legs, so that was likely. As my eyes finally opened I understood two things: firstly, why I was so groggy and secondly, that I was in deep shit.

I was hanging upside down, swaying gently, hands bound behind my back by what felt to be thick metal chains. I ventured a quick look up at my feet, *yep still there,* bound in thick steel chain and hanging through a loop in the chain on a big metal hook. A single torch fluttered near my head, casting a circle of light around me and leaving the rest of the room in darkness. The effort of raising my head elicited a groan and something out of the corner of my eye moved in response. The blurry, black shape soon emerged as a dark, shadowy figure that strode towards me, hooded and cloaked and wielding a disconcertingly bloody knife in hand.

"Greetings Calidan. I see that you are awake. Good."

My tongue felt thick and unmalleable in my dry mouth as I tried to talk. "Whe...where am I? What's going on?"

"Sssshh, don't worry yourself over it. I'll get to you in good time. Just stay here and relax. I'll be back shortly." With that the figure slowly retreated, gliding back into the surrounding darkness.

"Wait, who are you? Why did you kill Korthan?" I yelled, rage filling me anew.

The figure didn't respond and simply walked away.

A blinding pain erupted in my side, shocking me from unconsciousness. Gasping, I flinched away from the source of the pain - the figure was back, standing with the now bloodier knife in hand. He, for I assumed it was a man from the sound of voice, had slashed a shallow cut along the ribs on my left side. Far from a mortal wound but certainly enough to send agonised pain responses to my brain.

"Awake again Calidan? I thought I might have lost you there, leaving people upside down tends to be bad for their health."

"Fuck you!" I spat, wanting nothing more than to choke the life out of Korthan's killer.

"Dear, dear Calidan. Where are your manners? Something you will have to learn is-" I gasped as the blade bit again into my flesh, slowly scoring down my leg, "to respect the man with the knife." Fresh blood dripped down my chest, pooling slightly at my neck before sliding further so that my vision soon turned red.

"Why?" I asked again, after spitting out my own blood.

"Why what?"

"Why kill Korthan?" I yelled, "he was no threat, he was just an old man!"

"Calidan, you seem to think that I need to have a reason to do this. Perhaps I just like killing and the thought of torturing a sweet old Imperator to death is like ambrosia to me. Did you think of that? Indeed, Calidan. Have you stopped to think at all?"

My brain froze.

"Ah, I see that you're finally cottoning on. Yes, I killed Korthan because he meant nothing to me, you were the one I was after Calidan. The boy with the big, smart brain, the Great Heart bonded. The boy who will tell me everything about the Empire and the Academy that he knows because he is a child, and I know how to make a child talk. Just ask your friends."

A chill went through my spine. "My friends?"

A hand reached down to my face, "See for yourself," and spun.

As I slowly rotated around my screams grew ever louder. Hanging, one by one, were the other members of my dorm. Sophia, Scythe and Rikol were upside down, hundreds of lacerated cuts along their naked bodies, pools of dried blood under their feet. One look at them and I knew that they were dead. Ella and Cassius were hanging upright, tightly bound. Both their faces were heavily bruised and their torsos, arms and feet bore similar wounds to the others. My heart felt split in two, my comrades, my brothers and sisters in arms were dead or dying. I felt so impotent. Who was this man? How had he known about the Academy and moreover how could he get in and remove us without anyone knowing? I had to know. I had to know everything about him so that when I got free, and I would, I would be able to track him to the ends of the earth for what he has done.

And make him pay.

The masked figure laughed as I screamed. "Yes, scream Calidan, scream as loud as you like. No one will hear you here. Scream for what you have lost, your innocence, your friends, scream for your dreams of vengeance, of taking from me what I have taken from you. Let despair fill your heart! I'm going to peel apart your friends in front you, and you're going to watch. You're going to watch them die Calidan and there is nothing you can do about it." The masked man paused. "I could be persuaded to grant them a quick death though, they'll certainly be asking for one by the end. Would you grant them that Calidan? Would you grant them that small mercy? A quick death in return for a small amount of information - sounds easy doesn't it!"

My hate must have shone in my eyes because the man laughed out loud again. "Now, now, don't be hasty in your decision Calidan, you can't take it back once you've decided. Why not watch me whilst I play first?" With that he drew a wickedly curved blade and walked towards Ella, heedless of my screams, my fury, my tears.

For hours he tortured her. Every scream, every beg for mercy like a knife thrust in my heart. Cassius howled, throwing himself against his bonds but to no avail. His eyes became dull as he found a hole inside himself from which to hide from his inability to protect the one he loved. The screams had become an endless cacophony of hateful sound and it was a few minutes before I realised that they had stopped. Just Ella, unconscious and bleeding, and Cassius watching the tormentor with dull eyes.

"So Calidan, were you watching?"

My mind was numb. Blank. A huff and a slap across the face.

"That's it Calidan, no going into shock for you. I need you with me now. Here." A sharp pain flashed across my chest and I arched in agony, screaming. He flicked something at my face, wet from blood. "The more you don't concentrate the more you and they will hurt, Calidan, so please do perk up." He stopped my spinning and pointed over at Ella. "Are you going to spare her from this Calidan? Are you going to tell me what I want to know?"

"What do you want to know?" I bellowed. "You haven't even told me?"

"Everything Calidan, I want to know everything. Everything about life in the Academy, your training, what you do, how you live. But first things first, why not tell me about your little expedition to the desert? What did you find?"

How did he know? That expedition was a secret, no one on board the ship or hired from the city knew that we were

Imperators, just a well-funded expedition group. So how on earth did he know? The memory of the High Imperator ordering all information related to the expedition to be kept silent, and not to leave the room resounded in my brain. Did that mean that this tortuous individual was also an Imperator, had he been in that very room with us? But if that was the case why would he need to know about the Academy? It made no sense! Either way I knew that I couldn't speak, couldn't reveal anything about the Academy. Silence was drilled into us - reinforced again and again over the first few years of training to not mention anything related to being an Imperator or the Academy itself. It was, after all, one of the Empire's most closely guarded secrets.

And so I chose to hold my silence.

Each noise, each gasp, scream, sob that stemmed from that decision cut through me. And remain with me to this day. Of the many terrible and shitty days that have followed that remains the worst.

And believe me, there have been a lot of bad days.

Cassius looked at me, his eyes heart wrenching. Asking me to end it. The rag in his mouth stopped him from speaking, and he had long ago gone hoarse from guttural, bestial screaming. Aside from the bruising and cuts that he had received before I awoke Cassius had not yet been touched, as though the torturer knew that whilst I loved Ella dearly, Cassius was my brother. I had no doubt that in that deep, twisted mind of whoever it was inflicting this pain on us, Ella was the starter and Cassius was the main course.

But still I held my silence and still the screams continued. I berated, I yelled, bellowed, cried and swore at this remorseless creature, but still I kept the Empire's secrets.

"You're doing well Calidan, I have to say that you are lasting much longer than I expected. Do your friends know how little they mean to you deep inside your heart?"

Hateful, ignorant words. Words designed just to hurt. My friends meant everything to me.

"If they knew Calidan, they would abandon you. They would walk away, just like everyone else. And rightly so, because look how easily you abandon them! Leaving them to this world of pain and suffering."

*Shut up! Shut up! Shut up!*

"I would help you if you would let me Calidan. I would end this pain. Just talk to me."

*Liar. Filth. Tyrant. Tormentor.*

"Calidan." Strange, the fiend's voice sounded softer.

"Calidan please." More feminine?

"Calidan, please, do what he says. I can't take it anymore!" My eyes snap open, Ella was watching me through hooded eyes. Tears had created rivulets down her cheeks, washing a gully through the blood and grime that swamped her once beautiful face. Her eyes were piercing, a rare moment of cognition in this hateful world.

"Please Calidan. Tell him something, anything!" Ella screams.

I close my eyes and wall up my heart. None of us are getting out of here alive.

A sigh.

"I can see that this isn't working for you Calidan. It isn't enough to get you to talk. Admirable, but wasted."

A noise of a blade biting through flesh. A gurgle. I opened my eyes. Cassius was wide eyed watching as Ella's lifeblood spilled out onto the stone floor. With a swift blow the fiend had ended her life, cutting smoothly through her jugular. Her eyes held mine, filled with betrayal; as well they should be for I had abandoned her in her hour of need.

A final gurgle and silence. Nothing but fresh blood dripping onto the floor to add to the orchestra in this room of death. Cassius didn't move, his heart was gone, broken. Only when he too went under the knife did he react, screaming through his cloth filled mouth. Each noise, just like before, sent shocks right through me.

"Stop it!" I whispered.

"Sorry, what was that Calidan, you have to speak up!"

"STOP IT!" I roared, fury blazing in my soul. Struggling against my bonds yet again but still to no avail.

"Why should I stop it Calidan? Are you going to talk?"

*Should I talk? Is it worth talking about the Empire, the Academy, even if all it grants is a faster death? What if he is lying? What if I talk and all that happens is that the torture continues?*

My brain was at a stalemate so I did the only logical thing that I could do as the fiend's masked face drew near.

I spit in his eye.

In retrospect that wasn't the wisest decision. It did, however, prevent the personification of evil from turning his attention to Cassius again for some time. The strangest thing was that as I had done it, I could have sworn that there was something akin to compassion in that eye, just before my beautifully aimed glob of bloody saliva detonated like a miniature explosion of justice.

Small things.

Compassion or no I still ended up being tortured. With each new injury the monster asked me a question, the same as before, the same as he had asked whilst he tortured Ella. I found that the threat and action of him torturing me wasn't as unsettling as it had been whilst watching it happen to Ella. I was able, between episodes of blinding pain, to become almost numb to the fact that it was happening to me. Lethargic almost. Perhaps accepting of the fact that I was going to die and my only satisfaction would be to not give this piece of shit anything.

The problem was, the torturer recognised this too. That is, after all, why he had Cassius still hanging there. Flesh wounded, eyes dull, happiness gone. And that is why after two hours of my own torture I was screaming harder than I had done during. Screaming as Cassius screamed. The air taught with his pain and fury. If pain was a physical force then that torturer would have been ripped asunder, unfortunately for us it was just wasted breath.

"Calidan, he will die Calidan, won't you do anything?"

*Shut up you piece of filth, just shut up!*

"Calidan, look, do you want his thumb? Here! I heard he was good at the sword...probably not anymore."

*I'll kill you; I'll kill you; I'll kill you!*

"Just tell me what I want to know Calidan and this stops. It all stops."

*Stop the screaming, too much screaming, Cassius, Cassius, Cassius!*

"Tell me Calidan. What did you find at the desert site? Tell me!"

*Nononononononononononononononononononononono!*

"Talk Calidan. Talk and it stops. You're only doing this to yourself."

*You bastard, you monster, you vile, wretched piece of horseshit!*

"How about an eye? Shall I take an eye Calidan?"

*NoNoNoNONONONONONONONONO!"*

"No!" I screamed as the poker neared Cassius's eye. "Skyren! ASH! seraph! I'll talk! No more! I'll talk!"

The screaming stopped and silence fell. I opened a tear-filled eye and saw nothing but blackness. Nothing in front of me, no Cassius or Ella, or Sophia, Scythe, Rikol. What was going on?

A blinding flash of light and I knew no more, a disembodied voice that sounded disconcertingly familiar echoing in my head as I passed out.

"Everyone breaks Calidan. Everyone. Part two lies ahead. Pick up the pieces of yourself and reforge them. Hone yourself into what you need to be to survive..."

# CHAPTER 4

## *Survival*

The wind rustled through the trees, causing goose-bumps to rise on my skin as it blew past; a cold voice in the air.

*Wait, trees?*

My eyes shot open. White light seared my retina, but not the same light as before when I had passed out, a different light; natural. A bright sun sat overhead, offsetting somewhat the otherwise cold air. A few sparse fir trees jutted out of the ground nearby, their branches overfilled with snow. I was lying under another fir on a bed of old, dried leaves and branches in what seemed to be a gully.

The wind blew again and I shivered, noticing for the first time that I was still naked. A closer inspection revealed that I bore no injuries from the torture seemingly seconds beforehand. I looked fit and healthy, with no scars and plenty of fingernails.

*What the hell just happened? Has someone healed me somehow?*

Even my enhanced healing from the bond with Seya would have left scars. I tried contacting her but there was nothing except for the faintest touch of her presence in my mind. And then it all came flooding in and it didn't matter how cold it was. For a good twenty minutes I just sat and cried. Sobbing over and over again for my lost friends. Wanting to just curl up

and die. But it was not to be. Something in my brain refused
to just let me give up and accept death; a smouldering core
of rage at my tormentor. The man who I had sworn to track
down, no matter where he lived.

Track down and extract vengeance.

Shivering, I pushed myself to my feet and winced as splinters
of wood dug into my soft soles. *Survive.* That is what that
voice had said, and that is what I would do, regardless of the
hollowness of my soul. First things first; shelter and fire. I
risked a climb to the top of the gully, peering out to see what
lay around me. It was not a satisfying scene. I was surrounded
by white for as far as I could see. Snow swirled through a
strong wind and the nearby ground was broken only by a few
more rocky outcroppings, but whether or not they were similar gullies to what I was in I could not tell. The swirling snow
made visibility poor but I thought that I could glimpse trees
further down the slope. Something to discover once I had my
priorities in order.

Climbing carefully back down I returned to where I had
awoken. A search of my sleeping place revealed nothing of
value. Nothing that is, except for a single piece of broken
glass. Perfect! Thanks to the fir trees there was plenty of dried
wood available, certainly enough to keep a small fire going
overnight. Another check revealed that sadly there wasn't
any kind of cave or hollow to provide further respite from
the wind, meaning that I would have to build a shelter or
risk freezing to death. Moving to one of the other fir trees I
carefully dislodged the built-up snow and snapped off several
large branches. Propping them up around the base of my fir
tree provided a small amount of cover from the wind and allowed me to concentrate on building a fire before venturing
out to reinforce the shelter.

Making the fire proved annoyingly more difficult than I had
hoped. Even with the many occasions I had done this when
living on the mountainside with the Tracker, the shifting sun
and scratched piece of glass made creating a flame frustrat-

ingly difficult. After far too much effort in which I could have sworn I could hear the Tracker's mocking voice, I managed to spark a flame amongst the small pile of broken twigs and leaves I had gathered and basked momentarily in the success. Feeding the small flame with twigs and leaves before moving to larger branches soon ensured that I had a constant flickering flame that quickly made me feel warmed through. Before night completely fell I moved out to the other firs again, breaking more branches to further cover the small shelter and finding a particularly large branch to begin crafting into a spear. I didn't know where I was or what was around and in that type of scenario it always paid best to be careful.

Returning to the fire I covered the shelter with the collected branches, making a very basic green shack around the base of the fir tree with a fire at the entrance. Confident that I couldn't do much more tonight, and hoping that the weather eased up the next day to allow for exploration I settled in for the night, using my time before sleep to trim away any extraneous protrusions from my intended spear, snapping them where viable and using a small stone with a broken edge to sharpen the end into a hopefully lethal point. Once done I planted my spear beside me, its point toward the entrance to my hovel and, placing my back against the tree, I closed my eyes and slept.

*"Tell him Calidan please!"*
*Nononononononononononononononononononononono!*

I awoke with a start, uncertain as to what had triggered my wakefulness. It was still night but dawn was not far off. I extended my senses but couldn't find anything out of place. I settled back, aiming to get a little more sleep before I heard it. A noise that sounded like the undying scream of a foul beast. It echoed around the hilltop, reverberating around the gully and making it hard to pin its location down. Whatever it was I had not heard anything like it before but I hoped that I didn't have to meet it in the flesh. Whatever could make a noise that deep and loud was probably big. Very big.

I listened intently but no more sound was forthcoming. Re-solving myself to the fact that further sleep was not going to come I got up and revitalised the banked fire with some more small branches and carefully aimed breath before breaking out into the wider world.

It had snowed overnight, the ground was covered with fresh, unmarked powder. Well, unmarked aside from the small paw prints that ran along the side of the gully. *Rabbit* - my stom-ach growled at the thought. Instinctively I shifted into mov-ing like the hunter, spear held low and loose, powder barely crunching as I slowly spread my weight through it. The cold soon became unnoticeable against my feet but I knew that I would have to find materials to make footwear soon. Frost-bite was a very real concern.

*There!* The tracks led into a small hole, almost hidden within the snow. Questing out with my senses I found three large rab-bits huddled within the warren, and what's more there only seemed to be two other entrances. Silently I made my way back to the fire and taking two well-lit branches walked back to the warren. Making sure the sticks stayed lit I slowly placed them inside each entrance and swiftly made my way back to the third outlet, hands at the ready. Before long the rabbits started twitching, the scent of smoke and fire awakening an instinct of danger. Soon the first rabbit darted for the entrance and right into my waiting hands. A swift snap and it was laid aside, just in time for the other two.

Three well fed rabbits made for a good meal with some food left over to be dried along with their hides whilst I made shoes out of bark. It was a trick that the Tracker had shown me long ago, and whilst a full hide shoe would be infinitely better the three rabbits wouldn't provide enough fur to make them. Stripping the bark from the fir trees I was able to make a some-what shambolic base and after some tricky interweaving of the bark, combined with a large amount of cursing, something resembling a shoe sat in front of me. Nothing compared to the completely functional and yet somehow aesthetically pleasing shoes that the Tracker had been able to make, and yet once wrapped in rabbit hide and filled with some fur they weren't half bad.

Alright, they were terrible. They rubbed my feet raw - even with the fur - and were downright uncomfortable to walk in, but they kept my feet relatively dry and warm and that was worth the inconvenience.

It was on the second day of my stay when running low on decent firewood that I trekked out from the gully, armed only with spear and rabbit shoes. A funny sight if anyone had been around to see me, my genitals swinging freely as I trekked out into the snowy mountain side and probably looking very much like a pale, hairless ape.

Unfortunately for me someone, or perhaps more accurately something, was indeed watching.

At first I roamed around the various rocky outcroppings to see if there was anything of use. Sadly that was all they seemed to be, outcroppings. No more gullies, trees or firewood, just rock. With that dead end I moved out towards the forest at the base of the hill. It seemed a likely place to find food and shelter. Hopefully there were enough big animals, maybe a deer or two, that I could fashion some proper clothes from.

I continuously held my senses out as I moved, looking for a new shelter and hunting at the same time. Despite my inability to contact her, the bond with Seya still seemed to be there, albeit on a reduced level. Where before I could likely have sensed the steps of a deer within a mile of my location I was now down to a fraction of that. Whilst Seya had mentioned that distance would reduce the effects of the bond, even deep within the desert my abilities had barely been impacted, so I either had to be extremely far away from Seya or something was forcibly impacting our bond.

*Or both.*

I could only hope that she was okay.

Shaking my head to clear my thoughts I continued into the

forest. There were more rabbits hidden at various points but I was hoping to bag bigger game before having to settle for rabbits. That said, I was worried about killing an animal and not having a fire ready to protect the kill from scavengers or bigger predators. Whilst I couldn't sense anything nearby I didn't want to take any chances.

It was by complete accident that I stumbled across the cave. Walking past the exposed rock face I nearly didn't notice the tiny slit until the whistling wind convinced me to have another look. Certain that there was nothing inside and that it widened further in, I committed to fitting through the gap, scratching my bare flesh on the harsh rock through the tight squeeze.

Inside was...perfect.

The cave was about fifteen feet in width, maybe twenty in length and had only one entrance - the tiny opening I had just consecrated my flesh on, with little sign of animal use. My decision of a campsite had practically been made for me. I could barely keep my excitement contained, a place out of the snow and wind! *Cassius would have loved thi- Cassius*. My heart clenched and I forced that image out of my head. With my burgeoning excitement gone I extracted myself from the cave and began the arduous task of collecting firewood and fitting it through the awkward cave entrance.

That night I had a pleasant fire in the cave eating more charred rabbit. Sadly no bigger game had come into range of my senses, but I was confident that given time I could find some. With a good, sturdy and defensible shelter like this I felt confident about my immediate survival and could set about laying stores and building up my equipment before moving off in search of civilization.

The creature called again in the night, a rampaging shout that echoed through the forest; silencing any wildlife that was braving the night-time air. Even in the cave I heard the undulating noise; seemingly reverberating through the rock. Clutching my spear close I sat in preparation, watching the entrance closely before sleep claimed me again and I sank back into my nightmares.

Two days into my stay at the cave I made my first proper kill. A deer, unsuspecting of my approach, had been gently pulling at some snow-covered foliage. My spear took it in the chest, the strength born of somewhat diminished Great Heart still causing the hurled spear to pierce through to the other side of its torso, killing it instantly and partially ruining the hide that I had been after. Annoyed at myself and imagining the Tracker berating me over not controlling my power better, I hauled the deer over my shoulders and began the three-mile trek back to the cave. My annoyance at my strength vanished immediately as I knew most humans would struggle to drag the deer that far, more likely opting to skin and gut the deer at the location of the kill and consequently risking being vulnerable in an unknown location.

On my fifth day I killed another deer, having roamed four miles to find it, and feeling warmer than ever thanks to the deer hide 'jumper' - if you could call it that - that I had fashioned for myself. In reality it was effectively the deer skin wrapped around me with holes for my arms, held together using stitches from the deer's sinew and bone for needles. My time in the cave years before with Tracker and Cassius had given me plenty of opportunity to learn such things from the old man and both Cassius and I had learnt well. The wolfskin clothes that had served on our journey down the mountain and across the Endless Sea to Forgoth had been made by our own hands. For the time being my legs and crotch still went uncovered but with this second kill I would have a decent set of winter gear.

One mile into the walk back to the cave as I dragged the deer carcass behind me I realised that I was being hunted. A four-legged shape slipped from tree to tree, its movement sinuous and fluid and completely unknowing that I had cottoned on to its hunt. When it had moved to within fifty feet of me I set the deer down and grabbed my spear before turning to face the lion. The mountain lion held a look of surprise on its face as I jumped in front of it and roared, my eyes wide and savage; the roar bestial. Or at least it should have been. If I had been at the Academy then the shout would have shaken the trees around me, my Great Heart enhanced lungs and throat making for a monstrous sound. It was certainly loud, but instead of immediately forcing the cat to cower like I had intended the roar had been within its levels of normality.

Which meant I was still potential prey.

The cat stepped forward, claws extending from the furred paw like gleaming razors. She was hungry and wanted the deer.

I gripped the handle of my homemade spear more tightly and prepared for the inevitable. This kill was mine and I was not giving it up.

The lion took another pace and growled, the vibration low and menacing. In turn I bared my teeth and snarled, slightly bending a knee and bringing the point of my spear in line with the lion. It was then that my senses flared and I felt the second lion stalking in from behind me. With a roar I swivelled and swept outwards with the spear, the point passing just in front of the second creature's face and causing it to leap backwards out of reach. Time was against me now. One mountain lion I was fairly sure I could take on, having been on the receiving end of attacks by a much more terrifying cat many times over the years, but two was a real threat. With my reduced speed and strength those claws and teeth could spell a messy end.

The first lion sensed opportunity and ran for my back, hoping to make a quick kill. Another swing of the spear and it danced away at the last second, padding just out of reach with a rumbling growl. A shift of claw on stone and I flung an arm up, the teeth that were aimed at my neck raking at my elbow and the impact sending the both of us to the ground in a tumble. There was a loud *snap* and a juddering howl as the spear point dug into the lion's underbelly, the haft breaking against the ground. Immediately the weight lifted and the cat limped away, backing into the undergrowth with a trail of blood.

I didn't even have a moment's respite before the other cat was on me. Sharp claws raked down my arm, leaving bloody tracts in their wake and jaws clenched down onto the bone of my shoulder. I howled with pain and bucked, trying to throw the weight of the cat off me, but it clung on with clawed tenacity. I hit with my left and felt something break under my fist but the lion refused to let go, its jaws just clenching harder into my flesh.

Wedged under its body, with panic rising in my chest and a complete lack of weapons at my disposal I did the only thing available to me and bit deep into the cat's neck, clenching down hard and ignoring the foul taste of blood that trickled into my throat.

The trickle became a torrent as I kept biting down. Wedged where I was the cat couldn't manage to get a better grip and end the fight and now time was on my side. Slowly but surely the cat's movements began to slow and eventually stopped entirely, leaving me thoroughly mauled and liberally painted with blood.

It was at this point hindsight suggested that I should have left them the deer.

Groaning in pain I told hindsight to sod off and slowly shifted out from under the body of the cat, my shoulder screaming at me every time I moved it. With weary legs I picked up the hard-won body of the deer and slung it over my unmarred shoulder before setting back off in the direction of the cave. Weaponless and almost broken I had to trust to hope that I could make it back unnoticed by any more denizens of the forest and as much as leaving the mountain cat coat behind pained me, I didn't have it in me to carry both. I continued the trudge back to the cave, completely unaware of just how far the sounds of the fight had carried, of how it echoed through forest and rock before finally reaching waiting ears.

Thankfully I reached the cave without any more misadventure and was able to restart the fire without too much trouble. As much as I wanted to collapse to the floor and rest I knew that infection from the cat's teeth and claws could finish the job that it had started and so I set out again in search of anything that could prove useful.

Half of the plants I didn't recognise in that place. Thankfully after searching in the waning light I managed to find some snow-covered willow, which I knew to have some medicinal properties. Staggering back to the cave I washed the wound out with snow and chewed on the bark before collapsing into a fever filled fugue.

I'm fairly positive that without the bond with Seya pushing whatever small amounts of healing it could my way I would have died in that cave. For two days I was feverish, in and out of consciousness and wracked with shivers. In normal times the cuts on my arms would have healed in a matter of hours, the deeper wounds in a few days. As it was the cuts only fully healed some three days after the mountain lion attack and my shoulder was still giving me problems a week later. I could barely remember how I had felt before meeting Seya and the many benefits she bestowed on me, but I imagined it was somewhat similar; weak, frightened and much more human. Which I am sure is exactly what was intended.

# PRESENT DAY

I haven't had much luck with caverns in my life.

I have a working theory that if an Imperator finds a cave or cavern then there is almost guaranteed to be some kind of evil beast within even if they weren't hunting one, and as I ran through the cavern frantically brushing off the tide of scarabs that were threatening to engulf me despite my wavering seraph shield a small part of my mind grinned at having been proven right yet again.

The sound of rushing water filled the desperate gloom and before I could give my brain chance to consider the host of even more disturbing creatures that could live within its waters I drew breath and took the plunge, leaving the horde of beetles to angrily chitter on the stone walls behind me as I was swept downstream. The world disappeared, becoming only a battering of rocks and rapids as the river flung me through the bowels of the mine. My shield was the only thing that kept me alive, both from the percussive impacts and because of the layer of oxygen that I had trapped in there with me. Finally the river spat me back out into daylight and with heaving breaths I dazedly made my way back to shore before collapsing in a heap for an unknown time.

A thunderous rumble shook me from my exhaustion.

*No, please no,* I thought wearily. *He can't be that pissed at me.*

The crashing grew louder and I threw myself to the side as a tail slammed the ground where I had been resting.

*Goddamnit.*

Cassius stood before me in all his demonic glory, armoured scales covered in blood and gore. He had given up on slaughtering the running slaves in order to come after me - that if nothing else cemented just how cunning the skyren personality within him could be, let alone just how keen its senses were to have tracked me down; I doubted that even Seya could have done that so quickly.

A howling roar split the air and Cassius pounced, flinging his several tonne body through the air with unbelievable ease. I flung my battered and bruised body aside again, wincing as I hit the ground. Rolling, I drew Asp from my side and sent a line of power hurtling towards the descending claws. Cassius twitched aside at the last second, the cutting line of energy scoring a mild line across his arm. *He remembers,* I thought grimly. *He's encountered Asp before.*

Cassius swivelled and his tail ripped the ground apart, pelting me with dust and stone. Only my senses saved me as I dropped to my knees underneath a swiving strike that would have cleaved me in two. Rolling forwards I sliced the length of his foot with Asp, the blade cutting deeply into his flesh. Bellowing in pain Cassius stamped downwards, the force of the blow lifting me from the floor. I cut again and found myself spinning through the air to crash into the water, the impact sending me to a much more pleasant place that didn't have an angry lizard trying to kill me.

A blinding pain erupted in my shoulder and I gasped as my senses came back to me. Cassius's tail spike was embedded deep inside my shoulder and the pain was overwhelming as he lifted me out of the water, his predator's eyes showing immense satisfaction at having captured his prey. Spluttering with pain I grabbed his tail and forced my little remaining seraph into the tattoo on my hand, burning the inscription into the meat of his tail and causing Cassius to screech in agony. Willing it to work I channelled as much seraph as possible, whilst holding the spike into my shoulder whilst he began to flail and flooding the skyren's body with my intent. Frantic movement sent me clutching the tail and I pushed every ounce of seraph I could muster into Cassius before a flick of his tail dislodged me and sent me crashing through the undergrowth. In a tumble of limbs I hit the ground and knew no more.

# CHAPTER 5

## *Reality*

Nine days after I had found the cave I was fully kitted out in tough deer hide clothing. My rough rabbit hide shoes had been remade with deer hide and I wore deerskin trousers. They wouldn't win any fashion contests but so far hadn't fallen apart. There was a veritable store of venison in my cave, much of which I was smoking to ensure that it lasted. All in all I had plenty of food and stores but didn't have a clear plan of action and so settled for ranging further and further afield in order to get a good view of the surrounding land. This was my furthest ranging yet; a good eight miles in an easterly direction from the cave, armed with spear, two bone knives, venison and a flask of water made out of hide and stomach lining. As I walked I began to notice a strange scent in the air, something that I couldn't immediately place but it quickly became overwhelmingly pungent. Several of the trees seemed to have been liberally sprayed with it, much like how certain animals mark territory, and many of the trees had large and deep claw marks with several that had been completely shredded. I had no idea what I was dealing with but decided that knowing one's enemy was the better course of action and so continued on.

Moving stealthily, I crept from tree to tree like Seya had

taught me, my senses on full alert. Something was over the next rise. Something strange, unmoving and apparently dead. I shuffled silently over to the ridge and looked down. Beneath me was the grisly scene of what appeared to have been an epic battle between presumably a human and what I could only guess was a troll. The ground was flattened for several metres in every direction and in the middle was the mighty creature. It was leaning forwards in an upright posture, held up by the four wooden spears that jutted the beast. My heart throbbed in anticipation and fear. Trolls were not something that I had come across in my training at the Academy...they were fairy tales as far as the average person knew. Who had managed to kill one? I had to track them.

It didn't take long. One individual was lying in the bole of a tree and breathing heavily. I could tell by the sound of his laboured breathing that he was in pain. I crept closer, sneaking into the glade and flitting like a shadow between cover, before freezing in shock.

Scythe was sitting against the tree.

Impossible. I had seen my friends dead. Watched them die. How was Scythe here? What was going on? I got so lost in the swirl of emotions that I didn't hear the presence approaching until a spear tip landed at my back.

"Don't move."

I moved. Instinct flared and I spun, knocking aside the spear point as I dashed towards the treeline unleashing the full strength and speed of my bonded self. I snarled as I ran, the savage bestial side of me rising up. That couldn't be Scythe! Scythe was dead. I heard her voice calling my name but ignored it. Ella was dead too. They were all dead. It was all a lie! I ran back to the cave and huddled back inside, content to sit within my nightmares, within what I knew was real.

Any sane person would think that to go back to the source of your insane, unreal visions would be ill advised. Frankly I'm not too sure that I was sane at this point, (nor am I fully aware if I am now for that matter), and so I returned to the same site

the next day, taking a wide and circular route that allowed me
to approach from a different angle. The troll was still there.
Still dead. The fake visions that definitely weren't real however weren't. Mildly disappointed that my brain couldn't conjure up more distractions of my deceased friends I set off back
to camp.

Imagine my surprise then that my visions awaited me in the
cave.

"Calm, Calidan! Peace!" pleaded Ella as I brandished my bone
knives menacingly towards her. I knew I could never bring
myself to hurt fake Ella but the other part of my brain that had
conjured her didn't have to know that.

"I told you he wouldn't see reason. You saw his eyes!" grunted
Scythe, his ankle heavily sprained and leaning on a crutch.

"He looks the same as you and I did when we first saw each
other!" Ella replied, holding her hands out towards me placatingly, "...just a little more savage."

I couldn't argue with that. I was too busy with surviving to
not be savage. Doing what the voice said.

"Get out of my head," I said, snarling. "You aren't real! You're
dead, you're all dead!"

"We are real Calidan. From the looks of it we have all been
through the same thing," replied Ella softly, continuing in the
same tone that you would use to calm a frightened mare. "I
thought you were dead. That Scythe and everyone...that Cassius was dead. I was tortured until I talked-" she broke off in a
sob.

"It's true Calidan," said Scythe. "I didn't believe it first and neither did Ella. We spent the first few hours after meeting poking
each other to make sure that the other was real. We both woke
up in the forest, in separate areas but came into contact when
out hunting the same deer."

Lies. Had to be lies.

Fake Ella approached slowly, like she would a wild animal.
"Calidan. Please. We're your friends. We aren't going to hurt
you."

"But I watched you die. Piece by piece," I whispered. "How can this be real?"

"We think what we all saw was fake. Part of the test," murmured Ella, her voice soft and warm.

"Test?"

"Scythe and I are fairly sure that this is all part of the fourth-year test. That they sprung it early to catch us off guard. I don't know what all that torture was about - maybe seeing if we can keep Academy secrets? But I'm guessing that it stopped when you broke and then you woke up here?"

I nodded, numb.

"The same happened to us. Please Calidan, we are real. Just touch me; you'll know." She came closer, arms spreading wide. I held myself rigid as she slowly, gently, embraced me in a hug. "It's me Calidan. It's Ella. I've missed you so."

Slowly I felt the warmth of her, the realness. If this was insanity then it was a much better existence. Carefully I embraced my long-time friend, held her and breathed in her scent as my walls came tumbling down one by one. I embraced her as I cried. As I sobbed out all the pain and anguish until I could cry no more.

And then I slept.

\* \* \*

When I woke it was with trepidation, part of my brain wondering if it had been somehow tricked, that it would all turn out to be a lie. But no, there they were sitting by the fire and toasting some venison, my friends. My whole, unscarred, unbroken and thoroughly alive friends. That dawn is one of the happiest that I can remember. The feeling of contentment in having been proven so wrong, that my friends were indeed alive and that the others were likely alive and surviving somewhere around here - a thought that Ella and Scythe readily agreed with.

"Yes, I mean, why wouldn't they be close by?" continued Scythe as he tore into some venison. "If this is the fourth-year exam then it would make sense for the entire dorm to be experiencing the same thing. To survive out here in what appears to be troll country."

"I had been meaning to ask about that," I said softly, "it definitely was a troll?"

Ella and Scythe nodded. "As far as we can guess anyway," replied Ella. "It fits the description after all and was extremely tough to kill. It only slowed down after the third spear!"

"Hah, I'm just glad that not all the stories are true!" I exclaimed, before stopping at the unspoken question on their faces. "In the tales, you can only kill a troll using fire. They say its flesh keeps healing but burning it stops the regeneration."

The two of them looked at each other. "That would explain much of what we saw," said Scythe slowly. "I engaged it with a sharp piece of wood, hit it in the eye before it knocked me away and caused me to sprain my ankle stumbling like a fool on a rock. It tore the spike out and after a few moments the eye looked as good as new!"

"Shit" I breathed. "This is going to make things more difficult."

"What if it isn't dead?" questioned Ella. "What if the flesh can only heal when whatever has hit it has been removed? It ran onto our spears, drove them deep. Perhaps if those spears were removed the troll would wake up?"

It seemed impossible, but we had all seen impossible things. "Fire seemed to slow the regeneration of that skyren back in the desert," mused Scythe slowly. "It could well be possible."

"In that case," I replied, "we need to prepare properly if we are to find the others. We obviously can't carry flaming spears everywhere we go, so let's put our heads together and think."

After some tinkering we came up with a relatively workable solution. By placing hot coals on top of a small log, it soon burnt through into the middle of the log, creating a method for carrying fire embers. We wrapped kindling and animal fat around some of the spears in the hope that if we had a few minutes before a fight we could spark the spears to flame. It wouldn't last long but hopefully the fiery tip would be enough to inflict some permanent damage to an inquisitive troll.

Leaving Scythe well stocked with water, wood and food, Ella and I set out in search of our friends, aiming to continue what I had started and walking in ever increasing circles from our location. For three days we scoured the countryside and found no sign of human presence but plenty of indication of trolls. Fortunately Ella was almost as skilled as Cassius in moving through the natural world, and far more skilled than either of us when moving in a city, and so we moved like shadows in the night, ensuring that nothing was aware of our presence. Or so we thought.

I hadn't heard the strange howling since my first few nights in this place and naturally assumed that it was the sound of a troll. It was strange then that when I heard a troll roar for the first time, it sounded nothing like what I had heard. We tracked the beast by the grunts and bellows that resounded through the small valley that we had come across. Small streams crisscrossed the ground and plenty of fir trees provided good cover - a decent place to hole up if I hadn't found my cave - and precisely what Rikol had thought before an angry troll found his scent and chased him up a tree.

It was shaking the giant fir furiously; the tree creaking ominously. Rikol was trapped at the top and looked utterly miserable, wrapped in a fur pelt but without any noticeable weapons. He was stuck up there until the troll got tired or we intervened.

"What do you think?" I whispered to Ella. "Wait or attack?"

"Attack," she replied. "Trolls aren't exactly the cleverest of creatures, it could have been shaking that tree for a day now for no reason other than it just enjoyed it!"

Together we set about rewrapping our spearheads and nursing the glowing embers into life, ensuring as we did so that we were downwind of the troll - trolls, it was rumoured, had an excellent sense of smell.

We conferred silently about our plan of attack, arguing back and forth in whispers until a plan had formed. It was, like all good plans, very simple. Kill it before it knew that we were there.

Drawing on all of my expertise in hunting and my supernatural skills in remaining quiet, I sprinted silently towards the troll, hoping that its grunts and roars would cover the minute sound that my feet made. With my flaming spear held loosely in my hands I jumped, arcing through the air before slamming the fiery point of the spear through the beast's head and with enough force to pin it to the tree. Dead.

"Calidan?" Rikol's voice trembled as he sat in the tree, peering down at who had saved him. "Is that you?"

"Rikol!" I called, "Come down, it's safe."

"How? You're all dead!"

I grinned wolfishly before proceeding to coax my friend down. Ella emerged from the tree line shortly after with armfuls of dry wood. We were taking no chances. An hour later we left the valley with a stunned Rikol and leaving behind a burning troll corpse.

I would say it was the smell of success, but I wish it wasn't. Burning troll is not something you get off your skin.

Unbeknownst to us, we weren't the only people aware that Rikol had been trapped at the top of the tree. Large blue eyes watched us leave, a glimmer of recognition filling them. Recognition...and hatred.

# CHAPTER 6

## *Differing Views*

### Ella

"Hone yourself into what you need to be to survive."

Ella's eyes flicked open and she drew a heaving breath, hands scrabbling at the burning blade in her side. When she didn't touch any metal her movements began to falter, her breathing reducing from panicked hyperventilation to deeper, gasping breaths. After a few moments her eyes adjusted and she realised that she was no longer in that terrifying room of despair but sitting on the cold floor of a cave. Light streaming in from above showed her that it was still day time outside.

*What in the Chains is going on? Is this another trick?*

But no, there were no hanging bodies, no flickering fire light and...

She inspected her body in the ray of light.

No wounds.

*Where were the wounds?*

Eyes wary and mind racing she slowly stood and made her way to the cave entrance. Surprisingly her body felt strong, like she had just woken up from a deep sleep rather than been hanging upside down for what had felt like days.

The world outside was covered in white and snow slowly swirled through the air. A gust of wind caught her and she shivered, wrapping her arms around herself and taking a step back inside.

*Okay, in a cave in the snow covered middle of nowhere. I'm not dead and I don't look like I've even been injured. So either I just hallucinated the whole thing, I've been healed or it was something else. Does that mean the others were still…?*

*Was Cassius alive?*

Tears welled up out of her eyes and a sob erupted from her chest before she shook her head angrily. *That's not useful right now Ella. Force it back. List out the situation and break it down. You have a cave, that's shelter which looks pretty useful right about now.* She cast her eyes around the cave, looking for anything useful. *Number of sharp rocks but that's about it. No water, no food and no clothing. So those three are the priority. Get on out there and find it. If Cassius is dead then he wouldn't want you moping around and if he is alive then you're going to show him how a city rat gets things done!*

With a determined grimace Ella stepped out into the outside world, tucking her face against the swirling snow and armed only with a rock. Instantly the temperature plummeted and she began to move quickly, keeping her body as small as possible against the wind. Deeper into the forest the trees were thicker and the ground was littered with autumnal leaves, providing some scant comfort from the cold of the ground. Bundling up any dry sticks that she could find she began ferrying them back to the relative safety of the cave, desperate to have enough for a fire before she lost the light. Once she had a big enough pile she set to work, putting into practice the survival skills that her time with Cassius, Calidan and the Academy had taught her.

Two agonizing hours later she transferred her precious ember to a small pile of dry leaves and silver birch and blew softly, until with a spark of light it caught. Piece by piece she built it up until the fire was casting light across the interior of the cave.

Sitting back with an exhausted smile she allowed herself a moment of peace. The wood she had used had been slightly damp meaning that it had taken even longer than usual to make the ember, something that her raw hands could attest to, but she had managed it in the end. With a groan she reached over to the last branch she had brought in, a sturdy and thick staff nearly as tall as she was, and started scraping away at the tip with a rock. A rock was all well and good as a weapon, but unless she could throw it she was at a disadvantage against practically any predator that might be out here. *Although...*she mused, her mind returning to the Academy survival training sessions, *if I find the right kind of bark, throwing rocks might be a very viable plan. Something to keep an eye out for.* With that in mind, a spear beside her and a glorious fire to keep her warm she curled up and closed her eyes, pushing the gnawing hunger in her belly to one side. She had had plenty of experience to do so over the years and within minutes was fast asleep.

* * *

## Scythe

Scythe slid down the embankment and jumped the icy brook, his feet crunching against the snow. Behind him he could hear the thudding of hooves and angry snorting as his pursuer lost sight of him. He continued to run, putting as much distance behind him as possible and trying to concentrate on his foot positioning rather than whether the sounds that followed were getting louder. With a grunt he pulled himself up the other side of the embankment and rolled behind a tree where he gasped heaving breaths before forcing himself to be silent. Heavy thuds cracked the snow on the other side of the brook, the pace slow and accompanied by a lot of grumbling. Snorts

filled the cold air and Scythe knew that if he looked out behind him his pursuer would be watching, instead he closed his
eyes and held his breath, willing his enemy to go away.

Eventually, after what seemed an eternity sitting in the cold
with only his bare flesh as protection, he heard the creature turn and trot away, its snorts shuffling into the distance.
Scythe let out a breath of relief. *I see why people get gored by
boars now,* he mused as he cast his eyes over his surroundings,
*that would have been an unpleasant way to die.*

He had woken up in the lee of a small tree, quickly realising that he was unarmed, unhurt and unclothed on the
outskirts of a snowy forest. The frigid air stopped the tears
from falling as he had endeavoured to find something, anything for warmth and protection and his chattering teeth had
been enough to scare the grumpy old boar into action. Barely
minutes into waking up he had been on a run for his life and
bitterly regretting the times he had laughed at the stories of
people getting killed by boars. It had seemed so silly - when
there were things out there that actively hunted humans getting killed by a normal sized boar seemed somehow foolish. A
great boar yes, but a normal boar?

*Scary bastards.*

Scythe got to his feet and set off into the forest, keeping an eye
out for any sturdy branches and dry material that he could use
to make fire. He desperately needed to get warm and quickly.
Arming himself with a knobbled piece of wood that felt like
it would make a decent enough club, he kept his eyes moving
as he walked, well aware that a moment of inattention could
spell his end and not wanting to find himself on the receiving
end of a boar's tusks, or worse.

Breaking through into a thicket of trees he found a tiny glade,
surrounded on all sides by thick firs. Nodding to himself
Scythe swept out the pile of branches and debris from under
the largest tree, collecting it in a small pile for later use, and
then began hauling in larger branches to rest against the trunk
to form a basic lean-to. Once done he stripped some of the

bushier fir branches and entwined them through the logs until he was satisfied that it would provide a decent level of protection from any errant gusts that made it through the surrounding trees. Just outside of his shelter he collected all of the swept-up items into a little pile and started making the basics for a fire.

A small gust drifted through as he worked and he shivered violently before redoubling his efforts. With the amount of dry tinder and wood available he quickly had a small flame going, its warmth sending thrills of pleasure through his frozen body. As he settled down to defrost himself he reached up for a couple of the fir cones and detached them from the branch. *Cassius once told me the seeds were edible,* he mused as he set about opening the cone, *I really hope he wasn't joking.*

* * *

## Ella

Ella loaded, twirled and fired at the cavern wall, cursing again as the rock went wide from her intended target. She had used slings before but never one that she had formed out of cord she had wound from bark fibre. So far though it was holding up and she was confident that given a few more practice shots she would understand the quirks of her new weapon and then the small creatures of the forest would have reason to tremble.

After finding a small stream and drinking her fill she had attempted to hunt rabbits for the majority of the previous day but their quick steps and well-hidden burrows had ensured that they eluded her. The silver lining of her misadventures however was that her journey had helped her find the bark of a tree that now formed the sling she had spent the majority of the evening making by flickering firelight. Given enough time she had plans to make cord for snares, so even the fleet footed rabbits couldn't escape.

*Crack.*
Another rock, this time a little closer to where she intended. A grim smile.
*Crack.*
Again.
*Crack!*
Again!
Satisfied that she had a functioning tool and confident that she could place a rock in the direction she wished it to go she stepped outside and went on the hunt, armed with spear and sling in one hand and a couple of rocks in the other.

Seven misses and forty sailor worthy curses later Ella succeeded in striking a rabbit a glancing blow with a small stone, stunning it for long enough for her to run over and stab it with her spear. Jubilant at her victory Ella picked up the rabbit and slung it over her shoulder to carry back before pausing for a moment and sniffing the air. She could have sworn that there had been a hint of smoke on the wind but after a few minutes of searching the sky with no more scent forthcoming she moved on, taking a slightly different path back to her cave to log any more useful materials as she passed. She had food, she had fire and she had shelter. She gave a wild grin, *who said surviving off the land was hard?*

❊ ❊ ❊

### Scythe

"Get off you little bastard!" Scythe roared with a furious swing of his club. The wolverine snarled as it danced out of the way before coming back to latch onto the corpse of Scythe's prey. The goose had been drinking from the brook and its arrogant nature had spelled its end as Scythe's club met its skull. Happy with the kill, Scythe had paused for a second to take a drink from the brook and turned around to find the goose being dragged back into the cover of the forest by a very aggressive tiny bear.

"That's mine, you prick! Mine!" he shouted again as the wolverine continued its backward haul. Keeping its keen eyes on him it didn't slow or stop, just continued its inexorable pace back into the forest. Somewhat awed by the sheer audacity of the little beast, Scythe swung again, hoping that his display of intended violence would be enough to put it off. The wolverine didn't bat an eye, somehow knowing that the blow wasn't going to land. Hunger made him press forward, the club coming down to strike the beast's side, causing it to wrench a chunk of flesh out of the goose as it went sprawling.

"That's right, get out of here," Scythe growled, content that any sane animal would leave before things became too heated. A snarl from the wolverine had him swivelling in surprise as it launched itself at him, sharp claws drawing lines of blood down his legs.

"Get off me you little shit!" Scythe roared, trying to kick it loose but struggling to find any purchase on the scrabbling animal. Awkwardly he brought the base of his club down on the side of its head, hitting once, twice, three times before the animal backed away, its steps unsteady. Scythe pressed his advantage, all thoughts of letting his foe live gone as he raised the club with both hands and swung it down, connecting solidly with its skull with a crunch. The wolverine flopped limply to the floor as Scythe stood over it, breathing heavily. After several gasping breaths he bent down to pick up the goose and then, after a moment's thought, slung the wolverine over his shoulder too. *I hate the outdoors,* he muttered silently as he began the walk back to camp. *Nothing is ever easy.*

In the past day he had expanded his lean-to, further covering it with more branches and leaves to try and cover the small gaps that allowed the night time air in, as well as laboriously digging a fire pit to allow for easier cooking. Water he had in close proximity, but food so far had been relatively scarce aside from the plentiful cones that he had in his glade, the

seeds of which seemingly hadn't made him ill yet, something
to thank Cassius for when-
*No. No I can't. Cassius is dead. Gone, just like the others.*
With a strangled sob Scythe flung his dinner down to the
ground and furiously began to pluck the feathers from the
goose, doing everything he could to concentrate on the activity at his fingertips rather than the screaming in his mind.
Once the goose was plucked, gutted and cooking over the fire
he turned his attention to the wolverine. Its pelt looked thick
and warm, and whilst it wouldn't be enough to cover his torso
completely it would be a damn sight better than wandering
around naked. With a sigh he picked up the shard of flint that
he had been using as a cutting tool and set to work as the smell
of cooking goose filled the glade.
"Scythe?"
Scythe shook his head. The nightmares were coming more frequently, even in his daydreams.
A choked sob echoed through the glade. "Oh gods it is you.
How are you here?!"
Scythe continued to work, his hands scraping away at the
bloody flesh on the underside of the hide with the flint blade,
doing his best to remove the excess.
"Scythe? It's me." This time a footfall sounded close by and he
swivelled, the flint blade extended. In front of him was a face
he did not ever think he would ever see again.
"Ella?" he murmured, confusion and wonder in his voice. "But,
you're...?"
"Dead?" the ghost of Ella replied. "As are you, I saw you get
killed. All of you get killed." Her voice trembled as she spoke
but she didn't come any closer, perhaps as untrusting as he
that she wasn't seeing an illusion.
Scythe shook his head. *It wasn't real? It had been so vivid. So life-
like. That couldn't be true, could it?*
"No," he muttered. "No, you're not real."
A small grin broke through the tears trickling down her face.
"That's what I thought at first, but then I wondered why my

imagination would have you cooking a goose of all things it could have chosen." She took a step closer. "Look at me Scythe. A good look. I'm as real as you."

Scythe did as she asked. She was covered in badly stitched pelts of rabbits, with small pouches hanging off her left side that clinked as she moved, a sling and a spear in one hand. What's more, he realised with a wrinkle of his nose, she absolutely reeked.

It was the final thing that did it for him. Whilst he was sure his damaged psyche could fool him with images he didn't believe it would be good enough to replicate such odour. He doubted he smelled much better but the number of small rabbits that Ella had killed and somehow attached to herself made for a thoroughly pungent collection.

He broke into a tentative grin. "It's good to see you Ella," he rasped as he stumbled to his feet. Stretching out his hand he wrapped her in a bone crushing hug and cried and cried and cried.

* * *

## Ella

"Gods that stinks," Ella groaned, holding a hand to her nose.

"Almost as bad as you did," Scythe murmured jokingly, a wolverine pelt wrapped around his shoulders.

"Prick," she retorted with a grin. "Whilst I might have smelt bad, I looked to be in a much better position than you, Mr 'I'm so good at living off the land' Scythe."

"Not all of us had a cave to start with," Scythe grumbled darkly. "Just boars and things with sharp claws."

After their reunion Ella had brought Scythe back to her much more defensible cave, the two of them working hard to improve their weaponry and collect food for winter. Scythe now carried a spear with a fire hardened point and a sling similar to Ella's and the two of them had spent more time scraping the skins of the animals they had slain along with smoking the furs to try and avoid the cloud of bugs that was attracted whenever they went outside. Armed with their slings they had been a menace to the local game and fowl population, on average scoring a kill out of every three attempts and smoking the meat to try and ensure its longevity.

With their immediate food and equipment problems solved for the past three days they had been scouting the forest, looking for anything that might suggest the presence of someone else. The fact that they had found each other proved that what they had seen hadn't been real and whilst it didn't help with the memories and the nightmares, it gave them the fervent belief that the others would be somewhere close by.

Eight days since waking up they had come into an area of the forest that held lots of damaged and broken trees and a scent that was beyond pungent. One that neither of them remotely recognised, but the amount of damage and the deep claw marks scored in the bark of the trees had them on their guard and moving warily.

A low grunting hoot thrummed through the air and instantly they both tensed, crouching low to the ground. "There it is again," Ella whispered. "What makes that kind of noise?"

"Whatever it is, it sounds big," Scythe replied softly. "And we already know that something around here has big claws. What do you think? Go around or see what we are dealing with?"

"I would rather know what we are facing," Ella said. "It might be that we don't need to deal with it, but you never know."

"Know your enemy," Scythe echoed in approval. He adjusted his grip on his spear and stepped forward with a nod. "Let's get this done then." With his practiced eye for tracking he took the lead, Ella following up with her sling at the ready. Some fifteen minutes later they knelt at the top of a small rise, eyes wide at what they saw in the hollow beneath.

"What are they?" Ella whispered in a mixture of awe and horror. "They're huge!"

"I haven't a clue," answered Scythe. "Safe to say that they look bigger than our spears could tackle right now. I suggest we avoid this area unless we absolutely have to be here. They look big enough whilst sleeping so I hate to think what they look like when upright!"

Nodding her head in agreement the two of them made to slip away. Creeping from the overhang they retraced their footsteps, eager to get back to the perceived safety of the rest of the forest. A heavy footfall resonated from up ahead, accompanied by a low grunting hoot, causing them to freeze momentarily in panic. Sniffing sounds filled the air and another footstep thudded, closer this time. Quickly they cut off from their original trail and lost themselves in the deeper undergrowth, hoping that the creature would pass them by.

It was not to be. The sniffing continued, the sound thick and syrupy, like the owner had a bad cold. As it reached where they had turned off the trail the sound increased in frequency, the creature recognising the more recent scent and a low grumbling hoot reverberated through the trees.

Ella swore under her breath as the footsteps started moving in their direction. Sharing a glance the two set off again, hoping that they could get far enough away from the creature that it would lose interest or to find a stream that would allow them to get rid of the scent they were leaving behind.

Whatever the creature was, it was tenacious. The thick and treacherous terrain that was slowing Ella and Scythe down seemed to hold no barriers for it, the sound of splintering trees echoing through the canopy as it continued its inexorable plod. Each footstep brought it closer, its pace increasing as the scent got more fresh, doubtless able to smell the hint of panic and fear that both of them were leaving behind.

"It's on us," Ella wheezed, "we need to do something!"

"I'm thinking," Scythe growled, his eyes wild.

A wide framed tree loomed out of the foliage and a terrible plan snapped together. "I'll be bait," Ella said, adjusting her direction towards the tree. "If it goes for me, use the time to

fashion any weapons you can and strike when you get an opportunity. If it goes for you I'll get it in the back and we go
from there."

"That's a terrible pla- wait!" Scythe barked, alarm in his voice
as he realised Ella was no longer by his side but climbing up
the branches of a tree.

"Just go!" wheezed Ella as she climbed. "And if this works,
don't leave me up here!"

Scythe gave an angry grunt and dashed further into the trees,
leaving Ella to sincerely hope that the creature didn't have the
power to knock over her tree.

Barely thirty seconds later the strange beast arrived, long
limbed with a fat belly, short snout and pungent odour that
had Ella's eyes watering in moments. It sniffed the air and
came to the base of the tree, its head reaching the second row
of branches, before grumbling to itself and beginning to move
in the direction that Scythe had taken.

"Oy, shit for brains!" Ella shouted as she flung a stone from her
pouch at its head. "I'm up here. I'm the one you want to eat.
Got it?"

The beast tracked the sound of her voice and small, beady eyes
locked onto her position in the tree. If it felt the rock it didn't
seem to show it, but with an excited roar it leapt to the tree
and began to batter it, sending twigs and branches crashing
down on top of it and causing the tree to sway ominously.

*Best hurry please Scythe,* Ella urged as she clutched onto the
trunk of the tree. *I'm getting tree-sick.*

* * *

## Scythe

Scythe continued running until he found a small clearing that
would allow him the space to move around unhindered. If
the beast was as large and lumbering as it looked then speed

would be his advantage. Hearing Ella shout behind him and the accompanying roar of the creature put extra spark into his efforts. Scanning the area he found a couple of thick spear length logs on the floor which he rapidly used a piece of rock to sharpen points onto. Some of the bigger logs he jammed into the ground, scrabbling at the loam until it gave way. Every now and again he heard shouting from Ella, letting him know that she was still alive and so giving him more time to prepare. Soon enough he had six logs embedded in the ground at an angle, each of them with a hastily sharpened point that could snap off as easily as penetrate the creature's hide. Amongst the semicircle of stakes was a number of broken shards of wood that Scythe hoped would slow down the beast's movement, but they could just as easily shatter into useless fragments of wood. He looked around for other things he could use but a scream from Ella accompanied by a splintering *crack* that resonated through the forest sent him running.

The troll's incessant shaking and clawing at the tree was taking its toll. Shattered timber lay at its feet, the thick trunk of the tree slowly narrowing and subsequently increasing the tree's sway much to Ella's dismay. The branch directly below her had cracked, causing the startled scream as it broke away and plummeted to the ground below. Scythe took this all in as he looped behind the beast and then swept forward, spear at the ready. At a flat sprint he buried the point of his spear into the base of the creature's spine, the tip piercing through its hide and burying the shaft of the weapon deep into its torso, eliciting a pained roar from the beast and an angry swing that sent Scythe scurrying back out of reach. He tried to reach for the spear that was still embedded in the beast's back, but with a sharp *crunch* the troll slammed the haft of the weapon into the side of the tree as it turned, snapping the end of the spear off and leaving the point deeply embedded in its flesh.

*Well damn,* Scythe thought with a grimace. *That didn't last long.* So he did the only thing available to him.

He turned and fled.

With a roar the strange creature followed, the shard of wood embedded in its back doing little to slow it down.

Scythe ran as fast as he dared through the grasping undergrowth, knowing that one fall or twist at this point would likely spell his death. Making it to the small clearing he cleared the smaller shards of wood and spun, lodging a rock in his sling as he did so. The beast ploughed into the wider space and continued straight at Scythe without slowing. Whirling the sling, Scythe released and swore as the rock went wide. Grabbing one of the smaller sharpened stakes in one hand he stood behind one of the larger logs and hoped that the creature was dumb enough to impale itself in its fury.

Without remotely slowing the troll ran into the raised log, the impact causing the wood to crack in half and sending the troll to the floor in a tangle of limbs and blood. Scythe stood for a second, astonished that it had been so easy. Then the limbs began moving and it slowly pulled itself back to its feet, the thoroughly crushed log left on the floor.

*Ah. Of course it wouldn't be dead.*

The beast swung a razor blade hand at Scythe, causing him to dive out of the way. Raising his smaller spear he stabbed out at the creature, cursing as the hastily made point crumpled under the impact and doing nothing to penetrate the creature's thick slabs of muscle and fat. A curse and another dive as the beast swept forward and then Ella was there, her spear lodged into the side of its neck. Gurgling growls sounded from the beast as it tottered around the clearing, Ella frantically trying to drive the point of her spear deeper. As the creature spun, its arm rising up to swipe at Ella ineffectually, Scythe picked up a jagged splinter of wood and sprinted towards it, leaping through the air at the last moment and burying the shard deep within its eye. It howled in agony and a flailing arm sent Scythe careening away with the bloody shard in hand, to land heavily on the floor, leaving him breathless and sending searing pain through his ankle.

Pushing the pain aside Scythe rose to his feet and ran to one of his log spears. "Come on!" he screamed, hoping the beast would react to the sound.

The beast spun, the mind-numbing agony thundering through its eye socket sending it into a frenzy. Ella finished driving the spear as far as she could and then dropped off its back, rolling as she hit the floor and immediately ducked into a sprint towards the nearest log. Scythe shouted again and the creature lumbered in his direction. It ploughed into the larger spear, the tip driving itself deep into its chest, Scythe's foot on the log helping keeping it in place for the impact. A shout and Ella ran forward, one of the log spears levelled at her side, thrusting the point into the flesh of its back and driving it further onto the spear in its chest. Scythe followed suit, assisting Ella in grabbing another of the embedded spears and driving it into the other side of the creature, pinning it in place whilst it thrashed weakly, blood coating the floor beneath it. Finally they drove another spear deep into the top of its chest and lodged the base into the floor, leaving the unmoving beast propped up like a doll.

Gasping heavily Scythe collapsed to the floor, the pain that he had pushed down amongst the roar of adrenaline remerging with a vengeance.

As Ella bent down to help drag him away from the corpse of the beast he pointed at its face and ground out between gritted teeth, "I could have sworn I got rid of that."

Ella followed his finger and paled. Where she had seen a blood-filled socket thanks to Scythe's attack with the wooden shard, now there was now a red veined eye.

"I-it's a troll," she said softly, as though fearing that it would wake.

"What makes you so sure?" Scythe replied, half crawling to lie against the bole of a tree where he sat with a sigh.

"Well unless it's a Great Heart or a skyren I don't know of anything else that regenerates," she said softly, stepping away from the beast and coming to inspect his ankle.

"Which means it could still be alive," Scythe murmured, grimacing as she inspected the swelling around his ankle.

Ella spared a look back at the impaled troll. "It regenerated its eye pretty quickly; I would hope that it would be moving by now if it was going to and we did a good job of sticking it in place. Let's just not stick around longer than we have to eh?"

Scythe gave a tight grin and a nod, pain flashing over his features. Ella glanced around and frowned. "I'm going to go and find you something that you can use as a crutch. Hold tight and don't move. I won't be long."

Scythe grunted in agreement and closed his eyes, letting his mind drift. When he opened them again there was a savage figure staring at him in undisguised shock.

*Calidan?*

"Don't move!"

He moved.

# CHAPTER 7

## *Raid*

"Did you see it?" Scythe asked cautiously, hand on a spear.

"See what?" I said as I slowly squeezed into the cave.

"Something was out there a few hours ago, it tried to get in."

"A troll?" asked Ella, catching the conversation as she moved in whilst leading Rikol by the hand. Scythe was about to answer when he caught sight of Rikol and limping over he caught our little friend in a bone crushing hug. "Good to see you," he said when he finally let go.

Rikol just looked at him, eyes revealing the depth of emotion held within. As the tears began to fall we said nothing, knowing exactly how he felt.

Scythe turned back to us. "I don't know. If it was a troll then it was different to the other one. Less snuffling and grunting. It was as though it was testing whether it could get in and then, once deciding it couldn't, gave up."

Ella and I looked at each other. "Not what a normal troll would do I think," said Ella, "the other one stayed after Rikol for some time."

"Three days," Rikol whispered, causing our heads to turn towards him.

"What was that Rikol?" I asked.

"Three days it stayed at the bottom of that tree."

We all locked eyes.

"Definitely not a normal troll," agreed Scythe.

"So what now? Keep looking for Cassius and Sophia?" asked Ella.

"Of course we keep looking! Why wouldn't we?" demanded Scythe, frustrated at the notion.

"Hold on Scythe, I'm not suggesting we aren't trying to find them. It's just that this forest is a big place and it has been pretty much luck that we four have managed to find each other," said Ella placatingly. I nodded - Ella was right, even though I could cover a large distance relatively quickly I still couldn't be completely positive that I hadn't missed someone...especially if they didn't want to be found.

"So perhaps it is best to sit tight here and signal them to come to us?" continued Ella.

"Not a bad idea," I mused. "Build a smoky fire and wait? The problem is that we don't know who or what else might be attracted to investigate that fire."

Rikol peeled himself away from the pile of dried venison long enough to muffle, "Well we know that something already knows where we are based. The only other things that I've seen around here are trolls and deer...and going by my recent experience if a troll thinks that we are inside this cave then it is going to wait a long time outside before giving up."

"That would be problematic," said Scythe, his flash of anger cooled. "The entrance is narrow, which is excellent for defence, but if a troll is waiting outside...we can't use spears around that corner. We would eventually be forced to leave for water and that would lead us right into its waiting maw.

"How about building the fire further away from the cave?" I ventured. "I'm reasonably certain that trolls aren't particularly intelligent, so we could build a large fire and leave directions to make our way here?"

"Sounds viable," agreed Ella, nodding. "Hopefully it won't

take them too long to come and join us."

"Are we agreed?" I asked, looking around the group. One by one the others nodded their assent.

"Excellent. Let's rest up and then tomorrow we start the fire."

"Calidan, Calidan wake up!" A hand roughly shook my shoulder and jolted me out of sleep.

"Whaargh?" I blurted out, half confused with dream and reality. I sat up slowly and noted the complete absence of light outside. "Rikol - it's not yet morning. What's wrong?"

"I couldn't sleep," he replied as he shook the others awake, "so I went outside to go for a walk. There was a sound on the air, a clanging noise like metal on metal so I climbed up a tree to get a better look. There is an orange glow to the south, like something is burning."

I looked at the others who were still rolling around in the pitch black and rushed to my feet. "We should check it out."

"What about Scythe?" said Ella, hands waving in the dark.

"Leave me and check it out. I have enough water and food here to last me a few days...I would only slow you down," he replied.

"You're sure?" I asked.

"Positive. Go. If it's Cassius and Sophia then they may need help. If it's not then it might be others who are either friends or threats. Either way we need to know - it's worth the risk."

I clapped him on the shoulder and dressed rapidly before helping the others to find their gear.

Ella hugged him tightly once ready and Rikol gave him a squeeze before I led them from the cave into the starlit world outside, leaving our injured friend to sit alone in the darkness. Rikol was right. I could hear faint clashes and shouts carrying in the air and the smell of smoke and charred flesh tinged my nostrils. If my senses weren't somehow deceiving me then there was a battle taking place ahead. Swiftly we moved towards the commotion, traversing snow filled undergrowth and frozen branches at a speed unmatched by all but the hardiest woodsman. After the first light of dawn started to tinge the sky I called a halt, allowing the others to catch their breath and have a small bite to eat. To my best guess we had travelled roughly eight miles in three hours, punishingly swift when travelling cross country in snow and ice. The smell of smoke and ash was much stronger now, though worryingly the sound had begun to die down. No longer could I hear the constant clash of metal, instead I could make out faint screams. One side had likely won. Hopefully the side that involved Cassius and Sophia if they were there.

An hour later we emerged from the forest in a fog of ash. Slowly and stealthily we walked forward, eyes on the burning pillars of the fort that was slowly emerging from the smoke in front of us. A once wooden palisade and twin towered fort was now burning merrily in multiple places, charred ash in the rest. Corpses littered the floor along our route, massing in one area just inside the smashed gates. Most of the bodies were thickly muscled men, carrying large two-handed axes and wearing thick furs. I realised with a start that they looked strangely like Kirok had when the giant bastard had arrived at the Academy.

Ella held up a hand as I started to move on and began to pat down some of the bodies. Realising what she was after Rikol and I quickly joined in, searching the corpses for any weapons that we could use. After a few minutes of tense searching, all the while hearing the screams of those fortunate enough to still be alive but not to have fled, we came up with two daggers apiece. To a man the corpses had battle axes - too large and heavy for Rikol and Ella to wield, but each carried a sharp knife, presumably for the kind of close quarter alley work that sounded like was taking place inside the fort.

"What's the plan Calidan?" whispered Rikol. "Are we going in?"

"It's a risk," Ella returned. "We don't know anything about them, who these people are, whether they are good or bad, anything at all."

I grasped the handle of a discarded axe, its former owner no longer needing it, and gave it an experimental twirl. "We should try and move unseen, find out the truth of what is going on. But if we see rape and murder," the two took a step back at the look in my eyes as I growled out, "then don't get in my way."

I did not know these people, but memories dogged my every step. Memories of fire and blood. Of darkness and death. Only this time I was not a young and helpless child. This time I could fight.

And make them pay.

*  *  *

Flitting from corpse to corpse we slipped through the unguarded gate. The inside was a charnel house, bodies sprawled across the floor; each frozen in agonising death. The fight for the gate had been fierce by all accounts; presumably someone in the fort had been awake enough to rouse enough fighters to counter the initial night attack. Or at least attempt to counter.

The defenders of the fort were similarly as tall and well-built as their foes, many armed with axes but several looking to have used swords and shields. Shield maidens were also among the bodies, not just women picking up weapons to defend their homes and families but women with fitted armour and sharp blades. Looking at the number of axe wielding corpses around each one, they were a force to be reckoned with.

Ella, Rikol and I each picked up a sword, the other two also taking shields. I shrugged off the idea of defence - I was feeling vengeful and broken, a warring rage of emotions within me and a shield did not fit into that mindset. Adronicus would have called me a young, emotion filled fool before slapping me around the head - and he would have been right to do so. Either way I buckled a sword onto my hip and continued forward, great axe in hand. Rikol and Ella followed closely behind, weapons hanging loosely but ready to move at a moment's notice.

Once we moved past the gate, bodies started to become more sporadic. Instead of seeing shield maidens and the bodies of fighting men in their prime we began to see the corpses of women laying over their dead children, old men hacked down in their homes. As we moved into the second alley a scream came from above us on the second floor of a solidly built wooden structure. Quickly I dashed inside, darting through the shattered door and leaping over the filleted body of an older man who had died defending it. I sped upstairs and with greataxe in hand spun amongst the three men who were approaching a heavily pregnant woman attempting to hold them off with a sword. One spin was all it took, the force of my blow shearing through armour and blades alike. It took the two lower men through the chest and the man closest to the woman through the spine, neatly shearing each body in two in a bloody swathe of gore.

Wiping my face I moved forward and found myself with a sword pointed at my chest.

"Back off Calidan," ordered Ella as she and Rikol caught up, eyes widening at the dripping walls. "You don't look like the friendliest of men right now." I looked down at myself and noticed that my clothing was sodden with blood and nodded, letting Ella walk past, hands in the air.

"We aren't going to hurt you," Ella said, trying the Andurran language. "Can you understand me?"

A burst of language came from the woman's mouth, certainly not Andurran but making Ella and I lock eyes in amazement.

Switching languages fluidly, Ella spoke again and this time the woman reacted, eyes widening before speaking, "Ah so you speak Meredothian, excellent. I am Beonica, First Shield of Rathnor. I thank you for your aid." She gave us an appraising look. "Who are you?

"We come from the Andurran Empire," Ella responded, "and are out here for a test of survival."

"Survival? Well your examiners must want you dead. None come to this land if they can help it." She kicked the corpse of the man next to her. "War is often the least of our concerns."

Rikol had been following our exchange with growing consternation. Finally he interrupted - bursting into conversation in Andurran, "Why do I feel like I'm being left out here? What language are you speaking?"

I turned to him and clapped him on the shoulder. "Sorry Rikol, I forgot you didn't know it. It's the language that an old friend of mine taught Cassius and myself, and then Ella when we got to Forgoth."

"When you got to Forgoth? That means..." his eyes widened, "the Tracker?"

I nodded. Somehow we had ended up close to where the Tracker came from. A land that he hadn't revealed much about, only that it was cold and filled with danger. Looking around I realised that he may have been understating that simple statement somewhat.

"Yes, the Tracker" said Ella. "Now let's find out what's going on and make sure that we survive this mess." She turned back to Beonica and spoke rapidly in fluent Meredothian.

Beonica nodded. "Yes these men have been an enemy for a long time, but never more than raiding parties. They are known locally as the Hrudan. Recently they have been more and more aggressive, pushing further into our lands than ever before. We've been alert since one of our trade routes ceased functioning."

"Ceased functioning?" asked Rikol as Ella translated.

"Trade just stopped coming through," Beonica replied. "Several scouts and war bands have gone out to investigate but none have returned. Since then we have had a watch through the night. Luckily they managed to catch this lot," she kicked the corpse again, "approaching. But they still broke through."

"At a heavy cost from the looks of it," I murmured, to which Beonica flashed a vicious grin.

"Yes, they will have paid a hefty price. But even so they seem to have more numbers than ever whilst each person we lose is another blow to our population." She indicated the outside city with a wave of her hand, "What is happening out there tonight...it is likely this place will never recover, even if we drive the Hrudan off."

"Well, we will save as many as we can," said Ella, "and attempt to remove these Hrudan. Before we go, have you seen anyone similar to ourselves over the past few weeks? Either a boy, similar in height and age to Calidan," she indicated me, "or a young woman, several years older than us with long blonde hair?"

Beonica brightened. "You speak of Cassius and Sophia! They have been indispensable since they arrived some fortnight ago. Cassius has been training some of the women in sword-play - our men still hold to the quaint idea that axes are better - and Sophia has been providing a masterclass in the bow. Where they are now I do not know, but it is likely that they were helping with the defence of the fort. Find them and give them my thanks for their help, and not just for today. They are excellent friends to our people."

"We will Beonica," Ella responded, a proud glimmer in her eyes, "find yourself somewhere safe to hold up."

"Safe? If I were any less pregnant I would be out there showing you young pups how to properly kill a man! Get out of here you mysterious younglings!" with a grim chuckle she shooed us down the stairs before barring the door.

"A strange person," Rikol said as we double checked our equipment and began to move back to the streets. "Not particularly saddened at the death around her."

"I think she is sad, but they seem to be a tough people for whom death is a close friend, whether by fighting, starvation or predation," Ella replied. "I imagine looking straight ahead is the best option at such times. Either way, Beonica is the First Shield. Looking at the number of bodies at the feet of the women in this fort I imagine that means that she would be a great person to have on our side, rather than as an enemy!"

With that we slipped out into the blood-soaked night.

# CHAPTER 8

## *Warband*

Blood spurted as Rikol caressed the man's throat with his blade. A stifled gurgle wound its way from behind the hand he had placed over his mouth and then the man went limp. His prey, a girl barely into two digits of age, lay on the alley floor, naked and motionless, blood seeping from the wound on her head where the brute had hit her. Checking for a pulse Ella shook her head sadly before standing and moving on. In the past hour this had become a common occurrence. Bodies and corpses littered the road, some still warm enough for the attackers to be having their way. Only a few had we seen still alive, either bleeding enough to have been left behind, or being toyed with and wishing for death. Each time their tormentors fell, their focus on their fun giving them no indication that we were near before our blades hit home. We were as shadow, swirling through ash clouds and firelight and leaving only corpses in our wake.

Deliverers of retribution.

Leaving the girl in the alley we stepped out into the main street, our bodies bathed in the flickering light of the burning keep. Taking point, I expanded my senses and focused on the next axe wielding bastard. It had served well so far, fulfilling our need to unleash our vengeance on these marauding monsters. What I hadn't yet managed to do however was locate either Cassius or Sophia. Several of the Hrudan bodies we had come across had been expertly filleted with sword or bow, but we had no way of knowing whether this was the work of our friends or the local defenders - after all they, like us, would be using local and scavenged equipment.

Sensing a group of men surrounding a building up the road I indicated my friends to follow. Together we slipped through the falling ash, unsheathed weapons in hand. As we rounded the corner I held up my hand and we paused to scope out the lay of the land. A low-slung wooden longhouse lay besieged by seven Hrudan. A fire had been started at one end of the building and the seven men were waiting, three covering the exits and the other four spread out near the front door - allowing the smoke to do their work for them and drive the people inside to their waiting blades.

As we watched, one of the raiders passed in front of the open door, briefly silhouetted by the outside light. Instantly an arrow sped out of the building and embedded itself in the warrior's throat. Gurgling and grasping futilely at the barbed shaft the man fell to his knees and slowly slumped sideways to the ground. The remaining three men watching the front door shouted in alarm and moved away from the open hatch. From the looks of the limbs lying in the doorway a frontal assault had already been attempted and been vehemently denied, explaining the approach that the men were taking.

With my senses open I could detect several figures inside the longhouse but the noise and smoke were impeding my ability to sense scent and listen - making it difficult to get a completely accurate picture. With a nod I indicated that it was time to see what was going on the old-fashioned way.

We moved.

Three daggers sped through the air, two flung by Rikol, the other by Ella. Each caught one of the rear watching men completely unaware and like puppets with cut strings they crumpled. With swiftness telling of years of experience in fighting for their lives the three men in front of the longhouse spun, axes to hand yet completely unprepared for my downward swing.

One slice, two halves. The first man fell.

To the remaining men's' eyes it must have been a surprising scene. A somewhat lanky youth dislodging a greataxe with uncanny ease from the split corpse of their comrade. To their credit, they didn't falter in their charge, though whether that should be classed as bravery or stupidity I do not know. Ducking the first swing I spun, keeping my axe held solidly at my chest. The blade parted the leather jerkin of the first man before tearing through skin, flesh and bone. By the time the first man landed on the floor, right leg removed at the hip, the second was met with an ascending uppercut that caught the hilt of his weak attempt to parry, splintered its way through and entered his lower jaw.

I flicked the blood off the axe and waited for Rikol and Ella to join me at the side of the door as they collected their blades. Filling my lungs I spoke loudly, my voice reverberating through the air. "Your attackers are dead, we mean no harm - Beonica sent us," first in Andurran, then in Meredothian.

A pause.

"Calidan?"

"Sophia?"

A shout of delight and some quickly spoken words and then Sophia emerged from the door, smoke curling around her form. As stunning as ever, she looked strong and lively, wearing figure fitting leather armour and carrying a beautiful ash bow. Tears trickled down her face as she walked and embraced me in a long hug.

"Perfect timing," she whispered, kissing me on the cheek before turning to hug Rikol and Ella.

It had been a long time coming, but the dorm was nearly complete.

Once the hugs and celebrations were complete Sophia introduced us to the three other people who had emerged from the

longhouse. Two women and one man, all three carrying bows. "Ryese, Llenya and Merkin," Sophia spoke, indicating her companions, "they are what remains of my archery unit."
"Archery unit?" Rikol questioned.
"Cassius and I got here together. We had found each other not too long upon waking in this place. That was a mindfuck as I imagine you know." Nods all round. "So it wasn't just us, that's something," she murmured.
"We reckon this is the fourth-year test," said Ella.
"That's what we reckoned too. Anyway I'll keep this short, the streets aren't safe and we need to find Cassius." She took a brief drink from a water skin and sighed heartily. "We found this place and they were good to us, saw that we needed help. Cassius spoke the language - as I hear you and Ella do, Calidan - and we were allowed to stay in the fort. These people pride themselves on their fighting and hunting skills and once they saw what we could do we were each approached by numerous people. Calidan started teaching a core of sword wielders how to improve their skills and I began working with those who enjoyed the bow. Before last night I had twenty-two in my group...now I have three."
"Have you seen Cassius since the fighting started?" Ella asked, tension in her voice.
"He was leading his unit with the defenders at the gate. If he wasn't amongst the fallen then he will have beat a fighting retreat to the keep. We aimed to get there too but got cut off."
I looked at the keep, grimacing at the fire lashing up the wooden walls. "Is there a fallback position past the keep?"
"Caves underneath the keep. One passage in and only wide enough to fit one man. If Cassius made it there then he could hold the passage for as long as he wanted. It's one of the reasons why the First Shield has pushed learning the sword on her brethren, the passage is too narrow to effectively wield an axe."
"That's our destination then," I confirmed and turned to her archers. "We go to rescue those in the keep, stay or come along

- you decide." As one they hefted their bows and fell in step. A warband of seven to relieve a fallen fort. It would have to be enough.

# CHAPTER 9

## Differing Views II

### Sophia

"Hone yourself into what you need to be to survive."

Sophia opened her eyes and immediately shut them against the burning light. A thin layer of diabolical snow reflected the dazzling beams with a vengeance directly into her retinas. Gasping at the sudden attack she blinked rapidly and then forced herself to open her eyes again.

*Snow?* she thought sluggishly. *Why am I outside?* Her brain chose that moment to fire up properly and alarm bells rang as she rolled, looking for the twisted killer that had done so many terrible things to her friends. The needles of a fir tree stared back at her, a thin veil of protection against the elements in the small hollow she found herself. There was nothing else, no evil being, no torture chamber, nothing at all. In fact the only thing that her current situation held in common with the chamber was that she was still very much naked.

A gust of frigid wind caused her to shiver violently and she clutched her arms to herself, seeking any warmth that she could. *It doesn't matter why I am here or how,* she thought through chattering teeth, *I just need to get warm.*

With that in mind she crawled out of her little hollow and scanned the horizon, looking for any tell-tale signs to iden- tify where she was, or any elements of civilization. Except for frozen tundra and fir-lined forest she found little and she began to trudge towards the forest boundary before a small dark smudge on the horizon caught her eye. *Smoke?*

Locking the location in her mind she continued her walk towards the forest, figuring that she could follow its edge until she was forced to leave it to investigate the cause of the smoke. Having grown up in the Ryganthian steppes, her people were used to living off an otherwise hostile land and so she had little in the way of concerns for surviving in the short term. Indeed she welcomed the challenge, embracing it for the ability to lose herself in pure survival rather than in the haunting memories of her recent past.

Two days later she walked out of the edge of the forest clad in deer skin with a fox pelt that covered her shoulders and a makeshift bow held loosely at her side. It wouldn't last too long once the wood began to dry out, but for the short term it provided relatively decent accuracy over a short distance. Put any of her clan in a survival situation and they would likely be looking to craft a bow before sourcing water. It was part of her heritage - she *needed* the feel of a bow in her hand - and it had already proven its worth, allowing her to snag the buck she now wore around her before it could bolt. With an easy lope she set out to investigate the source of the smoke that she had seen two days before. It was thicker here, easier to spot and relatively constant, meaning that it could only come from a settlement. With any luck it would be a place where she would be able to find help and figure out where in the world she was.

* * *

**Cassius**

*"Hone yourself into what you need to be to survive."*
Cassius awoke to coarse laughter, the sound of it sending shivers through his body at the thought that the demon was back for more. He kept his eyes shut, knowing that opening them would just give him more bloody horrors to see, that the swaying of his body on the rope would just keep making him nauseous.

*Wait.* He wasn't swaying. There was cold earth under his body. Opening his eyes to the blinding light above he found himself the subject of scrutiny. Two heavily built men stood above him, axes held in hand whilst laughing in astonishment. At first he wasn't sure why but as the cold air began to send shivers down his spine he realised that he wasn't wearing an inch of clothing. With a start he moved to cover himself up, in doing so causing the two to laugh even harder, but now the laughter had a menacing edge. Mirth at someone insane enough to be naked outside in what was apparently a snow filled tundra, but the laughter wasn't a joyous sound, nor was it friendly.

Cassius eyed the two men warily as he slowly made to stand up. A burst of language came from one of the two, the man who had spoken looking at his companion and gesturing in Cassius's direction, prompting another bout of laughter. The same man shook his head as if in disbelief and gripping the axe more tightly he took a step towards Cassius who raised his hands non-threateningly whilst moving back a step. He didn't have a clue what was going on, but it was quickly becoming clear that he had moved from one hostile environment to another.

Another step and another step back. The man's face grew hard now, the chuckle low and menacing. A third step and this time Cassius moved forwards instead of away, stepping into the man's guard, one arm going to maintain control of the axe hand, the other jabbing straight knuckles into his opponent's throat. A kick to the crotch as hands came up to scrabble at a damaged trachea and he stepped back, twisting the arm and driving the man to the floor, coming back up with the axe in hand, his eyes already on the second man who had barely moved in the moment it had taken Cassius to dismantle his colleague.

Eventually he got over his surprise and with a bellow he leapt forward, sending a whistling slice at Cassius who danced lightly out of the way, circling around the slow-moving man at his feet. A shout on the wind and an arrow arced down from the sky, hitting the second attacker like a thunderbolt, sending him spinning to the floor. Cassius spun from the direction the arrow had come from, raising a hand to his eyes against the glare of the sun. Three figures were moving in his direction, bows held out and arrows loosely knocked. Cassius raised his hands and took a few steps away from the first man he had dropped before lowering the axe he had collected. Against bows in a land with little in the way of cover he didn't have much hope of dodging. He kept his hands raised as the archers approached, fur wrapped figures swiftly closing the distance. One kept a bow trained on Cassius whilst the others checked the two on the floor with the wounded man Cassius had taken down being rapidly stripped of weapons and bound.

Low orders were muttered and Cassius's ears perked up. Seeing his reaction his guard lowered her fur hood, revealing a curious look on hazel eyes.

"Interesting way to introduce yourself to a lady," she said in the Tracker's language, her voice low and husky. She reached down to the body at her feet and threw Cassius the man's cloak. "Come on boy, you get to meet Jadira. I imagine you have quite the story to tell."

❋ ❋ ❋

## Sophia

The black smudge Sophia had seen two days before had turned out to be a fort, smoke drifting lazily upwards on the morning air from numerous cookfires and braziers. She had watched the fort for some time, trying to get a feel for the people who lived inside, and by the reflection that kept catching the sun she had no doubt that she was being scrutinised in turn.

*Well, I can either go and live in a forest or go and see what these people are like,* she thought dryly. *No impaled people on spikes, no raging pyres or blood-soaked signs so hopefully they're open to outsiders and not cannibals.* She cast one last look at the forest behind her, a part of her attracted to the idea of running back in there and losing herself in the simplicity of it all, but she was an Imp and if she was lost in some unknown corner of the world then it was her duty to get herself unlost so that she could return to the Academy, so pushing aside her last remnants of hesitation she started forward towards the fort.

As she walked across the snow, features that she hadn't been able to make out at distance began to be clearer. The fort was a mixture of wood and stone, thick wooden beams supporting the outer battlements above a solid stone base. Judging by the roaming guards, the parapets were at least large enough for two to walk side by side and the top of the wall was easily thirty foot in height, providing any guard an enviable view over the relatively flat landscape. Furthermore, the place was *large.* The walls stretched for a substantial distance in either direction and looked to extend far into the distance. It was certainly no temporary fort but something that had been developed to be a place to call home. She only hoped that for a short time at least she would be allowed to do the same.

She tensed as she walked into bowshot, half expecting a shout from one of the guards and prepared for an arrow to the gut. When neither came she walked on until she was within easy bowshot of the walls and when still no shout came she walked to the foreboding log door that blocked the entrance. As she lifted her hand to knock, the smaller door within the frame opened and a fierce looking woman stepped out, a hand on the hilt of her sword. She barked a word, the inflection suggesting it was a question and paused as if waiting for an answer. When Sophia shook her head she sighed and tried another language before asking again in thick, heavily accented Andurran.

"Name?"

"Sophia," she replied.

The guard nodded as if that somehow meant something to her and stepping out of the door frame she indicated that she should enter. Ducking through the door Sophia walked into the fort and found a backdrop of wooden lodges, each cleverly constructed with heavy wooden logs that seemed to slot together. It was unlike anything she had seen in the empire and certainly nothing that her clan would ever use but before she was given more time to admire the buildings or take in the hustle and bustle of the seemingly thriving fortification the guard took her by the arm and led her further into the maze, driving her through the streets until they came to a door of a lodge no different from the others that she had seen.

Opening the door the guard ushered her through before closing the door behind Sophia, shouting only one word before she left. "Sophia!"

A small but powerfully built woman looked up from her conversation with a fur wrapped figure and smiled before speaking in flawless Andurran. "Sophia. Glad to meet you. I've heard a lot about you."

"You...have?" Sophia replied, stunned. "By who?"

"By me," replied a voice she knew all too well. Turning, she found Cassius coming in the door with a tentative smile on his face. "Hi Sophia."

✳ ✳ ✳

**Cassius**

Sophia stared at him like she had seen a ghost, which wasn't too far from the truth.

"You're dead," she whispered, taking a step back before muttering a line in her own language and making a strange hand motion as though warding herself from evil.

"He's not dead," said the woman from behind her, "and neither are you. Cassius is the reason that you were allowed into the fort. He described his friends when we had our first meeting and so when my guards reported a white-haired girl watching the fort I had Cassius go and take a look." She gave a nod at Cassius who inclined his head towards her.

"I'm incredibly grateful you allowed me to do so, Jadira. This is certainly Sophia and no, Sophia, neither of us are dead." He spread his arms out wide and took a step forward, "I didn't believe it at first when I saw you through their scope, but it's certainly you!" He took another step, then a third before gently wrapping his arms around her.

"I'm so sorry," he whispered in a voice suddenly thick with barely withheld emotion.

As she slowly wrapped her arms around him, as though wary that he might just vanish into thin air the dam cracked and Cassius sobbed. Suddenly Sophia's hold on him became that of a drowning person and together they sank to the floor in tears. Jadira gave them some modicum of privacy, looking over the maps that were spread over the table in front of her before clearing her throat when she sensed the time was right. A few moments later they were standing, eyes dried and cheeks flushed with the excitement of having a friend thought dead reappear.

"First things first..." Jadira began, directing her gaze at Sophia, "Cassius has told me what he knew. Said that you were tortured, that all of his friends were killed and that he awoke naked in the snow. What's your story?"

Sophia's eyes widened at the revelation and quickly added in her own version of events, highlighting how she had seen her friends, including Cassius die before her eyes.

Jadira nodded along as Sophia spoke, her eyes dark. "Okay, well as an impartial bystander I can confirm that both of you are physically here and very much alive, so unless you can be killed and brought back to life I'm going to suggest that what you saw was in your head. As for waking up naked in the snow? Sounds like someone is either playing a sick prank on you or throwing you in the deep end and seeing if you manage to swim."

At that both Cassius and Sophia shared looks.

"As it is, I could do with some more bodies around the place. As Cassius is all too aware, Hrudan forces are being found throughout my land in more numbers than I care for. My hunters tell me that Cassius managed to thoroughly disarm a heavily armed Hrudan warrior whilst naked and cold. If that's true then you've had training, yes?"

A hesitant nod from Cassius.

"Good enough for me. If you support my people with training I will see you fed, housed and watered until such time that your other friends arrive or you choose to leave. If you have other skills that would be useful feel free to make them known to me and I'll see you put to use. No idle hands or free meals here I'm afraid."

Sophia raised a hand and waited for Jadira to nod before speaking, "Bows are my speciality. I would put good money on being able to teach your best a thing or two."

Jadira gave her a thoughtful look before clapping her hands together in decision. "Good, I like that spirit. My archers are good, better than good in fact, but if the both of you are who I think you are then you might well just be able to show everyone something new."

At that Cassius and Sophia shared a look but said nothing, cementing Jadira's theory in her mind. "Excellent," she said with a laugh. "Cassius already knows where to get food and Jentar here," she pointed at the fur clad man sitting opposite her, "will sort you a place to stay as well as introduce you to the right people. I'll come and find you when I have a spare moment and see how things are getting on. Happy?"

The two looked at each other then grinned back at the smiling woman. "Happy," they said in unison.

* * *

## Sophia

The arrow thrummed through the air in a high arc, the fletching rippling in the wind. A moment later the furthest man crumpled, the shaft buried deep in his neck. The others with him spared him no glance and just kept running.

Three more bows twanged and two more men fell, the third arrow just missing as its intended target darted away at the last moment - a stroke of blind luck rather than intent.

Sophia nocked and fired again, this time the arrow taking the final raider through the chest and sending him tumbling to the ground.

"Excellent shooting everyone," she said softly as she started towards the fallen men. "All the shots were on target and accounted for the wind, nicely done." She directed her gaze to Yana, an archer who looked slightly crestfallen at having missed, "You would have hit had he not moved at the last second, nothing about your technique was off."

Yana gave a small grimace but nodded. "I would have got him with the second arrow."

"I know you would," Sophia replied with a smile, "but I wasn't going to leave those murdering bastards alive any longer than I had to."

Ten days since Sophia had arrived at the fort and raids by the Hrudan, the axe wielding killers who had chosen to pick a fight with Cassius the week before, had only increased. Jadira had said that they had long experienced such raids but the number was becoming too frequent, as though the Hrudan were here in force. There had been five separate reports of attacks in the past week with outlying hamlets and farms being targeted. The Meredothians were a hardy bunch themselves but the outlying farms had been targeted by more people than they could handle, resulting in a one-sided fight. Jadira had increased patrols of the outer areas whilst offering sanctuary to those who wanted to leave their homes until they felt safe, but for many of the farmers and solitary folk who lived out in the wilds of the Meredothian heartland it was their home - and they had no desire to leave.

The four that Sophia and the small unit of trackers had hunted for the past day had slaughtered a farm of five. Two adults and three children killed for a pittance of wine and food. Sophia didn't really know who these Hrudan were or why they had problems with the Meredothians but raiders were seemingly the same the world over and her clan had the same approach as those she had spent the last days with; root them out with efficient force.

Jadira had been true to her word, allowing Sophia and Cassius to stay within the fort, providing them with clothes and equipment as long as they helped support the people within. She obviously knew more than she was letting on, Sophia had a sneaking suspicion she knew about Imperators and an even larger suspicion that she was in liaison with the Emperor, but she had spent an hour judging their skills with blade and bow with a critical eye before ordering that they provide whatever pointers and training that they could to the rest of her people. Jadira's fort had guards but by and large Meredothians didn't have formal soldiers. They had skilled people in violence that was for certain, but it was generally an extra addition to another skillset, whereas the Hrudan seemed to be fighters first and foremost. Jadira had implemented a training regime when she took ownership of the fort to make a cadre of individuals who were fighters beyond all else, and they were excellent. Beonica, the First Shield, was the leader of the troops and was an excellent fighter. Initially Cassius had been wary that she might have been against the sword skills that he could demonstrate but her eagerness for new tools within her repertoire had her training alongside her team, regardless of her pregnancy.

If the fighters that Beonica led were great, the hunters who doubled as guards were a step above. Food could be relatively scarce in the surrounding lands and consequently the ability to take a bird on the wing was highly prized. Jadira's hunters were sharp eyed and keen of hearing and their tracking abilities were the main reason that the Hrudan perpetrating the raids on Jadira's people were being punished. Unfortunately the hunters were so useful that they weren't often at the fort as guards but were out doing what they did best. As such Sophia was spending most of her time with hunters in training and bringing them up to speed. Yana, Merkin and Illien were three of her trainees, each of them already skilled with archery but with just enough rough edges for Sophia to be able to mould them into something better.

Approaching the fresh corpses with a critical eye Sophia gave a nod of satisfaction. Each enemy had been struck cleanly through the torso, impressive work considering the distance had been near three hundred feet. Quickly and efficiently the team checked the dead for anything of value, particularly anything that would suggest where they were coming from or why they were ramping up their attacks, but aside from some dried meats and a couple of wine skins they had little worth taking. The Meredothians seemed disciplined to utilise the armour and weaponry of the Hrudan and Sophia was more than happy to leave the heavy equipment where it lay, instead beginning the long walk back to the fort, eager to get back to the warming fires.

\* \* \*

**Cassius**

"Form up," Cassius barked. "At my tempo, second sequence. Ready? Begin." He delivered an overtly slow series of moves, moving as though in treacle and grinned at the gasping and shaking team that followed him, their muscles aching with the pace.

"Doing such activities slowly may seem counter intuitive," he said once he finished and they collapsed on the floor, "but you are putting your muscles under much greater strain than just flicking through the motions. Do it slowly first, repeatedly, before finishing your session with the faster versions, your muscles will thank you for the warm up and for the extra exercise." He gave them a wink, "Once you stop trembling, that is." For the past ten days he had been training those who had been interested in the finer points of swordplay. Interestingly the majority of those who had taken him up on the offer had been female, with Beonica laughing at his puzzlement by simply explaining that most Meredothian men were idiots bound by tradition to hit things with an axe. The real fighters were the women, often quicker on their feet in the snow and that could make all the difference in a battle.

As Cassius urged his trainees back to their feet a low horn sounded out from one of the fort towers. The deep noise reverberated through the buildings, feeling like it was thrumming through Cassius's chest until it trickled into nothingness. At first there was no sound and then like a lightning bolt had struck the fort burst into activity.

"What's going on?" Cassius yelled as his erstwhile troops deserted his training session, scattering in all directions.

Stopping long enough to explain, Isma said, "The long horn means enemy spotted. It wouldn't have been sounded unless there were many. Everyone is to arm up and prepare for assault." She thought for a moment and then spoke again, "You should check with Jadira or Beonica as to what to do."

"No need," Cassius replied with a grim smile. "You're my trainees, I'll stand with you."

"Find us at the gate!" Isma shouted as she ran to get her gear. Sprinting quickly into the ordered chaos that had overtaken the village Cassius found Sophia in the bunks they had been allotted, and together they quickly strapped on any protection that they had been offered, which largely amounted to furs, blades and bows. Stepping back onto the street Sophia gave Cassius a clap on the shoulder before running off to the nearest tower overlooking the gate. Cassius turned and followed the street down to the main gate, joining his sword bearers.

"Isma," he shouted above the din. "What's the situation?"

"Hrudan forces on the horizon," she reported. "Looks like enough for a full-scale attack. They'll be here before dark."

"Have they attacked before?" he asked, leaning against the nearest wall.

"A couple of times, but they are usually raids. Enough men to climb the walls during the night and steal what they can. From the sound of it this is a full-scale assault," Essel offered.

"So they know that the Meredothians have good archers and they're still some distance away..." Cassius mused more to himself than the others. "If I were you, I would take what rest you can. I doubt we will see much action until nightfall."

"Already ordering my people around young Cassius?" a voice asked in a clipped tone. Looking up he saw Jadira descending from the nearest tower, her face drawn and grim.

"My apologies," Cassius said, hands held high, "I meant no offence."

Jadira waved him off and motioned for the soldiers to stand down. "No apology needed as your assessment is likely correct. They have felt the sting of our arrows many times and unless they have some secret that I can't discern they would barely reach the walls of our fort with the numbers they have in the daylight. They will come at dark. Stand down for the moment, eat and rest. You will be the breach guard. Anything gets through that gate or forces a breach, you close it." She locked eyes with everyone in the unit one by one. "Do me proud."

A clang of fists on chest pieces resounded as the Meredothians saluted their leader. With a final nod at Cassius, Jadira headed in the direction of her map room and following her advice he set off in search of food.

It was going to be a long night.

＊　＊　＊

## Sophia

Darkness fell and with it the shifting line of watching warriors started the steady jog towards the fort. Flaming arrows roared out of the keep, rippling through the air to land in the surrounding snow, providing just enough light before extinguishing to judge whether the shadows approaching were troops or tricks of the eye. Shouts, challenges and war cries began to fill the night as the Hrudan approached, the thump of heavy boots sending a rumble through the air. One by one the twang of bow strings sounded as sharp-eyed hunters started to take their toll and screams began to add to the encroaching cacophony.

Sophia nocked, released, nocked and released again. The half-seen shadows that had been moving towards the base of the wall stiffened and fell, and she gave a small grimace of satisfaction before turning her attention to the next shifting movement. A rattle of hail on the battlements startled her for a moment until she heard the short scream of one of her fellow archers and saw her drop to the floor below. The Hrudan had ranged weapons of their own it seemed and the archers were far enough away as to be invisible to the fort's occupants. They didn't appear to be picking their targets but it served to keep the defenders' heads down, slackening the rate of fire and allow the Hrudan troops to get closer to the wall.

"Keep firing!" bellowed one of the archers. "Do not stop!"

"Troops at the base of the wall!" shouted another.

Sophia poked her head above the parapet and saw a long shadow snaking its way through the flickering flames. It took a moment for her brain to make sense of what she was seeing but when it did she ran to the other side of the tower and screamed at the guard below.

"Ram incoming, brace the gate! Brace the gate!"

Cassius took one look at her panicked face and sprinted with the other breach guard to slam themselves against the thick log gate, muscles straining in anticipation of what was to come.

The ram appeared out of the darkness, a thick pine cut down with branches trimmed to be handles for the wielders, the men holding it thick of arm and back, their heads hunched over as they powered through the snow with their heavy burden. Arrows arced in, some finding targets and causing the load to increase for the others, but more missed; hammering into the snow or thunking into the wood of the pine. Over the last few feet the gasping breaths of the ram bearers turned into a deep roar as they charged the weapon home.

The boom of the ram impacting the gate shuddered the palisade behind which Sophia crouched and sent Cassius and his breach guard flying back, only to fling themselves back at the gate before the ram could hit again.

Sophia looked over towards the gate, spotted her target and in one fluid motion rose, aimed and fired before sinking back down behind the wall, her target dropped with an arrow lodged in his neck.

"Make way!" shouted a voice and she pressed herself into the wall as two huddled past carrying a heavy pot. They reached the top of the gate and then with a heave sent the contents of the pot over the side. Instantly the smell of cooking flesh rose to Sophia's nostrils and the screams rose to fever pitch.

The ram fell silent for a blessed moment of respite, but the Hrudan who hid at the base of the wall in relative protection from the archers ran to pick it up again, quickly starting their work anew. The resounding *thuds* started again, but quickly became accompanied by splintering *cracks* as the gate began to suffer. A fresh wave of arrows hammered into the dual towers surrounding the gate, trying the prevent the archers from hitting the ram crews and then the night lit up as the Hrudan archers lit their arrows, sending them blazing into the wooden walls of the fort, concentrating primarily on the towers until they resembled a crackling bonfire. The defenders hurriedly threw buckets of water and snow on any fires that they could reach but soon the blazes on the tops of the towers were raging out of control.

Another splintering thunk and this time there was a cry from the streets below. Sophia stuck her head out and saw that the head of the ram had broken through part of the gate, leaving a gaping wound where the once sturdy log had lain.

That was the only thing that saved her life.

A low *clunk* sounded as something rolled into the tower. Sophia turned just in time to see the burning wick fizzle down to nothing and then the world went white.

\* \* \*

### Cassius

Cassius ducked as a blast came from above, seeing someone get flung onto the roof of the nearest lodge and heard the screams that followed. *Black powder,* he thought grimly as he ran to brace the gate again but the ram got there first. This time the entire gate fell inwards and the breach guard scrambled to get out of the way, some making it in time, others not so lucky and being crushed by the falling timber. Howling war cries the Hrudan charged through the now open gate, butchering those that were on the floor and aiming to flood into the fort.

Desperately Cassius dived into the melee, shouting for his

breach guard to form up and get back into the fight. His sword soon became slick with blood as he fought like a man possessed, taking wrists and throats as he battled to stand above his fallen friends. In the tight press his smaller sword made for a better weapon than the great axes that the Hrudan needed room to swing, but their size and power began to take its toll. The movements of Kaschan were largely impossible, the floor slick with blood and bodies, and too many people surrounding him to be able to dance out of the way of attacks.

He felt, rather than saw, the impact of his allies coming back into the fray. The Hrudan reeled back as shields smashed into the line, forming a wedge that drove deep into their ranks in order to him. A hilt of an axe caught him in the face and his attacker snarled as he made to follow up before an arrow lodged itself in his eye socket, his corpse kept upright in the press of people. A hand grabbed Cassius's shoulder and pulled him back, dragging him behind the line of shields and giving him a moment's respite. Giving himself a quick once over he had numerous cuts and scratches but none of them deep, and as far as he could tell the majority of the blood that covered him was thankfully not his. Looking up at the roof he saw Sophia firing into the press of people, her clothes charred and face covered in smoke but her will to fight unbroken.

A shield bearer fell, great axe splitting her head like a log. Respite over Cassius stepped back into the line, his sword seeking out the exultant axe wielder and leaving him gasping over a severed windpipe. He fell back into the mechanical nature of his swordplay, block and counter strike, covering those nearest to him when he was able and punishing the enemy for every mistake. For a moment he dreamt that they could hold the breach, that they could keep the Hrudan from progressing any further and then the line wavered from impact and he realised what Sophia had been trying to scream over the din of battle.

"They're over the walls!"

The gate was not the only point being assaulted and the more dexterous warriors had managed to climb the walls, removing the guards and pouring into the fort in enough numbers to throw the tide of the battle for the gate into the favour of the Hrudan.

Seeing this and seeing the shield bearers begin to fall, struck from blows from the side without opportunity to defend themselves Cassius made the call.

"Fall back!" he bellowed. "Back to the keep!"

The Hrudan surged forward as the defenders began to melt away, axes catching many of those who tried to run and leaving them broken on the floor. With his immediate group Cassius sprinted twenty paces before turning and as one slamming back into the chasing warriors, the ferocity of the impact breaking up the attacking force enough for them to break off again, leaving three dead Hrudan and one dead shield maiden.

Bit by bit they began to carve their way back to the keep, collecting any Meredothians who they met on the way. The retreat became easier as they moved, the chasing warriors lost in the glee of loot and slaughter. Screams resounded through the air as those who hadn't managed to retreat began to suffer at the hands of the aggressors but Cassius couldn't stop to help or they would all be lost. He clamped down on his emotions and swore to save all he could. In the keep they could hold until it was over.

One way or the other.

# CHAPTER 10

## *Relief*

T he keep was a raging blaze. Rising above the rest of the fort large parts of it were burning merrily away and bodies littered the path up to the main gates. Thankfully these were primarily the corpses of the invaders and had been killed by blade and feathered shaft. Here and there were larger groups of fallen where the defenders had turned and counter charged their pursuers. Judging from what my senses were telling me, the attackers had numbers to spare, whereas for each defender lost the chances of anyone surviving this assault dwindled. I just hoped that Cassius had made it to the caves.

We sprinted up the hill, dodging bodies and removing pockets of resistance where we could. Sophia's allies proved themselves to be as good a shot as the woman herself. Many of the targets we engaged fell before the rest of us lowly melee fighters could close with them, arrows unerringly embedded in throats, eyes or craniums. As we ran past each archer would scavenge the arrows they had fired, re-utilising them if they weren't broken and even with that tactic they were running low. Barely four arrows apiece. A pity that they didn't have more for my senses told me at least thirty men, maybe more, were inside the keep and moving deeper inside the building, hulking brutes one and all. The burning gates flanked a scene from a nightmare with the steps to the keep slick with blood and viscera; bodies strewn all over. The attackers had paid dearly for entrance to the building.

Eyes sharp and noting each fallen body we entered the flaming building, weapons held ready. The first to fall was an invader that exited a side room, wine flask in hand. His face registered nothing but pure shock that there was something pointy in his chest. A shout came from ahead, a questioning tone. After a period of silence, another shout - angry this time. Boots stomped down the hall towards us. As the bulk of the aggressor came into view an arrow embedded itself in his shoulder. An angry grunt from Ryese - the top most fletching had come off mid-flight and altered the trajectory of the arrow. The wounded man spun and shouted before a second and third arrow hit the base of his neck and back of his skull. He crumpled to the ground.

I silently wished that the man's shout hadn't been heard.

Unfortunately my luck had never been that good.

The person commanding this attack wasn't entirely stupid and had committed a rear-guard to ensure that the keep wasn't relieved by counterattack. This rear guard now formed up around the corner of the hallway, out of sight for arrow shot, but not from my senses. The keep had been designed with defence in mind, the main corridor twisted and turned at various points. From the corpses strewn around the place it had served its purpose. Now those same defences were working against us, allowing the ten-man unit to wait in relatively safety around the ninety-degree bend. I relayed what I knew and motioned for the archers to watch our backs. Ella, Rikol and I strode forward; it was time to get messy.

We halted at the edge of the corner. The ten men were in two ranks, each person shifting in anticipation. Unfortunately, whilst the idea was sound the reality was flawed. Unlike soldiers with shields who can cover the comrade next to him, soldiers with two handed weapons are not best suited to holding positions. They are line breakers; shock troops employed to shatter defensive lines and best work in open spaces. A corridor with room for perhaps three people to actually swing a weapon? They were their own worst enemy.

Rikol edged one of his blades around the corner, using it as a mirror to judge the enemy placement. He held another blade loosely in his right hand, Ella held a further two. Nodding at each other they both darted forward and loosed their daggers, three of which embedded themselves in the chest or throat of their intended targets. The fourth ricocheted off the blade of a greataxe raised in protection. As the rest of the men charged I swept forward, axe held across my shoulder. Ducking into the mass of men I sheared through two in one swing before being forced to leave the axe embedded in the chest of a third. Rikol and Ella came forward, flowing past each other in perfect Kaschan form, two strikes each and two men fell. The remaining two swung wild, chest shattering swings but the blows were easy for my companions to avoid. Ella spun and slipped past the head of an axe, embedding a blade in her assailant's eye before kicking the final man in the side of his ankle whilst he was distracted, the brief moment of uncontrolled focus giving Rikol all the time he needed to drive his blade into his opponent's throat.

Sophia emerged behind us, leading the rest of the archers who looked somewhat stunned at how quickly we had dispatched the ten men.

"Good job," was all she said as she walked past, an arrow loosely mocked to her string. "My turn to take point". A normal person would probably argue that an archer is a terrible point man, especially in confined quarters. But we Imps had all seen many times just how fast Sophia was. And it wasn't just speed, it was her uncanny accuracy whilst firing as a purely reflexive movement. Honestly, I wouldn't want to test my speed against her archery.

With Sophia leading the way forward we fell into step behind her, weapons at the ready and archers at the rear. I left behind

my borrowed greataxe and instead drew my sword. As fond of
it as I was growing, as these fallen men had just found out, axes
weren't always the best choice. What was ahead was likely to
be knife work; a close, confined melee. Our specialty.

We passed into the great hall. Vast timbers crossed over the
ceiling holding old flags and tapestries. It looked like it would
have been a homely place were it not for the tables that lay
upturned in a concentric ring at the far end of the room. Approaching, it became clear that there had been an attempt at a
barricade. More bodies lay sprawled around the tables and the
floor was precariously slick with blood and splintered wood.

"Let me guess, the entrance to the caverns is past the barricade?" said Rikol.

"Correct," replied Sophia, "looks like someone was trying to
buy some time."

"No sign of Cassius thankfully," said Ella.

"I wouldn't say that's entirely accurate," I replied. "Look at the
bodies, several have sword cuts - rare enough here - that are
very well placed. Throat, heart, lead arm. I would go so far to
say that this is Cassius's work."

Tears welled in Ella's eyes before she nodded, "Let's move."

Following Sophia, we moved past the barricade and through
a curtained door. Several more bodies lay in the hallway, two
leather clad attackers and one female defender, her sword still
in hand even in death. Slightly further down the hall were
wooden steps leading down. Together we descended into
the gloom, the foreboding atmosphere lit only by a periodic
torch. Moving forward I took over from Sophia, trusting my
senses to warn me of any incoming attack. The wooden steps
soon became stone. Narrow and difficult to navigate steps
that had been carved into solid rock.

"Not far now," came Sophia's whispered voice. She was right;
I could hear a cacophony of noise coming from further down
the stairs. Sounds of fighting with the associated grunts of
pain and blades on steel, and further on cries of fear and panic.
Finally we reached the bottom of the stairs and emerged into a

scene reminiscent of the paintings of heroic last stands found in any noble's house in the Empire.

Bodies lay strewn across the floor, with a veritable pile close around the entrance to a narrow passage through the rock. Cassius stood alone, breathing heavily and holding the entrance against a wave of furious attackers. Cuts lacerated his face, close calls each, and he was keeping his weight off his left leg. Even as we arrived he lunged forward, showing no sign of his injury and speared a man through the throat as he raised his axe. Another to add to the pile.

Perhaps twenty men were waiting to engage Cassius. But as Sophia had said, the choke point was extremely effective, forcing a one-on-one situation. If this had been one of our training sessions, Adronicus would have seen that Cassius didn't have a shield and lambasted him whilst we riddled him full of blunt arrows. Thankfully the attackers were either too prideful to use anything other than their axes or had lost all their bows - something that favoured our friend. Something that I have learnt time and time again over the years and have used to extreme effectiveness is that if you need a small choke point holding then Cassius is the man to do it. His skill with the blade meant that unless you got around him or did something particularly unexpected he wasn't going to be going down easily.

Unfortunately, in battle unexpected things happen all the time.

As Cassius began to withdraw his sword, a particularly large warrior kicked the corpse of his companion forward, preventing Cassius from easily withdrawing his blade as the body came in his direction. A brutal punch from a massive fist struck my friend's face as the warrior came forward, charging over the corpse and preventing the sword from being dislodged. Cassius swayed, the blow having rocked his senses, but as the fighter moved to strike with the hilt of his axe, Cassius launched forward and buried a knife in his wrist.

Bellowing with agony, the warrior dropped his axe, seized

Cassius with his good arm and cruelly head butted him before dragging him back out of the crevasse and throwing him into the circle of men. And in doing so finally noticed us.

So intent were the men on the fight with Cassius that they hadn't noticed the quick dispatch of their comrades and the newly arrived force at their rear. Seven corpses lay on the floor by the time Cassius was flung into the mass of rage filled men. Or more accurately, rage filled men, and us.

A pause filled the air as the men realised that it wasn't their comrades standing next to them, but young, gangly youths. Their gazes slowly lifted from Cassius, taking in our clothing, weapons, age and the corpses at our feet, before one by one their brains confirmed that no, we weren't friendly.

When the pause was at its peak, I spoke up. "Morning!" I said brightly, before stepping over Cassius and stabbing the man nearest to me in the neck.

Chaos ensued.

Ella and Rikol joined me in front of Cassius, our blades out and stabbing furiously. Sophia grabbed Cassius and with the help of the three archers, dragged him clear to the base of the stairs. Once they had him to safety they turned and with their remaining arrows began a murderous fire. The big warrior grabbed the man nearest him as two arrows whistled towards his face, utilising his friend as an impromptu shield before crashing forward into the melee. A thunderous punch caught Rikol on the side of the head as he moved to dislodge his knife from the armpit of an armoured opponent. A knee followed the blow, doubling him over and a mighty kick sent him sprawling into the brawl. The giant strode through the fight, five men drawing close around him, their axes at the ready.

Kaschan, for all its excellent qualities, is not best suited to engaging an organised unit. Practitioners of the art are masters of utilising weaknesses, drawing enemies into dangerous situations where our movement and skill sets can wreak havoc. Such fighters are wasted against an organised battle line where the shoulder-to-shoulder discipline of trained soldiers prevents gaps from occurring. For a second it looked as though the giant and his men would succeed in forcing their way out of the cavern. They moved as an organised unit, capitalising on our engagement of the others to force their way towards the stairs.

Then Sophia struck. Arrows spent she dropped her bow and darted forward, blades in hand. She spun past a descending axe from the leading man, gashing a wrist as she moved and waited for the opportunity that came in the form of her archer team's final two arrows. Expertly aimed, the two men closest to her fell. In an instant she was within the group, unleashing tightly controlled savagery with her daggers. Axes raised and fell, only to find nothing but air as she danced.

The distraction was all Cassius needed. Picking up one of the axes he hefted its weight, the great axe massive in his young hands. He paused, watching the fray, biding his time. With a sudden whip-like movement of his body he flung the axe, snapping it towards the large brute as the man turned towards Sophia whilst she was busy embedding her dagger in his comrade's eye. His boulder of an arm stopped mid-swing and instead reached up to clutch in vain at the axe buried deeply in his spine. Like a felled tree the man toppled, hitting the ground with a resounding thud.

Much of the fight went out of the remaining men as they saw their leader fall, but instead of surrendering they continued battling on, lacklustre though it was. It didn't take long for us to finish the job.

I had just finished pulling my sword out of the last man's torso when I was enveloped in a crushing embrace.

"Good to see you alive and well Calidan!" Cassius exclaimed, breaking off his hug when my face started going purple. "Good to see all of you," he said, scanning the room before growing more solemn. "Scythe? Is he-"

"Fine," I jutted in. "He hurt his leg so stayed behind to let us move more quickly."

Cassius nodded; relief plainly written on his face. "Good to hear. How did you find us?"

"A story for another time perhaps," I answered as Ella finished removing her dagger from a fallen enemy and rushed Cassius, grabbing him in a tear-filled hug.

Leaving my friends to their long yearned for reunion I regrouped with Rikol and Sophia.

"Nice work getting through that last lot," I said to Sophia, nodding my head in the direction of the fallen giant.

She smiled in appreciation of my words but directed me towards her three archers. "Couldn't have done it without these three," she said. "Their shooting made the opening."

After a round of congratulations, hand shaking and hugs Rikol voiced the obvious question, "What now?"

"I will head into the caverns and let them know that the immediate threat is over, and to get more men stationed at the pass," said Cassius, extracting himself from Ella. "Then we should use Calidan's skill set to locate any survivors and hunt down any stragglers."

"Sounds sensible," answered Rikol, Sophia, Ella and I nodding in agreement. Sophia thumbed her bowstring and cast a gaze at her archers before looking back at Cassius. "See if you can find some arrows back there?"

He nodded.

Ten minutes later we left the keep, the pass to the caverns now guarded by a grizzled soldier with one eye, and stocked with fresh arrows in our quivers.

The hunt continued.

# CHAPTER 11

## *Jadira*

A stubborn silence reigned as the surviving members of the fort began picking up the pieces of their lives. Bodies of friends and enemies were dragged to a growing pyre in the square and wounds were tended in a hurriedly set up triage centre...and as I watched it all I realised just how scarily pragmatic these people were.

"It's not the first time these people have been attacked," Cassius observed, handing me a bottle of something eye-wateringly strong. "From what little I have learnt of them they will likely morn in their own time; preparing for the next attack comes first." Pragmatic, just like Tracker.

"How often have these attacks been happening?" I asked.

A feminine voice broke in before Cassius could answer, "Raids are a normal way of life up here, but they've been getting worse." Turing we saw Beonica slowly making her way over. The First Shield looked well, grinning broadly as she approached. She hugged Cassius, my friend returning the embrace with warmth, before coming to me. Pausing for a second, as if weighing me up, she lunged forward and grabbed me in a hug before I could react.

"Thank you," she said in my ear.

'You're welcome!" I wheezed. The woman's grasp was bone-crushingly strong.

Releasing me she stepped back, smiling. "Fortuitous indeed that such fine young men and women like yourselves turned up lost all the way up here. And here I thought the Emperor had forgotten us!"

"The Emperor? You know him?" Cassius asked, surprise evident in his voice.

"Know him? No. We aren't part of the Empire; the clans have never been one for bowing to another. But we are trade partners, and if there is one thing that the Andurran Empire can't abide it is the interruption of trade. So when the attacks began getting worse Jadira sent a rider to the Empire. We weren't sure if anything would happen, but here you are."

"Jadira?" I questioned.

"The chieftain," Beonica said simply, "and also the person who sent me to find you young heroes. It seems that it's time for you all to meet. Follow me."

As Cassius and I trailed after Beonica I leant over and murmured, "What do you make of the idea that our test was engineered to help these people?"

He paused for a minute then shrugged. "Does it matter? I imagine that if the test is intended to be dangerous and yet relations can be improved at the same time...why not?"

He made a fair point. But if that was the case then why place us in the forest with the trolls? Why not just give us to the clan to help with the defences, surely that would have been enough to fulfil the requirements of the test? I sighed in frustration, drawing a puzzled look from Cassius, and tried to settle the feeling of unease in my gut. Whatever the reasoning behind this test, I was positive that defending the clan wasn't the whole of it.

✳ ✳ ✳

Jadira turned out to be a woman in her mid-thirties, short yet lithe, with hair tied back in a warrior's knot and carrying a sword with a well-worn grip. Her brow was furrowed in concentration as she frowned at a map spread across a large table. As we approached my senses flared. She had obviously seen some fighting earlier in the day; like myself she still reeked of blood.

Looking up at our approach her frown eased and she spoke in flawless Andurran, "Ah, our wayward saviours, I see Beonica found you. Good. Pleased to meet you at last." She indicated the bench in front of the table, already filled with Ella, Rikol and Sophia. "Please, have a seat. I was just giving your comrades an overview of the surrounding area." Sitting swiftly, she continued. "As I was saying, this is the location of this fort. We are about two days walk from the next major clan encampment and often the first line of defence against the Hrudan who tend to approach through this," she indicated an area on the map, "pass. The Pass of Eredon. It is the most direct route to the other side of the mountains and to the lands of the Hrudan." She paused to take a drink, the sweet aroma of honeyed mead caressing my nostrils.

"As Beonica has probably told you, these attacks used to be far fewer, with less assailants, perhaps only one every two or three months. It was more akin to a raid, a test of mettle for the Hrudan. Now however, we are being hit two or three times a month, each time by more men. Where they are getting their numbers from I do not know. The Hrudan are much like us, a system of clans that more often than not fight each other. For the attacks to have increased to this extent and ferocity...I can only assume that something has happened in their homeland. Perhaps they are being driven out or that the clans have united. But every scout that I have sent out hasn't returned."

*Uh oh. Are you going where I think you're going with this?*

"Sophia and Cassius have been a massive asset the past few weeks. And after the events of the past day... I know that you can all handle yourselves better than anyone here."

*You are, aren't you.*

"I wouldn't ask if the situation wasn't so dire."

*Here it comes.*

"But we are in desperate need of assistance. Can I ask you to scout the pass?"

*Goddamnit.*

I pasted on a smile and looked at the others who nodded in assent. "It looks like we're at your disposal."

Jadira smiled and began to speak, but I held up my hand. "Firstly though, we have a companion in the forest who needs assistance. We need to bring him in and get him some help before we plan the next move."

"Of course!" Jadira replied. "What's the injury?"

"Badly sprained ankle," said Rikol. "We're probably going to need a stretcher to get him through the trees and undergrowth."

"Tell you what," Jadira began. "If I send a few men with one of your party to find your friend, the rest of you can stay here and we can plan your approach. Deal?"

I began to speak-

"I'll go." Rikol. Everyone looked at him and he shrugged. "Of the three of us who know where he is, Calidan and Ella are the better at strategy. You can fill Scythe and myself in when we return."

"You're sure Rikol?" Ella asked. He nodded firmly.

"Done," said Jadira. She motioned over one of her men and spoke swiftly in Meredothian. "Rikol, if you follow Rygaard here he will take you to collect a few others and then you can be on your way. There will be hot food and drinks awaiting your return."

Rikol nodded and stood up. "Best plan this well everyone," he said as he began following Rygaard. "If we all die because I let you lot be in charge of the stratagems I will be mighty pissed. See you in a bit."

Once he left Jadira pulled out a box of flags and markers. "Okay. Time for some planning." She started placing locations on the map, surrounding the pass. "We have suggestions that the Hrudan have placed a forward encampment at our side of the pass. Fires have been seen at night in the area. This is unusual in itself - usually the Hrudan retreat through the pass to their lands once a raid is completed."

"Where is the closest Hrudan fort?" asked Ella.

"Here." Another flag placed down. "Roughly a day's march from the exit of the pass. Two other clans are located here, and here," another two markers, both a fair distance from the original. "However, we have had no scouts return from the region in five months so much could have changed."

Sophia held up a hand. "Sorry Jadira. Before we go any further...what would you have us do? Scout the pass and return?"

"If you can make it into Hrudan and find out what is going on, what the cause of these incessant attacks is, then that would be the main priority. If not, the scouting and impediment of any forces currently stationed in the pass is the secondary objective."

I raised a hand. "Can we shut the pass?"

Jadira looked troubled and shook her head. "We would prefer you not to damage anything in the pass."

"Why?"

She sighed. "The Pass of Eredon is a sacred site to the Meredothian people. It is where a mighty warrior, Eredon, took upon himself to venture into the ice caverns and defeat Mendrok, the spider queen. It is said that their battle is what caused the cavern to split and create the pass into Hrudan."

Silence.

I held up a hand.

"I'm sorry. Did you say spider queen?"

Jadira nodded.

"As in, large spiders? How large are we talking? The size of a mouse, a cat?"

Jadira's gaze widened. "Do you not have Tumulk in your country?" I looked at the others and saw that like myself we were all shaking our heads. Jadira grinned ruefully. "Just another monstrous creature that lives here in our lands then eh? Fear

not, the Tumulk have not been seen in the pass in large numbers for many years. You should be fine."

I pressed the point. "How. Large?"

She looked me up and down. "The average one, including legs?
Probably about your size. They are basically standard spiders
in every way except larger."

Oh how I wished Rikol was with us for a sarcastic comment.

Ella rolled her eyes. "Anything else you would like to add?"

Jadira shifted uncomfortably. "Well...many of them also have
three-inch fangs and a venomous tail. But that shouldn't deter
a group of killers like yourselves. Not unless you're afraid of
spiders?"

Silence reigned.

Now, none of us had a specific phobia about spiders. I've long
thought that humanity must have been tormented by them in
the past to account for the sheer number of people terrified by
a tiny house spider. Coming from remote villages, Sophia, Cassius and I had dealt with plenty of spiders. Ella and Rikol were
street rats and that, again, meant that spiders had been commonplace. But still...giant spiders? That sent a shiver down
my spine. And a glance around the room confirmed that none
of the others looked particularly pleased.

*Oh well, comes with the territory of being an Imp I guess.*

I tried to ease the tension. "If the Hrudan have been using the
pass then they must have done something about the Tumulk.
If it is the main arterial route to move troops into a neigh-
bouring region then you wouldn't want half of your men being
eaten on the way!"

The others nodded and Jadira spoke up. "You're right. As I said
they are not usually seen in large numbers but keep to the war-
rens below the main cavern. I imagine that if you went down
there you would find more."

Cassius spoke up, "Okay, let me see if I can sum up. One, we
remove any Hrudan encampment this side of the pass. Two,
we attempt to get through the pass to see what is going on in
the Hrudan lands. Three, we aim to destabilise the units there.

Four, we don't blow the pass. And five, we aim to not get eaten by giant spiders. That about right?"

Jadira nodded.

Cassius smiled at his less enthusiastic team mates, "Sounds kind of fun. When do we leave?"

Of course he would be enjoying the idea.

We spent the rest of the day cleaning blades, preparing equipment and acquiring decent clothes whilst we waited for Rikol and Scythe to return. Leather jerkins replaced the deer hide clothes we had made whilst in the forest, and we were gifted wolf pelt cloaks to keep us warm in the ice caves. Amongst ample provision of food supplies each of us received a number of blue flowers; if crushed into a poultice they apparently treated the spider venom. I sincerely hoped that none of us would need it.

We were in the midst of acquiring new weapons and sharpening old ones when Rikol returned, Scythe hobbling alongside.

"This is bullshit!" he exclaimed when we explained the situation. "Let me strap my leg up and join you!"

I shook my head. "It's an ice cave filled with evil bastards and giant spiders. We may need to move swiftly; I don't think your leg can handle it."

"He's right Scythe," Sophia said, resting her hand on his shoulder. "Stay here and rest that leg of yours. We will be back before you know it."

"When are you leaving?"

"First light."

Scythe looked around. "Well, if my reunion with you lot is to be this short then I'm going to properly save the speeches for when you're back from the caves and go and do the fun stuff with my lady!"

Ella nodded along, grabbing Cassius's hand tightly whilst Sophia blushed at the friendly laughter.

"Before I go though, you should know that our mysterious and inquisitive friend returned almost as soon as you left the cave," continued Scythe. "It left about half an hour before

Rikol returned."

"Any better idea as to what it is?" I asked.

He shook his head. "Still sounds like a troll to me. But a very strange one at that." He pulled Sophia to her feet and grinned at her. "I'll keep an eye out whilst you're gone, but in the meantime if you excuse us, I'm going to feast my eyes on something else!" With a passionate kiss, he and Sophia got up and left, shortly followed by Cassius and Ella who were presumably going to their own romantic rendezvous.

That left Rikol and me. I turned to him, only to see a sword pointed at my head, "Don't you be getting any ideas now, you hear?" he said. "I know that I am a beautiful and ridiculously attractive individual but I don't swing that way. Just admire me and leave."

I snorted and clapped him on the shoulder. "Come on, oh attractive one. Let's grab a beer, you can regale the northerners with your tales of rescuing princesses and fighting dragons."

"Now you're speaking my language!" cried Rikol. "Lead the way, my liege!"

A night of passion, alcohol and laughter helped begin to ease the pain of the past weeks. The smiles came less frequently, but the laughter was still genuine. The scars of the test cut deep, but we would survive it.

Or so I thought.

# PRESENT DAY

The Emperor stood in his office, the behemoth of a man holding the tiny request form in his hand. Turning as I entered, he threw the letter onto the desk in front of him.

"You wanted to see me?" I asked pointedly. I had no time for decorum with this man. Not these days.

"Indeed I did my boy! That letter there is, I believe, the fifty third request I have had from you to go hunting a very specific monster. Does that sound about right?"

I sighed and began to turn away. "I have better things to be doing than be denied agai-"

"-I'm inclined to grant your request."

I stopped dead.

"After all this time...why would you do that?" I asked, hope warring with suspicion in my chest.

He shrugged. "Perhaps your incessant requests have worn me down. Perhaps I think it fruitful to rid the world of the...what do you refer to it as? The red eyed skyren? Or perhaps the planets and stars are aligned to make me feel particularly generous as of late. But ask yourself this...do you really care?"

I awoke to a crackling fire and a shadow of gigantic proportions looming over me. Wide, chaotic eyes watched me with a hint of worry as a finger the size of my wrist poked me in the side.

"Ow!" I snapped, rubbing at the rapidly bruising spot. "Stop that! I'm awake."

He poked me again, a rumble of noise in his throat.

"Awake and alive," I confirmed, "as I can see you are too. Congratulations."

A beatific smile spread across Cassius's face.

Sitting up, a bite of pain lanced through my shoulder and I hissed, feeling the open wound that the skyren's tail spike had caused.  With a groan I reached for my supplies and began checking them one by one, thankfully finding all the blades intact. Oathbreaker Cassius already had next to him, the blade gleaming in the firelight, it was probably the first thing that he had picked up on reverting to normal. After a few frustratingly painful movements I had my first aid kit in hand and set about cleaning and binding the wound. Cassius knew I was wounded but he didn't have the capacity to look after me, resulting in far too much experience in learning how to deliver self-care. Luckily a constant administration of my green seraph would help the wound heal quickly and without complications.

Ministrations done, I tentatively touched my Imperator jacket and finding it to be largely dry I flung it to Cassius. "Here," I said as he caught it, "cover yourself with this if you get cold." Another innocent smile and he carefully curled the jacket onto the top of his head before sitting down next to me.

"Glad to see you haven't let it win yet," I murmured softly as he sat. "We'll have to find you something to wear as soon as possible. Honestly if you're going to change at the drop of a button then we need to find a way that you keep your clothes intact. Ridiculous really."

Cassius rocked back and forth, careful to keep the coat perfectly piled on his head.

"I know, I know," I sighed. "It isn't your fault. We both know who is responsible for this, we could have at least got him to sort something out clothing wise - looks like the Emperor isn't quite so infallible as he would like us to believe."

Silence.

I nodded in agreement. "Or he just doesn't care."

Reaching into my sack I pulled out a soggy piece of jerky and began chewing thoughtfully, trying to place our position on the maps I had filed away in the back of my mind. Come dawn we would be back on the road and we needed both supplies and repairs - not easy to find in thyrkan controlled territory.

"Best get some sleep," I said to the big man before laying back down to nurse my bruises, "as tomorrow we find the Under-trail."

For some people, hunting thyrkan, being chased by your demonic friend and surviving a close encounter with a beetle infested mountain and a fight with a demon would be the most memorable points of their lives.

For us?

...It was just another day.

# CHAPTER 12

## *Pass of Eredon*

T he Pass of Eredon was an eerie place. A stunning glacial blue, it shimmered with strange light and sound bounced off every surface, reverberating and reflecting a million times before fading. Somewhat disconcertingly there had been no sign of men in the poorly built encampment at the entrance to the pass. Tracks led out from the pass, not in. Wherever the Hrudan were attacking from, it wasn't from here. Even so, we decided to push forwards, through the ice caves and to the Hrudan lands. I imagine the experience of walking through the glistening blue was weird enough for my friends, but for me, with my extra sensory capabilities? I could have gone quite mad in there. Each footfall echoed into the distance until it sounded like one made by another. I could hear the ice groaning and shifting into the deep, until I could imagine something living inside the ice. And every now and again, I swore I could hear a soft, bristly scurrying.

That said, it was a beautiful place. Every different shade of blue imaginable streaming out into the fractaled distance. Icicles hung suspended in the air and frozen stalagmites rose out of the floor. It was unsurprising that it was a place of spiritual significance. It felt like you could learn a great deal about yourself just by venturing through the cave.

And in a way, we did. We all learnt to hate spiders.

There it was again. "I'm sure that there is something alive in here, moving around us," I said softly to the others.

We all stopped. Nothing. "Any idea where?" asked Cassius.

"No. The ice makes it hard to track. At first it sounds like it is coming from above, then beneath."

"Well if Jadira is right about the spiders, it would probably be like them to live in the walls," Ella supplied. "We should probably keep our weapons close and hope that they decide to leave us alone."

It was about all we could do, and so we continued forward, hands close to blades at all times.

I still couldn't find any recent tracks making their way back through the ice caves away from Meredothian lands. "Perhaps Jadira has more on her hands than raiding," I ventured. "It could be that this is an invasion."

Cassius knelt down and scratched away at the ice floor. "I don't know if there have been the tracks of enough men to warrant an invasion force. Roughly sixty Hrudan were killed during their attack on the fort. If we assume that the same force has been conducting the increasing raids then Jadira and her people have killed near enough two hundred...do you think there has been that many pass through here?"

"It's difficult to tell. The ice changes shape often enough to remove most tell-tale sign. It's possible a large force pushed through and the ice has healed since their passage."

Sophia spoke up, "Or perhaps the Hrudan attacking Jadira's people have found another way through."

A troubling thought.

Two hours into the pass and the colours changed. Light should not have easily reached the inside but the walls still glowed as if lit from within. Deep blues and purples spread out and throbbed, once again giving the impression of being alive. The walls of the path maintained a surprising consistency. Whilst the tunnel twisted and turned, the width and height of the walls remained the same; big enough for the six of us to walk abreast and then some. Whether a marvel of nature or a feat of engineering I did not know. Either way it was impressive.

Four hours into the cave and the walls began exhibiting hues of swirling greens and even reds amongst the plethora of blue. The scurrying noises had continued intermittently, as if one creature continuously paused and listened before moving again...or many creatures were picking up our presence and moving before letting us leave. Another disturbing thought. I just hoped that the creatures were not as dangerous as Jadira suggested.

A fool's hope.

Five hours in and we reached a junction. The first that we had seen. One path led to the right, and seemed to stay on the same level. The other led on a downward gradient. After a quick discussion we decided to go right. Some track marks remained that came from that direction, and so sensibly we decided to follow them - until we hit a dead end.

Not a natural dead end either. It looked like a cave-in that had frozen over. Massive amounts of rock had fallen, blocking any avenue of exit and the approach was now shielded by ice.

"Well...gives more credence to another route, don't you think?" smirked Rikol. "Looks like this was a waste of time."

"Not really," admonished Ella. "We know this is blocked and so can concentrate on locating the other route - if any."

"What do you mean?"

"Perhaps the men who have been attacking have been staying in the Meredothian lands because they can't go back home? It could be possible that the raiders were all that was able to get through here before the pass sealed."

"Sounds plausible," I added. "No tracks leading back because they knew there was no point. Interesting."

"What about that side passage?" Cassius asked. "Shouldn't we go down there and see where it leads?"

"You know the horror stories that we tell at the Academy, Cassius?" Rikol asked. When Cassius nodded he continued, "What you're suggesting to do is pretty much how each of them begins. 'Let's all go down into the spider pit! I'm sure it will be fine! Ahhhh! Spiders! Who could have guessed?!' ME. That's who."

"But we should check it in case there is another route-"

"But nothing! I told you last time in the desert that it was a monstrous death pit, and did any of you believe me? 'It's fine Rikol. Everything is long dead Rikol. Stop worrying Rikol.' And look how that turned out."

He had a point.

I turned to him. "Okay, what would you have us do?"

He smiled grimly. "Camp here and then head back out. We know it's defensible as there is only one-way in."

We all looked at each other and nodded. Decision made.

"Oh and one last thing," Rikol added as we started making camp. "No ghost stories."

*  *  *

All in all the Meredothian camping gear made for a decent night's sleep. Good, warm tents and thin but very toasty furs allowed us to sleep in the middle of an ice cavern without need for a fire. A useful thing too, as an ice cavern by its very name doesn't hold much in the way of wood for kindling. I took the first watch, a completely uneventful experience that was incredibly relaxing. The ice somehow still retained light, even though the sun must have set, and the patterns were almost hypnotic. After a few hours I was relieved and went to sleep with dreams of colour.

*Skittering*
*Bristles*
*Eyes*

I jolted upright, sweat coursing down my back and cursed my brain for being unable to sleep properly. Realising that I wasn't going to sleep more I pulled on my boots and went out to let

Rikol catch a few more winks...only to stop dead in my tracks.

Rikol hung suspended in the air, slowly rotating, his eyes holding nothing but sheer, unadulterated terror.

Craning my head up I could see why. Standing over the tents, each leg like a fur coated pillar, was a spider.

Using my magnificent powers of deduction I ascertained that it probably wasn't a normal spider.

Black eyes dotted the top of a large, bristling torso, Rikol's rotating image reflecting in each of the glittering orbs. Mandibles the size of my forearm quivered next to a fanged mouth and a large stinger extended from the base of its abdomen.

I slowly began moving my hand to my sword and froze as my reflection lit up in the glittering eyes. Shit.

"WAKE UP!" I roared, my voice thundering through the cave, and sprung forward to shear my blade through the nearest leg. Or tried to. The blade stuck half way and before I could dislodge it I found myself in the air, hanging onto the blade and staring into a glittering reflection of terror.

Bumbling sounds emerged from the tents as the others woke up, hastily buckling on weapons and boots. The spider danced in pain as I grimly held on to the blade, its remaining legs trampling through the tents and knocking them asunder. One by one my companions were free to see what was going on. Free to gasp in shock. All except Cassius who ran to the next nearest leg and slashed, twisting the blade as he did so to avoid my fate. The spider hissed in fury and lashed out with the leg that he struck, flinging him through a tent and sending him crashing into Sophia. With its other leg it dashed me into the wall hard enough to crush the ice, causing me to lose my grip on the blade, then began to vanish back through the tunnel, taking poor, potentially prescient Rikol with it.

By the gods it was quick. By the time we had given chase it had pulled from view. Its legs somehow finding some scant purchase on the floor and surrounding walls, allowing it to propel itself along at a tremendous rate. Whilst we were wearing the sturdy boots that the Meredothians used for ice exploration we couldn't hope to move a fraction of the speed. Ella recognised this first and stopped our headlong chase.

"It's gone, hold up!" she shouted as we sprinted and slid after the long-vanished spider.

Cassius looked at her incredulously. "Why are we stopping? It has Rikol!"

"I know, but it's obvious that we aren't going to catch it. Even Calidan wasn't anywhere near matching its speed on the ice. We know that it is likely going down that other path - it stands to reason as we didn't see any other openings on the walk here. So we should approach this carefully and not rush headlong into anything."

She had a point. Long experience has since confirmed to me that rushing into the lion's den is a bad move. Mainly because as an Imperator what is inside will be much, much worse than a simple lion.

I nodded. "Good thinking. Let's collect our gear and make our way to that other path entrance."

Thirty minutes later we were back at the descending pathway, fully attired and prepared. Or close to it; my sword was still embedded in that foul creature's leg.

"Going by what we saw, our best bet is probably the eyes and abdomen rather than the legs," Sophia confirmed. "Let's take it slow. Spiders are ambush hunters."

Weapons out - in my case twin daggers - we paced forward to face the foe and rescue the friend.

Unfortunately we had hoped for foe singular.

Perhaps a mile into our descent the walls began to glisten differently to those above.

"Ugh." Cassius said, wrinkling his nose and rubbing his hands. To our inquisitive faces he simply shrugged and said, "Webs."

He was right; the entirety of the hallway was covered in strands of cobweb. Suddenly walking became much more difficult, each step began to take twice as long as the webs snatched at our boots with surprising strength.

"This is not going to help us if we need to fight," grunted Cassius as we thumped our way down the passage, all traces of stealth gone.

"Er." I raised my blades. "Funny you should say that..." The cobwebs in front of us were vibrating relentlessly as my eyes picked up a wave of legs coming towards us. The tumulk had arrived.

Arrow after arrow slammed into beady eyes, bodies falling from the ceiling and walls to join the growing pile on the floor. Sophia was in fine form. Protecting our archer we ducked and weaved as the table-sized spiders swarmed us. Unfortunately that was largely all we could do. The swift movements of Kaschan were impossible whilst on the webbed floor and that made the fight much more desperate. In seconds we were overwhelmed, covered in ichor and flattened by sheer numbers. A wave of legs, fur and fangs covering our faces until all we knew was endless stabbing.

After what felt like a lifetime the pressure eased and the wave of nightmares ended.

"What just happened?" Sophia asked, covered in thick green ichor.

"I have no idea," I replied, wiping goo off my face. "Anyone hurt?" Surprisingly, no one was.

"I think they weren't attacking us at all!" groaned Ella as she peeled herself off the floor. "Perhaps they were running from something?"

I cocked my head as a faint reverberation rang through the air. "I don't think you're far off the mark there Ella. Something is ahead."

"The spider?"

"I don't know." With another groan I shouldered my pack. "Let's go find out."

# CHAPTER 13

## *Arachnophobia*

The cobwebbed ice tunnel eventually opened out into a large cavern. It would have been quite pleasant if it hadn't been a spider infested hell hole. Mummified prey hung suspended from the ceiling. Some had four legs, some two. The tumulk, it seemed, were not as opposed to catching humans as Jadira had suggested.

More strangely was that there were remains of several spiders scattered around. Fresh remains judging by the smell. Legs torn off, limbs removed and green ichor splattered everywhere.

"Do spiders eat each other?" Ella asked aloud.

"I'm sure some do. But do you think they do it without eating their prey?" Cassius replied. "It is different to the neatly organised prey hanging from the ceiling. More like unnecessarily violent than skilled hunting."

We continued on in silence, each concentrating for any possible threat; whether spider or otherwise.

A trail of spider body parts led the way to the next cavern, their bodies ripped asunder. None of us had a clue as to the cause. Whatever had done it was obviously powerful and utilised brute strength over blades...spiders were bad enough and so I whole-heartedly prayed we didn't meet something new.

But as usual, the gods either paid no attention or, much more likely in my view, thoroughly enjoyed my pain.

Inside the cavern was the remains of a giant spider. Its colossal limbs ripped free from its body, its abdomen ruptured and eyes removed as if plucked from the head and casually tossed over a shoulder. Whatever had done this had gloried in the violence.

"What on earth?" Sophia whispered the question on everyone's lips.

"Do you think that was the same spider that took Rikol?" asked Ella.

I scanned its scattered legs. "Can't see a sword, but it could have easily come loose. Too many claw marks to make out if any of the damage was done by us."

"Calidan, that giant spider shrugged off one of your attacks pretty easily," Cassius said, his expression grim. "Whatever did this was immensely powerful."

"A troll perhaps?" suggested Sophia.

"It would be the likeliest culprit," I agreed, "but trolls tend to keep to themselves. Why would one suddenly come into the spider caverns? Plus that spider was as quick as it was strong. Trolls are generally pretty lumbering creatures. If I had to guess I would say the spider would have the advantage in a fight..."

Silence fell as the others pondered my words. Finally Cassius spoke up, "Does it matter?"

We looked at him, shocked.

"So what if there is something ahead of us that we don't understand? We are knowingly going into spider infested caverns to rescue Rikol. It doesn't matter what gets in our way, we will cut it down and see it crawl before us. Understood?"

The dorm looked at each other, strength and solidarity reaffirmed thanks to Cassius's speech. With a grim-faced look at everyone he set off, blade held over one shoulder. One by one we followed him into the next cavern, following the trail of broken limbs.

More mummified prey and more dead spiders. It was becoming a regular disturbing sight. Thankfully the trail ensured that we didn't get lost. More and more side tunnels were appearing, turning the spider caves into an interconnected warren. By unspoken agreement we continued following the broken spiders, perhaps presuming that whatever was causing the destruction would head for the next set of spiders, and hopefully Rikol.

A reverberation caught my attention. Holding up a hand I stopped the others and another reverberation filled my senses. Something down the tunnel was making tremendous impacts.

"I think we're close to whatever did this," I said to the group, indicating the ichor covered floor. "Be ready."

Nodding, they continued forward, following my lead. Angry and emboldened we pushed ahead, ready to clash with whatever monstrosity lay before us for the sake of our friend, but we could never have guessed what we found.

It was a troll. Or something akin to a troll. Humanoid with bulging, misshapen muscles. Around ten feet tall it had a mouth filled with curved teeth, dexterous hands and a pale blue skin. A light patterning of white fur spread across the beast's back and chest, but not the thick, heavy mantle of fur that trolls possessed. Nor did it seem to have the lumbering movement of a troll, it danced lightly on its feet, smashing through the legs of the gigantic spider that it battled. Whatever else it was, it was obviously a brutally efficient killer. Dodging the spider's massive leg blows, it spun past the stinging abdomen and tore off the appendage. The spider's hiss was one of extreme pain, which only grew louder when the beast jumped onto its back and rammed the stinger home into the top of its skull. Limbs trembling in a frenzy the spider collapsed in its death throes. But that wasn't enough for the misshapen creature. It stabbed again and again, driving the stinger deep into the spider's brain and making a hole into the spider's head big enough for its hands to get into. Then it released the stinger and, putting its hands inside the spider's head, it pulled. Piece by piece it broke the spider apart until it was standing in a heap of broken parts, its blue skin covered in green ichor. Standing on top of the pile it roared, a strange sound that I recognised instantly; the uncanny roar I had heard in the forest. That was disconcerting. Was it following us?

The beast stopped its roar and shuddered, breathing heavily. Its head flicked from side to side, its arms twitching erratically, as though wanting to go in two directions at once. After a minute the twitching slowed and it turned, scanning the room and spotting us at the tunnel mouth. Expecting an attack we tensed, blades out, but the creature just looked at us with one vividly blue, intelligent eye. An eye that I couldn't help thinking held a vast amount of rage, yet...recognition?

What's worse is that as it turned away I could have sworn that it winked. A feeling confirmed when Sophia murmured, "Did that thing just wink?"

Good, so it wasn't just me losing my mind.

Stiffening as though it sensed something nearby, the troll-beast unleashed another roar and raced down another tunnel. "Did that just happen?" Ella asked to a chorus of dumbfounded nods.

"Some kind of intelligent troll I guess...but it doesn't act like any troll I've heard of," Cassius said. "But we should leave the guesswork until we've found Rikol and got out of here."

Once more we set off into the tunnels. The beast seemed to know where it was going which I hoped was a good thing as I couldn't smell or sense Rikol nearby so following it seemed to be a better option than not. Perhaps it would give us time to figure out if the strange creature was a friend or an enemy. Considering its extremely violent dismemberment of the spiders I would settle for the enemy of my enemy, but I couldn't shake the sense that it somehow knew us.

Another mystery to solve.

The labyrinth of ice continued. Mazes of tunnels criss-crossed around us. Without the troll leading the way we would have been hopelessly lost. As it was I wasn't sure I would be able to lead us back to the entrance. The entire area smelled of strange troll and large spider, making it hard to distinguish our route through the stinking mire. This should have been a worry, but every single one of us would have gladly lost ourselves in the labyrinth for a chance to save our friend. And so forward we plunged, casting aside doubt and fears, following only the echoing roars of the troll and keeping eyes open for Rikol.

It wasn't long until the grunts and roars of the troll changed, the echoes that reverberated along the tunnel sounding angrier, and soon my senses picked up the chittering that I had come to associate with the eight-legged locals. The sounds ramped and crescendoed until I was positive my senses had failed me. Surely there couldn't be that many spiders.

Stalking into a vast cavern, flanked by my friends, my jaw dropped open. The troll was an island in a sea of brown, green and grey. Spiders of different sizes were assaulting it from all sides, their glistening mandibles grasping for its flesh. Behind the waves of legs were several giant spiders, threading their way towards the harried troll. Behind those spiders was a creature of nightmare.

And that was saying something considering the predicament we were in.

This spider dwarfed even the already gigantic ones that we had fought before. Thick black hairs thrust out from its articulated legs; each bristling appendage as wide as my arms outstretched. The torso was vast, an undulating, disgusting mass of flesh and horror that rippled each time the behemoth took a step.

"Fuck. Me." Sophia breathed seeing the monstrosity. "That thing is huge!"

The others simply nodded, wide eyed in amazement and horror. "How about we go round instead of through?" Ella suggested carefully, not taking her eyes off of the spider queen.

"I wish we could," I replied, expression grim. I pointed at

the ceiling behind the spider. Following my finger the others squinted, gasping as they saw several rows of hanging people, wrapped in web.

"Is Rikol in there?" asked Cassius.

"I can't see for certain, but it seems as likely a place as anywhere else," I answered.

"Fan-fucking-tastic," whispered Sophia, loudly enough for everyone to hear. Wry smirks appeared on our faces and for a moment the terror of the situation lessened. She continued, "So what's the plan Cal?"

"Well firstly, not getting eaten," I began, the other nodding sagely as though I was imparting great wisdom. "Secondly, I think that as the troll thing didn't immediately try to eat us, we might want to try and support it in this fight. But I still don't recommend getting close...whilst it didn't instantly try and kill us it might just be saving us for later." Again more nods. "Sophia, if we find which one Rikol is, you reckon you can hit the web holding him up?"

Sophia grimaced, "I can't see it from here, but if it's relatively static then I would imagine so. But we don't know the properties of the web, something coming out of a spider that big might not get easily cut."

A valid point.

"We haven't got much in the way of other options," voiced Ella, always the voice of reason. "We won't know until we try, if it fails then we'll come up with something."

"Agreed," I replied. "I think we should skirt around as much as possible and when we see an opening - and Rikol - Sophia can take a shot and one of us can try catching him. Then we get out of here as fast as possible. If any of that fails then watch each other's backs and try not to die. Good?"

Nods all round.

"Well then," I twirled my blades. "Let's get to it."

We struck out from the cavern entrance, keeping close to the edge in an attempt to avoid the notice of the swarm. We didn't need to have worried quite so much - the spiders only had their many horrible eyes focused on the strange troll that was wreaking havoc on their population. It stood surrounded by a mountain of broken and twitching limbs, gleaming claws eviscerating every spider that came close, green ichor spraying like an intermittent geyser. But for every one it killed another took its place, and its claws could only be in so many places at once. As we watched several spiders jumped onto its back, stingers stabbing and mandibles flexing. The troll roared in pain and swung, its claws catching one of the spiders but leaving two still attached and just out of reach of its flailing arms. Proving that it was no normal troll, the beast picked up a nearby corpse that wasn't completely crushed and swung it like a club behind its back, using the extra reach to knock the spiders loose in a splatter of squelching limbs. Spinning, it scythed through the nearest ranks, a whirlwind of angry death. And for a time it looked like an effective strategy...until they started dropping from the ceiling.

In an instant the troll was covered. The momentary distraction allowed a fresh flood of the surrounding arachnids to surge forward, enveloping the creature in a wave of stabbing limbs and bristly legs. Blood of a different colour began to spurt in greater and greater amounts and the troll began to visibly slow; tiring from blood loss. Sophia paused and a second later an almost continuous flight of arrows sped into the mass, the power of Sophia's bow allowing each one to cut through multiple bodies before stopping. Her shooting never ceased to amaze the rest of the team and myself - whilst we were all passing fair with the bow, Sophia's archery was masterful. Her first few arrows cleared the spiders off the troll's face, allowing it to once again see the most immediate threats, and the next few tore off those attached to its back, providing it a brief respite. Even from a distance we could see the gaping wounds on the beast's frame immediately begin to knit together and it once more entered into its windmill spin, this time keeping an eye on the ceiling, an ichor coated paw reaching up to bat a descending spider out of the air every now and then. As its wounds healed its speed began to pick up until it was once again back in fine form.

Sophia nodded to herself and trotted along after us. "I can't do that again," she said as she caught up. "My quiver only holds so many and I doubt rescuing Rikol is going to be as simple as we're all hoping."

She was right, it wasn't.

Whether the gigantic spider queen could see us - something that from the rheumy look of its oozing eyes I very much doubted - or it had a connection to its spiders or some other sense of which I wasn't aware, after Sophia's intervention a large percentage of the surrounding wave of spiders peeled away from the troll and began heading in our direction.

"Heads up!" Cassius yelled pointing at the ceiling.

"Circle up!" I barked. "Sophia in the middle - keep those things off our heads. Keep moving towards the rear of the cavern as we go, we don't want to get bogged down."

The whistle of arrows punctuated my order and the closest spider fell from the ceiling, legs writhing around the shaft of wood in its chest.

I had time to once again admire the shot and then they were upon us.

Not for the first time I regretted leaving the battle-axe that I had utilised when clearing the fort. Its massive double-edged blade would have been extremely useful to cut swathes through the surrounding enemies. Shit, my sword that that bastard giant spider had hopped away with in its leg would have been good too. *Pretty much anything other than daggers,* I thought grimly as I hacked, sliced and spun amongst furred limbs. I usually quite enjoyed dagger work, as when against human enemies it required a speed and accuracy above most other weapons. Against an endless horde of spiders however? Not the best.

That was mainly because there was no ability to move easily, no dancing out of the way of scrabbling limbs to strike from behind. Instead it was just a plethora of stabbing, over and over, cutting and thrusting into anything that came my way. The axe at least would have knocked corpses away, the sword providing that extra bit of reach to stay away from the vile creatures, knives just meant that very quickly my vision turned green as I became an advertisement for spider ichor. Ella was faring similarly; Cassius having moved closer to her to provide support - a wise move. I was finding it difficult and I could hit hard enough to split each spider in two without much effort. Their bodies didn't seem to have the hard carapace of the giant spiders, for which I was immensely grateful - I had no desire to have a repeat of my earlier misfortune and be reduced to using my hands to punch spiders to death...though armed only with daggers, it more often than not felt like I was anyway.

Out of the corner of my eye I could see Cassius slashing with his sword, each swing of the blade hitting multiple opponents and slicing off limbs with wild abandon. Ella was next to him, laying into the spiders that Cassius missed and finishing off those he had crippled. Each of us was covered in thick, green ichor from the close encounters, all except Sophia who was still raining death at those on the roof, causing a hail of broken arachnids to fall, their corpses crushing their brethren beneath. I could barely see the troll anymore, the immediate volume of spiders that needed stabbing blocking my vision, but I could hear its continued and full-throated roars.

Despite our best efforts, we were slowly grinding to a halt, the incessant multitudes giving us no room to breathe, let alone walk. We had our backs to the cavern wall which provided a little protection, but Sophia was low on arrows and there appeared to be no end to the horde.

"This isn't looking good!" bellowed Cassius as he cut a leaping spider in two. "What now?"

I looked around frantically, trying to think of something, anything that would help - but nothing came to mind. Thankfully Sophia kept her head as a sudden bloom of flame behind me caught my attention. Sophia had stopped shooting and instead lit a torch, thrusting it at the nearest spider. It hissed and frantically attempted to back away. Instantly a gap appeared around the torch where the spiders no longer approached, afraid of the fire but not of the steel we had been embedding into their chests.

Ella touched Cassius on the shoulder and disengaged from the fight, pulling close to Sophia and grabbing another torch. Quickly a second flame appeared and together they did more for us in the next few seconds than the past few minutes of blood, sweat and tears had; they succeeded in driving back the horde.

"Thank fuck for that," Cassius said, breathing heavily and wiping sweat away from his brow. "That was getting pretty dicey back there."

Ella smirked and pulled away a strand of spider fur away from his face. "I guess you could say that it got a little...hairy."

The groans that elicited soon gave way to some much-needed laughter. Incongruent, perhaps, with our predicament but sometimes laughter is the best medicine. The troll continued roaring and slaughtering its way through the spider swarm as we chuckled and I fervently hoped that we didn't have to fight it. The mountains of dead spiders behind and around it made our own trail of dead look paltry in comparison. For the moment though, we had breathing space. Breathing space that was ringed with bulbous eyes that glistened in the firelight.

"Everyone okay?" Cassius asked once we had stopped laughing.

A chorus of nods and affirmatives.

"I have two arrows left," confirmed Sophia, checking her quiver. "So keep your heads up for spiders dropping from above, I can't afford to waste a shot that we might need to save Rikol."

That wasn't good. So far we had only been surviving because of Sophia's ability with the bow preventing angry spiders from landing with their stingers on our heads.

"How many torches do we have?" I asked, keeping my eyes on

several giant spiders that had turned away from the troll and were slowly advancing our way.

Sophia quickly patted down our bags whilst keeping the flame held high. "Seven, including the two lit," she answered.

Seven torches. Seven torches to get us further into an ice bound cavern, rescue Rikol and escape - all without getting eaten by small spiders, giant spiders, a monstrously oversized eight-legged queen freak of a spider or ravaged by a raging troll...thing. No matter which way I looked at it, it wasn't great odds.

But I guess overcoming massive odds is what Imperators are all about. It's what we're trained for. To do the impossible.

I steeled myself and pointed my sword towards the hanging larder that hopefully contained our friend. "We move together, nice and slow. If the torches start dying, get a new one up as soon as possible."

Ella waved her torch at the nearest spiders and together we all stepped into the gap made by the recoiling beasts. Bit by nightmarish bit we inched our way through the sea of limbs, the incessant hissing and spitting of the creatures marking our every step. The further we made it the more thankful I became that the spiders didn't have the ability to spit venom or some other twisted concoction like some of the monsters we had heard about in the world. If that had been the case, we surely wouldn't have survived.

They did have something else to fire though. Something sticky, white and very unpleasant to get on your face.

Our journey through the swarm was going relatively well until the giant spiders got within range. By which I mean we had moved all of fifty feet and no one had yet died. At first they tried to pierce the ring of fire with their mighty legs, but a thrust of the torch was enough for them to recoil, leaving behind a deep hiss of frustration. And so we continued on, delving into the masses and burning a path to Rikol.

Whether it was the giant spider itself or the monstrous queen that dreamt up the thought I do not know. But I had barely a moment of warning to shout and tug Sophia to the ground before spiderweb as thick as my wrist shot out of the dark above our heads. In an instant the two other giants decided to join the game and our world became a spinning haze of fire and webs.

Have you ever tried Kaschan whilst holding a flaming torch? It's a tricky business. You attempt to move swiftly in the standard evasive patterns but if you move too fast then the torch starts guttering and you have to slow down. And when the torch starts guttering in the midst of a thousand hungry mandibles you realise something vastly important.

Life is bollocks.

One of the watching ceiling spiders would have had an interesting view of intermittently fast and slow swirls of flame dancing around the cavern floor as Sophia and Ella sped up to dodge web and slowed down to keep their torches alive. It probably would have looked quite pretty, but in the end it was only a matter of time before something got through.

That something was a thick cord of web which lanced out of the shadow to strike Cassius in the stomach. The first I heard of it was a strangled cry and I whirled to see him vanishing into the edge of the torchlight. Roaring with anger, I leapt forward and caught his outstretched hand, pulling with all my might. He screamed as the fibres of the web pulled taught but didn't break, leaving him as the centrepiece of a tug of war. Quickly Sophia and Ella darted into view, bringing the circle of firelight back around us, but their blades made barely a dent in the thick cord. With my muscles corded, veins popping and Cassius screaming I barely saw Ella move in and thrust her torch directly at the web. I felt however, an immediate loosening in the hold on Cassius and pulled harder, determined to get him back. The torch seemingly melted the web strands, not burning them as such, but they vanished and dissipated before the heat, quickly leaving Cassius back on his feet, sore chested and gasping for air, with a heavily bruised arm from my grip.

But there was no time to rest. Threads continued erupting from the nearby giant spiders and I quickly realised that the way things currently were we were going to take forever to get near to the larder. I flung a third torch at Cassius, who lit it quickly, wincing as he did so. I pretended not to notice. If he knew that he wouldn't be able to keep up then he would have said, the Imperator Academy does not make for stupid Imps.
"We run," I barked, ducking another thread. "Stick together, but charge as fast as you can with those torches lit. We have to do this fast or not at all." Everyone nodded, faces set in grim determination. "Go!" I roared, flexing my lungs to their full. The shout was like a thunderclap in the cavern, causing the momentary silencing of the hissing around us. Quickly we set off, sprinting into the mass and relying on the fear of the fire to drive the spiders away from us faster than we could run. I brought up the rear, hoping that I could grab anyone in time if they were struck by the spider silk and trusting that I had the reactions to dodge anything that came my way.
That sprint reminded me, in some strange way, of running through the forests at the Academy. The extending branches of the enclosed trees made you feel like you were sprinting through a tunnel, giving an even greater sensation of speed. Replace branches with spider legs and it was a pretty similar sensation, just filled with infinitely more peril.
The spiders drew back, throwing themselves backwards to get away from the onslaught of flame. The giant arachnids continued firing strands of web but fortunately nothing came close enough to worry about - the jumble of retreating spiders around us providing something of an effective shield. Swiftly we drew close to the hanging larder, looping around the rear of the queen beast whose attention was solely on the advancing and seemingly unstoppable troll. The smaller spiders kept pace with us, and the giant ones were seemingly content to turn back after the troll.
Or at least, that's what I thought.
The furious run combined with the constant movement, hiss-

ing and web slinging of the spiders around us wore on my senses and so when the web struck me squarely in the back and I started being lifted into the air, I was just as surprised as anyone.

"Go! Get Rikol!" I yelled as the others started to turn. To their credit, they paused only for a split second before continuing the run to the larder, leaving me to deal with the gigantic, yet sneaky, son of a bitch that was perched on the ceiling and hauling me in to be its next morsel.

It was a weird feeling, ascending through the air like that. If it didn't end with sharp teeth and disgusting mandibles it could have been quite pleasant. As it was I struggled to try and see my opponent, but I was hesitant to flip over and embroil myself yet further into the spider silk given how strong and sticky it was and so I hung relatively still, my limbs hanging loose but ready, hands clasping my ichor covered daggers and my neck craned as far back as possible trying to judge the distance to the ceiling - if it was anything like the one that took Rikol I could likely expect a large stinger ready to meet my innards when I reached the top.

In short, I had one shot at getting it right.

I concentrated on my senses, drowning out the sibilant spider sea beneath me, the panicked breathing of my friends as they desperately began looking for Rikol amongst the swinging larder and the roar of the thing-troll as it continued to eviscerate everything that fell into its hands. Slowly, carefully, I searched for my prey; breathing in its scent, listening for its breathing, the movement of its hairs, a tell-tale muscle twitch. My foe, like all spiders, was very difficult to detect but by straining to my limits I could just make it out. I kept limp, letting the arachnid think me incapacitated or resigned to my fate and when I judged the time was right I struck upwards, driving my daggers into the flesh of the creature above me, and, hoping that the carapace was as hard as the one that had stolen my sword, I twisted, levering my body as close to the creature as possible and avoiding the thrust of the deadly stinger by mere inches. Quickly I wrapped an arm around the bulbous flesh surrounding the stinger and with my other hand wrenched out the supporting dagger; trusting the stinger to hold my weight.

Thankfully it did.

It also made the spider go berserk.

Have you ever seen a rodeo? Imagine that but upside down, on the roof of a hundred-foot-tall cavern, oh, and the mount is a giant spider. In other words, it was pretty fun. I stabbed repeatedly into the flesh of the stinger before realising that cutting apart the only thing holding me to the roof might not have been the wisest of ideas. So using each thunking drive of the dagger into its soft flesh I crawled up the length of its sting, leaving gooey green trails that dripped down onto the masses below. The spider hissed and screeched, attempting to crush me against the roof with the mass of its stinger but it couldn't quite get the leverage. It tried to pull me off by reeling in the web, but I had my grip locked down tight. Slowly and stabbily I made my way to its underbelly and there I set to work with gusto. Ripping, stabbing, shredding and tearing I clawed my way deep into its guts, the creature scurrying along the roof this way and that in an effort to rid itself of the pain. I didn't care. I just kept cutting until I was hitting bits that looked important and then I cut some more. Eventually the creature began to slow with deep, pained shudders emanating from its body. And then I enacted the second part of my plan - curl up inside the spider and hope for the best.

The fall actually wasn't that bad. A juddering impact that resulted in an exploded spider. Getting spider blood up my nose? That was unpleasant.

I stood up out of the gory mess and attempted to wipe some of it off, flinging it from my eyes in thick globs. It was when I looked up that I realised where the spider had fallen.

Right between the troll and the queen.

She, for I presume she was a she, was a grotesque sight. A bulbous mass of hideousness that groaned, hissed and squelched its way closer with ponderous steps. I suppose that she could afford to be ponderous though, for she was *fucking gigantic.* I could see myself refracted in several of her rheumy, black eyes and knew that she was watching me. Doubtless she had earlier thought the troll more of a threat, but landing in the carcass of a spider may have given her cause to re-evaluate me. Just what I needed.

Balls.

To make a bad position worse, there were several giant spiders that flanked the queen and I had had enough of their shit already. I could hear the troll behind me, still bloodily roaring its way through the smaller citizens of the cavern. It was one tough bastard, that was for sure.

I cautiously took a step backwards, feeling behind me with my toes through the gooey, slime covered floor for solid footing. If I could let the troll take the brunt of the spiders' interest then I could possibly get out of the cavern with the others without having to do more fighting. Another step. Still no movement from the watching spiders. Maybe they were just going to let me go? That would be nice.

A third step, and my watching admirers acted almost as though on cue - in an instant all hell broke loose.

The great wobbly spider queen let out a deep, ear throbbing hiss and her lackeys sprang into action sending flying tendrils of web in my direction. Quickly ducking and weaving between the threads I sprang sideways, narrowly missing a furred leg that crashed down near my head, and then my world was a dance of crashing pillars and stingers. As more spiders joined the fray I knew I had to do something to change the dynamics of the situation. Every now and again I could see a bobbing flame making its way steadily along the cavern which gave me hope that my friends were still alive but I didn't have the time to make out if they had Rikol with them or not.

And then with a mighty roar the dynamics changed.

The troll had flung itself through the air. This by itself was interesting - whilst most normal trolls had similar character-

istics to gorillas they tended to do very little jumping; preferring to lumber around in an angry manner until something
made its way into their mouths. Granted they could put on a
turn of speed when they wanted, but rarely would they soar,
majestically through the air. Especially majestically. Trolls
don't do looking good.

This one did. It had flung itself thirty feet through the air, its
arms outstretched and claws extended. Looking like a blood-
soaked nightmare it landed on the queen's face and dug in.
Ichor splattered as eyes popped with a satisfying sound. The
troll's mighty claws raked at the gigantic face and its powerful arms levered back to deliver more brutal cuts. The queen
shook, wobbled, hissed and grunted, attempting to dislodge
the tenacious creature but to no avail. The troll held on
grimly and just kept tearing. In under a minute half the eyes
on the queen's face had turned into mush and the troll quickly
shifted positions to deliver the same to the other set.

The howls of the queen sent the spiders harassing me into fury.
They forgot all about me in their haste to get to the creature
that was tormenting their squelchy leader and a quick look
around the cavern confirmed that the now much reduced sea
of spiders was converging on the queen as well. The others
were free and clear, sprinting down the cavern with an unmoving, grey wrapped figure on Cassius's shoulder. I ducked
out from the fight and bolted for the cavern wall; the surrounding spiders taking no more notice of me than of a speck
of dirt so intent they were on stopping the hurt to their queen.
In a matter of moments we were back together, the others
greeting me with grim nods and quickly we made our way
to the tunnel entrance that we had arrived in. Rikol bounced
along on Cassius's shoulder wrapped in spider silk, alive but
unresponsive with his face pale and grey and his skin giving
off a strange odour. Some kind of poison I surmised. Hopefully
it would wear off and not leave him long in a state of unconsciousness.

We reached the tunnel entrance, leaving behind us a battlefield. Spider corpses coated the floor, some in scattered ones and two and in other areas there were mountains of dead, and over it all was a liberal coating of green ichor. But thankfully, it was over.

Except it wasn't. All thanks to Cassius. *Cassius and his integrity.* We reached the tunnel and he put an arm out to stop me. "What about him?" he asked.

"What about who?" I replied, knowing full well exactly what he was asking and trying in vain to put a stop to it.

A roar of rage and pain echoed through the cavern and we turned in time to see the troll wrenched off the queen's face and disappear under a pile of stingers.

I sighed. "Oh, you mean him."

Cassius, his face grim, handed me his sword. "He gave us the opportunity to save Rikol. The least we can do is return the favour." His eyes roamed over the blood-soaked girls and unconscious friend on his shoulder and his face turned apologetic. "In this case though, by we I think I mean you. You know I-"

I held up a hand and cut him off, "Save it. The curse of being amazing. I know." I jerked my head up the tunnel. "Go, all of you, get out of here and get Rikol help." I turned back to the cavern floor, in what I assumed was a significantly heroic posture. "I'll see what I can do here."

# CHAPTER 14

## *Asp*

One thing about Imperator training is just how hardened you become to events, activities and swallowing orders. Sophia and Ella didn't so much as argue as I turned away, just turned and continued the mission. We all knew that emotion at this point - this deep in such a desperate and perilous mission - would do little to help. Besides, no matter what we had each said I don't think any of us were one hundred percent sure that what we were doing was real. There was always an underlying uncertainty - after all how can you know what is true when your mind has been tricked in such a realistic way? But real or not, that troll had whether by intent or coincidence helped us save Rikol and so it was time for me to return the favour. I hefted Cassius's blade, twirled it a few times to get a feel for the weight and with a wild grin plastered on my face to cover my fear, sprinted out into the cavern anew. The first positive was that the troll was still alive; if the noises emanating from the spider mountain were anything to go by. The second positive was that we had been completely ignored by the spiders. All their focus was on the beast that had injured their queen, which meant that I had free reign to approach how I wanted. Judging by what had happened earlier with the troll, if it was unhurt for a few moments it would soon regain its full strength and so my plan was decided for me. Afterall, there was only one sure-fire way to attract the attention of all the spiders that were currently stabbing and cutting at the injured creature.

I dashed through the outer ranks of lesser arachnids, keeping my blade close and relying on my senses to keep my feet fast. I doubt most of the spiders I passed registered my approach before I was gone. I sprinted through the towering pillars of the giant spiders, resisting the temptation to slice upwards. The queen was the target and I couldn't afford to get bogged down fighting my way towards her. The less the surrounding spiders knew of my presence, the better.

Getting there, in the end, was almost too easy. The spiders were practically hypnotised in a frenzy of killing whoever had dared harm their queen. I imagine that I could have strolled through the surrounding legions of eight legged monstrosities and not been bothered. Their mistake.

The back end of the spider queen was an unpleasantly gooey place. She dragged some kind of sac behind her that was seemingly made up of a thin, sticky membrane that protected tiny little spiderlings within. At least, that's what I guessed they were as I clambered up along it, step by sticky step with my face far too close to the disgusting film - if I survived I knew that I would be having flashbacks to this moment for a tremendously long time. I certainly wasn't wrong.

I eventually reached the top of the sac and crouched upon the top of the spider queen, covered - and I mean *covered* - in goo. Spider ichor, sac goo, blood and viscera - I had it all. I had no time to give in to my disgust however and forced my revulsion to one side as I began moving along the top of the arachnid. After a painstaking journey and covered in ichor and bristling hair, I reached the top of the queen's head and crouched down behind the range of its eyes.

My perch atop the spider queen's back allowed me to survey the chaos that lay beneath. Thousands - or what appeared in my adrenaline addled mind like thousands - of dead spider corpses littered the ground, soaking the floor in green ichor. The troll was still going, despite bleeding from hundreds of wounds as his regenerative abilities worked hard to keep it alive, but it wouldn't be long before it succumbed.

Gearing myself up for what had to come next I took a deep breath, drew Cassius's blade and swung over into the damaged face of the queen. Hissing sounds, like hundreds of snakes being thrown in a bag, emanated from its mouth as I began to systematically stab any remaining eye that the troll had missed. I hung on for dear life as the queen began to buck and rear. It wiggled and jibed - trying to dislodge whatever was sticking a needle into its vast eyes. With manic laughter I began enjoying myself, perforating each segmented eye with a deluge of stabbing and hacking; relishing the juices and spatter that poured out of each wound until the eye finally went dark and then I would move onto the next.

In a short time the spider queen realised that it could not dislodge me alone, and it began sending it spiderlings to crawl along its body to try and attack me. Luckily, my panther honed senses made sure that I was aware that they were coming. Those that approached met a grisly end.

The roars of the troll began to lessen and so I forced myself to move faster, slicing my blades in long lines across its rows of eyes, popping each one. Sadly, I was wrong to think that defeating something as big and dangerous as this spider would be as easy as that. Shimmering power began to gather around the spider and the hairs on my arms and neck stood up like in the air before a storm. Currents of purple light shimmered across the thick hairs of its body. The energy sparked and crackled and began moving in random arcs between its follicles. Knowing that it was likely my death I grimly continued hacking away. My mission was not yet over and if I left the spider its eyes we would be in trouble regardless of if I saved the troll - if the queen was still around it could send its minions to hunt the others down before they got out of the ice caves.

I continued my work, hoping upon hope that whatever the purple light was it wouldn't do as much damage as I thought it might. When it hit the pain was indescribable. Intense agony that - if I hadn't already been subjected to mind altering torture earlier - I surely would have crumbled. Screaming aloud, I hacked and sliced, venting my pain and fury upon the beast beneath me. The sparking energy shimmered along the metal blade I held in my hand, turning it into a blaze of purple that sizzled the eyes of the queen, turning its own magic against it. Soon there was nothing left that I could do. My insides were likely a charred and broken mess, my hands blackened along with the rest of my own skin. Even with the regenerative powers gifted to me by Seya, my body was crumbling beneath the spider queen's assault. With a final, agonised swipe I managed to darken the final segment of the queen's head, rendering it completely blind.

And that was as far as I could go.

With a gasp, the blade fell from my charred hands and I slipped from the thick hair of the beast to plummet to the floor below, landing on something soft and squishy that left a vile taste in my mouth. The spider queen was stamping in pain and horror, its wild hissing like a pit of snakes. Its legs flailed wildly, each one capable of sending myself or the troll flying into the wall and most likely into the next world. I could only watch through bleary eyes as one of those legs came perilously close to my torso. Relief turned to panic, turned to mind bending agony as just as I thought I was safe it rose up and with immense ease crushed my foot to powder.

If I'd thought I had felt pain before, this was a whole new level. I would like to say that my scream was a manly thing full of grit and determination - but that would be about as far from the truth as it could possibly be. It was a high pitched, wordless thing composed of sheer agony. Every nerve ending in my brain exploded in pain until, blessedly, I blacked out. When I came to, seconds or eternities later, a small part of my mind hoped that I had missed the rest of the battle. Sadly, as is often the case in my life, things rarely turn out how I want.

My eyes opened and I saw the spider queen's leg descending again; no doubt she had heard my piercing scream and pinpointed my location, seeking to take revenge for the loss of her eyes. The great foot descended and squelched the spider that had been my cushion, my last second roll flinging me out of harm's way. Thus began the strangest game of cat and mouse that I had ever partaken in, a surprising claim to fame considering that I had a giant cat as a training partner.

As I rolled weaponless amid the dead and dying spiderlings, trying to avoid the tree trunk legs of the spider queen, I soon discovered that some of the spiderlings were still alive enough to complain about my treatment of them. There were only a few, however even that small amount was enough to pose a threat - and that is how I found out how it was to bite into a spiderling with my bare teeth. I felt a strange satisfaction in being able to fight so effectively whilst down one limb. I knew that what I was doing was long beyond the scope of most humans, possibly even beyond the scope of Tyrgan with his tyrant blades, and that my broken and charred body still functioned at all was a wonder. Seya's regenerative powers were nothing to be sniffed at but I didn't want to test if they would be enough if one of those errant tree trunk legs hit me dead centre. As I continued my desperate rolling I could feel strength slowly beginning to return. Though just a trickle, it made the dodging ever so slightly easier, or as easy as dodging with one foot could be. Casting my eyes wide, looking for an advantage - anything at all that could help - I saw a telltale glint of metal shining from one of the mummified larders hanging from the ceiling. With my weapons long gone it was as good an option as any.

I rolled my way across the broken spiders, my ankle sending mindless waves of pain radiating through my body. Powering off my remaining foot, I jumped the short distance to the hanging larder and dragged it to the ground. The web was thick and sticky, and I imagine if I had the strength of a normal human I could have found myself in a very precarious situation indeed. Quickly I managed to tear a gap for the hilt and grasping it I hauled the blade out of the thick webbing. Just in time too for the spider queen had heard my liaisons with its harvest and multiple legs were thundering towards my position, likely moving faster than I could roll. Aware that I was about to die, I raised the blade and thrust it at the closest leg, sidestepping as I did so. If I had had time to admire the sword that I pulled from the larder, I would have noticed that it was a thing of beautiful construction. A curved blade the length of a standard military sabre, its edge gleaming with razor sharpness and the blade itself seemed to glow with an inner light. As I thrust towards the leg I felt something pull inside of me and something flashed; a gleam of light that extended out from the blade and was gone in a second. Instantly I felt tired, drained in a way that I had not felt since before meeting Seya. Exhaustion was the better term; every single cell in my being felt like it was slowly switching off.

Whilst I focused on the workings of my body and the strange new exhaustion, I realised that I wasn't yet crushed to death. Looking up I saw the leg that had been descending to crush me was no longer there. Instead the limb was sheared through and a black, blistering substance was eating into the stump of the spider queen's leg. I noticed then that the high-pitched screeching that I had been hearing and assuming was part of my brain going to sleep was in fact the spider queen's screams. Acrid smoke billowed out of the spider queen's leg and sizzling sounds could be heard underneath its hissing screen. Unfortunately I did not have time to admire my apparent handiwork as the queen flailed crazily, overcome by anger and pain. A leg came out of nowhere and took me in the side of the chest, breaking bone and sending me cartwheeling across the room. When I came to a stop everything hurt. I struggled to breathe, the bone in my chest having perforated my lung. Blood spattered my hand as I coughed; a wet, thick sound.

Vision swimming, I tried to sit up and promptly passed out.

I was in and out of consciousness over the next few moments or minutes or hours; time is a weird thing when you're concussed. I recall seeing the spider queen moving in my direction, I saw a hazy figure standing before me and I remember bright bursts of light, and then I saw no more.

# CHAPTER 15

## *Recovery*

Waking up after being knocked unconscious is a very strange experience. Especially if the place you end up waking is not the place you remember being last. It makes you realise that you were either far more hurt than you had previously thought or were so tired that your body had no choice but to shut down and sleep. In my case both applied. I woke in a comfortable bed covered by thick furs, with a warm, mellow feeling deep inside my chest. I was aware of the pain that still wracked my body and knew that I should be screaming in agony but it was kept at bay by something strange and wonderful. I didn't know what it was but all I knew was that I wanted more.

I only realised that I had verbalised those thoughts aloud when a chuckling figure moved into the edges of my vision, his young face seemingly aged with worry. Cassius.

"The medicae did say that it was potent stuff," he said as he sat on the side of the bed. "I have a feeling that it's a mixture of poppy and alcohol, something that is certainly going to leave you feeling in a good mood." He sighed a deep and long sigh. "A reward, I guess, for someone who managed to get beaten up quite so badly as you."

I coughed and reached for the glass of water next to my bed.

Calidan quickly sprung to his feet, grabbed the water and guided it to my lips. After quenching the desert that was my throat, I nodded at him thankfully and spoke.

"What happened?"

"What do you remember?"

I thought back to the battle, my memories after my injury fragmented and splintered. "I got hit by the leg," I said slowly, thinking. "No, wait. I grabbed the sword, the sword that was hanging in the larder. The spider was going to hit me and I moved to deflect it. Something happened and its leg was gone and this black...bubbly...something was moving up what remained. Then it hit me and everything from then on is a bit of a blur."

Cassius's face was grave. "I saw you get hit," he said in a hoarse voice. "I honestly thought you were dead. I didn't think anything alive could survive the impact that you took."

"You were there?"

A nod. A grim smile. "Of course I was there." A spark of humour lit his eyes. "I knew that left on your own you would end up getting yourself hurt, if not killed. So I saw the others into the main tunnel and then came back just in time to see you grab the blade and stand against the spider queen. You swept the blade up, and for a moment you glowed, then the spider's leg simply...cut."

"What do you mean I glowed?" I said incredulously. "It's not something I often go about doing."

"I mean what I said," Cassius said casually. "I mean what do you expect? You went and picked up what I'm fairly certain is a tyrant blade, one that seems to forcibly draw seraph from you and use it to fuel its attacks. I'm pretty confident that's why you were so tired, it expunged your entire seraph pool."

"...Then the other person?"

He nodded. "I saw what the blade had done, I figured it was our best shot at staying alive. Whilst the queen was flailing in pain I sprinted, grabbed the sword, and did my best to figure it out."

"You stood against the queen? Alone?"

"She was hurt, blinded and mad with pain," he replied with amusement in his voice. "But yes, yes I did. Though I certainly wasn't alone. You forget our muscular and troll-like friend. Between the two of us we managed to drive her deep into the tunnels where she is either dead, dying, or licking her wounds. Either way I managed to pick you up and drag you back to the others."

I looked at my friend with awe. "If you wielded that sword and you didn't collapse, then your seraph pool must be…"

"Massive, apparently," Cassius replied with a laugh, "and yours my small, panthery friend, is tiny. Good to know that you can't beat everyone at everything! And that reminds me." He reached over to his side and deposited a sheathed blade on the bed. "This is yours."

I reached down and slowly removed the blade from the sheath, examining the exquisite workmanship with a careful eye. "It's a magnificent blade," I murmured softly, before sliding it back into its sheath. "And it's yours."

Cassius gave me a stunned look. "You can't be serious! That's a tyrant blade! You don't just give those away."

"A blade which you have proven far more capable of using," I replied calmly. "You saved my life down there Cassius. I might have been the one to find the blade but you're the one who used it to defeat that beast. As far as I'm concerned you have far more right to this weapon then anyone. Besides," I gave him a wink, "I can't keep having all the fun. It would be good to have someone else who can take a few of the beatings every now and again."

He scoffed. "Pretty sure I can give you a beating right now!"

I glanced at my bandaged form and wiggled my little finger. "I confess I'm not at my finest form right now. But I do have a functioning finger. Prepare for a whooping."

It turned out that laughing with broken ribs was a distinctly painful experience. Worth it.

Cassius didn't reach for the sword that lay on my lap, just sat by my side whilst I drifted in and out of sleep, updating me on the fort and the Meredothians when I was coherent enough for it and indulging me in drug induced nonsense when the blessed doctor came to refill my supply of whatever potent concoction she used. In my more lucid moments I asked after and saw the others, all looking battered, bruised but very much alive. All but Rikol who was feverishly sweating out whatever poison the spiders had used to keep him immobilised.

And, every now and then, I asked about the troll.

Cassius would stiffen slightly whenever I mentioned it. An almost imperceptible tightening of his muscles that I doubted even he knew he was doing. It didn't take me too long to probe through his defences and discover what ate away at him.

"I'm positive that I knew that creature, or whatever it used to be," he said slowly, perhaps expecting me to laugh him out of the room. When I didn't he continued less gingerly. "Something about its..."

"Its eyes," I finished, nodding. "I felt exactly the same way."

"It's fucking eyes!" Cassius exclaimed, and that was when I knew that this had been eating at Cassius whilst I had been recovering. Cassius wasn't much for vulgarity.

"What happened to it?" I asked, before we delved deeper into the topic of how or why we both felt like we knew a strange troll out in a place we had never before been.

Cassius's eyes narrowed in recollection. "It was hurt. Really badly hurt. But it still kept on fighting. Its raw power was astonishing, able to tear through the chitin of those giant spiders where even you had trouble. I think the only reason we survived was due to the focus of the spiderlings being on that beast." He shook his head as if clearing his thoughts. "Anyway, it was torn and bleeding, its flesh cut to ribbons and it had been stung so many times that I honestly was surprised that it wasn't keeled over and bubbling poison. But whatever else it might be, it's a troll. Its powers of regeneration are ridiculous. So whilst I picked up your sword-"

"Your sword," I interjected.

"The sword," he conceded, "and fought the spider queen, the distraction provided the troll with enough breathing room to begin healing. By the time I had driven the queen off, most of the cuts in its flesh were nothing more than scars." He paused a moment to gather his thoughts before continuing. "The spiderlings lost all sense of coherence when the queen fled, as though her pain or fear overwhelmed any intelligence that they might have had. They fled or attacked in aimless fashion. The troll ripped through them all with a vengeance. A massacre."

"They deserved it," I replied firmly.

"Perhaps," Cassius shrugged. "Or perhaps not. Should predators be destroyed just because they follow the laws of their nature?"

"Should trolls be destroyed, should the beast that murdered our village be destroyed?" I said rhetorically in return. "My answer is yes, if it threatens me or mine. That holds for a lion in the endless sea as much as it does for some demon from a different world."

Cassius considered this a moment before replying. "Would you kill the lion's cubs?"

"No."

"Why?"

"Because they hadn't done anything to me."

"A fair reply. You would kill that which seeks you harm, but not seek vengeance against anything else. Well...this troll slaughtered everything that remained in that cavern," Cassius said heavily. "Everything except you and me. It chased after the weak, the wounded, and glorified in their deaths. It enjoyed it."

"Sounds like most trolls I've heard of," I replied. "They aren't exactly known for being squeamish about killing."

"But they stop. They kill primarily for food, not for sport," said Cassius. "This troll roared in delight as it shredded spiders leg by leg. Something that I don't think its kin would do."

"If they are its kin," I murmured darkly.

"Agreed. It's no troll that I have ever heard of or seen before. But we both felt that sense of recognition, something about those eyes that seemed so familiar. Plus even in its frenzied rage it didn't kill us. Suggesting that for some reason it wanted us alive, whether by pure chance or because it needed to, I do not know."

"...So where is it then?" I asked slowly. "What happened to it?"

"It...it..." Cassius broke off, frustration evident in his face.

"It what, Cassius?"

He sighed. "It came and watched over you. It let out the biggest growl when it realised you were breathing, almost like it was relieved and frustrated at the same time. At first I had the blade at the ready, though I was so tired that my arm could barely hold it steady, after all it was covered in spider ichor and I had just seen it peel a spider apart like a grape and eat it, but it made no move to hurt you. Just sat and watched until I recovered enough to move you. When I did it made no move to assist, just followed me out of the ice caverns as though keeping guard against potential threats. Ella and Sophia had set up camp a little way outside, waiting for us. The troll made sure I arrived there safely and then peeled off, heading back into the woods. I don't doubt it kept watching, tailing us to the fort."

I stared at him blankly, my brain struggling to process what he was telling me. Eventually I realised he had stopped talking and was waiting for a reaction. "Cassius," I began, "to the best of your recollection, have I ever met a troll before, or anything that resembled that creature?"

He shook his head firmly.

"And to the best of mine, you haven't either," I continued. "I'm fairly certain a run in with something like that is something that we would have told each other. So we've either met it before and lost our memories, met something like it that makes us think it is familiar, or met it when it didn't look that way."

"For the second one," Cassius added in thoughtfully. "That would suggest that it's just a very helpful and friendly troll that decided not to kill us because *we* think *it* is somehow familiar."

"Doesn't exactly sound realistic, I know," I replied. "But none of this does. Considering what happened to us earlier, I'm having a hard time believing that this is real and isn't all some extended figment of my imagination at this point."

"Me too," said Cassius, "but we have to work on the basis that it is real for the time being. So unless something glaringly obvious happens that makes us realise that this is all some illusion or dream then that leaves us with option one or three; lost memories or a change of face."

"Well, I'm not sure that we are going to find the answer by ourselves," I replied with a yawn. "Maybe the others had some spark of inspiration or understanding that we didn't." Ignoring Cassius's shaking head I continued, "And if they didn't then I think we're just going to have to treat it as a strange unknown, something that can't be explained until the world, fate or whatever god is watching over us decides that it can be."

"So just ignore it?" Cassius asked. "Forget about the strange creature that assisted us? What if," he dropped his voice, "what if it is another Great Heart?"

"A Great Heart troll?" I said sceptically. "From what little Korthan told me about known Great Hearts, I would doubt it. I would also imagine it would have a smarter way of communicating with us than eviscerating countless spiders in various disturbing ways. But then again, I could be wrong." I held up my hand to forestall Cassius's reply, "Even if it is a Great Heart, what then? It hasn't bonded with anyone it came into contact with otherwise we would be having a much more intelligent conversation with it in this room. As such I don't think we can do anything about it at this point except remark upon it when we get back to the Academy."

Cassius pulled a face. "I hate leaving mysteries unanswered!"

That got a laugh out of me. "I'm pretty sure you're usually the one giving me this talk!" I said with a grin. "You're the sensible one and I'm the hare-brained schemer remember?"

He looked at me with a bemused expression. "I'm not sure any of us can be called 'sensible' Calidan. I doubt anyone who decides to be an Imperator can justifiably be called that."

"And yet you manage it," I retorted. "Good job!"

A snort. "Prick."

After an amused chuckle I turned back to work. "Have we talked about the potential for another route to the land of the Hrudan, or the possibility that the Hrudan couldn't retreat with Jadira?"

He nodded. "They have scouts out looking but nothing yet. They're keeping a set of eyes on the pass in case the spiders come out looking for vengeance or if the Hrudan have some method of getting through that blockage, but in my view they aren't getting through that without some pretty heavy equipment. In my view, if the Meredothians get hit hard again then the Hrudan have to have another pass available."

I rubbed my temples to try and clear some of the drug addled haze that the doctor largely kept me in. "How large is the area that we're in?" I asked finally. "The Meredothians think that the Hrudan can only come in via the pass, which makes me think that we're in some kind of plateau or valley?"

"You're in the Meredothian heartland," Jadira said as she pushed her way through the door hangings and into the room. "The mountains on the northern and eastern sides are seen as largely impassable, hence why the pass is so important."

I tilted my head at her. "Jadira, good to see you."

She nodded back at me. "And you, young one. It seems like your trek into the pass made for more mysteries than sense. The spiders haven't been that active in years. I apologise for sending you and yours into that nightmare."

I regarded her for a moment, noting her undisturbed heartbeat and her slow breathing - either she was a remarkable liar or she hadn't known that the pass was a death trap. "You couldn't have known," I replied warmly. "Just give Rikol a few pints to cheer him up. Being filled with spider poison can't have been much fun."

"There's a few waiting for him when he is up and about," she confirmed, giving a toothy smile. "Good thing you had some of those antivenom supplies, else he might not have made it judging by the amount of venom in his blood. It was damn near black!"

"He's tougher than he looks," I answered with a wry smile, "and has a habit of surviving dangerous situations, though I'm sure he would rather do it without getting injured at all. You mentioned being in the heartland, how large an area are we talking?"

Jadira pursed her lips for a moment, calculating. "We're up against the eastern mountains here as you know. If I wanted to get to the far edge of Meredothian land in the west during summer then I would say roughly five weeks of hard walking, though the heartland truly ends about four weeks in, everything past that point is barren and hard to live in. The northern range is a six day walk from here, to go south from there would require you to be walking for around two weeks to get to the furthest edge of the heartland."

I did some rough calculations in my head and my eyes widened, "That's a large chunk of land the Meredothians have, how come I haven't heard much about your country before?"

Jadira shrugged. "We tend to keep ourselves to ourselves. Outsiders tend to be a pest, like the Hrudan or trolls. The heartland keeps us sustained well enough and what little we do require from external sources we trade for, but in small numbers. Your Emperor is certainly aware of who we are, our numbers and size, after all, he sent you to us."

"I'm still not positive that we are the people you requested..." I began, but Jadira snorted and shook her head.

"You arrive from nowhere and save our town from attack, you offer support and go hunting for Hrudan, and you're from the Empire. Sounds like what I asked for from my end." Her eyes crinkled with humour, "Whether or not you knew that you were meant to do those things is another matter entirely. I'll let you take that up with your Emperor when you get back to him."

Cassius snorted and shrugged at me. "You never know, she might be right," he said. "This could all be some part of our training. In fact I would argue it is more than likely - at the very least I doubt the Academy has just up and lost its students. That said, at this point does it even matter why or how we are here? We should help these people where we can and then head back to the Empire."

"You're right," I said softly, causing Cassius to take a step back in amazement.

"I'm...I'm right?"

I gave him a sardonic look. "Yes, you're right and you know it. Stop being an ass."

He put a hand to his head and feigned a swoon. "This must be the drugs talking. Calidan agreeing with me? This happens so rarely I had forgotten what it felt like. Pure, sweet, unadulterated bliss."

I sighed and gave an apologetic glance to Jadira. "He will go on like this for a while. For some reason he likes to think I don't listen to what he says." Ignoring his outraged spluttering I carried on. "If you could start putting together supplies for a journey, we would be happy to assist in locating these Hrudan once every member of the team is up and about. In the meantime, if you have any maps of the local area, please bring them so that Cassius and I can have a look."

Jadira nodded and stood up, poking her head out of the fabric door to the room for a moment and then turning back. "I had a feeling you might want to look at those maps, but Ella, Scythe and Sophia have already stolen most of them. The doctor said you would be seemingly fine with multiple visitors from now on, so you can tap them for sources of information. I'll see you later." With that she walked out of the room but held back the curtain as three of my favourite people entered.

Ella had a ring of bruises and mild lacerations down her right arm, yet the smile on her face suggested she wasn't too hurt.

Waving, she came in, giving me a punch on the shoulder and sitting next to Cassius. Sophia looked as radiant as ever, cuts and bruises notwithstanding. She gave me a kiss on the cheek then stepped back to make way for Scythe who, using a crutch to support his injured leg moved to my bed and did the same thing...just directly on the mouth. My protestations were ignored to peals of laughter and soon we were chatting animatedly amongst ourselves, the maps of the surrounding area forgotten whilst we basked in each other's company.

It took three more days before Rikol awoke; the spider venom coursing through his veins thoroughly ravaged his body even with the antivenom that Jadira had given us. We were all overjoyed to see him awake and for the pallor of his skin to slowly be returning to its normal hue. It was a good thing he took a while to recover as it meant Scythe wasn't needed to be up and about – his ankle was a serious mess, a swollen foot attached to an even more swollen ankle and I was happy that he had decided to listen to reason and stay behind during our foray to the caves. A lot of people tend to think that courage is not listening to your body despite any issues you might have and pushing through the pain. In some cases I agree - you push yourself for competitions, you push yourself to be the best, and that is far truer at the Academy than anywhere else I've come across - however when you're out in the field and your friends' lives on the line, you have to listen to your body. It takes courage to understand when you're not fit enough to do the tasks required. Thus it was with great joy when Scythe was finally able to put down the crutches and gingerly start exercising his ankle and foot.

All in all we were a bit of a mess.

As soon as Rikol awoke we surrounded him with hugs, tears and laughter, yet in the quieter moments that dark side that I had seen in the forest still came to the fore. He was no longer the kind and witty, yet sometimes cutting joker. He was very much a cynical sardonic man whose wit could cut to the bone. Obviously we were very much alike. Doubtless being poisoned by a giant spider didn't help one's humour very much. And he wasn't that overjoyed to learn that there had been a lot more of the spiders within the caverns.

"Why is it always monsters with Imperators?" he sighed exasperatedly. "Why not more fighting with humans, humans I can deal with."

"Nature of the beast, I imagine," said Scythe. "There aren't that many humans that are of the same threat as the beasts that can be encountered in the world."

"I wouldn't be too surprised to find that the empire and the Emperor use more traditional methods of hunting humans," Ella added. "Why go through all the trouble of training Imperators for threats normal people can handle? They leave things like the little spiders to us."

Rikol's face was like stone. "Little? A little spider?" He grimaced. "If that was little I hate to see what you fought down in the cavern."

"Maybe we should go down there and show you…" Sophia said smoothly with a mocking grin, but judging by the pale look on his face we knew that Rikol would never go to those caverns again…and rightly so. Through a mixture of Sophia's effortless social grace and Scythe's rude charm the subject was swiftly changed to safer topics, first and foremost being that of the upcoming trip to locate the whereabouts of the Hrudan. A topic that led into many late-night discussions, planning sessions and tip gathering from many of the locals. All of which, as it turned out, was to be largely for naught in the face of something that none of us had enough experience to be involved with…a Meredothian winter.

# PRESENT DAY

What happens when an invading force conquers a rugged and mountainous region filled with warriors, hunters and trackers? The Undertrail, that's what.

The thyrkan had advanced so rapidly in their initial conquest that pockets of resistance had been left behind. Those hardy Hrudan, Meredothians, ash folk and wyldeans who had resisted the insidious might of the Enemy and yet failed in or decided against retreating. The information sources of the Empire kept us fairly well abreast of the relative locations of activity, but for security reasons the names and exact locations were known by a very select few and any information that we did collect was quickly outdated as the members of the Undertrail ebbed and flowed, never staying in one place too long in order to survive.

Originally the nobility of the Empire scoffed at the idea of a resistance movement and their effectiveness. That soon changed when Lionel Helmhast led his heroic and ill-advised advance into thyrkan held territory to 'put paid to the thyrkan threat'. Three thousand household knights met their end that day, surrounded and consumed with the loss of only some two hundred thyrkan. As if in mockery of the attempt, the Undertrail managed to bring a landslide down on a thyrkan encampment, wiping out over a thousand troops. Since that day the nobility have left the war plans to those more knowledgeable and actively supported the Undertrail to the best of their ability, sending food and supplies along little-known paths until the entirety of the thyrkan controlled sector became almost like a rabbit warren and thyrkan forces became used to night-time raids and poisoned supplies.

The Undertrail was how we had got into the area, and it was the place I hoped to get more supplies, repair Cassius's armour and more information - If anyone had seen a red eyed skyren it would be one of its many leaders. The Academy was well known to the Undertrail, and those of us who specialised in monster hunting had spent the last few years training those who would and could be trained on the most effective methods of dispatching their foes. Each time I had been here I had searched for the red eyed demon and each time I had met with no clues. But this time was different. This time I wasn't going to stop until I ended it once and for all; for I had no other mission. No other reason to be here than to end it. The Emperor in all his blind, shit eating wisdom, had either finally grown tired enough of my incessant requests to go and do to the skyren what it did to my village, or had secret plans of his own.

Likely both.

And so he had given us leave to go and do what we do best. He seemed confident that we would find the beast that we were hunting but hadn't offered up more than vague comments to keep heading north and that we would know when it was near. As cryptic and dickish as ever really.

We walked for two days, stalking through the blighted lands and avoiding thyrkan patrols. When we walked into the closest Undertail encampment under watchful eyes there was a smattering of bemused laughter at the sight of a man as large as Cassius walking naked. The bare steel in his hand and the sheer size of him quickly served to make it nervous laughter. I clarified our credentials and soon had warm food whilst clothes were stitched together to fit Cassius's frame. The local

leader, a woman by the name of Anzan, didn't have any information regarding a red eyed demon but did have plenty of
useful details regarding the increasing thyrkan patrols in the
area. She also didn't have a forge, meaning that Cassius would
have to continue going armourless for the time being, but she
pointed us in the direction of Scourge, a larger Undertrail encampment dedicated to removal of the thyrkan. I had been to
Scourge twice before and knew the commander well enough
but as its location changed every few months out of necessity
it was difficult to know where it was without recent information from the locals.

After a day of rest we moved out with a small caravan that
was heading to Scourge and were happy with the accompani-
ment of extra blades. Three days later we were in the latest
location of Scourge - an abandoned mine within the base of
Mount Woathan and the mine rang with the rhythmic beat of
the blacksmith reforming Cassius's armour.

Issan, the commander of Scourge, was an ex-ranger of the
Hrudan with enough scars to almost rival me. He had proven
to be a solid and dependable leader and through his guid-
ance Scourge had survived, grown and managed to repeatedly
strike back at the thyrkan threat. He had no news of a red
eyed demon but plenty of rumours related to slave camps and
the horrors inflicted on humanity. The one thing that he and
everyone else in Scourge could agree on was that the further
north you went the less likely you were to come back. This
had been a common theme throughout the Desolate lands and
doubtless for good reason.

Issan was never one for missing out on an opportunity, especially one that landed two Imperators in his lap, and so
through some wheedling, the promise of extra supplies and
liberal drinking I ended up agreeing that we would help him
strike against the thyrkan commander of the region, a move
that he was adamant would help destabilize the thyrkan hold
in the area. It would certainly be the boldest move that
Scourge had made yet, but as I sampled the firewater in my

clay cup and smiled at Issan's enthusiasm I could only wonder if it might be one move too far.

Afterall, the thyrkan were nothing if not vengeful.

# CHAPTER 16

## *Heartland*

When we finally set out on the march to determine the whereabouts of the Hrudan incursion it was late autumn, with snow laying down more thickly with each passing day. Scythe's leg still had a slight hobble, giving him a slightly jerky gait, and my reknit ankle burned in the cold, but Jadira reasoned that if we didn't leave we wouldn't have time for searching before we got snowed into the fort. She gave us roughly three weeks before the snow became too heavy and warned us of blizzards that could freeze a man solid in minutes. Truly the Meredothian heartland was a holiday destination like no other.

Strange really. It might have been an inhospitable place populated by even more inhospitable beasts, but, despite my griping, I found myself resonating with the land we were walking through. Yes it was dangerous, yes it was cold, but there was a stark beauty to the scene that I hadn't realised my soul had missed. The others huddled within their furs, but the two mountain born felt a previously unknown weight lift off their shoulders, for like no other place since entering the grassland of the Endless Sea, the Meredothian Heartland felt like home. A distant cousin to the grand mountain Cassius and I grew up on perhaps, but the relation was there. We strode with light steps, ignoring the bemused looks of our friends as we laughed, cajoled and chattered as animatedly as they had ever seen us, breathing in the crisp air and stunning landscapes with a vivacity much like a white sand addict in the Chains.

We marched north, hugging the foot of the mountains. It was as Jadira had said, much of the mountain range looked largely impassable, or at least requiring so much effort to traverse as to not be worth it. Sheer rock faces soared out of the ground, passable to a dedicated climber with spools of equipment and rope perhaps, but to a group of Hrudan encroaching onto enemy territory and armed for battle? Not likely.

Every now and again we would see caves or fissures in the rock and ice and we would creep in expecting a whole host of troubles; the least of which was the Hrudan. Thankfully, aside from one somewhat irate bear who decided that we weren't worth the effort of trying to eat we didn't run into anything too dangerous on our explorations. Rikol's face was drawn and pale whenever we explored a cave, as though he was constantly expecting a spider to crawl up beside him and stab him in the back. Considering that was pretty much exactly what happened last time I couldn't quite blame him for it and it said much about his character that he was able to follow us into the caves at all.

We set out with a range of plentiful supplies that Jadira had given us, lots of dried food, wood and kindling for starting fires. She warned us not to eat the snow to quench our thirst but to melt the water in a series of pots that she provided. I wasn't entirely sure why - surely snow was just frozen water - but memories of our parents stating the same thing was enough to stay our hands and warn the others off too. What many outdoor people don't tell you is that after a few days dried food becomes a real chore to eat. Your body starts craving fresh meat, fresh vegetables, and you begin to incessantly look for anything that you can forage. Thankfully we all had a fair amount of experience of surviving off the land - some of us more than others. Cassius and I were back in our element, reliving the time that we had spent with Seya hunting and living on the mountain - just with a lot more adult responsibility and less childish freedom. And, of course, without my cat.

I could still feel Seya. Our connection was there and seemingly whole but for the last few weeks it had been a drawn and pale imitation of itself. I missed her terribly. It's one thing to be surrounded by friends, but to be missing a part of your soul? Everything felt more dull, less vibrant and alive, and I don't think it was just a decrease in the magic of our bond but the simple fact that Seya - funny, witty Seya - wasn't there. The others missed her too, I knew that much. Our time at the Academy had meant that they had grown extremely close to Seya, giving her treats and scratches and wrestling with her at any opportunity. They asked me about her, where she was, what she was doing, but soon stopped when I explained that I knew as much as they did; that she was alive but far away. I didn't know what was stopping her from joining me and so I could only hope that she was not in pain.

We were coming towards the end of the second week when we finally came across some sign. Nothing much to a layperson's eye perhaps, but thanks to the skills instilled in Cassius and myself by the Tracker it was easy to infer that it was the remains of a once heavily used camp. The trail was hard to read, days or even weeks old, and it spread in every direction. Reasoning that those that pushed into the heartland were some of the incursive teams that have been attacking the Meredothians, we decided to keep with those that came from further north. The trail had been worn fairly heavily through the icy landscape - footprints that would have disappeared in a single night of rain had instead remained frozen in the grass, giving practically perfect conditions for the trained eye to track, and very tricky problems to get rid of for any party, as we well knew having struggled to do so over the past week.

"There's something about this trail..." Cassius said, crouching down beside the rutted ground. We all gathered around expectantly, but he just kept combing the ground.

Finally, Scythe couldn't keep his quiet any longer. "Well, what is it?" he asked.

"It's...getting cold."

The party groaned as Cassius cracked a grin.

"Really?" Scythe said exasperatedly. "That's the third time in as many days!"

"And it gets you each time," Cassius replied, his smile broad.

Whilst the party devolved into good-natured bickering I smiled and closed my eyes, opening my senses to the world around me. The crunch of ice-encrusted grass, the rustle of the wind across the furs of my coat, the creaking of distant boughs under the weight of snow, it all became that much clearer and more vivid- I froze, the only trees in view didn't have a large weight of snow pressing down amongst them.

"Down!" I roared, grabbing Scythe and Ella, the two nearest to me, and flinging them to the floor. I heard a muttered curse, sensed the snap of bowstrings, the flexing snap of wood, and an arrow rocketed towards where I had been a split second before, a second narrowly missing Ella. Just the two as far as I could tell, and I could sense the hurried movement of a man in the brush further ahead.

"Calidan?" Cassius shouted with a questioning voice.

"Two," I replied, already moving. "I'm fairly positive."

Instantly the group were up and on the run, their movements trained and confident. We had done exercises in the Academy designed to maximise our chances against snipers, and our movements consisted of erratic stop and start sprints that twisted and turned, all while closing the distance as quickly as possible. It was much harder in open terrain rather than the streets and buildings we often practiced in, but at least you didn't have to worry about arrows coming down from floors above you. We rapidly closed in on the two men in the thicket of trees, angry Imperators-in-training moving like hungry wolves. I was right, one of the men had been trying to make a break for it, the other wasn't moving - or at least wasn't moving away - I could sense that he was scrabbling to knock another arrow to his string, panic and adrenaline making his actions more erratic and prone to error. As for the other man, he was going to be out of the thicket and away before we were close enough to catch him.

"Sophia!" I cried, pointing in the direction of the rear of the thicket in case she could see me. "We've got a runner, far end of the trees, bring him down, alive if possible!"

I heard a grunt and felt Sophia change direction ever so slightly, unlooping her bow as she ran. I continued past the unmoving man, leaving him to the others in case I could assist in catching the runner. On even ground and drawing on the power of Seya's bond I would be much faster, but his lead was substantial and it was possible that he was trying to lead us into a trap - something I could hurtle straight into. Thankfully however, Sophia's bow was a thing of sheer beauty and power and she wielded it like it was an extension of her body. It was a rare day that anyone saw her miss. I had no doubt that she would be able to bring him down before he was out of range. I rounded the edge of the small thatch of trees and saw the man sprinting, his head tucked low with his arms pumping furiously. He was clad in a variety of leather with his bow slung over one shoulder and a hatchet tucked into his belt. As far as I could see there was no chainmail, no large war axe - nothing, in fact, that I particularly attributed to a member of a Hrudan warband; he could be anyone.

My brain sparked. "Wait!" I roared to Sophia whilst putting every ounce of speed I had into my legs, hoping that I could make it in time and knowing that it was futile. Even one bonded to a Great Heart can't outrun an arrow in flight and Sophia's fingers had already loosed. I slid to a halt next to the man in time to watch blood froth from his lips, Sophia's arrow having embedded itself deep into a lung. I held his gaze as he died, my hand on his shoulder in a small attempt to offer what support I could. Though the man had shot at us I couldn't bring myself to be angry, particularly when I was fairly positive he was Meredothian.

Sophia and I returned to the cover of the trees as quickly as possible, lunging through the grasping undergrowth and all the while hoping that Cassius had done his usual - and very un-Imperator like - thing and stayed his hand. I gave a sigh of relief as we arrived to find the rest of the group standing around the second attacker but it was easy to see why they had not cut him down and why he hadn't run like the others. The stump of his leg was eminently visible with dirty bandages stained black with blood. More worryingly were the black lines spreading up from the wound and into the meat of his thigh.

"He's Meredothian," Cassius said softly as I arrived, his eyes turning further downcast as he noticed the bloody hands I bore. "Thought we were more Hrudan coming to finish them off."

"Doesn't look like he needs much finishing," Scythe said grimly. "That's blood poisoning. He will be dead within a day, two at the most."

"You killed Cannae," a wearied voice rasped in Meredothian, the tone not accusatory but matter of fact. The man's eyes had found my hands and the fresh blood that coated them.

I inclined my head. "I did," I replied in the same language, ignoring Sophia's glance. "I believed him to be Hrudan and running to return to warn of our approach. I gave the order to bring him down and only when the deed was done did I realise the error. I am sorry."

The man raised his hand and waved my apology off. "We shot first. We thought that we were likely to die when we saw the number of you, and knew it when we saw you move. Fighters one and all. Cannae and I are hunters, not blooded killers. I should hate you for killing my brother, but I have nothing left to grieve."

"What happened?" said Rikol, crouching down beside the man. His face held no emotion but his voice was soft, gentle.

There was silence for some time and then the man began to speak. His eyes were haunted as he relived the memories of the last few days. Days filled with fire, swords and death. He spoke

of how his village, a relatively meagre collection of huts that
kept to themselves, came to be set upon by a small but experienced band of men. His brother and himself came back to the
village following an unsuccessful hunt to find people they had
known their entire lives dead on the floor. At this Cassius and I
shared a look, the horror that we had known that day was new
and fresh for this man, front and foremost in his mind whereas
for us it was now just a deep, soul-wrenching ache to which we
had become accustomed. If he lived - and that was doubtful
looking at his leg - I fully suspected that he would die in some
violent spat and a needless waste of life further down the line.
He spoke about how the men, the Hrudan, were still in the
village, still raping and still murdering. Our ears perked up
when he spoke about how he saw some people being dragged
away, thick ropes binding their hands and wooden contrap-
tions locked around their necks. He spoke about how he and
his brother had done what they could and attempted to find
survivors before trying to extract vengeance. He shakily, yet
proudly, talked about how they had shot down at least one
man, their arrows striking true and the Hrudan falling to the
ground and lying still. This had given them away and for the
past two days they had been chased, though he imagined that
the trail was now somewhat cold. As a parting gift their pursuers had managed to cut him with an arrow - the wound shallow and barely noticeable, but a fierce burning soon began to
rage within his leg and it became clear that the Hrudan used
poisoned arrows. By the time they were safe enough to deal
with the injury the wound had been black and putrid and the
only thing they could think to do was to remove the limb. He
spoke and rambled, his voice getting weaker until he drifted
into fevered sleep.
I looked at the group. "Thoughts?"
"Sounds like the Hrudan are slavers," Scythe muttered, eyes
dark.
"Slavers aren't the only thing to come out of the deep North,"
Cassius said softly. "Tracker said that the people he was forced

to work for were not Meredothian," he looked at me with a fierce light in his eyes, "could it be they were Hrudan?"

"Could be," I replied. "But we don't know enough to declare war on the Hrudan populace for demon summoning and human sacrifice. What we do know is that they, or at least a segment of their population, are aggressive and intent on either claiming this country or raiding it whilst inflicting wanton violence. Anything else?"

"He's brave," Ella said, speaking up. "To cut off your own foot without something to numb the pain and no medical experience? Brave."

"True enough," Rikol interjected, "but it doesn't look like it did him all that much good in the end. Either that poison got further into his flesh than he expected or his leg has become fouled. Those black lines are a very bad sign."

"Agreed," said Scythe. "We all know that he won't last much longer. If we had come across him a little earlier perhaps we could have done something, but at this point?" He sighed and shook his head. "Probably best just to ease his pain."

"We aren't leaving him," Cassius stated firmly. He raised a hand to cut off Scythe's response. "I will not leave someone out here to die, I will carry him."

"Where?" said Ella, moving close to grasp his hand in hers. "Where will you take him?"

The fact that Ella didn't say 'we' was telling. She hadn't lost her sense of toughness or her street smarts from her rough upbringing and consequently had an astoundingly practical nature. Cassius was the only one who was driven by his need to save others. He always was the best of us.

"You won't take him," I said bluntly. "It's too far, we are miles from anywhere and we don't know where we are headed, let alone the fact that it is going to be dangerous. We can't risk our best swordsman being tired if we suddenly get attacked."

Cassius looked devastated, as though I had betrayed some inherent value that he held most dear. At that point in my life he wasn't quite used to that.

And I guess, neither was I.

I walked up to the unconscious man, gathered him into my arms and stood up, turning as I did so to lock eyes with them all.

"I will take him."

# CHAPTER 17

## *Avalanche*

The man's name was Kernighan and when he was in a more reasonable state of mind he was quite an amusing bloke, cracking sardonic jokes at any available opportunity. Even Rikol, lost as he was in his own bitter thoughts, cracked a smile here and there and began to join in, one bitter and broken boy to a bitter and broken man.

Kernighan was aware that he was going to die. He had accepted it before we arrived. Village life anywhere in the world, let alone in the Meredothian heartland during winter, was hard. Though he only had perhaps thirty years under his belt he had seen enough people come and go to know that death more often than not came at the behest of the infected wound or sickness than it did at the hands of blade or claw. With pained breaths he directed us back towards the torched remains of his village - a distance we made in just under a day of hard walking. His fatigue ridden eyes watched blankly as the broken and burned walls came into view, the village nestled at the base of a small hill, the blackened wood stark against the snow-covered landscape. Broken bodies lay where they had fallen, frozen in rictures of pain, many of them savaged by beasts that had found the grisly feast.

With a glance the group spread out, weapons at the ready in

case of straggling Hrudan - or more likely scavenging wolves - but nothing moved. The dead village was silent save for the cawing of crows. Little remained of the buildings; everything had been smashed and then burned. Kernighan, mercifully, was unconscious for the majority of the time that we spent there hunting for clues. For those moments that he was awake he was silent, watching the remains of his village and home with haunted eyes. With no immediate tracks and the light long since faded we set up camp on the other side of the hill, huddling together against the cold with only a small banked fire and some hide tarpaulins for warmth. It was a long and restless night as Kernighan struggled in his sleep, wrestling with fever dreams. Only in the deep hours of the morning did he eventually still, allowing some rest to be had by those not on watch.

He died during that night. It wasn't unexpected but it was still surprisingly impactful. We hadn't known him long and he had started our relationship by attempting to kill us but carrying an injured man through snow and ice tends to quickly build a relationship. We buried him on top of the hill overlooking the remains of his home, said a few words and then moved on. Whilst it might not seem sentimental the biggest thing we could do to honour his memory was to find the band of men who had done this and send them to join him in the great beyond.

As you might imagine, the tracks around the burnt village were almost completely unintelligible. People had run, died and been dragged back through the mud and blood through-out the village and to top it all off there was a few days of fresh snow on top. Circling further from the village however, we began to find signs of the group that had passed through. It looked like it was maybe a dozen strong, which might not seem like enough to take out a village, but a dozen armed men with mail and weapons versus thirty scared and unarmed vil-lagers? Easy prey.

The tracks led further to the north east, the Hrudan moving

slowly, hampered presumably by the fresh addition of slaves. The tracks of the slaves were heavy, hindered as they were by the yoke that Kernighan had seen round their necks. Periodically we saw waste that had been dropped just off the tracks, all in a line indicating toilet stops for the slaves. Unpleasant for them but a useful tracking tool for us. That said, the Hrudan really didn't seem to be minding their tracks in the first place, perhaps because they were on their way out of the Heartland and thus heading home, or because they thought they had this entire area of the Heartland to themselves. Either way it made our lives a whole bunch easier.

A good thing too, because the sheer amount of bad weather that started rolling in made our days miserable. Jadira's words about how bad the weather would get roughly three weeks after our departure from the fort were proving strangely prophetic. The only consolation was that the Hrudan party must have faced the same difficulties. Snow was becoming a real problem, both in terms of the cold and in terms of depth. I was able to wade my way through the majority of the snow drifts due to my height and strength but some of the smaller members of the party, Ella and Rikol in particular, were starting to struggle. More and more frequently terrible snow storms struck, rolling across the empty skies with astonishing speed to strike with unmitigated fury. On these occasions I began to rely more heavily on my senses and consequently took the lead, tying the others to me and taking the best route to shelter. When the storms hit the snow was so blindingly thick and the wind was at times so powerful that you couldn't see more than a couple of feet in front of you, rendering us effectively deaf and blind to the world. For one day in particular we were kept in a tiny shelter that Cassius and I fought to create against the wind. How to dig a snow hole was something that our fathers had taught us at a young age, not that we had needed to use the technique before, but it proved surprisingly warm, if not particularly cosy, and I credit it with keeping us alive for that day. When we got out of the snow hole the next morning the snow was so thick that it came up to our waists. Cassius and I put our heads together to recall everything and anything that our parents had taught us years earlier before trekking to hunt down some saplings that had survived the ravages of the winter and lashing them together with strips of hide into oval shapes to create a terrible mockery of a snowshoe.

Terrible and yet surprisingly effective. I'm not sure if our parents would have been proud or scornful considering that what we had created did not remotely represent the art that they had once taught us. But most importantly to us was that they worked, allowing our feet to sink into the snow by a couple of inches rather than down to our waists. Our going was slow but infinitely faster than the speed we were doing before. By this point largely all signs of the Hrudan party had disappeared, covered under mounds of snow. The landscape had changed completely, becoming a barren, frozen wasteland filled with howling wind. Where I had once been in awe of this stark landscape I was now purely focused on putting one step in front of the next and being as warm as possible. I imagine that for the others it was much worse but complaints were few and far between with everyone lost in their own miserable worlds.

Judging the right direction to go in was far more difficult than before. When the sun was overhead and with no storm howling on our faces, it was possible to see far into the distance and locate the mountain range that I presumed the Hrudan were heading for. As soon as the clouds rolled in and blinding snow filled the sky, travelling by landmark became impossible. Often we would find that once the weather lifted our direction had changed considerably and we would be forced to add further miles onto our journey. What hope we had for finding the Hrudan party swiftly soon became hope that we would find the party at all. Eventually, after five frostbitten days after leaving Kernighan's destroyed village, we gave up any hope of finding the group and our aim became purely to reach the base of the mountains. We were covering probably six, maybe seven miles in a day, each one longer and more arduous than the last. Hidden features of the terrain, like ravines or tree roots that snared your feet under the snow became punishing. Obstacles that would take no time at all to bypass in the summer took forever when covered in layers of snow; instead becoming deadly traps, just waiting for someone to slip and hit their head whilst in the depths of a blizzard. Thankfully however we managed to navigate these obstacles without injury and eventually, perhaps four weeks after we had left the fort, we reached the base of the mountains, far behind our original schedule thanks to the diversion caused by both the weather and Kernighan, and began a slow trek along the base; keeping an eye on any potential passes.

It was a long, tedious and dangerous job. Something I'm sure Jadira understood full well when she gave it to us. The majority of the mountains that we travelled past consisted of sheer rock faces and so would be extremely difficult to bypass, but every now and again we would be forced to follow some twisting turning attribute of the mountain that looked like it might be a path. Each one led on some perilous journey up steep and exposed routes that inevitably ended in nothing at all. Our only protection on those climbs was the thick rope that we tied around ourselves and the hope that if one fell then the others could haul them back in.

The main problem however, was that for all that Cassius and I were mountain born, we hadn't been exposed to weather of this magnitude, or at least not whilst we were fending for ourselves without the experience of our village and relatives to guide us. No one in the party was particularly well suited to this environment or had relevant experience in the many dangers of the mountains.

And that is how we all nearly died.

We were climbing up one particularly steep section of mountain; in hindsight it was something that was more like a mountain goat's trail than a route that heavily laden Hrudan could follow but we had undertaken to leave no stone unturned. Consequently we pushed far up the mountain, twisting and

turning along narrow precipices, facing sheer drops and slippery surfaces with nothing but hide boots, our thick rope and
sticks we had brought for walking. It was difficult, dangerous,
and extremely stupid, but we were Imperators in training and
we had a job to do, reckoning that our skills, our abilities, and
above all our reckless youthful optimism would keep us safe.
It turns out that nature cares nothing for what you believe.
It only cares about what you do and how you do it, and
climbing a mountain whilst shouting at the top of your lungs
was certainly not the way. Unfortunately that was how we approached it, shouting at each other against the wind. Roaring
at the top of our lungs to make ourselves heard as we clambered up the steep rocks. And eventually, nature decided to
make us pay the price.

What a bitch.

The first I sensed of it was a tremor in the rock, a shaking that
I couldn't attribute to the cold in my hands. Next I saw peb-
bles shaking and rolling their way down the hill, and then I
saw snow pouring off the top shelf of the mountain. Like a liquid torrent it thundered its way towards us, ripping boulders
and rocks off the mountainside and carrying them along in its
wake.

"Avalanche!" I roared, desperately looking for somewhere for
us to hide. *There's got to be something, somewhere,* I thought
frantically. We were exposed, stuck on the side of a mountain
with no quick means of descent aside from the very obvious
and direct route by which the avalanche was intending to take
us.

"The cliff!" screamed Sophia, pointing at the closest rock face
that jutted out from the mountain. It was sheer and there were
not many easily visible holds, but it was overhanging which
meant that we wouldn't get snow raining down upon us from
above - as long as we could hold on. I had my doubts, the rock
looked slick and we were not equipped for climbing, but there
was no other option.

Quickly we sprinted for the cliff, throwing aside gear that

was slowing us down and removing the fur gloves that were keeping our hands safe from the cold. Even if we survived we were going to be in a very precarious situation indeed. Sophia reached it first, her nimble fingers quickly finding holds on the rock face, her boots scrabbling at the rock as she tried to hold herself in place before moving further out to make room for the others. One by one we shifted onto the rock face, fingers holding onto the smallest of holds with the energy of desperation. The 'death grip' I had heard it called when discussing mountaineering in the Academy with some Imperators. It was meant to be a bad thing, something that ensured that you tired out your arms much faster than if you trusted your arms to hold onto the same bit of rock with less ferocity - but I doubted that even those Imperators could have clung in the same situation and not been squeezing with all their might.

A quick glance showed me that everyone was managing so far. Ella was surprisingly at ease in this environment, her strong hands and small figure lending itself well to traversing the wall, and I doubted it was the first time that she had taken up climbing, particularly when growing up in the Chains of Forgoth. Scythe too, seemed in his element, his strong arms and powerful figure keeping him in place. Rikol, much like Sophia, was scrabbling for purchase for his feet, not trusting his fingers to keep him in place. Cassius was pressed up under the rock face and straining his feet against the wall whilst keeping his torso tight, with his fingers embedded in a small pocket the tension in his body all that was keeping him from slipping. I had my hand wedged deep into a small crack that extended above my head, the other hand was out wide and hanging off a small outcropping. The rock was sharp, slicing into my fingers so much so that I could feel blood welling. Doubtless the others were experiencing exactly the same. I held my breath, hearing the roar coming closer and closer until it felt like the entire rock face was going to collapse due to the weight of the sound.

And then the avalanche hit.

The rock trembled, shook and groaned under the impact of the snow. All of our attempts to hang on suddenly became that much harder as blinding white erupted around us, threatening to suck us down if an errant leg or arm was misplaced. Splintering rock could be heard as boulders large and small struck against each other before launching off the edge of the cliff to explode below. Anyone caught in the flow would have to face a drop of near a hundred feet onto solid rock and if they somehow survived that they would inevitably be crushed, swamped and suffocated by the deluge of rock and ice. We were surviving by pure luck and, judging by what I could see of Rikol, quite literally the skin of our teeth. I could only hope that the snow ended before our strength gave out.

Screaming got my attention, the sound almost lost in the thunder around us. I could see Ella reaching for Rikol whose face was blanching almost as white as the surrounding snow as both his feet scrabbled for purchase against the slippery rock, one hand loose and dangling, avid panic in his eyes. Ella's hand reached, touched, missed and touched again as Rikol flailed until she finally grasped his wrist. Panting heavily he clutched in his panic, threatening Ella's safety like a drowning swimmer might a would-be saviour. She wobbled, a minor motion that sent shivers down my spine. Scythe was moving to assist, reaching out a hand to help haul Rikol back on to the wa-

Rikol's foot flared too far and hit the wall of snow. Instantly he disappeared, sucked into a world of white. The sudden jerk was too much for Ella's fingers and she too vanished into the snow.

"Hold on!" Sophia screamed before the rope went taught and Scythe whipped from the wall, bloodied hands pinging off the sharp rock. The rope strained and pulled at my torso and my hands screamed as I clung on with every inch of strength left to me. Sophia and I were opposite sides of the rope that held us tight, if the two of us could hold it we could potentially haul in the others once the avalanche ceased.

And then Cassius, taking the brunt of the weight on an awkward hold, lost his grip and was plucked from the face with a roar of despair. Sophia and I locked eyes a split second before she disappeared; gone like she had never been. I screamed as the weight on my body pulled my legs from the wall, my hand that I had jammed into the crack as deep as it could go was the only thing keeping me from joining my friends and the only thing potentially keeping them alive. I could feel the tendons quivering in my arm and could hear the joints popping in my shoulder as my ligaments, tendons and my entire body screamed against the punishment. For all my strength and power, holding the combined weight of the entire party against the indomitable might of the avalanche was never going to end well.

With a barely audible but very physical sensation my shoulder dislocated. My scream became one of pure agony. My primal instinct was to let go instantly, yet I wasn't sure I could do so even if my instinct overrode my reason. My hand was wedged deep into the rock, rivulets of blood running down my arm and onto my neck as my skin tore against the sharp edges. One by one I could feel things - likely very important and highly needed things - *ping* all along my shoulder and arm as my muscles stretched and tore even more.

My screaming was a mixture of pure animal panic and fury at this point. I could feel my arm shredding, my hand a raw and bloodied thing. If the snow kept on coming then I was positive that dislocation would be the least of my worries, but I could do nothing except hang on for as long as possible. Hang on and hope that they could survive the thundering torrent. I cursed and screamed as my arm continued to separate, howling until my vision began to go grey, until, with more sickening crunches from my shoulder, my body went limp and my vision black.

I woke up what felt like hours later but was just minute-like seconds. I was no longer on the wall; my hand must have relaxed enough to escape the crack I had wedged it into. I was trapped in a world of white, a shifting and tumbling universe where I could not determine what was up and what was down. Soon enough the motion settled as the avalanche died down, its anger spent. Thankfully the weight of the snow pressing down on me was not all encompassing. Heavy and terrifying yes, but not unbearable. It gave me hope that my friends could be saved. The snow around me was stained red, and though I couldn't move my head to see my arm, any attempt to move it was met with agony. Gritting my teeth I lifted my good arm and slowly began to dig.

Digging yourself out of snow, especially many layers of snow, is exhausting. Not as bad as trying to dig oneself out of sand - a recurring theme in my nightmares thanks to our ill-fated trip to the desert - but close. I imagine that if I didn't have Seya's strength to draw on I would have taken far, far longer, or simply not managed at all. The rising panic was the worst. The feeling like you're completely trapped, locked in place, with stifling air convincing you that you're going to suffocate. When I finally broke free it was an exuberant feeling, the taste of fresh mountain air flowing into my lungs bringing unbidden tears to my eyes. I lay there for a second, gasping, feeling battered, bruised, and completely unable to do what I had to do next. Pushing all that self-pity aside I slowly dragged myself to my knees and felt for the rope around my waist. Extending my senses, I could feel the muffled thumping and the frantic scrabbling of some of my friends as they tried to escape their icy prisons. More worryingly was that at least two of them were unmoving. Gripping the rope tightly I made my way over to the next person in the chain and began to pull.

After what felt like an eternity later I had everyone out. Scythe had been the first and though he was battered and bruised he had been able to assist me in retrieving the next in the chain. Three hands made it a lot faster than one and quickly we had been able to retrieve Ella and Rikol - a good thing too because both of them were unconscious and whether due to impact or asphyxiation we weren't sure. Cassius and Sophia took a little longer. Both were awake and actively trying to get out of the snow, however they'd been buried very deep and it took time to get them out whilst at the same time trying to take care of Rikol and Ella. Eventually everyone was out on top of the snow and more or less in one piece. Surprisingly, I was by far the most injured. The others have various cuts and scrapes and the majority of their bodies would be one gigantic bruise in the coming hours but, whether by some divine providence or just pure luck, they were more or less intact with no seriously debilitating injuries. On the other hand, I looked like I had just come out of a war. With my arm hanging loosely - the dislocation causing me to look lopsided - and blood covering my clothes thanks to the flesh on my arm that had been torn to ribbons, I had given the others quite a fright.

I bit back a scream as Cassius lifted my arm out in front of me until it thunked back into the socket with a horrible jolt. "Sorry," he muttered as he finished tightening the strips of tattered cloak around my lacerated arm. "Best I can do to stop the bleeding for the moment. As for your shoulder I suggest not moving it for as long as possible. Dislocation is one thing but I can't do anything for any internal damage." He gave me a small grin. "Besides there's nothing to say that you aren't going to die of infection in the next couple of days so might as well not worry about the shoulder eh?"

He was jesting and I forced a smile, but we both knew that without supplies we were in a sticky situation. Somewhere on the side of the mountain were our packs. Packs that contained food, water and weapons. As it was we were stuck on the side of an inhospitable mountain with fresh injuries, damp clothes and no supplies which was a delightfully unenviable position to be in. With night drawing in, we needed to figure out a solution and fast.

With a pained grunt I hauled myself to my feet, Cassius's arm offering me steadying support. "Normally," he said as I began to move, "I would tell you to sit back down and not move your arse until your arm was fixed. But with your healing as reduced as it is, time is going to be our enemy. Just...try to take it easy?"

I barked a laugh at that. "Not sure that I have much say in the matter," I replied with a small grin. "The mountain does as the mountain wants and currently that seems to involve giving us the middle finger. We need to find our supplies and we won't last long exposed like this."

"Agreed," he said with a nod. "There are snow clouds on the horizon. We best get shelter sorted before we look for any further supplies. Snow hole?"

"Snow hole," I echoed with a nod. "Though this time, I think you guys will need to do most of the digging."

In the end it didn't take us too long to get the shelter sorted. We buried ourselves into the fresh snow as close to the overhanging rock face that had saved us as possible. Whether or not that was a good idea I didn't know, but we were rapidly losing the light and the adrenaline pumped adventures of the day had us all weary. By the time it was complete it was pretty much all we could do to crawl inside and fall into exhausted slumber. Outside the snow raged; howling wind shrieked across the mountain range and coated any exposed surface in white, yet for all its fury it went unnoticed.

Unnoticed by all but one.

# CHAPTER 18

## *Unseen Helper*

Punching my way out of the snowhole was remarkably similar to clawing my way out of the avalanche. For a moment the same panic rose in my chest; the once comforting walls of the night suddenly imposing, confining. Desperation tingeing my movements I struck upwards, outwards and then I was free, my good hand breaking through the crust and into the outside world, my panic instantly easing. Strange how such a simple thing can make the difference between being a mindless, panicked animal or a functioning human being. Now that my nerves had settled I patiently cleared out the rest of the snow that blocked the entrance before slithering out into the sun.

The world below was a thing of beauty. The sky was clear and the sun dazzlingly bright, gleaming rays reflecting and refracting off the ice and snow to coat the landscape in a kaleidoscope of colours. Honestly, if we weren't sitting in an avalanche zone I could have stayed there for days watching that vista. As it was I saw something else that raised my eyebrows and a whole host of questions. For sitting some ten feet in front of the entrance to the snow hole, a light dusting of snow failing to disguise the brown leather, was one of our packs.

"Well...that's surprising," Ella murmured from behind me as

she extricated herself from the den and walked over. "Did we
miss it in the dark?"

"No way," I said. "Absolutely no way. I mean..." I gestured exasperatedly at the pack, "it's right there! We would have basically been lying on top of it when digging the snow hole!"

"What's the matter?" came a muffled voice from within.

"It appears we have a mysterious benefactor," Ella replied
dryly, moving aside to make way for the others. One by one
they crawled out, gasped at the view and then goggled at the
innocuously placed bag.

None of us approached it for a long time. Whether due to
the deep suspicion of all things good inherent in all Imperators and their ilk or in case it might have been some kind
of hunger and snow induced mirage I couldn't say. Eventually
Cassius grabbed his sword, walked up to the quietly waiting
bag and with a finesse refined through years of sword practice
he tentatively poked it in the side. When nothing happened
he crouched down next to the bag, gingerly brushed away the
snow and opened the top. He spent a few moments looking inside and rummaging through the contents, before standing up
and brushing snow from his knees.

"It's Rikol's bag," he said, eyebrows furrowed in thought. "All
his stuff. Food, clothing, weapons - it's all there. Untouched."

"Before I realise that I haven't regained my sanity," said Scythe
slowly, "can we all confirm that there is no way in the seven
pits of Arshuderan that we each missed this pack last night?"

"No way," said Sophia, her voice dripping with incredulity.
"We all stumbled and walked across here last night, kicking
aside snow and fighting the weather. The visibility wasn't so
bad when Calidan first got us out from under the snow that we
wouldn't have seen this."

Rikol looked up at the rockface above him. "Another avalanche in the night?"

Ella snorted. "Disregarding the fact that we would likely all
be dead, why would your pack be somehow above us waiting
to be swept down by another avalanche?" She shook her head.

"No, this wasn't some random coincidence...this was placed here."

It's what we had all been thinking but hearing the words out loud set cautious eyes to scanning the surrounding mountainside, hunting for any sign of whoever was seemingly looking out for us but to no avail. Even with my enhanced senses the storm strength winds the night before had removed all scent or tracks; ensuring that there was nothing left to go on except pure guesswork.

"So..." I said, slowly drawing out the word once everyone had studiously examined the pack and the mountain and found them both wanting. "Anyone want to hazard a guess?"

"Could someone have followed us up here?" Sophia asked, her voice suggesting that she didn't think it likely.

"Without any of us noticing?" Cassius replied. "The weather wasn't that bad until after the avalanche. It was bright and sunny, and the route we took up didn't exactly leave that many places to hide." He paused to consider his next words. "Perhaps from above us? It would explain why we didn't see whoever it was earlier in the day."

"Potentially," Scythe mused. "But if they were friendly then why not just help us out by introducing themselves or waiting until we discovered this pack and then doing so? Just seems like a strange way of doing things."

I nodded my head in agreement. "So we have someone or something that seemingly wants to help us without being seen. I'm fine with that for the time being. Plus," my nose sniffed the air, "I think that he, she or it wants us to go back down the mountain."

"How do you figure that?" Cassius asked.

I pointed down the mountain. "Because the only thing I can smell that isn't us is sun-baked leather and it's coming from where we came." I looked at the others and then up the route we had been attempting to take. "I think that we can agree that a force of Hrudan couldn't easily make it over this part of the mountain. Without supplies we aren't going to last long and things will be difficult enough as it is unless our friend intends to deliver all our packs to us. I suggest we head back down the mountain and find what we can to help us survive."

It took a few minutes of discussion but eventually everyone agreed on the course of action and we slowly began making our way back down the mountain, slipping and sliding along the treacherous surfaces. Along the way we found Sophia's bag placed on an exposed outcropping that was easily visible in the noonday sun. Ella's bag we found at the base of the mountain just as the light was beginning to draw to a close. We built another snow hole, ate a little of the dried food within the three rescued packs and fell into another exhausted slumber.

After an uneventful night we once again emerged, blinking, into the bright morning sun. The cuts on my arm had begun to close up, scabbing over in a grisly process that entailed no end of itching. My shoulder throbbed incessantly but I listened to Cassius's advice and kept it as immobile as possible. I knew just how long a normal human would have been out of action with such an injury - even with my reduced healing speed and judging by the recovery from the mountain lion attack I figured it would be a few days rather than months before I regained full mobility.

It had been nearly four weeks since we left the fort and the weather was continually becoming more punishing. Considering our situation, which had been growing steadily more dire even before losing our packs and nearly dying in an avalanche, it was prudent to turn back and head towards the fort and its relative safety as soon as possible, which was something that we were all more than happy to do. However when scouting the surrounding area for berries to complement our meagre breakfast I found one of Cassius's knives pinned into a tree just north of our tiny camp and beneath it was a crudely drawn arrow pointing further along the mountain range in the opposite direction to the fort. We dithered for a little while but in the end there was only one choice that could be made. We were all far too determined to find out who was leaving this information and supporting us to turn back now - we just had to hope that there would be more supplies somewhere ahead.

And supplies there were indeed. A whole train of them.

Two days of walking following badly hacked signs in trees had us hiding in a small forest and watching the tell-tale smoke signals of multiple campfires curling into the sky not a half mile away. Our hidden benefactor had not yet been revealed though I had a sneaking suspicion growing within my chest as to the identity of our friend. Brush crackled to my left as Cassius slithered his way back through the undergrowth, freshly returned from his scouting. The others were further back and waiting for the two of us - thanks to Seya's training we were the two best at moving silently through the undergrowth - to return with news.

He nodded at me, his expression grave. "Hrudan, no doubt about it," he whispered.

"How many did you count?"

"Roughly sixty men by my reckoning," he replied. "Looks like they are busy trying to fortify the approach to the mountain. I couldn't get close enough for a proper look but I would put money on the pass being up there."

I nodded in agreement; his numbers tallied with mine. "Looks very much like the Hrudan want to keep their foothold on the heartland doesn't it?" I murmured. "Reckon that the Meredothians know of this?"

"Some must have, though whether it is just small communities that live nearby or they have been killed for their knowledge or even colluding with the Hrudan, who can say?"

"Well, we're certainly in the middle of nowhere as far as I can tell," I said with a sigh. "No sign of any forts or villages nearby. And Jadira certainly didn't know of any places of note up here."

Cassius gave a wry smile. "Kinda reminds me of home - there weren't that many who knew of our village if I remember rightly. Just that one trader who visited every now and again.

Could be that there are places like that dotted around here that are hard to find. It's certainly no part of the Empire that's for sure, otherwise there would be fortified locations all over the place along with their many roads, people and associated stink."

I almost laughed aloud; Cassius has never been a big fan of the vivid smell of Andurran cities. "Should try going into the capital with a nose like mine," I replied softly. "No wonder Seya tries her utmost to stay out of the cities, she can smell them from miles away." My thoughts turned towards the big cat and her absence at my side. *Seya, I hope you're well,* I thought and then with an effort I refocused on the task at hand. "Thoughts on the approach?"

Cassius shook his head. "Difficult. They've cleared any nearby trees and there isn't much brush that hasn't been trampled or cut down. Getting close would have to be done in the dark, unless you somehow managed to use the cliff faces and climbed laterally to get above them." He gave a pointed look at my scabbed over arm which was healing rapidly but still covered in lacerations. "Something that you aren't going to be doing, that's for sure."

I grimaced. "Agreed. It looks like a tricky approach and as soon as they are alerted they hold every advantage. The only thing that comes to mind is rushing them under the cover of darkness, but against sixty men that seems foolish."

The two of us bounced ideas back and forth for another minute and then headed back through the undergrowth to where the rest of the group lay in wait, hidden from prying eyes. It didn't take long to fill them in on the terrain and the forces arrayed against us and soon we began discussing ideas for how to remove the Hrudan threat. None of us were for a direct assault, the weight of numbers on the enemy side was far too much of a threat for our small force. Sophia suggested returning to Jadira and coming back with more men, but that was quickly dissuaded due to the distances involved and the length of time it would take to get there and return.

We talked, planned and squabbled late into the night before finally turning in with our approach undecided.

We awoke just before dawn to Rikol shaking us awake. "Something is up at the camp," he hissed as we all groggily shook off the last vestiges of sleep. Minutes later we were overlooking the encampment and watching with curious eyes as men finished up attaching horses to laden carts. Just after dawn three carts and a detachment of twenty men left the fortifications and began a slow walk west, fighting against the snow with every step.

"A supply train," Sophia whispered, her eyes alight. "They must have more men further west. Another camp perhaps. This is our chance! We could hit the train, take their supplies and that leaves the men here with less troops and an easier target."

She wasn't wrong and she knew it. It would be a dangerous play, for twenty men strung out along the wagons was still going to be a difficult job, but we desperately needed new supplies. *And not just food, but clothing too,* I thought, looking at my blue tinged hands. Even with no deaths and relatively minor injuries that avalanche had cost us far too much and it was only with the packs retrieved by our mutual benefactor that we hadn't lost fingers or limbs to frostbite. In the end it didn't take long to reach a decision.

"Let's do it," I said to nods all round.

Three hours later we were roughly four miles from the encampment and following the supply train as they fought against the elements. Whilst Cassius and I had been good naturedly griping about the Andurran Empire the previous day it was easy to see the benefits of roads over dirt tracks. The wagons were becoming bogged down every few paces, the snow hiding multitudes of dangers and sending the beleaguered troops mad with frustration. It didn't take long for the soldiers guarding the wagons to become complacent with more of them being drafted in to assist with lifting the wagons out of ditches than keeping watch. We drifted like ghosts

alongside the train, waiting for the ideal opportunity. It didn't
take long before the perfect moment arose. The supposed trail
that the wagons were following moved into a thicker part of
forest, a place where more competent guards would have been
on high alert, but these ones were worn out and tired from the
incessant problems with the wagons and so made our job far
too easy.

Slowly we spread out until we were just ahead of the wagons,
closing the distance until we were standing behind trees bare
feet away from the track. The unknowing soldiers trudged
past, heads bowed against the snow and hauling or pushing
the wagon loads. Our attack took them completely by surprise. We closed in from all sides, moving silently with blades
bared. The first few kills were quiet, taking those at the rear
of the train so the ones upfront were unaware of the attack. In
a perfect world we could have done the entire thing quietly,
however death is a messy business and people tend to scream
if you don't place your blade correctly. An unfortunate soul
got a blade stuck in his ribs rather than the heart and his
wheezing cry of pain turned the others towards the sound. Before they'd even had time to discern what they were seeing we
were upon them. They were slow from fatigue and cold whilst
we were relatively fresh and, more importantly, were desperate for supplies. We ripped through them like a warm knife
through butter. Arrows thrummed, blades sang and men died.
Against that number of warriors it should have been a messy
and desperate fight, particularly considering their armour.
And if we had been fighting them head-to-head on an open
plain we would have been at a sore disadvantage. Here their
armour counted for little aside from having wearied them
during the trek through the tundra, and the close quarters
meant that their axes were difficult to use - not that we gave
them much opportunity. A few short and bloody minutes
later we were victorious, breathing heavily and resting
against the heavily laden wagons whilst wiping blood coated
swords against anything that wasn't sprayed with gore.

"Well," panted Rikol as he systematically wiped his multitude of knives against the cloth of the wagon, "that went better than expected."

"And what did you expect?" asked Sophia dryly.

"Oh, most of us dead or grievously wounded. Six of us against twenty didn't exactly make for good odds," he replied with a sardonic smile.

Sophia snorted and continued hunting for arrows that she could reuse, calling back over her shoulder as she moved, "Ever the optimist eh Rikol?"

"Always."

I moved up to the wagon where Cassius was slicing through the ropes that held the protective tarp in place. The others soon joined and quickly we had the tarp off and the contents exposed. And what contents they were! Boxes of dried jerky and smoked meats lined the first cart alongside heavy woollen cloaks and thick furs. The second wagon held whetstones, bows, axes and even an anvil. The third held barrels of musty grain and boxes marked with black rope. Whoever had been intending to receive these items was obviously in the process of entrenching themselves within the heartland and logic dictated that they had set up a relatively large encampment if they had been sent an anvil to begin forging new supplies. Cassius levered off the lid of one of the black twined barrels and stared inside before lifting a hand to his nose, black grained sand running through his fingers.

"Black powder," he murmured, wiping his hands free of the explosive dust. "Someone's planning on blasting something for sure."

"Slaves," Ella said quietly. "The slaves from the village - could be they didn't go back through the pass. Could be that the Hrudan have them mining."

"Could they do that without the Meredothians knowing?" Scythe asked.

"Don't see why not," she replied. "It's a pretty big slice of land and seemingly sparsely populated. What if instead of just raiding via the pass the Hrudan decided to set up shop and not leave?"

"What does it matter?" asked Rikol. "Our goal is obvious." He shrugged at our questioning glances then carried on. "We forget about the Hrudan on this side of the mountains and focus on stopping more getting in - or out. We seal the pass and let the Meredothians do the rest."

"We could be leaving people to die," Cassius murmured quietly.

"And those slaves could be in the camp at the pass right now," Rikol shot back. "This is all hypothetical. We should work on the evidence," his gaze took in the wagons, "and the equipment that we have."

"He's right," I said, refusing to wilt under Ella's glare. "We would waste time hunting for wherever this caravan was headed. Time that we could use to stop more Hrudan from coming through the pass. It solves our mission with Jadira far better than I imagine she expected." I settled my hand on the black powder. "We blow the pass using their own tools and bring the mountain side down on their heads."

We discussed it some more but in the end Rikol's idea was the only practical solution. We had the Hrudan location, enough supplies and warm clothes to keep us happy - our clothes were tattered and grimy enough that we gratefully wore whatever we could find that fit - and barrels of blasting powder. If we did this right then the Hrudan wouldn't know what hit them. The only downside was that we soon realised the pain and frustration that the Hrudan caravan had felt as we endeavoured to get the wagons turned around and headed back. My senses helped find the worst of the snow-covered holes but even so it was a rough and tiring journey.

Several hours later we were within a mile of the Hrudan controlled pass with the wagons hidden off the trail and black powder transferred into sacks that we carried - with no small amount of trepidation - on our backs. Trying to sneak into a fortified enemy encampment to blow up the surrounding mountain side was going to be hard enough without attempting to do it whilst rolling barrels of black powder along the way. I entertained brief fantasies about donning the dead men's' clothes and walking straight into the encampment but I doubted even the Hrudan would be that stupid as to just let us waltz in without showing our faces. We would have to do it the hard way - either sneaking through the camp or climbing the jagged and sheer rock faces that soared high above the encampment. Looking at the thickly scarred parts of my arm and feeling the dull throbbing in my shoulder I knew which choice I preferred. Not to mention that if after all her training Cassius and I got caught sneaking through a camp of humans I was fairly sure that Seya would disown me. But then again, it wasn't us two that I was concerned about. The others were stealthy, sure, and their fun and games with Seya over the past couple of years had only served to enhance their skills, but they hadn't achieved the same level of mastery that only those who had spent months being hunted, pounced, licked and otherwise preyed upon by a giant panther did. Unfortunately there was nothing for it. We needed all the black powder we could get and sending in a larger team once and once only likely had a higher chance of success than two people sneaking in and out of the same camp multiple times in one night.

I don't know if Cassius shared my concerns. His confident face gave nothing away as we prepared our explosive sacks and began to walk, crawl and scramble our way to the camp. Once we reached a close enough distance where we could just about see the sentries we stopped and settled in for some much-needed rest. It was going to be a busy night.

# CHAPTER 19

## *Assault*

Roughly two hours after full dark had descended we slowly broke the crust of ice that had formed on our fur coated huddle and stretched out our cramped limbs before turning our eyes on the not-so-distant camp. It was less of a camp and more of a fortified approach to what we all naturally assumed was the mountain pass. The truth was that we had no idea if we had found the mountain pass or not. It could well have led into some subterranean mine for all we knew but after weeks of sleeping on rough ground and miles of hard travelling it certainly seemed like the best assumption, and if we were the hardened Imperators that we became later in life we wouldn't have bothered scouting the camp at all and just brought the mountain directly down on the heads of the Hrudan regardless of whether or not there were innocents within.

Thankfully however, at this point in our lives we weren't quite so hardened and calloused to causing suffering to those who might not have needed it. Whilst the most expedient method was to sneak into the camp and plant our black powder where it would cause the most devastation and retreat, none of us were comfortable with the idea that there might have been captured Meredothians within. As such it fell to

Cassius and myself to carry in black powder along with the others, plant it where it would best cause as much rockfall and damage as possible whilst the others did the same, and then instead of retreating to scout for any potential slaves and free them if possible.

As plans go it wasn't the best. I'm fairly certain that my plan with the great boar back when I was younger and being hunted by the Tracker was far more thought out than this. However we had to work with what we had and it wouldn't be the last time that our soft natures got us into difficult situations. What we didn't know, or only suspected at the time, was that there was a great asset on our side...just one that we weren't aware of and so couldn't count it in our deck to play.

With gentle pats of good luck we all set off, slinking into the darkness and utilising the terrain to hide us from any eagle-eyed sentries. We all went separate directions; aiming to approach the camp in as many different manners as possible to maximise our chances of success. The main difficulty was that the pass itself was - as you might expect - narrow. Consequently the fortified position that the Hrudan had built expanded outwards from the narrow pass, getting more concentrated the closer you got to it. If we wanted the explosives to be effective we needed to be within or above the pass itself, otherwise we might do damage but the route through would likely remain open and continue to allow Hrudan reinforcements to flood into the heartland.

Passing through the outer ring of sentries was almost too easy. My senses gave me too great an edge, allowing me to slip around sentries like a shadow. Even when the camp narrowed and there was a higher concentration of guards to available space I danced around them, at times close enough to reach out and touch, yet they had no awareness of my presence. The others, I knew, were having a little bit of a more difficult time and their progress was much slower. We had accounted for this, knowing that it was likely that Cassius and myself would reach the innards of the pass first, if at all. Indeed it was only three minutes after I had pinged a stone off a guard's helmet and slipped past as he was busy looking up that Cassius arrived, his face flushed with excitement and exertion. Together we crept through the canyon which was just about the width of a single wagon, the rock showing obvious signs of recent work. It was likely that the pass had once been much narrower but the Hrudan had worked away at it, widening the crevice where they could into an almost serviceable road. We followed the path for a good mile, ducking along its twists and turns. Once within the path itself there were actually fewer guards which wasn't too surprising once I thought about it - why would you need guards in a narrow pass when you have presumed control over both access points? Those that were around were about as attentive as you might imagine someone to be when in a safe location in the middle of the night and so were easy to pass by. Eventually the path began to widen and then we were out of the mountain...and if the other side had been a fortified encampment then on this side the Hrudan had built a whole damned fort.

"...Well. Shit," I said softly, casting my eyes over the thick stone walls replete with a considerable excess of seemingly attentive guards. "Looks like the Hrudan are on a war footing and have known about this place for a long time."

Cassius leaned in and whispered in my ear, "How much can you see?"

Whoops. I had forgotten that Cassius didn't share my eyesight. All he could likely see was the ring of braziers that flamed atop the walls of the fort. Whilst it was likely murder on the guards' night vision it certainly made for an imposing picture. What Cassius likely couldn't see was the size of the overall building - it stretched back into the gloom until even my eyes couldn't make it out. From our vantage point on the descent from the pass I could see over the walls and so could espy their width and, much more worryingly, see that there was row upon row of what I could only assume to be bunkhouses in the grounds within. All of this added up to one thing.

"The Hrudan have been planning this for a long time," I said after I recounted what I could see. "A fort like this doesn't just spring up. That looks like quarried stone which means that they have enough manpower to quarry that amount of material and haul it over here. If they knew about the pass and built this as a precaution against a Meredothian attack that's one thing. But you wouldn't have that many guards - especially as I doubt any Meredothians even know about this passage into Hrudan lands. Which makes me think -"

"-that the bunkhouses are all full of soldiers," Cassius finished. "If that is the case then my money is on Hrudan unleashing a full-scale invasion come spring."

I nodded grimly. "They will raze everything within the heartland if they have their way."

"Then we best stop it here and now," Cassius said, his eyes bright in the flickering dark. "We do our best to collapse the pass and then head back to Jadira as fast as possible. If she can assemble a force in time then they can hold the other side even if the Hrudan dig out the rubble."

"Sounds like a plan," I agreed. "Except..." I kept my gaze on the fort beneath me.

"Except what Calidan?" His voice held a note of warning - he knew full well what I was going to say.

"Except the Academy would tell us to find out as much as possible about our enemies wouldn't it. What would Kane think if he knew we had seen such a fort and turned away?"

"He would tell us well done for using our brains," Cassius replied dryly. "But I know full well when your mind is made up so let's get down there."

"Not this time," I said, holding up a hand against his chest to forestall him. "If I fail in this we still need that pass brought down. You need to take this," I thrust my twin sacks of black powder into his arms, "and make sure that pass goes off. If I'm not back by dawn, blow it."

He opened his mouth to argue, his face moving like a fish for a few moments and then with a grimace he slung both bags over his already laden shoulders. "Don't be late," was all he murmured as he walked back into the canyon - as he had said, he knew what I was like when my mind was made up. What can I say? Stubbornness runs deep in us mountain folk.

Turning away I trotted down towards the fort. Truth be told I felt lighter and more free than I had in some time, for instead of navigating the inhospitable tundra of the north eastern edge of the heartland I finally had a target in front of me, one that was unaware and ripe for the plucking. The Academy would want to know about these Hrudan, their numbers, the types of dress, the weapons - anything that would be useful to know about a potential enemy - and that fort in front of me represented the best opportunity to find this information. It also, much more frighteningly, represented the best opportunity for the Hrudan to capture and torture themselves an Imperator Academy student, though perhaps that was just my more recent brush with those morbid arts speaking. Rumour had it that the Asahani empire somewhere over to the far, far east didn't torture their captives, instead they provided them with lush rooms, complete with plentiful food and wine and thus received all the information they could have wanted just by listening to the not-quite-so-prisoner-prisoner talk when drunk and surrounded by attractive and attentive friends - which seemed like a pretty good deal to me. Somehow though, having seen the heavyset and scowling Hrudan rape and slaughter their way through villages already I didn't think they were in the same camp as the Asahani. Oh well. A man can dream.

Slipping through the shadows, I made my way to the base of the fort wall. It was made of large blocks of hewn stone, each one probably hauled into place by some team of unfortunate souls. If the Hrudan had any sense they would have laid out braziers on the ground outside the fort to make it easier for the guards to see any approaching figures at night, without any light to attest to my presence it was a simple matter to make my way to the base of the fort. Testing my fingers on the wall I found that I had enough purchase to lift myself up. The healing skin on my forearm pulled tight but didn't reopen and my right shoulder bellowed at me but it held my weight without any of my important bits deciding to disconnect again. Progress.

Swiftly and assuredly I climbed up the fort wall, pausing at the top to let a guard walk by before draping myself over the balustrade and merging into the shadows caused by the flickering braziers.

*Seya, eat your heart out*, I thought as I crept through the darkness. For a second I thought I felt a flicker of amusement but then it was gone. I shoved all non-essential thoughts to the back of my mind as I was forced to make a quick dive over the edge of the inner wall, catching the edge and hanging with my left arm, my right holding a dagger in preparation just as a guard passed above me. I listened carefully for any change in his heartbeat, anything to suggest that he had seen something, but he carried on completely undisturbed. Looking down I made the tactical choice and dropped the fifteen feet to the floor, landing softly with my knees bent to minimise the shock. Thankfully the shadows were thick and fast here, what little moon there was not having enough influence to peel them apart. I spent some time judging the surrounding area, trying to figure out where the fort commander would be based. If the Hrudan followed the Andurran method of military set ups then the fort commander would have a room to himself situated to the rear of the primary facing wall and that would be close to the kitchens - every good commander knows that being near the kitchens means warmth and food. The question was whether or not this fort was as fully developed as it looked from the outside, or whether it was in essence just one big wall. My money was on the former. The Hrudan had obviously put a lot of time and money into the construction of this facility and there was no way that they had missed out the commander's room. And so, keeping one eye on the tents filled with snoring soldiers, I set off to go and find the kitchens.

It didn't take long. Soon enough my senses were filled with the overpowering smell of flour and baked goods. Even in the early hours of the morning there was someone in there preparing for the next day's meals. It had been the same in Forgoth at the military camp that I'd called home for some time; the kitchens were never quiet. Military men were always hungry. It was a known fact. If the kitchens didn't prepare for the next day then they would inevitably run out of food halfway through the men's second serving and the grumbling would begin. Grumbling men meant that the day's activities would be more difficult for the officers who would in turn grumble to each other and through the chain of command said grumbling would elevate to the commanding officer who would - if they had any sense - go straight to the source of the problem and tell the kitchens to get their shit sorted.

My nose led me along the edge of the wall until I reached a series of out-jutting buildings. Following the scent of fresh flour I came to a series of panelled shutters and then to a heavy-set wooden door. I quickly checked the other entrances to the building, each of them protected by a similar door with no other easy access points. I had a cursory feel of the hinges and then, trusting to luck, I slowly tugged on the thick iron ring, attempting to tease the door open and hopefully avoiding any squealing hinges. The door was stiff, whether from the cold or from bad hinges I don't know, but it didn't come easily when I pulled. Cursing under my breath I put a bit more strength into it, tugging harder and harder until the door shuddered with a muffled crack and began to open with a slow grinding sound. I froze for a second, shocked at my own stupidity. The door had been barred from the inside and had only given when I had pulled on the iron ring hard enough to snap the wooden bar. *Idiot.* I listened closely, waiting for the sound of yells or panic, trying in vain to still my racing heart. I could tell that whoever was in the kitchens had paused from their activities to move to the passageway, obviously curious about the sound.

Quick as a cat I darted into the hallway and shut the door. Thankfully at this time of night no one had bothered to light the braziers that dotted along the hallway - it would have been a pointless waste of resources when only a few people needed to be up.

Firelight came to shine beneath the door that led off the passageway to the kitchen and another oak door creaked open as a matronly looking woman poked her head out into the hallway. The torch she carried did an admirable job of trying to beat back the shadows but in the end it was not up to the task of divining the entirety of the hallway to the door. The woman peered down the hall but seemed reluctant to step out. After a minute of peering and muttering to herself she scowled down the hallway and then retreated back into the kitchen. Safe for the moment I let out a long breath, aware of the adrenaline coursing through my veins. *That had been altogether too close.* Resolving to do better rather than merely throwing my life away for the sake of not checking if the door was bolted I moved on, casting my senses as far as possible, listening for heartbeats, following scents - anything that would allow me to pinpoint a potential commander's office.

In the end it was scent again that gave it away; a mixture of cigar smoke and brandy. The fort's commander was obviously a man who liked his little luxuries and the scent was fresh enough for me to follow all the way to his door. Inside I could hear him sleeping, a phlegmy and rasping wheeze. I gave an experimental tug on the door in a vain hope for the best but it refused to budge. I peered down the gap between the door frame and could just make out the bar of wood that held it in place. I gently slipped the edge of my knife into the gap until it rested just underneath the wooden bar. For this to work without waking the sleeping man I would have to be very quick and trust that the commander's attendants did a thorough job in keeping his office hinges well oiled. Once I had the blade in position I slowly began to lift. To my ears it sounded like someone was harshly scraping two bits of wood together but the sleeping figure did not stir. I kept my ear pressed to the door, listening closely for the moment I was waiting for. When it came and the wooden bar wobbled out of the top of the bracket that held it in place I tugged open the door as quickly as I dared and caught the falling piece before it hit the ground. Proud of myself for an incredible catch it took me a moment to realise what had been amiss. Then it hit me. The door hinges had given a very audible screech as I flung it open and the officer's breathing changed from rhythmic wheeze to a sharp gasp as he jolted out of sleep. I was on him before he knew it, driving the ridge of my hand into the side of his neck and sending his eyes rolling up into the back of his head. Safe for a few moments, I tore some strips of linen from the officer's bedding and stuffed it in his mouth before moving back to shut the door. Searching the room for any ropes I found none and so bound his feet and arms with more strips of linen cloth. They likely wouldn't hold very long but they would do in a pinch. Worst came to worst I could stab him, but here was another example of my youthful innocence making things harder for me; the thought of murdering someone in cold blood was still a sickening prospect.

It didn't take him long to come around. In some of the plays I had seen the hero punches the person in the jaw and that's the end of it for however long the hero needs. Life unfortunately doesn't tend to work that way. If you hit someone in the jaw and they are out for longer than a few minutes...chances are you've killed them. Hitting someone in the neck was even trickier; it gave a much higher rate of rendering someone quickly unconscious, but if done overly hard you could permanently injure or kill. Thankfully the officer was coming around within seconds but was still groggy whilst I finished binding his limbs. Ignoring him for the moment I searched the room, looking for anything valuable. The first thing I came across was one of the most useful finds, a large map of what I presumed to be the territory of the Hrudan complete with a somewhat detailed survey of the Meredothian heartland, including the location of Jadira's fort. Judging by what was drawn on the map the Meredothians had a larger village or fort about four days west of the pass and considering the number of crossed out markers it was likely that a number of local villages had met a grisly fate. There was even a marker where the ice caves were and the route through looked to be quite a long walk. Interestingly, sketched next to it was a skull which suggested that the Hrudan had encountered the spiders in the ice as well. An area marked with black concentric rings was in the northern part of the heartland, a place I would put money on being where the Hrudan caravan was intending to head before we ambushed them. There were a few more items of note that the Hrudan had found within the heartland but much more interestingly to me was the fact that the map contained a well-drawn and presumably not fantasy rendering of the lands north and east of the heartland. Lands that bordered the Andurran Empire. Lands that bordered the mountains that once harboured my home. If this was accurate then it seemed like a gold mine. I had little idea if the Emperor had maps revealing such data - knowing the Academy he probably had a couple of full-time spies ensconced in those regions - but something so up to date would certainly be of interest.

I rolled up the map and scanned the room, looking for anything else that might be worth taking. Spying a chest with a padlock I snapped the metal with a quick downward jerk and opened the box - the officer grunting through his mouth rags as I rummaged through it. Fortunately for him it was only personal items, nothing of any particular value to myself or the Empire as a whole. A few drawings of presumed loved ones, a locket of hair, a fancy but somewhat impractical knife - all useless to me. There was even a bag of crudely cast non-Andurran marked silver coins, interesting but somewhat impractical to take back with me as the bag clinked quite loudly. Some armour lay on a stand in the office, treated leather with metal vambraces and pauldrons. As much as I am meant to be an upstanding member of the Empire and decry any other

workmanship as shoddy...it actually looked quite good. The
leather was supple yet felt strong, the metal showed signs of
wear and impact but had obviously done a decent job at keeping its owner alive - something I valued much more highly
than looking pretty. I was half taken with wearing it but sadly
the commanding officer was much bulkier than myself and
the armour was sized to fit accordingly. I was still a growing
lad so with a heavy heart I turned away from the stand and
resolved to update those in the Academy that the so called
'northern barbarians' had some well-equipped armour that
would likely deflect an imperial blade or two, and that if they
got in range of our men the quality of the axe that I picked
up next would likely kill via the impact of being hit even if it
didn't cut. Shaking my head at the foolish idea of myself fleeing the fort whilst hauling a double-bladed battle axe I went
back to the table and absentmindedly picked up a few documents. I couldn't read Hrudan but there would be someone
either in the heartland or in the Academy who they could be
useful for - though knowing the many documents that Major
General Kyle used to have to sign it was likely that they were
just orders for requisitions and troop movement. Either way I
folded each one carefully and folded them into a pouch on my
belt.
I was almost done when I picked up a letter that I almost put
away before realising that I understood the language. It was
written in Meredothian and gave rough coordinates of a number of the villages within the heartland itself. Even though I
should have expected it - there was an entire country worth of
people within the heartland after all - I still felt a bolt of disap-
pointment strike my gut that someone would have the gall to
sell out their own kind. There was no signature, no revealing
mark of any kind that I could immediately use to identify the
writer but I kept the document anyway with the intent to give
it to Jadira in the hope that she would at least know that someone, somewhere, was acting against the rest of the country.
Finally I turned back to the fully awake officer. He was a big

man, almost the size of Kane in girth and probably broader across the shoulders too. He was busy trying to pry apart the linen that held his wrists and didn't bother stopping even when he noticed I was watching. It was somewhat admirable that - he didn't care because he either didn't mind if he died or because he knew I could have killed him in his sleep and was betting on me not having the balls to kill him now. I couldn't risk pulling out his mouth gag - one shout and the entire fort would be alerted and so I did the only obvious thing. I hit him again and used the remaining linen to reinforce my previous work. One final cast of my eyes over the room and then I was out, shutting the door as softly as I dared to attempt avoiding the squealing hinge. I looked down the corridor I had come from, knowing that the route back lay in that direction, but my feet took me the other way. What can I say? I always had a nose for trouble.

Moving swiftly but quietly I flitted down the corridor whilst using my nose to define what each room held. *Sleeping person, sleeping person, toilet, sleeping person, carpenter, I* checked off as I moved. Finally a familiar scent hit my nose and I grinned in pleasure. The smell of steel, iron and the harsh combination of sulphur, saltpetre and charcoal. Following the scent I went through a door and straight into the fort's armoury. Racks of axes and bows lay along the walls, gleaming and freshly oiled. Stacks of boiled leather armour lay on pallets in the centre of the floor and towards the back were three fresh barrels of what had brought us on this suicidal mission in the first place; black powder. With a mischievous smile I moved two of the barrels to the centre of the room and removed the lid from the third. Slowly I poured a thin trail along the floor, through the door and into the wood working shop up the corridor. Pouring the rest of the powder in the corner of the room I set about stacking all the many highly flammable woodworking items in the centre and then using the flint and steel from a pouch on my belt I sparked into the pots of resin until they caught and then ran like the wind.

Out of the corridor and back into the courtyard, along the inner wall until the stairway and then up onto the parapet with all the guards. I practically sprinted the distance, my feet making little noise on the hard stone. The smell of smoke caught up with me, the scent on the wind faster than my feet. A quick pause to let a guard walk past and then out, over the far wall and dropping the distance to the outside of the fort. I began moving more quickly, heading back up to the pass as the scent of fire filled the air. Soon I could hear shouting and alarm bells and bit by bit the hornet nest within the fort began to wake. I danced past one guard and then a second, both of them too busy looking at the beacon of fire that now lit the pre-dawn light to notice me. It was about this time that I realised the potential error of my plan - would the alarm make it to the other side of the pass before I did? If so I was about to face a lot of enemies in a very narrow stretch of land. I could only hope that I hadn't just made things much more difficult for the others.

I was twenty feet into the pass when a roaring explosion thundered behind me, nearly knocking me over as a torrent of sound rippled and rumbled down the narrow passageway. For a long second a somewhat less sane part of me wanted to turn around to witness the damage I had just wrought but I forced myself to keep moving, to keep my legs pumping along the crevice. I was nervous now. I knew thunder travelled far, that the sound of it could be used to measure distance and as such my best guess was that the noise would reverberate along the whole mountain range and do it far faster than my feet could carry me.

In other words, I was quite possibly screwed.

Regardless, I carried along, practically flat out sprinting my way down the rapidly lightening pass, relying on my senses and quick feet to keep me from careening into one of the twisting walls, or in the case of one very confused guard, a person. Leaving him slumped on the floor, unconscious but breathing, I continued my mad run, forcing any thoughts from my brain that weren't to do with my immediate survival, banishing anything that remotely suggested that it was almost certainly dawn and that the others would detonate the pass any moment, focusing only on my breathing and my pounding feet, tunnelling my vision. It turned out that wasn't the best idea when running through an enemy held encampment. I practically sprinted into a squad of six men who were marching two by two towards the fort I had just escaped - probably some kind of dawn patrol - and sent them sprawling to the ground, myself amongst them. I lay on-top of a very surprised Hrudan, gave him a gentle pat on the jaw and used his torso as a springboard to get back to my feet. Very soon I was running for my life with shouts of alarm and rapidly fading footsteps behind me.

As I neared the exit of the pass my nose became filled with the smell of black powder and smoke. Somewhere above and around me lay the bags of black powder, meaning that at least some of the others had succeeded in planting the explosives. The smell of the smoke was thick and oppressive, not the usual crisp wood scent of breakfast fires but that of heavy material burning. I could hear cries of alarm ahead of me and as I rounded the final corner I saw that the others had taken the art of improvisation to heart.

Within the fortified approach to the pass there had been a number of heavy cloth tents. The Hrudan likely hadn't had time to make everything a permanent building before winter set in and consequently had a number of heavy tarps battened down with iron pegs. On the way in they had rippled with the cold wind and provided a good bit of cover for any errant sounds that the others had made. On the way out they did the same job but as a flaming distraction. One of the group - my money was on Rikol or Ella - had been enterprising enough to take the time to find a source of flame, sneak to the tents and coax them alight. I would have been annoyed if this had been a stealth mission but that ship had sailed with my theatrics at the fort. Hrudan milled around the tents trying in vain to put out the roaring flames that hungrily licked towards the sky. An enterprising commander had organised for buckets of snow to be collected and thrown at the tents but not yet in enough quantities to threaten the fire. A quick glance over the rest of the camp showed that the other Hrudan were organised and alert with units of two and three moving around the encampment with bared blades. My blood ran cold. It could either be a precaution or they had seen one of the others. Hoping everyone was safe I briefly pushed out with my senses and looked for anyone freshly bleeding - of which I found several - and any smaller figures lying dead or injured - of which I found none. A silent sigh of relief and then I was running again, not bothering with dashing from shadow to shadow but relying on my speed and the distraction of the fire to cover my approach. I saw a flicker of light beyond the camp perimeter, like someone kindling a torch and then a duo of Hrudan walked round the corner of a building, had a moment of stunned silence as they saw my face and then promptly roared with alarm.

Keeping my momentum I rolled under the first swing of an axe, coming up into a spin with my leg outstretched to catch the back ankle of the second man and sending him tumbling to the ground. The first man reacted quickly, moving with rotation of his first cut to swivel and bring the blade down from his shoulder in a devastating cut. Throwing myself backwards I rolled to my feet and drew the daggers at my side in the same movement, noting the sound of tramping feet rushing towards my position as I did so. A shout from my left and I spun, reflexively shifting into the third pattern of Kaschan, my feet carrying me into the range of the descending axe, around and behind the wielder before putting two puncture wounds in his back. He coughed, a wet and bloody sound, then slumped to the floor. The other men approached more warily now, content to use time to their advantage. I moved back, trying to find my way out of the encampment but found the press of stone against my spine. Axemen surrounded me now, gleaming blades catching the dawn sun as it finally peaked over the mountains. Snarling, I made a dash for one warrior then spun and lunged for the one behind me as the half circle contracted. He deftly parried my lunge, pinging the blade from my hand with the haft of his axe. He looked pleased with himself so I robbed him of his satisfaction by breaking his knee with a kick. Inured to his howling I calmly picked the axe from his flailing hands and turned to the enemy before smiling a terrible smile.

"Come on then," I barked loudly. "Let's be having it."

What followed couldn't be called a battle or barely even a fight. It wasn't honourable. It wasn't pretty. It certainly wasn't anything worthy of a song. It was more like a taproom brawl that had spiralled out of hand to involve sharp implements and murder. The Hrudan had numbers on their side and each soldier was surprisingly strong, flinging their axes around with wild abandon. I stabbed two, crippled a third and maimed the fourth before being blindsided by a Hrudan who tackled me to the floor, using his superior weight to bring me down. After crushing his testicles with my hand, I had a brief respite to see a bright flame dart across the sky before the man's forehead came down to rock my skull, and then the world shook.

The ground shifted beneath me as bags of black powder erupted one by one in a chain reaction. Chunks of rock hurtled through the sky, arcing up and up before plummeting back down with frightening speed. A thick, black combination of ash and smoke gushed over the encampment, rendering visibility down to practically zero. The rumble of the explosion receded into echoes and was replaced by sharp, frigid *cracks* that splintered the air. They were the sounds that any climber would be terrified to hear. The sound of breaking rock. The men surrounding me were just as stunned as I was, one had fallen to the ground whilst the others had stumbled in the wake of the explosion and were choking in the wave of dust and ash. I caught the man atop me with a hook hard enough to

shatter his jaw and twisted, bucking my knees to get out from
under his legs. Impressively the man still had enough sense
in him to try and regain his balance but with my legs now
available I quickly shifted, propping a knee across his chest
and splaying the other leg out before pushing and sweeping
simultaneously; turning him over in one smooth motion. Another punch and this time his face became a mangled mess. I
managed to get one foot under me before being sent sprawling
to the ground by a stumbling warrior. My head spinning from
the impact against his hardened breast plate I rolled, flailing
with a leg and connecting with a crunch and a howl. I rolled
again, knowing that my legs would be jelly if I tried to stand,
and gasped as the same warrior I had just kicked fell onto my
chest, driving the breath out of my lungs. I bucked with my
hips, throwing him off and twisted to all fours. Slowly, head
pounding, I drove myself to my feet. And it was then I heard
the screams.

At some point the background roar of the collapsing rubble
had been overtaken by something more primal. Something
that bellowed its rage into the collapsing night. And frighteningly it was something that I recognised. A horrified scream
rent the air above the din and abruptly cut off. I stood for a
long moment, temporarily forgotten by the enemies around
me as shouts, screams and bestial roars filled the ashen sky.
Something flew through the air and I ducked instinctively,
narrowingly missing being bludgeoned by half a torso.

Yes. I had a very good idea of what was decimating the soldiers
within the smoke and ash - I had wondered where our strange
ally had got to. It seemed likely that it was the one who left
the sign for us to follow and find this encampment in the first
place which begged the question - who was it and how did it
know these things? And for that matter how did it know us?

I had some strong suspicions on that subject. The troll creature wouldn't be the first strange beast I had met that somehow served the Andurran Empire - Merowyn and her strange
inner travel companion being the first that jumped to mind.

Kane had alluded that certain Imperators had been subjected to the same process as Merowyn and that sometimes the creature won. I just couldn't shake the feeling that it knew me... which - if my theory was correct - meant that surely I had to know whoever it was at the core of that beast?

I shook my head as much to clear my thoughts as to clear my face of ash. Now wasn't the time to be considering what may or may not lie beneath the troll-like exterior of our seeming ally. The Hrudan were in trouble. At least temporarily cut off from reinforcements and reeling from the twin disasters of explosions and an angry troll, now was either the time to strike or flee. Moving to run and suspecting that attacking any survivors would be easier once the dust had cleared, I heard a bellow of pain and hesitated. With a sigh that turned into a hacking cough I turned and sprinted further into the dust, blade out.

Now that the rumbling and cracking of the pass had largely subsided the dust was no longer the impediment it once was. Focusing on my hearing I was able to move fairly rapidly within the swirling motes of ash, or as quickly as one could when there was still the threat of running head first into a stone wall. Either way it gave me an acute advantage over the remaining Hrudan who were making their way towards the troll. Most didn't see me coming.

Cassius probably would have disapproved. He didn't particularly like the idea of killing someone from behind. It was one of the first things the Academy had tried to hammer into us, that there is no such thing as a fair fight, just the living and the dead. We were actively instructed to fight as unfairly as possible. It was, after all, the very principle of Kaschan. It was actually one of the few areas where Cassius wasn't excelling, but then again with his sword work he didn't particularly need to fight dirty. I probably didn't need to either due to the benefits bestowed upon me by Seya but whereas Cassius rebelled against the idea of fighting dirty I was a quick and enthusiastic learner. Afterall, revenge was my driving force and revenge wasn't something that you could so easily accomplish with a sense of honour. Or at least not the revenge I had in mind which consisted of a substantial amount of gratuitous violence.

Eye for an eye and all that.

Put simply, men fell to my blade. I would like to say I was like a whisper in the night, a knife in the dark and all that romantic poetry that ends up embellishing folk heroes but in reality I was like a somewhat quieter though just as prone to coughing individual who could hear where his next opponent was. And as it happened, that was enough. I left a trail of dead or dying men on my way to the centre of the camp where the thunk of blades and claws on flesh still resonated. The Hrudan were making a good show of it, swinging their broad bladed axes with all the savage might that their corded muscles afforded, the axe heads parting fur and skin to bite deep into the troll's flesh. For it was the troll, that much I could be sure, in all its strange blue skinned glory, and just as it had with the spiders its powers of regeneration made it a foe beyond that of the men. Bloody wounds that would leave a human dead were healing in a matter of moments. Unfortunately for the men that surrounded the troll they didn't share the same ability. I watched through the dust as a warrior rushed in and swung at the creature's leg, his axe slicing through to the bone and sending visibly clotting blood into the air. The blade caught slightly as the wound began to heal and the troll's counter stroke removed his head in a very messy fashion, sending it flying through the air and leaving his body to join the visceral display that coated the ground. It had all the hallmarks of being a one-sided slaughter and if it had stayed that way I would have left the troll to its fun and gone to find my friends. Unfortunately the Hrudan, like all humans, possessed the same thing that made humans rise above animals time and time again. The ability to adapt.

It was clear that they had fought trolls before. Granted this troll was very different to the normal lumbering beasts of destruction, but it retained enough similarities that many of the same fighting moves could be applied. What was more impressive was that one of the men had recognised the enemy for what it was and given orders accordingly. Those men who ringed the troll knew that it was futile. I realised too late that they were there purely to keep it in place as bait. It was the other group of men hidden from my eyes but not my senses who were standing just outside the ring in a huddle that was the real threat. They finished rubbing something over the blades of their weapons and then with a *whoosh* the axe heads ignited. As one they turned and moved into the circle, each man taking the place of another who didn't have a fire coated weapon - who promptly disengaged and ran to where the men had been huddled, where I could dimly smell over the dust and blood some sort of flammable unguent.

This time when one of the men ran in and struck the troll the flame singed away the hair, sizzled through the skin and seared the cut of the blade, effectively cauterising the wound. The beast roared and swung a claw but the man dropped and rolled out of the way, wrenching his blade out as he did so. Unlike before no blood spurted out of the wound and the men watched with hungry eyes as the wound failed to close. A shared murmur of success and the men began to close the circle, flaming blades held ready. The troll was roaring, one hand patting at its leg in an all too human movement, surprise evident in its eyes. With its other hand it swung out at the approaching group, catching a man by the shoulder and sending him tumbling to the floor. It was when another blade sliced down leaving behind the scent of sizzling troll fat and a flash of fear in the creature's eyes that I knew I had to step in.

Three paces carried me to the closest man, my knife thrusting into the back of his neck and ending his life instantly. The downside to my plan was whilst the ash made me relatively difficult to spot, the flaming axe tumbling to the ground was enough to attract the attention of the three warriors next to me. I flicked my knife in the direction of the nearest, a well-

timed stumble as he drove through the ash saving his life as
the blade took him in the shoulder rather than the throat.
Committed now and hoping fervently that the angry troll remembered me as a friend and not an enemy I swept forward,
spinning as I moved, clasping the handle of the fallen axe and
delivering an oblique cut that swept a line of fire down the
front of the closest man. Stepping off line with the third I
drove the handle of the axe into the chest of the warrior who
had just recovered from being struck with the knife, sending
him stumbling backwards and leaving me free to strike at the
remaining member of the trio. He managed to parry the first
two blows, his skill with the axe greater than mine, but my
speed and strength kept him on the defensive allowing me to
press the attack until an uppercutting blow removed his jaw,
the follow up cleaving the unfortunate first man from neck
to groin. The overwhelming smell of cooking meat radiated
from the three bodies where the liquid fire still burned. I had
heard of the substance but had yet to see it in action. It was fas-
cinatingly deadly.

The troll didn't let my distraction go to waste and closed the
distance between himself and the closest foe with terrifying
speed. The man barely had time to scream before he was torn
asunder and the beast roared in challenge and fury before
charging into its next victim.

That quickly the circle that could have spelled death for
the troll was broken. Facing attack on two sides the Hrudan
warriors fell into disarray, fighting bravely but quickly suc-
cumbing to the whirlwind of fury and claws that was the
troll. Those that came towards me fought bravely but didn't
come in enough numbers to counter my physical advantages.
I danced between four men, cutting in swirling arcs - the flaming axe leaving fire trails in the air and by the time the third
man was dead the fourth was in the hands of the troll. Once his
screams were over the two of us stood in the Hrudan slaugh-
terhouse and caught our breath, eyes watching the other intently. I slowly and carefully put the axe on the floor before

holding my hands up to show I was no threat. I already knew that it recognised me - I wasn't dead - but I didn't know if it would react strongly to the flaming blades that had inflicted such damage. The troll glared at me with such raw hatred in its eyes that I felt inclined to pick back up the weapon. Forcing the impulse back down I stood my ground and locked eyes with the creature. Slowly the look in its eyes softened to a low bubble of anger and I no longer immediately feared for my life. Inclining my head in respect I spoke up, grating the words out past my ash parched throat. "Thank you."

For a moment the troll did nothing then stiffly inclined its head in an all too human nod, accompanying the motion with a grunt that I took to have the same meaning. We might not like each other - or at least it didn't like me - but apparently we could work together well enough and for that I was grateful.

"We're going to head back to Jadira's fort," I said after an uncomfortable pause. "You're welcome to join us."

With a snort the beast shook its head and stepped backwards into the still swirling dust, a hulking shadow for a second and then gone.

"I'll take that as a no," I muttered before picking up my knife and turning down the hill. "Grumpy bastard."

# CHAPTER 20

## *Winter*

In the end I think the troll had more sense than me, though it pains me to say it. I re-joined the others and we checked that the pass was fully blocked before joyfully heading off back in the direction of Jadira's fort. Lives saved and mission done.

How woefully, utterly unprepared we were for the deep of winter. We thought we had seen the worst it had to offer on the trip in, but the deep snows had taken their time in coming and made the trip back at best miserable and at worst murderous. Luckily we had the clothes and equipment that we had scavenged from the Hrudan and so comparatively we were much warmer, but even thick clad leathers and furs were no match for wading through waist deep snow day in and day out. After the second day of the journey we were exhausted and our clothes were soaked. By day three we were desperately searching for firewood to dry out our layers and save our extremities. By day ten we were on quarter rations. On day twenty-two we came across a half-eaten frozen deer carcass. We ate it half raw, barely waiting for the ice to melt before the might of our pitiful fire before ravenously tucking in. From day thirty-eight to forty-one we were stalked by wolves that were so hungry as to no longer be afraid of fire. We killed two, leaving one for the pack and one for us. I don't know if the pack ate their own but they didn't bother us again.

It was day fifty-two when we finally stumbled into the shelter of the fort. Each of us painfully lean, scarred, grizzled and sun-burned. One of us - I'll let you guess who - was missing two toes and another the bottom of an ear lobe. Jadira didn't recognise who we were at first and awe was on the faces of the Meredoth-ians as we piled into the first proper warmth we had experi-enced in nearly two months. It wasn't awe at our bravery in facing such a wintery onslaught, but awe at our complete and utter stupidity...and as I sat there nursing a hacking cough and frostbitten hands with warm mead I could not blame them in the slightest for such a reaction.

I think Jadira felt responsible for our sorry state as we did not want for anything for the remainder of our stay at the fort. She took our report on the pass, dispatched men to organise forces and fortify the Meredothian side of the canyon as soon as the snows lessened and then spent the rest of the time mothering us like only a hard-nosed Meredothian warrior queen could. Which primarily meant mead.

Lots of mead.

The rest of winter at the fort passed in a haze of food, alcohol, and most importantly, warmth. The team rarely left the blaze of the hearth fires, content to lay on the floor rushes in mead assisted stupor. Slowly but surely we built up the fat reserves that we had lost during the trek and began to look somewhat like our old selves, just with more scars and less append-ages. It took time but the gaunt features and serious eyes of those who had suffered for long, arduous hours slowly began to disappear. Yet that isn't to say that everything was forgot-ten and that we were once again our young teenage selves. Even within the confines of the fort, wrapped in the warmth of blankets and fires and fuelled by rich food and mead, we couldn't forget. The trauma that each of us had experienced in that place was more than we possibly could have expected. More so because we had been thrust into the fight, tortured and exposed without having any time to prepare...not that we could have prepared for such a thing, but you had to admire the Academy's gall at unleashing such an experience on its students. There was still a small chance that it wasn't the Academy who had kidnapped us of course, but it didn't tally with the very real feeling but seemingly non-damaging torture as well as us just so happening to end up at a location where our support could fulfil a promise of the Emperor. No. It had to be the Academy. The more I thought about it the more it all made more sense. I doubted that any of the fourth-year tests were the same and yet they probably all fulfilled some purpose of the Academy or Emperor and were equally horrifying - providing some measure of the team's ability to deal with pain, heartache and still being able to function to provide some important service to the Empire. It practically had the stamp of being an Imperator trial all over it and would go a long way to highlighting why no one back at the Academy had ever wanted to discuss the test; it likely brought back unpleasant memories and thoughts of friends now lost. Afterall, considering what we had been through I held no illusions that every single person or team came back.

The time we spent at the fort was, in all, time well spent. As winter began to release its grip on the country we began to emerge into the blinding light of the outside world, helping Jadira and her men to begin clearing the snow and ice melt, joining in to repair what the winter storms had broken and beginning to cycle back through the motions we had learnt to keep our bodies limber and weapon skills sharp. By the time spring was properly in motion we were back at our prior levels of physical prowess, the dust of the past few months shaken off and our skills resharpened. First up in the morning for fitness training and last standing for combat practice - sharpening the Meredothian skills in addition to our own. And so it was an early morning when we saw the eagle pass overhead, its leg bearing a message only for Jadira's eyes.

A message to bring us home.

# PART II

*Cards on the Board*

# PRESENT DAY

Simultaneous detonations echoed along the tree line, thundering away into the distance to be replaced by the terrifying sound of shifting rock. The landslide started slowly, a trickle of rocks and dust that slowly shifted into a torrent of mud, stone and despair. The thyrkan forces beneath us split in the centre and ran for the illusion of safety.

A nod and Issan gave a shout. Flaming arrows arced down from the mountain side and the remaining barrels of black powder hidden on either side of the path erupted in a blinding flash of light and smoke, sending thyrkan staggering back, bleeding and bruised and straight into the path of the landslide.

Issan and his small contingent of Scourge troops let out cheers at the sight, exultant in the crushing of the region commander. I kept my gaze firmly on the tumbling rocks. Whilst it would have been difficult to survive such an event the thyrkan had an annoying tendency to not die easily.

The thunder rumbled away as the rocks began to settle, the dust cloud thick and suffocating. I summoned from my small pool of seraph and sent a gust of wind to clear the dust from our vision. If they had surviving warlocks then it might not have been the smartest move, but having the ability for the ten strong team of Scourge citizens to feather anything that survived would be likely more useful in the long run. Besides, perhaps it was over, perhaps the rockslide annihilated everything in its path and all there was to do was celebrate.

A rock moved.

I let out a sigh and unsheathed Asp. *Nothing is ever easy.*

A flash of black light from between the gaps in the rocks and then I was diving, tackling Issan to the floor as the boulders were flung in all directions. When I regained my feet three thyrkan stood in a crater now void of any rock bigger than a speck of dust.

"Warlocks!" Issan hissed. "Had to be warlocks."

"They're not alone," I murmured, concentrating my senses across the debris field. *There!* A boulder was flung aside, sailing in a high arc across the sky. In its place stood a hulking brute of a thyrkan.

"Reaver," I confirmed and Issan paled. Silly really - a warlock was far worse than a reaver in most situations. But I had to admit, reavers looked far more terrifying.

"Get your archers on those warlocks," I ordered. "Thunderheads first."

"What about the reaver?" he shot back.

"The reaver will be nearly invincible with warlocks backing it up. Take them down!" I had no wish for Cassius to meet the reaver head on again, if that happened then I would inevitably end up fleeing for my life yet again.

Black lightning crackled as the two warlocks began their retaliation. The third member of their trio which I could only presume was the commander of the region and intended target of this raid, stood in complete calm, analysing and watching everything that it could whilst the reaver let out a mighty bellow and began sprinting towards the hilltop.

The lightning condensed into orbs of arcing energy, each one vibrating with power that, having seen it in action before, would quite literally and very vividly melt flesh off bones. Thankfully Issan had come prepared. Arrows screamed into the sky, coming down to detonate in a series of thunderous flashes that blinded and deafened their intended targets. As I knew all too well from my seraph lessons many years ago,

the easiest way to kill a caster was to interrupt its concentration. The arcing energy released as the noise disoriented the
warlocks, loosing across the countryside in a devastating but
randomly directed show of power. Before they could recover
more arrows arced in, these ones fitted with heads heavy
enough to puncture armour. One warlock fell in a spray of
blood, multiple arrows punctured through its torso. The second dropped to a knee but still moved.

Still dangerous.

Two arrows arced towards the commander. A blade lashed
out faster than thought and sent them tumbling into the
ground. If I hadn't been watching closely I wasn't sure that
I would have noticed the creature move its action had been
that fast.

"Keep firing!" I bellowed over the sound of a rising roar as
the reaver made its way closer. As big and scary as they were,
something about the transition to reaver made the thyrkan
lose any inkling of intelligence that it may have had, which
meant that it was clawing its way up the loose rubble with all
the subtlety of a charging great boar and sliding back a foot for
every two it made.

As more thundering *booms* echoed across the valley I swept
Asp out in a wave of motion, releasing a blade of pent-up energy that screamed through the air to slice through one of
the reaver's legs. Smoke billowed as the wound immediately
began to fester with the black acid-like substance that gave
Asp its name and the reaver screeched in agony, the high-
pitched sound surprising from such a large beast. I gave a
grim smile. Without a warlock to support it I had the advantage. Raising my blade I began channelling power for a second
strike.

A black flash and screams began. I chanced a quick glance.
Two of the archers were simply gone; smoking patches of
earth where they had stood. Either the thunderheads weren't
enough or the warlock was adapting to the disorientation. I
looked back at the reaver and it had begun to move, crawling

on its three limbs almost as fast as it had been moving up the slope on two feet.

Another blast from Asp and this time the beast jumped, throwing itself into the air in a frightening display of raw power and leaving the energy to slice into the ground beneath it. I cursed; things were about to get more difficult.

Thankfully we had one more trick up our sleeve.

Behind the thyrkan warlock and commander rose an armour-clad figure. It had been risky, attempting to predict where the landslide would cover, but it had worked, leaving the thyrkan thinking that there would be no attack from the rear.

How wrong they were.

Cassius took one step. Two. On his third he broke into a jog, by his eighth he was in full sprint, head bowed low, Oath-breaker over one shoulder. Something alerted the thyrkan commander at the last second and he spun, raising two blades only to be sent flying as Cassius spun, the great sword of Oath-breaker slicing clean through the remaining warlock before hammering into the commander.

The reaver turned almost in mid-air and began clawing its way back to the commander. Like I said before; not the wisest of creatures. I sent two strokes of Asp after it, the first severing its spine just above its hips, the second opening it from shoul-der to waist. If that hadn't killed it then the bubbling black acid would finish it off. I sheathed Asp and turned to watch the show.

The thyrkan commander was incredible. Its swordplay was intricate and blindingly quick, the beast moved light on its feet and against any normal swordsman it would have left them in pieces. Fortunately for us, Cassius was not remotely normal.

The enhancements and transformation that the Emperor had put him through had done nothing to remove his uncanny skill with the sword and if anything his size and power had made him even faster. Blow after blow rained down on the thyrkan, each impact sending the creature staggering and keeping it on the defensive. It spun and cut, the blade scratching along the thick plate but not penetrating and an armoured boot caught it in the chest, audibly crunching bone and causing the Scourge troops to wince. Two steps to catch up as the thyrkan began to rise and another kick to drive it back down to the ground. The thyrkan held its blades in the air to block as it tried to shift the weight off its body but the power of Cassius would not be denied, his foot was as immovable as a mountain. The first strike buckled the thyrkan's arms, sending its own blades dangerously close to its face. The second blow forced the blades against its own body, the thyrkan letting out a roar of inept anger as it watched Cassius wind up for another blow. The third strike cleaved right through the creature's paltry guard, embedding Oathbreaker deep within its torso along with both of its swords. A brief gurgling cough and then silence.

Issan and the Scourge troops let out whoops of joy, hugging and celebrating at the victory. With the loss of only two people they had inflicted a blow on the thyrkan that would be felt throughout the region. Perhaps the Enemy would allow them that victory or perhaps these broken lands would soon rumble with the thunder of thyrkan armies. Either way I didn't intend to be there.

I clasped a hand onto Issan's shoulder and gave him a nod before walking down to join Cassius. A quick search of the corpses revealed little of use and so we set our faces north. If the red eyed demon was still alive we would find it.

Find it and kill it.

# CHAPTER 21

## *Home*

The trip back was a long one. The eagle had arrived a good two days before the carriage, the driver of which knew nothing about our mission and our activities, just hired from a staging output out past the west of Forgoth to pick up a group of Andurran teenagers. A strange enough request perhaps, but the purse of gold he doubtless received for the journey more than made him happy to do such a strange thing. Our goodbyes with Jadira and the friends we had made within the fort were long and heartfelt. There were many requests for us to come and visit, promises of mead to be shared and Hrudan to rout. Jadira gave us all hugs and newly worked leather vambraces - each of them hardened to deflect all but the most determined cutting edge but flexible enough to make wearing them not a chore. She shook off our remarks of thanks stating that if she had the time the gifts that we had received would have been much more valuable. As it was she swore that she would be sending a missive to the empire at the first available opportunity to receive trainers of our calibre to winter with them in order to improve the Meredothian fighting skills. I had half a mind to ask how much she would be paying for such a person, but I didn't doubt that the Emperor would offer our services cheaply if it kept the Hrudan threat from his borders. Once all the rounds had been made we climbed into the carriage and set off rumbling down the road. And rumbled.

...And rumbled.

Carriages, in case you didn't know this already, are intensely boring. At first you climb in and marvel at the wooden construction, gasp at the train of horses and articulate just how much more dignified it is than riding. About an hour later you take all that back once the potholes have worked their way through your buttocks and into your lower spine. Granted once we entered the Empire proper the roads were better paved, courtesy of the military needing efficient transportation systems, but by that point we were so broken and weary of travel that we would have killed for horses or even to walk. Five weeks it took us to make the journey. Five weeks of mind-numbing boredom and relentless motion. I didn't know how we were brought to the heartland in the first place - we could have been drugged for weeks or perhaps some kind of seraph related travel magic was used - but why the same method couldn't be used to bring us back was an oft heated topic during the long, long ride. During all that time we perhaps surprisingly and somewhat disappointingly only had one bandit attempt on the carriage and they were so laughably unorganised as to barely be worth mentioning. The only upside that I will grudgingly give to a carriage is the protection from the elements, but staying dry is not worth the broken back. Trust me on that.

To be entirely honest I shouldn't be the one to complain. I only had to ride in the carriage for three weeks, not five. Towards the end of the third week my bond with Seya that had been slowly getting stronger as the distance between us decreased rocketed in strength. A day later I was able to get fleeting thoughts through, but she didn't respond to my urging other than to give me a semblance of pride at her overwhelming speed. Not two days later she hurtled out of the woods onto the trail, causing the horses to panic and the driver to scream in terror. Her laughter filled my mind and an amused purr that we had all missed terribly and brought Cassius and myself to tears filled our chests. Seya was back.

Still saying nothing about the past months she cavorted, pounced and purred her way through the first joyful reunion and only several hours later, once I had taken her for a run out of sight of the still terrified horses and leaving the others to suffer the indignity of the carriage did she begin to speak.

"Drugged?!" I burst out angrily, kicking at an offensive looking bush.

*That is what it appears happened,* Seya replied softly. *I cannot remember any periods of relative lucidity over what seems to have been a considerable period of time. If what you tell me is accurate and this is one of the Academy's examinations then the most logical explanation is that they did not want me coming with you to upset the imbalance of power. After all, with me you would have solved these problems before winter had closed in.* She said it so matter-of-factly that I almost agreed with her before I realised it. Gods I had missed her prideful, beautiful face! My anger at her treatment went from explosive fire to flickering candle in an instant and with the emotion of the last few months sweeping up on me I threw my arms around her neck, pressed my face into the side of her soft fur and cried and cried...and cried.

She let me loose all the sorrow, pain and fear that I had borne throughout this harsh winter. She made no comment and just let her presence soothe me. Finally, after an interminable period of time my tears dried and I straightened up, the weight on my shoulders considerably lessened.

"Thank you," I said, wiping my eyes.

She leant forward, large eyes gazing intently into mine and then a thick dry tongue sandpapered my face. A chuckle thrummed through her that turned into an internal sigh. *Oh little one, I can tell that this has been a hard journey. Sit and tell me your story and I will tell you mine.*

And so I did. I sat, curled into my partner's chest and talked about everything that had happened since finding Korthan's body, the torture, the trolls, the spiders and the Hrudan. When I finally finished she nuzzled my head like a new-born.

*It is a long tale and one that speaks of great bravery and bigger foolishness. You took many risks Calidan. You need to learn to protect yourself better - I thought I taught you better than that.* She shook off my attempts at a response, stopping me from talking by simply pressing her tongue against my face. Disgusting. Laughing at my feeble struggles to get free she continued, *one thing I can confirm is that Korthan is not dead, which lends a lot of credence to this all being part of your fourth-year exam.*

I finally broke free, "Not dead?!" I cried happily. "You sure?"

*He was the first person I saw when I woke. Considering your story I believe the wily old fox might have done that on purpose so that you would know for sure that what you saw was not real.*

"That bastard," I murmured. "He must have known that the first thing you would do would be to come to me, so he showed himself to confirm that all was well and we didn't come back to the Academy prepared for the worst." I stopped for a moment and then snorted in frustration. "And he probably woke you now when we are still some time away so that we had time to come to terms with what the Academy has done and not knock down the doors in fury."

Seya yawned, exposing her arm length canines. *A wise move on his part. Like I said, a wily old fox.*

After an hour of lounging in the sun, enjoying the dappled sunlight like old times, we began chasing down the carriage. It didn't take us long, despite the carriage being drawn by four horses the driver maintained a consistently slow pace so as to save his wheels, but not the passengers, the trauma of the roads. With the wind blowing towards us it was a simple matter for Seya to prowl up behind the carriage and for me to jump in without alerting the horses or driver. The others reacted much the same as me to Seya's revelations, a mixture of rage at the horrors that they had put us through combined with relief that Korthan was alive and the confirmations that gave regarding the torture that had taken place. It probably says something about the Academy itself and the type of people it recruited that we didn't immediately throw our towels in the proverbial ring - though I very much doubt that we could have if we had wanted to. Whether we knew that we couldn't receive the training we wanted anywhere else or that we had just got to that level of indoctrination where we could and would suggest seemingly valid reasons for the Academy's actions, or knowing what we knew about Imperators we deemed it a logical approach and would do the same things in our instructor's shoes I do not know, but we returned to the Academy with our heads held high, the rage reduced to simmering embers, just as the staff had no doubt intended.

✳ ✳ ✳

### The Emperor

*The portal shimmered into life and the Emperor stepped back to make room for the traveller. When after a few moments nothing came through he raised an irritated eyebrow and sighed before sticking his arm into the portal and beginning to pull. With barely any sign of effort on his face he slowly stepped backward, revealing a heavily muscled blue skinned arm clutching his own and frantically scrabbling. Another step and the torso appeared, a third and the face of the blue skinned troll was revealed, its eyes wild and frightened with the Emperor's hand clenched tight around its throat. Claws that had rendered legion of spiders bounced off the Emperor's unarmoured skin, muscles that had fended off blows from the mightiest of mutated beasts proved ineffective against the Emperor's inexorable strength. With a long-suffering sigh he threw the troll into a nearby cage before locking the door.*
*"How many times do we have to go over this?" he said softly. "You are a tool. My tool. I expect you to come when I call. Otherwise I will stop offering you carrot and resort to stick."*

*The eyes of the troll widened even further and a frightened hooting noise rumbled out of its throat as it shook its head frantically.*
*"Ah, you remember the stick. Good. Don't test my patience again."*
*Frantic nodding.*
*The Emperor gave the troll a considering gaze. "Overall, you performed within my expectations," he rumbled. "I predicted a forty percent chance that you would turn on your one-time friends so congratulations on thinking that approach through. One doesn't keep a tool that can't be trusted." His expression turned thoughtful as he examined the many healed scars on the troll's body. "Still looks like you could do with some improvements. Your battle skills leave a lot to be desired."*
*The troll went wild, shivers wracking its body as it tried to get as far away from the Emperor as possible, flinging itself against the bars in an attempt to escape and causing denizens of further cages to roar and moan in response.*
*"Now, now, don't worry. It won't be today. You did well enough to earn a little rest," the Emperor said, seemingly completely unconcerned with the troll's response, his voice immediately silencing the occupants of the other cages. "The better you do then the less changes we have to make, so work hard."*
*Turning, the Emperor began to walk away from the row of cages, pausing only to remove the light with a flicker of will.*
*"Rest well and I'll see you again soon...*
*...Kirok."*

✳ ✳ ✳

"Welcome back my boy."
"Korthan," I intoned calmly, trying to hide the rush of happiness I felt at seeing his face. "The last time I saw you, you were dead. Glad to see that you're back to being only nearly so."
My old mentor laughed, a dry, rasping chuckle from an ancient throat. "I'll only die when you least expect it, just to make sure that it impacts you the most." He stepped forward and

held his arms out wide. "Good to see you lad."

I hesitated for a moment and then my resolve crumbled. Stepping forward I gave him a hug, cementing him as not a creation of my mind but a physical, living person.

"Good to see you too you old fart," I mumbled, trying to hide the tears that glistened in the corners of my eyes.

The return to the Academy had been strangely understated, Kane had just stood at the entrance to the gates when the carriage dropped us off and beckoned us in. 'Well done,' he had said gruffly, brushing off questions with a wave of his hand. 'Head to the Decompression Chambers, clean up, get a good meal and relax. I'll see you for a debrief tomorrow.' And that was that. So obviously I completely ignored his advice and immediately headed to Korthan's library where he had been seemingly awaiting my arrival, two whiskies poured out next to the deep-set armchairs that he preferred to recline in. Once we had settled in to chat, he in his comfortable robes and me still in my travel-stained furs and skins and exchanged enough carefully neutral pleasantries he finally took a deep taste of his drink before waving a hand.

"Ok, enough time wasting. Ask your questions and let an old man sleep."

I couldn't help but grin. I had missed the cranky old bastard terribly. I swirled the whisky around in my glass for a long moment, enjoying the touch of annoyance in the old man's face as I didn't immediately answer. After I had taken a sip of the delightful fluid I put the glass down carefully and looked him in the eyes.

"How did you do it?"

He raised an eyebrow. "That's it? No 'why' or tears or anger?"

"The anger is there," I assured him, "the tears were there too. As for the 'why?' I'm pretty certain I can answer that myself. The Academy needs to know that its Imperators can handle themselves and that they aren't going to break at the first sign of danger." I gazed thoughtfully into the glass, "Though whether they are now more predisposed to being brittle rather than tempered remains to be seen."

Korthan heaved out a long sigh. "Sounds about right. And if you have any better ideas for testing the mettle of our Imps then I'm sure that Kane will avidly discuss them with you tomorrow. So," an eager gleam flared in his eye, "let's discuss the much more interesting topic of how I did it. Theories?"

"Seraph," I answered. "Some kind of seraph attack that rendered me incapacitated and then transported us to the heartland...a portal?"

Korthan grinned. "Not everything is done with seraph young one, though it easily could have been. You're right on the portal front; there aren't too many ways to get a bunch of unconscious people that much distance without keeping them drugged for weeks. We thought it a better use of time to combine enough seraph to fuel a portal than invest the resources to get you up there. But knocking you out and what you saw? Nothing but plain old poison and method acting! Well," he clarified, "method acting and poison that simulates death. Surprisingly useful stuff that. More than you might expect."

Poison and portals. He made it sound so simple.

"Why the charade?" I asked after digesting his words. "What was the point?"

He raised an eyebrow. "I would have thought that straightforward. Despair. Horror. Heartache. All things that an Imperator is going to experience throughout their careers. Experiencing the loss of a comrade puts you in a frame of mind that little else can replicate, a frame of mind that – and have no doubt about this Calidan – you will experience for real in the future. How you act when your brain is dealing with that information, how you perform under such overwhelming sorrow, and how you operate when bad things are happening to you at the same time, that is what we need to find out." He gazed thoughtfully at me and then his expression softened. "It is a hard life we lead boy and the Academy's job is to push you to the point of breaking and beyond then forge what comes out the other side into a tool for the Emperor to wield. It isn't pretty, it isn't nice. But it works...for the most part."

For a long time I didn't respond. I thought about the horrors we had all witnessed and been subjected to, to the extent that we didn't know what was real and what wasn't. Was it really beneficial in the long term, or did it just scar us into being mentally numb? I thought back to Rikol's dead stare, the complete change in personality he had had since Darren's death. Would he have found his way back to his normal self if given enough time and support? Was this newer, darker version of him stronger in the face of adversity like the Academy hoped? Only time would tell.

"And... what if we had been broken? Death is one thing, but what if our minds had not been up to the challenge and crumbled?"

He stared at me, eyes weighing. "Then you would have been broken. Your mind in tatters from the strain. Some recover from such things, others don't." His eyes were intent on me now. "But you know that Calidan, and you're not one for asking foolish questions. So tell me, what is it you really want to know?"

Clever Korthan, he was always able to cut to the quick. "How much were we observed during the trial?" I asked, the question seeming to throw Korthan for a second.

"Relatively little," he replied, a curious look flittering onto his face. "Or, to put it more accurately, almost not at all. We have informants within the Meredothian community but when in the wilds you were largely on your own."

*Largely.*

"When you say 'largely'," I began, "that suggests you had someone out there with us at least some of the time."

"It does."

"Want to tell me who?"

"Not even slightly."

I took another sip of whisky. It really was excellent. "So it wasn't perhaps a blue skinned, intelligent troll that helped us survive when we needed it most?"

A fierce grin - he was proud of me for the question, which was an answer of sorts in its own way. "I can neither confirm nor deny the existence of any blue skinned troll that may or may not have provided support to you and your team throughout the exam." His eyes twinkled, "But it would be strange to think that such a creature would provide assistance of its own accord."

I nodded and gave a small grin that didn't reach my eyes. "Korthan," I said slowly. "That troll knew me, and I knew it. We have met before; I am sure of it! Can you-"

He held up a hand and cut me off. "Sorry lad I can't discuss anything of this nature with Imps. It is well above your pay grade. Just know that whoever, whatever this blue troll of yours is, it can rest easy knowing that it helped you out and in doing so served the Empire."

"But-"

"No 'buts' Calidan," His tone was harsh and his eyes serious. "This cannot and will not be discussed. Not here. Not now. Understood?"

Simmering anger flared into life in my chest but I swallowed the flames and nodded. "Understood."

He gave me a tight smile and leant back. "Good. Now tell me about the Meredothians."

We talked late into the night. Or at least late enough that by the time I left the library I was fairly certain it was more morning than night. Making my way back to the relaxing chambers and its bed that felt so familiar and yet so strange I collapsed and slept the sleep of the dead.

Kane didn't give us much of a lie in. At nine in the morning we were assembled in his office, coffees in hand, skins and leathers swapped for clothes that hadn't been hacked off an animal or stolen from the dead. All of us had woken up earlier in the morning and gone to the baths, taking the time to thoroughly scrub out the dirt, grime and bad memories of the past months. It might not have done much for the memories but at least we smelled more fresh.

Kane finished pouring the final cup of steaming black nectar for himself and sat on the edge of his desk, his gaze taking us all in, noting the changes in our physiques, the way we carried ourselves and - perhaps most telling of all - the differences in our eyes. Just as we began to squirm under the weight of his regard he spoke up, his voice deep and calm.

"You survived." It was a statement, not a question. "Congratulations. Not all do."

Silence.

He gave a sad smirk and took a sip of coffee. "I know it feels rough. That's because it is. The exam is different for every group and though we try to factor in the ability of the parties and the potential dangers they might face, it is largely guess work. And in the end that makes sense because often that is all Imperators have to go on. Rumour and hearsay. Often an Imperator doesn't have the chance to head back or call in support if they find that they are in a more dangerous situation with a more deadly foe than expected and so they have to improvise. Adapt. Overcome. Or die. The exam, as I'm sure you found out, encompassed that kind of situation and I am pleased to say that from the feedback I have gathered you have all performed admirably."

Silence again.

This time he blew a sigh out of his nostrils. "You know, no matter how many times I have had to do this moment, it never gets easier. If anything it gets more difficult, knowing what each fresh group is going to be in for, that it will be life changing and not always for the better. I've had teams come back and threaten to kill me - some have even tried - I've had teams who simply stopped caring at all, and I've had people who have accepted what the Academy did and does and attempted to immediately move past it. I can never predict exactly how it is going to turn out until I'm sitting here in front of you and so I can't make a speech that perfectly embodies what you are feeling right now and answers all your questions. So," he took another sip of coffee and rested it on his knee. "Ask away."

Rikol piped up first, his voice sombre. "How many?"

"How many what?" Kane replied, head tilted.

"...How many don't make it back?"

Kane took a deep, slow breath, his brow furrowed in thought. "The fourth-year exam has been going on for as long as anyone can remember. Korthan is one of the oldest members of the Academy and he says that he had never heard of it not being in place here. Put simply it's too useful to give up. It tests our Imps and it solves whatever minor crisis the Academy or the Emperor decides needs solving but that doesn't require a full Imperator. It's one of the reasons that we operate such a fluid system of instruction at the Academy, with the exam only happening when we deem you ready for it and when there is a crisis of the right magnitude for your skill level. All of which goes...a long way to not answering your question." A deep breath, as if he was steadying himself. "Out of every ten people to take the fourth-year exam, six return."

This time the silence wasn't out of frustration or anger. *Six?!*

'Six!" Scythe said incredulously. "Only six come back?"

"How many a year go on the fourth-year exam?" Ella asked quietly.

"Between ten to sixteen on average," Kane answered, eyes dark. "The mortality rate is fairly high. The burn out rate following the exam is relatively high too. It is not, as you were all repeatedly told prior to the event, an easy exam. It is dangerous, often deadly, and offers a no-holds barred glimpse into the day-to-day life of an Imperator."

"Why not prepare them more, give them more time, more knowledge?" Sophia cried; her face distraught.

"And would more time have made your trip particularly different?" Kane queried. "You all survived, which suggests that your skill levels were such that you were able to overcome the obstacles in your path. The completion of the fourth-year exam is a turning point in your time at the Academy. It shows that you are competent enough to begin external missions. Again, missions that are deemed to be too light for full-fledged Imperators to use their time on, but all will be dangerous in their own way. If we moved the exam to a later year then unless we increased the overall length of time to be spent at the Academy – which is unlikely considering the numbers we have to attempt to replenish on a yearly basis – you lose up to a year of real-world refinement." A grimace. "As harsh as it is, this exam separates the wheat from the chaff. Those who survive are deemed fit to continue into the later years of training and the others, well…"

"Die?" Rikol said sardonically.

Kane levelled a cool look at him. "Yes," he said. "More often than not they die. And that is a sad loss for the empire, a terrible loss for their friends and family and a huge loss for humanity. Those that don't are provided whatever support is in the Academy's power to give. Some end up serving the empire in other ways, others are…unsuited to serve."

"And what happens to them?" Sophia asked.

"They are looked after," Kane said carefully. "They aren't abandoned, if that's what you're asking."

"And all of them are turned into monsters?" I asked, voice neutral.

Kane went very still. He turned to look me in the eye. "And what do you mean by that Calidan?" he asked. There was a wary look in his eye as though we were discussing something very dangerous indeed.

"Just something that we discussed on the way home," I replied. "How we had a certain strange troll support us when we needed it most. A most unlikely scenario wouldn't you say?"

"Unlikely indeed," Kane said slowly. "But not completely impossible."

"Well yes, completely impossible," Rikol countered. "There has never been a single indication of an intelligent troll, everyone knows that they are there for one thing and one thing only; to eat you. So one coming out of the blue to help us over and over again is an impossibility."

"So why do you think the Academy has a hand in this?" asked

Kane.

"You mean aside from the Academy understanding the research behind combining Imperators with otherworldly creatures?" Scythe replied. "We've all seen it. You know that. So you may as well tell us what is going on."

Kane twisted his lips, lost in thought. "I know you've all seen things that generally Imps would not see or be made aware of for a long, long time. But there are certain elements that prevent me from talking about this. Other countries would kill and have killed for this information, and having been subjected to the type of treatment that you might expect to receive at the hands of another country's inquisition I think we can all agree that not knowing is the best defence."

It was a compelling argument and we all knew it. All of us could remember the terror and the pain that we had felt during the early days of the exam. Everyone breaks and the empire could then protect its most precious secrets by keeping the pool of people who knew them to a minimum.

"When would you usually tell an imp this information?" Cassius asked.

"Never," Kane said simply. "Only full-fledged Imperators would be privy to this, and even then it would be on a need-to-know basis. You already know a substantial amount more than several of the newer Imperators regarding the Academy's dealings with other...races," he finished tactfully. "As you might imagine we keep this information as confidential as it gets. It might not be too surprising to realise that there was quite a case for your immediate silencing following the events of your journey into the desert. Thankfully there was more than enough support, not least from the Emperor himself, to keep you around."

"Well that's just brilliant," muttered Rikol angrily. "You go on missions to unknown areas of the world and fight murderous kind of alive but not quite alive scorpions, find information that the Emperor himself wanted and lose a friend in the process but we still get nearly 'removed'? What does the Academy think it is?! What right does it have to decide that we should be killed for our knowledge?"

Kane snorted. "The Academy answers to the Emperor and the Emperor alone Rikol. You know that. You knew what this life was. The Emperor himself told you it would be hard, just like you were told that once in the Academy you are part of this for life - whether you want to be or not. The Academy will do what it must to protect the Andurran Empire and it does that job proudly. If you had been removed due to what you had discovered it would not be the first time that had happened. Some information is too important to let anyone know. Some information is best kept locked away, the key in the Emperor's - and only the Emperor's - hand.

"I can understand you being angry, I can understand the rage and horror at that statement. But the key fact that you all seem to be forgetting is that you *belong* to the Emperor. His word is law and if he says you die to protect something he deems important; it will be so." A fervent gleam appeared in Kane's eyes, his expression growing a little wild. "His knowledge, his power is beyond anything you might imagine. With his understanding and intellect the Andurran Empire has grown to what it is today and will continue to reach new heights...as long as we are ready to sacrifice ourselves to achieve that goal."

A pause filled the room, filling its nooks and crannies until it was fit to burst. Cassius took the plunge.

"I don't think any of us here think any less of the Emperor, but are you suggesting that he is more than human?"

'The Emperor is unlike other mortals," Kane answered. "I have seen him take a blow that would fell Adronicus in a heartbeat and shrug it off like it was nothing. I've known him for twenty years and would swear that he hasn't aged a day whilst I have got old and slow. He is- "

"-Very pleased to see you all."

# CHAPTER 22

## *Emperor*

T he thunderous voice rumbled through the office, cutting off Kane's words as the door to the room flung open with a bang and the Emperor strolled inside. He was clad in a finely crafted white silk shirt and blue corded trousers that must have cost a fortune, not just for the quality and dye but for the sheer quantity of the material required, and despite his lack of armour I could have sworn that the room shook with the force of his strides. He stopped next to Kane's desk and turned to take a seat on the edge of the desk next to Kane, who looked like he didn't know whether to be thrilled or alarmed. I could hear the wood groan under the sheer weight of the man. When he was settled his gaze scanned us all and each one of us buckled beneath the intensity of his regard. When under his gaze it was like being in the path of a charging great boar, you felt rooted to the ground and unable to act or think. After a few moments his eyes relaxed as though he was happy with what he saw before him and a wide smile spread from eye to eye.

"Children," he thrummed, "it is so very pleasing to see you. I've been keeping an eye on your exploits and have found your actions to be most satisfactory indeed. Congratulations."

We all stammered our thanks at his approval which he waved

off. "It is my thanks that you shall have and not the other way round. Kane here," he put a plate sized hand on Kane's shoulder and gave him an intent look, "knows that today would have been better spent in celebration of your efforts rather than a debriefing." Kane shrank back with a chagrined look. "So you have five minutes more of questions with me which I will do my utmost to answer as long as it doesn't impact national security and then you are to prepare yourselves for a visit to your mess hall where I have taken the liberty of inviting my chefs to prepare a most marvellous spread. I like to see my people rewarded for their efforts where possible." He paused a moment to let his message sink in and for the grins to reach our faces at the prospect of the divine food we had once eaten at the top of his tower in what felt like a previous lifetime. "So," he rumbled, "ask."

And with that option before us, with the ability to ask any question of the Emperor, the man that Kane had just billed as the most knowledgeable individual in the Empire if not the world...words failed. Minds blank we looked at each other dumbly, each hoping another would ask the first question.

"Come," he said gently after a good thirty seconds of uncomfortable shifting. "Fear not, ask your questions."

"The troll," I forced out and immediately Kane's face darkened. He moved to open his mouth but a raised hand from the Emperor forestalled him.

"The troll is an experiment. One of several. You have met the results of similar experiments before, Merowyn being one. In this instance much of the joined beast came to the fore, rendering speech impossible but importantly sentience and much of the person's individuality remained, resulting in a useful tool. As you have experienced its battlefield potential is outstanding, its ability to heal combined with its strength and power is a combination hard to rival." He seemed pleased with the troll much like a breeder for hounds would be for a successful litter.

"But," I said slowly, "but it was...is a person is it not?"

"It was. A broken and crushed person in no shape to be useful to the empire. Now it is something more."

"Who was it?"

His eyes met mine. "That, young Calidan, is not for me to reveal. I have no doubt that you will meet again and I will not rob that creature of its satisfaction for the grand revelation. Rest assured that the creature is not in pain and I have no doubt that it appreciates its new role in life."

A frustrating answer. Nodding my head respectfully I leant back against the wall to ponder his words. He had given us more than Kane but it still wasn't much, just a promise that we would meet again. I wasn't sure if that made me relieved or concerned. Probably a bit of both.

Cassius perked up. "The Hrudan. Did you know they were a threat before we were sent there?"

A thunderous chuckle shook the room. "Of course! Jadira sent me a request for support some time ago, but I have other sources of information that allowed me to predict the Hrudan plans. The Meredothians are sometime Andurran allies and I have been content to keep friendships and open trade routes with them for they act as a defensive buffer against threats to the Empire from the north west just by the act of being in the way. It benefitted me to send you over there as it provided a decent training exercise for you whilst suggesting that we were taking the Hrudan threat seriously which would strengthen their gratitude to the empire."

"And if we had died before reaching the fort?" Rikol asked, expression wary.

"Then they wouldn't have known you were there and I would have enacted another plan to support them...or taken advantage of the Hrudan threat," the Emperor replied casually. "These are the decisions that someone in my position must make, so hopefully you do not feel too badly wronged by the callous nature of it. At some point in the future I will likely have to ask one or all of you to die for this empire and I make no excuses for that. It is why I reward where possible."

His frankness was simultaneously calming and disturbing. That he could speak so easily of using us as expendable tools and yet go to the trouble of providing a feast that would be quite literally fit for a king was a strange combination and yet I think all of us felt reassured by just how frank he was about what may or may not be asked of us. If you were going to be used by someone better to have it known throughout rather than only find out at the end.

Scythe raised a hand and the Emperor nodded at him. "Time for the last question I think. What have you got to ask Scythe?"

Scythe visibly took a deep breath to steady his nerves. "The torture sir. It felt so real…more real than a lot of this to be honest. Was it truly necessary and how was it done?"

The silk clad giant paused for a moment, his intelligent eyes considering. "Necessary? Perhaps, perhaps not. Useful? Absolutely. Some say that you only really know who you are when faced with your own mortality. Over a long, long life I can safely say that I disagree. You only really know who you are when you are faced with the mortality of your friends. Do you place their safety above your own? Do you leave them to suffer to minimise the damage to you? An individual can often find it in themselves to bravely meet the end or give a last-minute desperate surge of action when threatened with impending death. That same individual might be rendered immobile at the thought of a colleague, family member or friend being killed in their place. From that perspective I believe that the Academy now knows much more about each of you and how you will perform under such intense pressure. There is an inherent risk in such an approach of course, however I firmly believe that the benefits outweigh the risks. It gives you an insight into how you may perform in a similar scenario, a benefit when capture and interrogation is not particularly uncommon for those in your line of work. Naturally there are downsides and mental damage is key amongst them." He gave a sad smile. "Such things are unavoidable when subjecting my best and brightest to such measures. Thankfully it is still relatively rare. Those chosen to attend the Academy are often robust both physically and mentally. As for how it was done it was a relatively straight forward illusion performed by Korthan who is particularly skilled in mental focused seraph techniques. It was a good test of his skills to perform it on all of you at once. I believe he was most pleased with how it went."

*Korthan.* It was hard to reconcile that the kindly old bastard had the stomach to inflict the mental agonies he had put us through. That said, he was an Imperator first and foremost and if the Academy commanded such a thing of him I had little doubt that he would do it. It was moments like this that made me wonder just how well I knew those closest to me. Whilst I might have guessed Korthan had the capacity to do it, after all an Imperator always has a dark edge, before the exam I wouldn't have thought that he would do it to me. In that capacity I could certainly say that I learnt something thanks to the fourth-year exam and that is not to trust blindly.

The Emperor gave a beatific smile. "Now, I think that is all the time we have for discussion. If you follow me we will go and dine." He stood up and the desk audibly heaved a sigh of relief. With an almost imperceptible nod at Kane the Emperor opened the office door and strode out, not waiting for further comments.

We paused for a moment, still digesting the information he had divulged and only broke into motion when Kane shook off a slightly perturbed expression and waved his hand.

"Hurry up everyone, go and enjoy your food. The Emperor is not one to be kept waiting. Unless he says otherwise your day is your own and the rest of the week is yours too. Relax and enjoy yourselves."

Free time! Life at the Academy seemed so relaxing compared to the constant battle for survival we had experienced until fairly recently. Even when recuperating in the fort the bone-shredding ice winds meant that any trip outside to the toilet was a hardship that no one should have to face. I had no doubt that come the next day we would be thrown back into the structured rigor of the Academy's training programmes but to have a whole day free to ourselves whilst at the Academy... that was a rare treat indeed.

It wasn't far to the mess hall and the Emperor strode ahead of us, his strides effortlessly eating the ground and requiring us all to half jog to keep up. He opened the doors and we immediately had our nostrils scintillated by sumptuous scents that had our mouths drooling. The inside of the mess hall looked much the same with the roaring fires still in place to push back the morning chill of spring. There were no other students inside - breakfast at the Academy was an early morning affair and one that was immediately followed by lessons or more exercise. This leisurely mid-morning meal was a treat unknown to myself and the others, although I had heard a rumour that the more well to do within the city were doing this more and more often, a meal that took the place of breakfast and lunch but was simultaneously both and neither. As far as I could tell 'brunch' seemed to be an excuse to drink early in the morning without any stigma. One can always rely on nobility to find new ways to justify alcoholism.

As we sat down the kitchen doors opened and row after row of serving staff emerged holding plate after plate of food. They poured out, their arms shaking with the weight of the trays that they carried, yet somehow managing to delicately place each silver plate along the trestle tables. And still it came, as though they had been planning on feeding the entire Academy rather than just our group. Having eaten the fort's winter stock of boiled grains, salted meats and roasted chicken during our stay at the fort - tasty enough fare but soon relatively dull - the vast array of cuisine laid out before us was a ridiculous and welcome sight.

Once the food had been brought, out came the drinks - mugs filled with the sweet, brown nectar that was coffee and our glasses with some kind of sweet wine. Satisfied, the Emperor gave an affirmative nod to the staff who disappeared as though they had never been. Gently clasping the tiny flute between his behemoth fingers he nodded to us all and raised the glass.

"To you, my young friends. Congratulations on passing your fourth-year exam. Here is to the future." With a clink of glasses we toasted and drank. The sweet wine tasted like blackcurrants and plum and sent a pleasant warmth winding throughout our bodies.

The Emperor murmured appreciatively and licked his lips. "A Rinevan dessert wine. They haven't been in the market particularly long but have been making waves with their flavour. It is good to see that the plaudits they have been receiving are well deserved."

We nodded in agreement as though we knew exactly what he was talking about and, not sure of the decorum for an Emperor held feast, we waited until he made the first move, the sense of anticipation building until we could barely contain ourselves. After what seemed like an eternity he stopped admiring the wine and turned to us, his eyes surprised as though he didn't know why we weren't eating.

"Ah," he said in a voice laden with amusement. "My apologies, please do not wait for me. Eat."

And with those glorious words we launched ourselves into battle.

I pride myself on being able to eat. Even without the vast number of calories that an Imp burns on an average day my bond with Seya meant that my ability to eat outshone anyone I had come across within the Academy and was a source of much disgust and fascination by many of my fellow classmates. Regardless, this was a fight I was doomed to lose. There were sixteen different types of bread, one so light and fluffy as to be akin to eating air, another so sweet and dense to be near full in one mouthful. Arrayed around the mountain of bread were platters of meats; hams, bacon and even a full glazed gammon. Surrounding that were trays of eggs cooked in nine different ways. I didn't even know that eggs could be cooked in that many methods but each version was gloriously tasty. Not to be left out were the sweeter items to counter that of the savoury. Cakes, biscuits, cereals, honeys, jams, marmalades - you name it, it was there. And as much as I tried to sample everything...in that epic task I failed. After nearly two hours of eating, the pace slowing to picking just for the sake of gluttony, we finally came to a stop, the Emperor chuckling as we rolled ourselves away from the table for fresh air.

"It was a good effort," he rumbled. "Rarely have I seen a finer attempt but I am afraid that my chefs see it as a challenge when they come to the Academy to make sure that the Imperators and Imps cannot finish everything on the table. So do not feel too disheartened."

Together we walked out into the Academy grounds and stood enjoying the fresh spring air. Around us Imps and Imperators walked, moving from class to class. When each saw the Emperor he or she stood a little straighter and ambles turned to purposeful strides. No one wanted the Emperor to think that they were anything but dedicated. Eventually he walked us to the gates of the Academy and turned, looking at each of us in turn before nodding in approval at what he saw.

"I am afraid that this is all I have time for today young ones," he said with a wide smile. "I hope that the feast provided to you goes some way to repaying a debt and clearing the sorrow of the last few months. I suggest that you enjoy the rest of your week, for soon I believe you will be back at your duties."

As he turned to go I spoke up, "Sir, if I may?"

He turned back and cocked his head, "Yes Calidan?"

"What happens now?"

"Now?" he asked, bemused.

"As in, if I'm not being too bold, we managed something extraordinary - do we just go back to training as normal?"

A slow smile spread across his face, lingering as though he found what I had said deeply amusing. "I do not deny that what you and your friends achieved was, as you say, extraordinary. Or at least I would not deny it if you were common folk. However you are in the Imperator Academy and here the extraordinary is, in fact, commonplace. So though you might expect me to instantly grant you the title of Imperator and send you off to work for me across the globe, no...no not yet. Not for some time young Calidan, though I do like the optimism. Once you have got back into some semblance of normality with your training Kane will see to it that you will be moved up to the fourth year and then your real training will begin. It will make the training you were receiving up to now look like child's play. So do your best." He winked and turned to leave. "You're all cards on the board now so I'll be keeping close tabs on you," he called over his shoulder as he walked through the gates.

"Don't let me down."

# CHAPTER 23

## *Serathine*

Once we finished our mandatory stay at the Decompression Chambers we were back to our regular training for the rest of the spring. Whilst we were all eager to be officially made fourth years, Kane reasoned that a period of normality following such an intense experience was the best approach and we took to the comforting familiarity with will. Adronicus was much the same, his swiftness, speed and power still startling despite having fought people who were of similar build. The weapon master had no compunction about throwing us back into everyday training, his devilish grin only getting wider the closer we got to being able to land hits on him. He showed interest in the ice spiders that we had fought, the eager glittering of his eyes suggesting that he would have relished the challenge. As for the Hrudan he was purely interested in their fighting style, weapons and martial quality. I had no doubt that he was already aware of the Hrudan but he just couldn't pass up the chance to learn more about a different culture and their fighting styles.

It was Asp however that truly blew his mind.

Cassius had kept Asp safely wrapped whilst we had been travelling in order to hide it from prying eyes. Now that we were at the Academy I had suggested that he take the time to learn how to use its abilities and there was no better person for him to learn from than Adronicus. When he first revealed the gleaming blade Adronicus's eyes glistened so much that I could have sworn he was tearing up. Soon Cassius was receiving dedicated one-to-one sessions with Adronicus on top of the rest of his training where they practised to unlock the abilities of the sword, or at least from what Cassius fed back he practiced to unlock the abilities of the sword whilst Adronicus alternated between shouting encouragement, abuse, and hitting him with blunt weapons.

Seya had started spending more and more time outside of the Academy. Whilst she didn't show any outward signs of discomfort or injury from her presumed drugging, she seemed much more wary of being back in the Academy buildings - something that I could not blame her for. From the Academy's perspective what had happened to Seya was straightforward. Simply put, she provided me with too much of a benefit to be allowed to participate with the fourth-year exam. In the Academy's eyes it was either Seya be removed from the equation or I forever stayed a third year. The annoying thing was that they didn't just *ask*. I could understand the reasoning - if Seya had refused to stay put there was little that could be done to stop her. Afterall, cats have minds of their own and their strange and inexplicable ability to flow like water meant that keeping them in one place was more difficult than it sounded. If I'd been hurt I don't really know what Seya would have done. She might have used it as a training experience for me or she might have been off like an arrow, unable to stop herself from running to my side. As the Academy hates uncertainty I could see why they went down the route they did but I couldn't forgive them for it. It was just another black mark in a small book that soon became a thick ledger.

It was midsummer when we became fourth years. We had all made the mistake of assuming that being promoted to the fourth-year grade was a matter of course post the fourth-year exam and that was an unwise assumption to make. The

promotion to the fourth-year grade was unlike the other cere-
monial moments we had partaken in up to this point all because of one reason.

Seraph.

Kane invited us all to his office and even included Seya who
curled up outside his open window. On his desk were six vials,
each glowing a deep emerald green.

"Come in and find somewhere to perch," he said gruffly as we
entered. "And don't touch!" he barked as Rikol leant in close.
"At least, not yet."

"What is that?" Scythe asked.

*Serathine,* Seya murmured, *I can smell it from here.*

*What is that?* I replied, curious.

*A substance that was developed a long, long time ago. I hear it tastes
foul and has a few unpleasant side effects but one very interesting
one. Enjoy yourselves.*

"-it's known as emeran," Kane was saying and I fought hard to
suppress a smile as Seya berated the Andurran language in my
mind. "It's used to awaken your seraph."

Stunned silence.

"...When you say 'awaken', what do you mean?" asked Ella
softly. "From what we heard of seraph from Ash she said that
only a few of the group have it and I'm fairly sure it's not alive."

"Alive!" Kane barked with a throaty chuckle. "I think not.
But if the Imperator Academy has learned anything over the
last decades it is that largely everyone has some basic level
of seraph ability. Whether it is because the only people who
survived the Cataclysm were, at least according to Ash, seraph
users I'm not sure, but it is fairly rare that what I am going to
ask you to do next doesn't reveal a pool within you, regardless of size. My best guess as to Ash detecting seraph within
Cassius and Calidan was due to the injury that Rya gave them.
Cassius was subjected to large amounts of black seraph and
managed to survive. Calidan was also exposed to it but I suspect Seya's seraph to largely be of the so-called Green type and
she flooded Calidan with that during his healing, hence the

designations that Ash gave. It is a guess, but the best one that I have." He shrugged wistfully. "A mystery to solve another time. Anyway, if I asked you now to reach within you and find your seraph pools, could you do it? Try."

He gave us a few seconds as we awkwardly tried to find something within ourselves that we weren't sure existed. "No one manage it? Didn't think so. You know when your seraph is accessible. You know it like you know that your arm is moveable and that you can bend your knee. You don't really know how you know...you just know. Make sense?" he finished with an infuriating grin.

"That analogy makes an annoying amount of sense," Sophia grumbled. "So how does this emeran-"

*Serathine*

"-drink work?"

"The ins and outs of it are beyond me and pointless to this discussion," Kane replied. "There are a relatively small number of people who are born with the ability to access seraph or who manage to access it during an exceptionally taxing moment in their lives. As you're aware, from what Ash told us people before the Cataclysm were starting to be born with it more and more frequently and it is true that with the testing we have done practically everyone has been able to have their seraph awakened." He paused for a moment, considering his next words.

"I'm not going to lie, it's an unpleasant drink – both in taste and in aftereffects. I suggest you take your vial and go and find yourself somewhere comfortable to convulse. Because you'll be doing that for some time."

"...Convulse." Ella said dryly.

"Yep," Kane replied happily. "A whole lot of it."

"Sounds...delightful."

He gave her a raised eyebrow. "You have a very strange idea of what is delightful." His grin broadened at her sarcastic eye roll. "Like I said, there isn't too much to discuss. If you want to be able to control seraph, drinking this is your best bet. You'll have a horrible time of it for the next day or so but afterwards you should feel something that has been there all along. Something that feels integral to your being and you will wonder as to how you possibly didn't feel it there before. So," he fixed us with an intense look, "like I said, choose your location wisely. You're going to spend the next twenty-four hours filled with regret."

He certainly wasn't wrong.

My location for drinking that evil concoction was in the forest that surrounded the Academy with Seya by my side. We found a nice spot under the grand bows of a billowing oak, Seya curled around me and I drank the potion. If I hadn't been tortured I would have classed it as the worst night of my life. What started out as a pleasant warmth in the centre of my belly became a spreading fire that lanced up and down my veins until I was convinced that I was going to combust. When the fire peaked uncontrollable shivering began, my teeth hammering so hard that Seya had to find a branch for me to bite down on until the flames began anew.

In short, after that night we all knew that if Kane said something was going to be bad it was going to be much, much worse.

# CHAPTER 24

## *Seraph*

"Breathe and focus inwards. Feel the pool within you. Follow how it flows throughout your body, filling each vein with light. Now follow from your pool to your hand, concentrate on the energy moving along your veins, flooding through your muscles, flowing until it is stored in your hand, until your hand can't contain it anymore and..."

"-explodes?" Rikol asked suddenly.

I couldn't help but burst out laughing and the flickering light that had begun to form at the edge of my hand dissipated before it had ever truly arrived. Sniggers and curses around the room suggested I hadn't been the only one to lose my concentration at Rikol's outburst. Instructor Laniel pursed her lips and frowned disapprovingly at Rikol who shrank slightly under the weight of her regard. I couldn't blame him, Imperator Erethea Laniel had a look that could bring Adronicus to his knees. It was like she could see right into you and found what was there disappointing.

"Rikol," she said calmly without any hint of anger or frustration, "please apologise to the class and reassure them that their hands will not explode when focusing seraph. That is, not unless they wanted them to."

Rikol mumbled an apology and the associated explanation

whilst Instructor Laniel nodded. "And why won't your hand explode unless you want it to?" she asked when he had finished.

"Because seraph responds to will," Rikol replied, his voice little more than a mumble.

"Because seraph responds to will," she echoed. "Correct. And few of us have the willpower to intentionally cause themselves damage. You might think you do, but unconsciously your body wants to save itself, to survive, and thus you put limits on your usage without even knowing. This is an important topic and one that, in a way, I am grateful that Rikol has brought us on to."

We all groaned inwardly. Instructor Laniel was nothing if not thorough and she made sure to dedicate a large part of each session to reinforcing seraph safety, even though we knew it off by heart.

"Your body places limits on your seraph usage," she continued, oblivious or uncaring of our bored looks. "These limits are there for a reason, much like lifting weights if you attempt too much without training for it your body can buckle or break. The good news is that much like a muscle your ability to use greater quantities of seraph is not purely defined at birth but can be improved. Yes Sophia?"

"But there are differences right?" Sophia asked, lowering her hand. "People do have different levels of ability with seraph, we aren't all born with the same sized pool?"

Laniel nodded. "Continuing the muscle and body metaphor, you're right, everyone is different. Just as someone might be a natural athlete, another might be a natural seraph user, gifted with a larger pool and the ability to wield and control it more effectively. But that isn't to say that person will always be better than someone born with a smaller pool. If that natural athlete didn't exercise whilst someone else did, eventually they would lose in a competition. It is much the same here. You might all have different levels of mastery over seraph at this point but whoever trains the hardest, uses it the most and drives themselves to become the best will succeed. Their pools will become larger, their bodies able to handle greater capacities of power. So," she finished with a pointed look at Rikol, "work hard and instead of being unable to make a light you'll be able to do much," she raised her hand and it thrummed with an orange light, "much more," and she began to paint. Her canvas was the air itself, her hand changing colour as she flicked her wrist again and again until she had created a surprisingly vivid image of Rikol with arms outstretched making a pool of light between his hands. We applauded as she finished and she smiled broadly.

"As much as the Academy wants you to be efficient with seraph to be more effective fighters," she said softly, "Seraph is not just for destruction. If you can think of it, seraph can help you do it. So think outside the box and put your skills to use. It will hone your skills and make you all more accomplished seraph users. Understood?"

Nods all round except for Rikol who sat completely still, his eyes wide in awe at the image that hovered in front of him. For a five-minute art piece Laniel had done an impressive job, the colour vivid and enthralling, Rikol's face seemingly more wise and noble as he wielded power beyond his current comprehension. Laniel gave it another minute and then with a wink at the stupefied Rikol she waved her fingers and the painting vanished into coloured smoke.

"That isn't half of what you could do Rikol," she said quietly at his desk as we all resumed our internal struggles to create basic light. "Work diligently and you could be more than you dreamed. You could have the power to change the world for the better," her eyes darkened for a moment as though filled with remembrance, "to save your friends from any danger, to be strong enough to save whoever you choose or be a harbinger of destruction to your enemies." She gave him a soft smile, the darkness that Rikol thought he had momentarily glimpsed dissipating, and stood up from the edge of his desk, patting his shoulder as she did so. "Just give it a shot. What's the worst that could happen?"

As she moved away I saw the look on my friend's face as he mouthed the words 'save my friends' to himself over and over. It was just the push that Rikol needed. From that point on he didn't disrupt the class with jokes, cynicism or wisecracks but dedicated himself to mastering seraph as quickly as possible. When we were outside of the class he spent any spare time funnelling seraph from hand to hand, working on mastering the flow of it through his body and at night I could often see the tell-tale glow coming from behind his curtain. Whilst we all worked hard to control the strange power that lay dormant within us, for Rikol nothing else mattered. His focus on other training lapsed, his mind elsewhere when practising the kaschan or weapons practice. He was repeatedly called out by Adronicus and the other trainers - even given a number of stern warnings by Kane - but it all paled in comparison to the look on his face when he produced his first piece of art with controlled use of seraph. His pool wasn't the biggest - that glory lay with Sophia if you didn't count my ability to draw on Seya - but his fine control soon outshone us all and he revelled in it.

Our passing of the fourth-year exam meant that restrictions on certain training methods had been lifted, with the introduction of seraph being the most important change. Whilst it was obvious that we had stumbled across the origins of seraph back in the desert it did not mean that the Academy was not aware of how to use it already. We already knew that both Kane and Sarrenai were users, with powerful control over their abilities. I didn't doubt that every single Imperator at the Academy had some elements of training in utilising seraph and now knew that everyone in the fourth-year category or above had at least a seraph pool thanks to the serum that we had drank. Those that didn't were likely kept as fourth years for further training in other disciplines but would be unable to be fully fledged Imperators.

Three months of seraph lessons combined with the daily rig-

ours of fitness, weapons and combat training meant that our
rake thin bodies from the hardships of the fourth-year exam
had begun to fill back out. In a relatively short time we were
feeling back to our normal selves, able to keep pace with
the other Academy students and able to compete within the
regular inter-form combat trials that Adronicus continued to
hold. The training we received in seraph didn't hone our bodies but improved mental acuity. Instructor Laniel discussed
concepts that were completely foreign to us, the theory only
making sense in practice. To be proficient at using seraph required a sharp mind, quick wits and the ability to adapt.
You could do practically anything with seraph, affecting the
world around you in whatever way you chose to imagine as
long as you had a pool of energy big enough to enact the
change you desired and the will to impose it. It was why, Laniel had explained, many Imperators stuck with the tried-and-
true methods of enhancing their blades or casting lances of
force or flame. They were easy to visualise which meant that
they were easier to will into being and had relatively small
drains on their pools, allowing for longer engagements. The
skill that Sarrenai had used when walking through walls and
into the literal belly of the beast back in the desert was much
more advanced in that it required an extremely strong sense
of self to be able to undo and rearrange your body just how
it was in another location. The seraph cost by itself was large
but the mental exhaustion and strain was the real problem,
as evidenced by Sarrenai's almost coma like state after the
final battle in the second year. The stories that Ash had talked
about, of people being able to rearrange the world to their lik-
ing, of being able to single-handedly crush armies - to have had
that amount of power was to have been someone of unbow-
ing willpower combined with unmatched intellect and a vast
pool of seraph...or methods to improve these attributes, just
like the Great Hearts were designed to be.
There were thirty-one students including ourselves who were
deemed to be of fourth year status. At least a dozen of those

students had been fourth years for more than two years and the majority of the students were older; most over twenty. It differed from the third year in the number of people in the fourth-year category and it both relieved and chilled me to realise that the reason why the third year didn't have people retaking the year was because anyone not at the required level would likely die in taking the test. The fact that there were fourth years who had been here for a long period suggested that progression to the fifth year was one of skill or learning and not of survival.

We knew most of the group already, having been subjected to countless defeats at their hands in evening combat sessions. We now trained with them in each session aside from seraph - in which we were still very much novices - and each individual's fighting prowess pushed, beat and moulded us into harder, better and more formidable versions of ourselves.

Sadly Rinoa, the flaming red head who had unceasingly defeated me in every combat session and whose presence gave me a reason to look forward to each beating, was now a sixth year and more and more removed from the normal activities of the Academy. I caught glimpses of her every now and again, a burning flash of red that caught my attention no matter the situation, but we would share little more than a smile. Whilst to me she was the most glorious being to have ever graced the earth, to her I was little more than a child. It would still be some time before she saw me differently.

Rivalry between the group was rampant. Those who had been held back were more skilled, older, more knowledgeable and held an inherent dislike for those who had hadn't yet earned their respect, something that those of us at the lower end of the scale desperately thirsted for. Our fights became vicious, each of us was more than skilled enough to kill and whilst trained to have the cold compassion of an Imperator anger and passion inevitably crept through, putting extra power into each blow. Even blunt wooden blades could leave dark bruises and broken bones. The instructors knew this was happening yet did nothing to dissuade it aside from stepping in if blows were getting too deadly. I suspected that the occurrence was not uncommon and that much like with Kirok and his actions in the first year this was another way to test and train students. The one rule in these combat scenarios was that we did not use seraph. Adronicus was adamant on that fact, declaring it as 'too dangerous for our foolish minds,' and any hint of seraph usage was met with his thick arm and a groggy visit to the medical centre.

He was right to do it too. The more we began to play with seraph the more we realised its overwhelming potential. It would be almost too easy to lose control in the moment and kill each other in a flash of destructive magic. Instructor Laniel made it a point to come to some of our training sessions in order to showcase the various ways that classic fighting could be rendered useless when faced with a skilled seraph user, carefully conducting skilled but controlled fights with Adronicus. Her favourite example of controlled power was to send a powerful cut towards his face, forcing him to raise his sword to parry and then allowing her sword to pass *through* his blade, just like Sarrenai had managed to travel through walls but without the showy side effects of blue flame, allowing her attack to travel unimpeded to rest on the edge of his neck. She showcased how by utilising seraph to enhance her muscles she could block the sharpened edge of Adronicus's steel greatsword with her arm, her wrist or even her finger and have the strength to lift him into the air with one petite hand. With a bigger expense of her seraph pool she could do the same thing without lifting a finger, lifting Adronicus into the air through sheer will and sending him cartwheeling through the sky much to our delight. Standard rules of engagement didn't apply to seraph users, their willpower, pool and mental acuity determining their effectiveness rather than physical prowess. Laniel always stressed that mental acuity - the ability to think fast, clearly and without distraction - was the most important part of being a successful seraph user. According to both instructors the fastest end to a seraph user was to break their concentration, to distract them so that whatever they were willing into being faltered and hitting them as hard as possible in that split second. That or assassination.

Understandably this meant that as lessons with seraph continued so did the style in which they were taught. For two hours a day we had lessons with Laniel on the theory behind using seraph and then we paired up to spend an hour practicing what we had just used. The reasoning behind the pairing was twofold, firstly to help each other understand the practical applications of the concepts we had learned earlier in the day and secondly to distract the other with liberal application of a pea shooter. It made for an aggravating yet fun method of learning that started to quickly produce results, all of us beginning to train our minds to ignore minor distractions at critical points. Granted, ignoring a stinging pea strike was a long way from ignoring an actual injury and with just one immediate threat on the horizon it was easier to focus yourself to ignore it. An actual battle, as we all well knew, would be filled with threats and distractions of all types. Being able to hold your will in place during such trying times would be an almost incomprehensible challenge.

"And that's why," Laniel explained, "Seraph users that focus on large scale, battlefield altering effects train to trust in the comrades around them to keep them safe whilst they concentrate. It's not something that as Imperators you will be expected to do. You're trained to act independently and not as a battlefield unit and- Calidan, you've got your mouth open, what is it?"

I shut my mouth abruptly and blushed. "I-" I flailed for the sentence but words failed me. Not often an issue in my case.

Cassius spoke up, a broad smile on his face. "I think Calidan hadn't considered that Imperators might not be the only seraph users around. His brain is struggling to cope with understanding how he didn't guess at that."

Laniel grinned. It was a bright smile that made her normally diminutive features seem larger than life. "That's not like you Calidan!" she exclaimed. "Did you honestly believe that the Andurran empire would be the only ones to have seraph users? Have you never heard the stories of shamans, witches or those Bedouin wizards who live out in the desert?" she laughed softly at my puzzled brow. "And those are only the ones who are known by the townsfolk, the stories told by peasants and villagers to keep their young ones safe. Most countries have forces dedicated to understanding and utilising seraph though they may not know it by that name."

Sophia stuck a hand up. "How many countries do we know of?" she asked when Laniel nodded in her direction.

"The Meredothians to a small extent," Laniel replied, brow furrowed as she concentrated. "The Hrudan have some forces who specialise in that area, I imagine you would have met some of them if you had stayed much longer in that region. The Sethani empire down in Arunsea has some particularly skilled wielders; they specialise more in large-scale battle magic due to the nature of the terrain. The Academy has ties with their schools, it is quite possible that you will be sent over there to receive some training from a different perspective. The Rodani maintain a standing force of seraph users embedded within their military command. They are utilised almost like our empire would utilise a cavalry charge, their skills designed to lance into and demoralise foes who have already been engaged - I hear it's very effective for shattering morale and routing enemy forces." She pursed her lips as she looked towards the ceiling. "I am forgetting something...what is it...oh yes!" she exclaimed, "Us."

At that everyone looked taken aback. "What do you mean, 'us'?" queried Scythe hesitantly.

Laniel sniggered. "Did you honestly think that the Emperor would only have his Imperators have access to seraph? Before you attempt to answer, that's a completely rhetorical question – of course he wouldn't." She locked us all with a steely gaze. "I know you all think that Imperators are special, that you are the be all and end all for the Emperor and the empire. And in most cases that is true. You are trained to be the best. To work as individuals or in pairs and achieve what no other force in the world could achieve. However the Andurran empire is engaged on multiple fronts and has been for many years; its fighting forces are widely regarded as some of the best in the world. The Emperor's elite units, often referred to as the Dragons, are regarded as the most terrifying units within our forces and are able to wear extremely thick plate armour because they are subtly empowering themselves with seraph. They are trained to utilise it to empower themselves and to smash through enemy ranks. Rumour has it that a single squadron of Black Dragon Knights can rout an entire army almost single-handedly. And whilst we don't show it off, the Emperor does of course have a cadre of seraph users who specialise in large-scale battle magic. If they are brought out onto the battlefield it means that the Emperor is intending to wipe all survivors out. No mercy. He doesn't like other countries knowing the extent of his power."

"And the common folk know nothing about this?" Sophia asked incredulously. "What about the troops in the armies who see the seraph users in action?"

"Of course some would talk," Laniel replied, "but a few rumours here and there are useful. They make their way to the ears of enemy spies and make their masters worry about the might of Andurran armies. Of course, those physically closest to the cadre are men loyal to the Emperor through and through; they know full well not to speak of what they see. If one does? They tend to find themselves either reprimanded...or removed. As for the common folk, like I said, many of the common folk still worry about ghosts and demons. I believe there is still a haunted forest near Forgoth thanks to Seya," she said with a nod in my direction. "They worry lots and know little, often deriding what they do not know. Why do you think so many stories of hermits, medicine men and witches have them out in solitary locations far from people?

Their seraph powers tend to see them reviled even if they help people in need, their actions too strange for the peasantry to justify."

She sighed sadly. "In all my travels I have come across a small number who are trusting and happy and willing to give a shot to someone who is strange and unknown. They are by far the minority. Listen to this and this and well for it is advice for life. For the most part the common folk just want each day to continue as the last, for there to be food in their bellies and to sleep undisturbed. Anything that takes them out of this natural order of things is a threat. This includes wise folk, witches, wizards, shamans, whatever everyone wants to call them, and yes," she gave us all an appraising glance, "Imperators on a mission for the empire. You will never feel welcomed, not once they know your true nature. You are a sign that something is wrong, that there will be upset in the near future." A flash of grief passed over her face as she spoke, as though she was digging up memories long buried. "Some might actively work against you. Revile you. Hate you. After all, Imperators don't always have the best reputation. Honestly," she said after a moment's pause, "I really do hope you have better experiences with the local populations wherever you go."

She noticed Sophia's raised hand and gave a slow nod.

"What did you mean by Imperators not always having the best reputation?" Sophia asked.

Laniel gave a dark bark of laughter, quickly cut off. "I sometimes forget how little you Imps know. Imperators are the burning knife that lances any boil that encroaches upon the empire. Sometimes that boil is murderer, sometimes a monster and sometimes innocent people."

"Innocent?" Sophia murmured in shock, dismay plainly written across her face, "Why would we kill innocent people?"

"Sometimes it is seen as the only solution," Laniel replied in a low voice, her eyes blank as she lost herself in memories. "Sometimes the definition of innocence is in the eye of the beholder." She roused herself slightly and cast a strange look on Sophia. "Tell me, Sophia, have you heard of a Ranulskin?" At her head shake Laniel continued, "A Ranulskin is a type of monster that breeds incessantly. It does so by finding hosts and injecting them with eggs. The larger the host the better, and humans seem to be a particular favourite. These eggs can be hard to trace and as the majority of hosts are attacked whilst asleep they have no memory of it. What would you do if, as Imperators, you were sent to remove a Ranulskin threat and there happened to be a settlement near where it was last reported?"

"I... I?" Sophia grasped for an answer but none came.

"Ranulskin eggs take five days to gestate. So if you can't spare the time to wait and see if anyone was infected? There is perhaps only one logical path." Laniel's eyes clouded again as she spoke. "To put the town to the sword in the name of the Emperor. Logical, but not an act that wins the hearts and minds of the locals...These are decisions that may well come to pass for you in the future, so when and if they do please choose wisely." Shaking herself, as though shaking off the echoes of a past long forgotten, she forced a smile to her face and clapped her hands. "Enough of that," she said brightly to the subdued room. "Rikol, please stand up and show us what you have been working on. I'm sure we all need something to lift the mood."

As Laniel forced us back into a more upbeat class I couldn't help but wonder if that story was something that she herself had been a part of. As I knew full well, survivors of an attack like that would only hold burning, unbridled hatred within their hearts for the perpetrator. There could be any number of survivors from that or other similar situations biding their time and building their skills all in preparation to strike at the Empire for the actions of years long past.

As it turned out, I was more right than I could have known.

# CHAPTER 25

## *Lessons*

Seraph lessons were not the only new addition to our curriculum. Lessons on history, politics, geography, they had all been there in some small shape or fashion in the first few years but the focus had been very much on the combat arts. Now they ramped up in earnest. Geography involved not just a wider understanding of where countries lay in relation to the Andurran empire but the detailed understandings of the terrain that surrounded our borders. We studied the locations of potential choke points and areas that could be used to funnel enemy troops or that we would need to pass were we to invade. Moreover we were taught the locations of villages, towns and people who might be sympathetic to a fleeing Imperator.

Politics was an area that made my head spin. Sophia, Scythe and Ella took to it like ducks in water, minds running amok with thoughts of courtly intrigue. It interested me, but in more of a strategic sense. Whilst I imagined courtly balls to be fairly interesting events I had no desire to ensconce myself in such a world for long periods. I was sure that the inevitable web of intrigue, constant threat of assassin's daggers and two-faced witticisms would quickly drive me mad. At the same time however, the study of human behaviour was enthralling.

Instructor Laniel, who also took this class, would feed us the latest news from her spies, which at times seemed almost petulant.

'Lady Afrulia has a taste for young men, strong spirits and impropriety.' 'Lord Hayden's eyes follow the most buxom of mature ladies, but trysts are through no action of his own.'

At first information like this seemed like somewhat strange insights into people's personal lives, however Laniel was quick to show us just how easily personal information could be used against the individual and thus the country. She highlighted that Lady Afrulia's impropriety was well known and that she would likely not be fazed by the threat of blackmail and so whispers into her ear from a young lover might be more rewarding. Similarly, Lord Hayden would be easily ensnared by Laniel's positioning of a well-endowed widower who just so happened to lift some incriminating material during a sordid encounter, his youth and lady wife leaving him vulnerable to blackmail. The fact that she could see the potential outcomes for each course of action, recognise which pressures to bring to bear upon the individual and predict how they would respond was, frankly, astounding. Whether it was experiential or an innate skill I wasn't sure but I endeavoured to become more empathetic in the way that I interacted with people, to better understand from their perspective my actions and consequently be able to predict exactly what they would do.

History was, unsurprisingly, spent with Korthan. He and I had already spent much time in discussion over the past few years and you would think that this would make him an amiable instructor. You would be wrong. Korthan did not like teaching. He knew it, we knew it, and he made sure that we full well remembered it. The bonus was that we could sit within his small library and digest the books within, the downside was that asking him questions on any subject that he didn't feel was entertaining was almost as deadly as asking a troll if you could have your arm back - you'd be lucky to still have all your features after the verbal tirade he embarked upon if your question was deemed too dumb to answer. Things improved somewhat when Kane, likely recognising just how Korthan liked to work, stepped in and watched a session. He ordered Korthan to take a more active role in our training. I say some-what because we still got the angry rants and bitter rancour but it did at least give us dedicated reading and resulted in a more cohesive knowledge for the group.

There was one final class, but it was for myself only. The class for Great Hearts.

The first I knew of it was when I was in the forest with Seya and she stiffened in alarm. A deep rumble, deeper than anything I had heard her make before emanated from her chest, vibrating the trees around her.

*What's wrong?* I asked in bewilderment. My senses couldn't detect anything amiss.

*Something comes,* she replied. *Something large.*

*Skyren?* I instantly questioned, my mind jumping to the giant creature that we had killed in the desert caverns.

*If it is, then it moves with purpose. It is coming straight for us.*

With that she leapt forwards and sped off into the under-growth, and though I tried to follow behind I could no more match her speed than a kitten match its mother. Twin roars shattered the forest air, sending leaves and branches spiral-ling to the ground. The first was Seya's; deep and throaty. The second was something I hadn't heard before. It wasn't the monstrous roar of a Skyren - or at least the one that we had encountered. It was more harsh, sharp. I sped towards the sound, leaping logs and undergrowth, knives unsheathed in my hands. If something was attacking Seya I would make it pay.

The roars died down but I could still feel Seya's wariness. She wasn't hurt, of that I was sure, but she was so focused that she didn't respond to any of my questions. Preparing myself for the worst I broke through the undergrowth and into the clear-ing where Seya stood, teeth and claws partially bared, body quivering with barely restrained power. At first my eyes were only for Seya and it took me a moment to register that the orange mountain in front of her was not a mountain at all but a gigantic orangutan. A round face with bright, intelligent eyes lay in-between thick shoulders that led to massive yet dexterous hands that I knew would possess the kind of crushing power that I could only dream of. Instantly I knew what it was and why Seya was so wary. In front of her was something that could truly be considered a threat.

In front of her was a Great Heart.

"Please, don't be afraid," a soft and creaky voice said from the trees. "We mean you no harm."

"Show yourself then," I said with as much of a commanding voice as I could muster.

"As you wish," the voice replied and from behind a tree stepped a woman. She was short and stooped with grey hair, her face lined with wrinkles. She looked almost as ancient as Korthan. "It's a pleasure to meet you Calidan, Seya," she said brightly, nodding at each of us in turn.

"Who are you and how do you know our names?" I replied, feeling Seya bristle at my side.

"Borza and I know a great many things," she chuckled. "Your existence is just one of them." She waved a hand to forestall my response, "Don't get your panties in a twist boy, I'm on your side. My name is Anatha, and as you might have guessed this is my Great Heart, Borza."

Borza casually waved a cartwheel sized hand as its name was called, its eyes still on Seya.

"In answer to your next question, the Emperor sent us here. It seems he felt you might desire a little instruction.

"Instruction?" I replied slowly, stupefied.

A broad grin spread across her face, "Aye, instruction! Hell's teeth boy, the Emperor said you were smart, tell me straight; had he been drinking at the time?"

I couldn't stop a smile from spreading across my face, I could almost guarantee that she knew Korthan. "You're one of the

Emperor's Great Hearts," I replied, awe in my voice. "It's an absolute honour to meet you."

"I should say so," she cackled. "It's been too long since we've been let out to play. Especially for something so simple as teaching, so I have that at least to thank you for boy." She paused for a second as if listening and I knew that her Great Heart was speaking to her, just like Seya did to me.

With amused chastisement on her face she continued, "Borza says I need to reign myself in and deliver the Emperor's message. He's not wrong, so stay there and shut up for a moment." She rummaged in a bag at her side for a moment before retrieving a small scroll. Clearing her throat noisily she began to read.

*"Calidan, your usefulness to myself and the Empire has not gone unnoticed. You're turning into an excellent fighter and a fine strategist. However your skills with your Great Heart leave a lot to be desired. A Great Heart and its partner are one of the strongest assets I have and I intend for you both to reach your full potential so that you can be of greatest use to me. Anatha and Borza's time with you will be limited and must remain secret, so make best use of the time you have together and do not reveal anything to anyone at the Academy.*

*I am counting on you."*

A shadow seemed to pass over Anatha's face as she read the scroll but whether it was just a trick of the light or something more it was gone as soon as she noticed me looking. Instead she gave me a gap-toothed smile.

"So there you have it, straight from the Emperor himself," she said. "Under no circumstances are you to reveal my presence here. If you do I imagine you will find yourself..." she pursed her lips in thought, "removed." She gave me another smile and a wink as she said it. "I will be in the forest just after noon every other day for one whole hour. Do not be late. Understood?"

I nodded and then spoke up. "May I ask a few questions?"

A wheezy sigh. "If you must."

"What is your role with the Emperor, how old are you and why do I need to keep your presence secret from the Academy?"

She laughed. It wasn't the cackle from before but a vibrant, joyous sound. "He did say you were inquisitive," she replied once she had her laughter under control. "Perhaps I should have put a limit on the type of questions you asked me." A snort, "But then again, he is trusting you with many things so perhaps some information can be freely shared."

Nodding to herself she walked over to Borza and sat in his lap, reclining against his stomach. Once she was completely at ease she began.

"I am Anatha. I am one of the Great Hearts within the Emperor's inner circle. We are kept close as..." she coughed and Borza tensed, but her coughing fit settled and she leant back again, a rueful smile on her face, "...our powers are uniquely suited to support the Emperor. As I said, we are rarely outside of the citadel. If we are then it is for a mission of grave importance, like killing a king or quelling a rebellion...or apparently teaching a child." A big wink. "As for my age, that is a horrible thing to ask. Did your elders never teach you better? Shame on you."

Just as my face began to colour she chuckled. "I've seen one hundred and five winters."

I gasped, "But you don't look remotely that old! You look... sixty? Seventy?"

This time she gave a mad cackle, avid humour in her eyes. "Well aren't you a charmer?" she said, wiping a tear from her eye. "Yes I look younger than I am, being bonded to a Great Heart gives you a long life. It would be longer except-" she broke off and waved her hand, "well, never mind why. Suffice to say I am old. And naturally in the view of your tiny brain that enhanced age of mine makes me very, very wise indeed." A cheeky grin. "So listen close when I speak and never ever contradict me for," she took a deep breath and raised her hands to the sky, adopting as powerful a voice as I suspected she could manage, "I am infallible and all knowing."

Silence echoed around the glade.

*I think she was right about being cooped up too long.*

I titled my head in amusement, *perhaps she has it backward, maybe the Emperor doesn't let her out because she is so...*

*Eccentric?*

*I would have gone with crazy.*

We shared silent laughter at the old woman's antics and when I opened my eyes I saw Anatha watching me with a suspicious glare. "You think it isn't obvious when you're talking with your Great Heart? You've got to get better at hiding your feelings and communication boy. It's too easy to read that you're talking to someone or something. And if I can recognise it then the Enemy can recognise it too."

"Enemy?" I replied with confusion, feeling like she had put particular emphasis on the word. "What enemy do you mean in particular? The Hrudan?"

"The Hrudan?!" she shrieked. "No, not the fucking Hrudan, what's wrong with you? The Hrudan are barely a piss stain in the annals of history. No boy. I'm talking about The Enemy." She finished the sentence with an expectant air.

"...And who is that?" I finally asked when it was clear she wasn't going to say anything else.

"That is well above your pay grade," she clarified with a smirk. "But rest assured that the small encounters and wars that the Andurran Empire conducts barely register on the Emperor's mind. His focus is always on the Enemy, planning stratagems, strikes and counter strikes unknown and unseen by practically everyone, but their effects reverberate around the world. This does segue nicely into my answer to your next question however. The reason that you are not to inform anyone at the Academy about my presence is that we suspect that someone inside is working with the Enemy."

# CHAPTER 26

## *Suspicions*

"What do you mean, someone is working with the Enemy?" I said, shocked. "Are you saying that you don't trust people at the Academy? It's the Imperator Academy for crying out loud, it's meant to train those most loyal to the Empire. How can it house a threat?"

"The Enemy is insidious," Anatha said softly, and I could see grief warring on her face. "It seduces, beguiles and entraps. You have seen it in action before I believe."

It took me a moment to figure out what she meant and then it clicked into place. "Rya," I breathed. I hadn't thought about her in some time now that the nightmares of a cavern of darkness and bone and the death of Brother Gelman had receded to be replaced by more recent horrors. "She came from the Academy...I remember her last words, 'they have my family.' You think someone here is responsible for that, don't you?"

"We do."

"Do you know who?"

"We have suspects."

"But you're not going to tell me?"

She gave a soft smile. "I can tell you haven't been in this game long boy. Do you honestly think Imperators and their ilk survive by just blurting out secrets to people they have just met? Whilst the file on you suggests you can likely be trusted I will make up my own mind before revealing any more. So you will know what I want you to know and no more. Understood?"

I scowled; arms crossed. Why bring me in so far only to hold me at arm's length? It was so frustrating!

She didn't respond to my angry gaze, just watched me, her eyes betraying nothing. Finally I relented. "Fine," I muttered. "Have it your way."

She gave me a smile that exposed her many missing teeth. "Excellent. I'm glad you see sense." She gave me an appraising look. "So... with a panther like yours I am guessing an increase to your speed, agility and strength and some more refined features like hearing and scent?"

I nodded, impressed.

She scoffed. "Idiot. That's the basic sum of everyone who has a Great Heart. They make you stronger, faster and a slew of other enhancements. Practically every animal has better senses than we do, so whilst the strength of the benefits might change - a bull Great Heart might bestow higher strength on its partner for instance - many of the basic aspects are very similar." She gave a lazy wave that encompassed herself and Borza, "You haven't met us before, what would you imagine Borza's particular talents to be?"

*To be a damned dirty ape*, Seya muttered.

I fought down a snigger. "Considering how mountainous he is, I imagine his strength is considerable, and whilst I haven't met any apes or monkeys before, I have read about them. I believe they are meant to be very intelligent. So perhaps that somehow improves your own as well?"

She gave me an appraising look. "Not half bad for an idiot. Yes, Borza is strong, incredibly so in fact. All Great Hearts are intelligent, as you know, and with the benefits of their long lives and large brains they are often more intelligent than any one human.

*Often?* Seya snorted. *Always.*

"Yet Borza is exceptional, even for Great Hearts. And yes, much like the associated strength and healing we all share, bonding with Borza has given me a boost to my own intellect. Whether it was a significant boost would depend on how intelligent I was as a child but as we bonded very young I can't remember a time without Borza, so you will have to find out for yourself. But enough of that." She shook herself. "The Emperor ordered me here to better your partnership with Seylantha and so that is what we will focus on."

"When you say better our partnership," I began curiously, "What exactly do you mean?"

"To make you a more effective duo and to make sure you are fully taking advantage of the bond," Anatha said simply.

"But-" I began.

"But Seylantha and I are one and the same," she cut in with a mockery of my voice. "We're perfect just as we are." She looked me in the eyes and spoke seriously, "No, you aren't. The Emperor has commanded you to learn. So learn."

I shrank back under the weight of her gaze. "Yes Ma'am."

"Good," she said, satisfied. "This training will get you to work more effectively as a pair until you're anticipating each other's needs. Your ability to draw on the bond will also be increased." She sighed at my hand that I had raised into the air. "Yes, idiot?"

"Can you explain what you mean by drawing on the bond?"

Another sigh, this one long and pained. "Drawing on the bond is the primary reason Great Hearts exist - or more accurately were created - as you know from your encounter with Ash. You do it every day at a level that you don't even recognise. This is what gives you your enhanced abilities. You've been severely hurt before, yes?"

I nodded.

"Did Seylantha mention anything to you about providing more energy to heal you?"

I cast my mind back. "She did," I said softly. "She also refused to let me provide her with more energy to heal her if the situation was reversed."

Anatha's gaze softened. "A commendable desire but your Great Heart is in the right of it." She tapped Borza's side. "Aside from being my partner in crime and best friend, Borza is essentially a giant well of resources. And I don't just mean seraph, though their seraph pools are massive and are the most intended option to draw from. Seya's ability to push healing into you is essentially her pushing her own energy into you, this abundance of life force pushes your body to heal itself at a supercharged rate. She does this at the cost of using her own energy, so if she used too much she could be left weak and defenceless...or even die. The reason why Seya told you not to do what you asked is because she is so much bigger and, for lack of another word, denser than you."

Anatha held up a hand and waved off Seya's growl. "Easy, I don't mean that in terms of intellect. I mean in terms of sheer mass and energy usage. Simply put," she said, fixing me with a steely gaze, "Seylantha can heal you because you are small and she has vast amounts of energy to spare. You are small and have limited amounts of energy - all of which you need to keep your own body running. Pushing your energy into hers is barely a drop in the ocean to her. She could consume your energy entirely and probably not recognise a significant change in energy levels. Does that make sense?"

Sadly it did and was my single worst fear. Seya getting hurt and myself not being able to do anything to save her had weighed on my mind ever since she had first forbidden that approach to me.

*But there had to be a way, right?*

"People have tried Calidan," Anatha said in a soft voice and I could tell she knew what I had been thinking. "Obviously people have. Great Hearts are more than any friend or lover. We know each other through and through. The pain at seeing your bonded hurt is unbearable, believe me. I know of not one person who has survived trying to bring their Great Heart back from serious injury. It is just too easy for one's life force to be snuffed out like a candle. But even so, with all that being said, if Borza were dying I couldn't honestly tell you if I would follow the rules."

I smiled at her for that. Perhaps she wasn't quite as curmudgeonly as I had thought.

She smiled back with eyes warm and full of compassion, and with a swift movement that vastly belied her age threw a stick at my head.

"But I am very old as you have already pointed out! I'm going to die relatively soon right? So who cares?! You're young so stop being an idiot and don't go attempting to save Seya when and if she gets hurt."

"Point made," I said stiffly as I rubbed my forehead. She had surprisingly good accuracy.

"I hope so," she replied as Borza let out a barking chuckle. "But let's not dwell on that because it is a sad and dark path. Healing is not the only thing that can be forcibly enhanced through the bond. Everything that you are currently feeling from your Great Heart is because of energy travelling through your bond. Your strength, speed and attuned senses. Each one is something that your body is taking from hers as we speak. And just like with health, Seya could push more energy down that particular path, making you stronger or faster than before at the cost of her own energy levels." She considered me for a moment, her gaze piercing. "I imagine that at this point you can hit hard enough to break men without much effort. My guess is Seya could uproot one of these trees quite easily." She turned her head to watch Seya's reaction. "Well?"

Seya looked at the mighty oaks that formed the forest that we were in, considering. *Their roots are strong and deep but I could topple one without too much strain,* she clarified. *They would be easier to swipe through.* She slowly extended her gleaming claws, pretending not to be watching Borza intently as she carefully cleaned each one. *One hit.*

I smirked. Seya was a cat above all else. She hated the thought that Borza might be stronger, but if it was true she would just bask in the fact that she would do everything *better*.

"You would be right," I answered Anatha. "Am I to assume that if I borrowed power from Seya that I could do the same?"

"Exactly," Anatha confirmed. "And at risk of leaving your Great Heart with less power. As you have probably found out the bond is more effective in close proximity. If you are on the other side of the world you can barely hear each other let alone transfer great quantities of energy. So if both of you are in a hostile environment then you have to make a tactical choice as to whether to draw on that extra energy. If Seya is involved in her own battle at the time it could weaken her and result in defeat. Even if she isn't she will be tired from the drain and will need to recuperate over the next few days."

*Did you know all this?* I asked Seya.

*Of course,* she answered, sedately licking a paw.

*Then why didn't you tell me?*

She stopped licking and swivelled her head to pierce me with those mesmerising orbs. I hadn't realised she could pull off sardonic so well. *You have got into enough trouble with just the benefits of the bond as they are. I can only imagine how much danger you will throw yourself into when you grow overconfident after punching through a tree that can't punch you back.*

*I wouldn't-*

*You would.*

*I-*

*You would.*

Sigh. *Yeah, you're probably right.*

A smug look. *Me being right is never in doubt.*

"Are you two done?" Anatha asked, jerking me out of my thoughts.

I smiled sheepishly. "Sorry," I replied.

"For communicating with your Great Heart? Don't be. You just have to learn how to do it whilst holding another conversation at the same time so that no-one suspects what you're doing."

"That sounds...impossible," I replied, brow furrowed. "Holding two conversations and being active in both at once, how would you focus on either?"

"Honestly, it might well be impossible for you, for, as you know, I've established that you are a simpleton," she replied with a shrug. "I've never taught someone how to better themselves at being bonded to a Great Heart before so I can only go by what I can do. And as I can do everything so much better than you it will be interesting to see where you fall down."

She seemed completely serious, even with the broad grin on her face. Perhaps she could manage to handle two conversations at once, it was doubtful but in the end the only real question was whether I could.

"So when does training start?" I asked.

A wicked grin crossed her face. "Right now."

# CHAPTER 27

## *Anatha*

Training with Anatha and Borza was mentally and physically exhausting to the extent that I was grateful for the breaks her absences afforded me. All of us pushed ourselves so hard at the Academy that the extra hour of training at times nearly broke me.

I say at times because training would alternate between trying to hold a clear conversation with Anatha whilst simultaneously trying to relay information to Seya as we separately moved through the forest. This was mentally taxing to the extreme but the only physical hardship was the stick or stone that would inevitably get thrown at me when my concentration slipped. Other days would consist of hunting and fighting, Borza and Anatha forcing Seya and myself to work together to try and bring them down. The latter reminded me of our time with Tracker, split second attacks from Anatha mid-conversation forcing Seya and I to react independently but maintaining knowledge of each other's actions so that we could counter attack effectively. Against any normal humans we wouldn't be remotely challenged, but Anatha by herself was anything but normal - her frail looking frame able to be filled with terrifying power - and when paired with Borza and the uncanny ability to predict each other's moves they were a terrifying force to be reckoned with.

It wasn't their combined power that was most difficult to deal with. Seya's speed more than made a match for Borza's overwhelming strength and if we were utilising the normal power of our bonds I was a fraction faster than Anatha, allowing me to dodge the majority of blows she sent my way. What Seya and I couldn't seem to beat was the speed of their thoughts and reactions. They moved almost as one being, casually defending and attacking with each other in perfect synchronicity. It was a level of understanding and unseen communication that a team of kaschan practitioners could only dream of achieving and they did it with no apparent effort.

Seya and I had fought against each other often but we did not have much practice with working together to defeat an opponent and it showed. When Borza and Anatha attacked it was an overwhelming deluge of attacks that left nothing to chance and no openings to take advantage of. Borza would seek to force us to defend against his might, using just his fists or whatever nearby log took his fancy to lay unrelenting blows in our direction. If we stayed still to defend then Anatha would take advantage of her small stature to slip around Borza's attacks and punish us from oblique angles. She would do it in such a way that she would know without looking where his next attack was coming from and already be moving to be a hairsbreadth out of the way, ready to attack. Compared to the two of them, Seya and I were babes in the wood. We could fight and we could fight well, yet we lacked the cohesion that made the duo so devastating. It was likely that we could fight and win in an ambush scenario - Seya's nature made such an approach her speciality - but Anatha and Borza weren't interested in what we could already do, they were there to punish and break until we were forced to become better versions of ourselves.

Little by little our abilities improved. Seya and I began to flow more seamlessly in combat, working to each other's strengths and weaknesses. It didn't happen overnight but much like

with our combat training with Tyrgan we slowly progressed
to the point where the fighting almost seemed manageable. In
a month of training we didn't win - didn't even come close -
but we began to be able to fend them off for longer periods of
time which I definitely counted as success. Anatha seemed to
come alive during these bouts, disparaging comments about
my ineptitude notwithstanding. She gave the impression that
teaching us was a chore yet revelled in being outside. I
couldn't help but feel sorry for her that she was spending so
much time within the citadel but she blankly refused to speak
of her time there and her normal day to day activities.

As promised, I didn't tell anyone about their presence within
the forest. It helped that the rest of the team were all focusing
on improving their own skill sets in their own time whether it
be martial, knowledge or seraph, and so my excuse of fighting
Seya for practice was easily swallowed and quickly forgotten.
During my other classes at the Academy I kept an eye out for
anything out of the ordinary, trying to locate any Instructor
that might have had reason to hate the Empire, and then
cursed myself for being a fool. I had no way of knowing everyone's personal details, their backstories or their motivations.
Even if I did, Rya's personal details had looked flawless until
she suddenly disappeared. As Anatha had said, the Enemy was
insidious and recognising that someone was under its sway
was practically impossible.

Considering her words on the 'Enemy' and its abilities I began
to suspect black seraph at play. Recalling Ash's words on
the history of seraph I knew that black seraph had the ability to cloud minds and control actions. Unfortunately that
knowledge earned me precisely zero benefits. I had no way of
determining who was a user of black seraph or if someone was
under its influence. As far as I knew the Academy had no such
thing as a seraph detector. Whilst the technology there was
cutting edge with the latest weaponry and methods of teaching it paled in comparison to the alien looking technology
that had been within the desert. The only place I could com-

pare Ash's complex to was the Emperor's citadel...

I frowned. *Maybe the Emperor would have such a thing as a seraph detector at the citadel? If so then we just needed an excuse to get all the Imperators into the heart of the Empire.* I made a note to ask Anatha when I next saw her if such a thing would be possible. *Could all the Imperators actually be collected together for one event? Even the ones on a mission?* The more I thought about it the more I realised that Anatha and I needed access to the Academy's records. If we could identify every individual who had had access to Rya during her time at the Academy and designed an event to bring them all back together then we could be on to something.

Even knowing that it was meant to be practically impossible to detect someone under the sway of black seraph I still felt like there had to be something that I could do. I began to have difficulty sleeping, anxious that someone, somewhere within the Academy was a threat. To help settle my nerves, or perhaps to soothe my conscience that I was doing everything possible to identify the enemy within our ranks I began to roam the Academy grounds at night. Often Seya joined me, the pair of us slipping around anyone returning late from the dining hall, moving as shadows in the night, and other times I casually strolled the cobbled paths of the campus, basking in the silence and shimmering starlight. Sometimes the early morning silence was broken by a disturbance, whether it was the muted cries of lovers having a tryst away from the prying eyes of their dorm or more frustratingly the angry shouts and pained grunts as students brawled in scenes reminiscent of our first encounter at the Academy. For these moments I would often stand and watch in the shadows, remembering Kane's reasoning behind Kirok. The first time I saw someone lift a cobble was when I first stepped in, sweeping his legs out from under him and grabbing the heavy stone as it fell.

"Cool off," I barked at the drunken boy's face. "You're not here to kill your classmates. Go and sleep it off."

As expected he and his friends didn't take the interruption

lightly, swinging and flailing with a complete lack of grace and skill. I sighed. *First years.* Had I really been so inept once? Diffusing the situation took less than thirty seconds. The hardest part was making sure that they weren't permanently injured, just bruised and damaged enough that their desire to inflict harm was outweighed by the need to curl up in a ball.

And that is how my reputation and nickname of the Academy Shadow began.

Fights between first years were something that could be easily broken up. After the first few interventions it simply became a matter of walking into view and both parties would instantly back down, knowing that it was foolish to try and fight me. The same could not be said of higher-grade students. You would think that fighting throughout the day would leave you too tired to want to fight further but the Academy had nothing if not students who were keen for a fight. Brawls between third years or above were rarer but they did still happen. And when they did they were much more vicious, though usually with less intent to kill. Only twice did I take it upon myself to step in. The first when it was a gang of third years against a group of first years. The overwhelming difference in skill annoyed me and so I stepped in on behalf of the first years. What resulted was an enjoyable fight of eight on one that tested my ability with regards to being able to put someone down with the minimal amount of fuss. The amusing thing was that I knew some of the third years having fought against them as a fourth year in evening sparring sessions. They had known as I stepped into the light that what happened next was going to hurt but the challenge was too much fun for them to back down. When they were all safely on the floor the majority were smiling or laughing, happy to have had a decent fight.

The second instance was much worse. Some sort of altercation had led to three groups of third and fourth years fighting with weapons. I didn't know the backstory but they were out for blood and by the time I got there two were already on the floor cradling wounds. This time I couldn't hold back, the threat of blades made the chance of someone dying too real. As the groups clashed I attacked from behind, knocking people unconscious where possible, disarming or breaking wrists and forearms where needed. Dancing between the blades felt so natural to me at this point that there was no hint of fear, just an overwhelming joy at the action of movement. I understood why Anatha had such a grin on her face when she fought - to be this good at something and not have the opportunity to do it regularly would be extremely frustrating. When I finished four people lay on the floor unmoving, six held limp arms and a further three lay in pools of vomit clutching their crotches.

As I stepped back from the carnage a familiar voice spoke up, "Can't sleep Calidan?"

Kane.

He was standing at the side of the dining hall with his arms folded, his body half coated in shadow. He nodded at the group of groaning Imps, "Nicely done. I wondered if you would show this evening."

"You knew this was going to happen?" I asked, frowning.

He shrugged. "They've been at each other's throats for the past few days. It was building to something, that's why we've been keeping an eye out. But I was hoping for the... 'Academy Shadow' to turn up and save the day instead of us staff having to step in." He nodded over to the other side of the courtyard and following his gaze I saw Instructor Laniel raise a hand in greeting before vanishing around the corner towards the medical centre, doubtless going to find the medicae. "Your night time habits have become known throughout the Academy. Kudos."

I snorted. "Seemed like a better thing to do than lie in bed not sleeping."

A grin. "Walk with me." It was an order, not a request.

Complying I fell into pace with him and we left the courtyard of injured students behind. No one was damaged severely enough that they wouldn't recover given enough rest. The

Academy medicae were some of the best in the empire at what they did and so I didn't feel too bad for resorting to breaking limbs.

"Something weighing on your mind?" Kane asked after a few minutes of silence. "You haven't been sleeping much lately."

"I don't know if it is anything specific," I replied after a few moments. "I don't feel particularly stressed or anxious but when I get into bed I just can't sleep. Going out and walking the Academy grounds just seemed like the better option. Getting into all that," I waved my hand behind us, "just kinda happened. I had to step in at times."

He nodded. "I know," he murmured. "You've done a good job, no-one seriously injured and only stepping in when things are going to get deadly. I have no problems with your actions. I just wanted to make sure that if there was something that you needed to talk about then you know you can talk to me." He locked me with a friendly gaze. "So tell me Calidan, is there anything you want to talk about?"

*Was he just being nice or is he searching for something?* I scrambled in my brain for a response. "N-no!" I blurted out. *Smooth Calidan.* I cursed. "I mean, it's appreciated but no thank you Kane. I don't know why I can't sleep but there is nothing that I know of that I need to talk about."

He regarded me intently for a few moments before nodding. "Fair enough Calidan, my door is open if you need me. I would suggest you take yourself to bed but as that seems to not be an option try not to get into any trouble for the rest of the morning, okay?"

"You've got it sir," I replied, relieved.

He gave me a grin and turned to go. Walking a few paces he stopped and turned as though he had forgotten something. "Oh, and Calidan?"

"Yes Instructor?"

"Tell Anatha I said hello."

My stomach plummeted. "A-Anatha?" I said, trying to keep the alarm out of my voice. "I'm not sure who you mean."

He snorted. "Anatha always likes to think that she is the cleverest one out there and she likely is. However because of her brilliance she often overlooks things, like how a seraph user of Laniel's talent doesn't need to physically search through a forest to see where you have been going. She should know that the Academy keeps tabs on its students. Especially now."

*Balls.* I gave in. "I'll let her know Instructor. Do you want her to meet with you?"

"No, no. Nothing of the sort. Your training with Seya looks to be paying off well so her visits here are welcome. As of this moment only Laniel, Korthan and myself are aware - that we know of anyway. If she wants to meet with me she can arrange it however she likes. Her rank is such that I couldn't refuse a meeting even if I wanted to."

I gave him a warm smile. "I understand sir, I'll let her know." It felt strangely nice to have someone else know my secret, even if it was Kane and not one of my friends.

"Good man," Kane said. "Don't let her bully you too much. But you've got a friendship with Korthan so you should know how to deal with crotchety old bastards."

"Korthan, sir?" I asked, confused. "What's he got to do with this?"

He looked momentarily taken aback. "Don't you know?" he asked a frown furrowing his brow. "No, of course you wouldn't," he muttered. "She wouldn't tell you herself." His frown disappeared to be replaced by a cheeky grin, "Well Calidan you get this one for free. Korthan is Anatha's youngest son." And with that he walked off into the night, leaving me dumbfounded.

*   *   *

"Kane knows," I said as I walked into the clearing. "As does Instructor Laniel and Korthan."

Anatha fixed me with a steely gaze. "You been talking, boy?"

"No," I replied calmly, keeping a close eye on Borza's meaty fists. "Kane said that you didn't think that a seraph user of Laniel's ability wouldn't be keeping tabs on me."

A crevasse of a frown opened up on the old woman's forehead and then she let fly with the most impressive string of curses that I had ever heard. By the time she was done she was blue in the face and I felt like I needed to wash my ears out with soap. Even Seya looked taken aback.

"Well," she finally said when she was done. "I guess it can't be helped. Time was that the Academy didn't bother to track its students by seraph so I..." she looked pained as she finished, "overlooked that avenue."

"I imagine that with the Rya case they are likely keeping much closer tabs on everyone," I replied apologetically. "Also, both Kane and Korthan say hello."

Her eyes narrowed at me once again and then she let out a heavy sigh. "So you know eh?"

I nodded. "Kane told me. I went and had a chat with Korthan. He said you and he hadn't seen each other in some time and usually kept in touch via mail. Why haven't you gone to see him?"

For a moment Anatha's gaze wavered, as though I had touched a nerve, but then it was gone, her steel resolve hardened. "Because if I go there and make contact now then I am not sure that I would be able to do what must be done if he is under the control of the Enemy."

"You would kill your own son?" I gasped, horrified.

"If I must. The Emperor has willed that the tainted here be rooted out and exorcised. The only way that I know to remove the control of black seraph is through either the sheer mental will of the host or death."

I thought furiously. "That can't be true," I replied after a long moment. "Cassius was hurt a couple of years ago, Rya hit him with a lance made of shadow. It spread through his body like some kind of disease. The Emperor managed to save him, to remove its infection."

"The Emperor is probably the one person in the empire who could do such a thing," Anatha said with a nod. "His control over seraph is astounding and his pool is practically limitless. From what I heard however the assault on your friend's body was not one of mental control, it was black seraph running rampant, warping and destroying everything it touched. Most seraph will do the same if flooded into a person. It is a horrible way to die." I could tell by the way she said the last few words that she was speaking from first-hand experience.

"Someone who has fully succumbed to control of the Enemy may not even know it," Anatha said softly, her gaze far away. "Someone like my son may have claws in their brain and not be aware. Those claws are directly linked to the black seraph user's will and that user has complete control. With very little threat to themselves they can manipulate the individual, force them to do things or, perhaps worse, force them to do things and not remember their actions."

"How is that worse?" I murmured, aghast.

She gave a soft snort. "I forget how little you know. The user of the black has to be actively controlling the target. As soon as their attention moves elsewhere the host can act as they will. If they let you remember the actions that you are taking that means that they do not need you once your mission is done. Otherwise they would just blank your memory and that way continually make use of you as a spy or saboteur."

"And what would they do once your mission is done?"

"Remember I said claws in your brain?" she asked. I nodded. "Imagine those claws raking through all that soft tissue. It's a messy and unpleasant sight. It is also the reason why it is so hard for someone to excise the control of a black user. The Emperor might have the skill, yes, but he would have to attempt to keep those claws from slicing into the individual's brain whilst forcing the black seraph out, whereas all the user has to do is leave whilst causing as much damage as possible. It is an almost impossible battle."

"What about the other method?" I asked.

She sighed heavily. "The other method is a very rare occurrence. The host has to come to the realisation that they are under someone else's control and to have the mental fortitude and seraph skill to be able to start picking apart the strands of black seraph within their brain without alerting the user. They may get away with it if the user does not check in with them for some time, but if the user comes back and finds their control fragmented then the host's usefulness becomes short-lived."

"Sounds like a nightmare," I whispered.

She nodded in agreement. "It is. It is why fighting against the Enemy is so consuming, both in terms of time and of will. Once you have seen friends become enemies enough times it drains you until you feel hollow." She looked old and withered as she said this, as though some spark of essential vitality was sputtering within her.

I moved close and put a hand on her shoulder. I didn't say anything and just stood there with her for a moment, providing her with what solidarity I could offer. A long second later she stood and wiped something from her eye. When she looked at me again she was once more Anatha, iron willed and steel spined.

"Tell me," I asked, "does the citadel have seraph detectors? Ash spoke of them, she said that they could detect different types of seraph."

Eyes curious, she tilted her head in thought. "Rumour has it that the doorway to the Emperor's inner sanctum is a seraph detector but it has not been operational within my lifetime. The doorway is ancient, whatever magic or energy was used to power the device failed long ago."

*Damn.* Though in retrospect it could never have been that easy. Life for me never was.

"What about if we could find a working version of whatever powers it? Or what about getting the Emperor himself to power it?"

She mused for a moment, fingers on her chin. "The Emperor is possibly the only person alive who may know what to do with such a device. I will have to ask. Your plan; I'm presuming that you intend for some kind of gathering within the citadel that requires every Imperator to pass through the seraph detector?"

"Every Imperator who had access to Rya," I replied. "Though every Imperator and every Imp would be most effective. There could well be more than one person being controlled, especially considering the time that has passed since the incident with Rya. If the Enemy is as insidious as you say then it is unlikely that they stopped with controlling her. Indeed why did they bother to control her at all if there was the option for more powerful Imperators available?"

"There are ways to prevent control by black seraph," Anatha answered. "Some basic defences that once taught provide some modicum of security - making it hard to gain control of someone from a distance. Every fully fledged Imperator has this ability. Direct control would have to come from being physically touched. This defence only comes out of power born of seraph and so is unavailable to anyone under fourth year at the Academy."

"Leaving the earlier years vulnerable," I said, brow furrowed.

"Vulnerable yes, but not as much of a threat," Anatha replied. "Rya must have had her seraph awakened to be able to use the abilities she did. That suggests the person who corrupted her had close access to her. Either that or the Enemy has a method of using a person as a conduit, as an extension for his own power - but I can only imagine the amount of seraph that would consume."

I remembered the coils of black smoke that had wrapped around Rya in the cave. Seraph was largely an internal power; certain side effects were given off when powering large abilities but it usually corresponded in a flood of light. That thick, black smoke had seemed almost *alive.*

"I think the latter might be more accurate," I said slowly. "And my guess is that Merowyn or Simone would say the same. The black smoke that wrapped around Rya, it didn't seem like it was a benefit for her. I think this Enemy was there, watching and interfering directly."

Anatha inclined her head. "We may never know for certain. We can only hypothesise at this point. If it is possible for the Enemy to do this then we may have to take extra precautions at the Academy. Corrupted Imps with advanced combat skills are one thing. Corrupted Imps who can be wielded as a channel for black seraph are another thing entirely." She gave a long sigh. "This would all be made much easier if we could replicate the seraph detectors. But that knowledge has long slipped from our grasp. More's the pity."

"Could the Emperor create a new one?" I asked. "Isn't creation by seraph a matter of will?"

"Theoretically yes," she replied. "Anyone could do it. But as I am sure that you have been learning in your classes, creation of something simple, like a shield, is much easier than something complicated. You have to have an innate understanding of what you are making. That means that in order to create a seraph detector out of seraph you need to fully understand how each part of it works, and believe me Calidan, technologies that came before the Cataclysm? They were on a whole other level. Humanity as it is now is barely a fraction of what it once was. I haven't the faintest understanding behind most of the technology at the citadel and I have been researching it for decades! If the overriding structure still works and it is the power device that has failed then it would be in our best interest to retrieve a functioning one."

"And do you know where one is?"

"Not yet," she replied. "But the Emperor has his ways. I'll have a talk with him and decide what our next steps should be." She shook her head and punched me in the shoulder. "But that is for next time. Get your arse in gear, it's time for training."

# PART III

*Revelations*

# CHAPTER 28

## *Journey*

I didn't see Anatha for two weeks after that conversation. She sent a message for me to practice taking strength from Seya and that I would hear from her in the near future and that was it.

Learning how to borrow energy from Seya was a strange process. It felt like I was stealing from her, even though she was adamant that it did not hurt and that her energy would replenish much more quickly than mine. Through much cajoling I finally managed to learn how to draw energy along our bond to fill myself with power. It was slow going and a long way from the rapid transfer that Anatha had said was possible, but it was very much a start. Boosting my strength made me feel like I could crush the world beneath my fingers and it was only Seya's sarcastic commentary that kept my ego from getting too inflated.

Speed was a strange one too. I was already fast thanks to Seya's bond but enhanced speed had me feeling like I was jogging through the forest faster than my previous sprint. The main downside was that it didn't improve my reaction time, meaning that I could seriously hurt myself if I went faster than my brain could handle. This was one of the reasons that Anatha and Borza's bond was so effective.

Two weeks after Anatha left I stood in Kane's office at his request. On his desk was a thick parchment letter complete with the gilded seal of the Emperor. He regarded me with curious eyes.

"What do you think this is Calidan?" he asked, pointing at the letter.

"Looks like a letter from the Emperor sir," I replied, feigning nonchalance.

"And do you know what this letter contains?"

"No sir," I said truthfully, with a shake of my head.

Kane picked up the letter, lowered some reading glasses onto his nose and began to read. "Imperator Kane, I seek a pair of competent fourth years to complete a negotiation with the Sunfa clan. They have something that I desire but will only deal in person. Relations are somewhat strained at the moment as the Sunfa are an obtuse and difficult tribe to work with, however I imagine that this will form the perfect opportunity for a learning session for a pair of competent Imps. I envisage this task will require someone with great will, great strength and most importantly a great heart to achieve success.

Find them, send them on horseback to the Anafor ferry. My contact will meet them there in three days."

He finished reading out the letter and took off his glasses, rubbing the bridge of his nose. "As you know we do send out our higher years for training, however it is usually with cordial relations in order to improve your knowledge of their home and learn certain etiquette. The Sunfa are a small clan that live in the Ellendar swamps of Mustovar. They tend not to trade with outsiders, preferring to be self-sufficient. As such relatively little is known of them. The Emperor obviously knows more than he is letting on in this letter and I can only presume from its contents that the mission's chance of success will be much higher if you and Seya go. Are you okay with this?"

I could barely contain my excitement. "Of course Instructor!" I said eagerly. "My thanks for the opportunity."

"Oh I doubt it is something that *I* have done that has provided you with this trip," Kane replied drily. "Out of your dorm who would you like with you?"

"Cassius," I said instantly. It needed no thought.

"I thought you might say that," Kane said. "You'll find him outside. Adronicus will make sure you're kitted out. You have two hours and then I want you out the door. Follow the high-road south following signs for the Anafor ferry. You'll be there in two days if you travel fast. The ferry will take you to Port Cambal and from there it is a four-day ride into Mustovar. The swamps are roughly a day's ride from where you will enter the country. Adronicus will provide you with a map, food, money and clothing. Take whatever weapons suit you both best."

He gave me an appraising look. "Whilst we are not directly sending you into combat this time Calidan do not mistake this for anything other than a real mission. I do not know who your contact will be at the ferry but they will have other information. Whatever the mission is I am sure that between you, Cassius and Seya you will be able to handle it. Just remember your training, plan your escape and leave violence as a last resort."

He stood and offered me his hand. "Best of luck Calidan, go in the Emperor's name."

Outside I found Cassius, his gaze uncertain. He brightened when he saw me and excitement lit his features when I explained the task ahead of us. He practically bounced as we headed back to the dorm to tell the others. Rikol was the only one who wasn't envious. I'm not even sure if he heard what we were doing or where we were going as he was that engrossed in whatever seraph project he was working on. We quickly gathered a few choice belongings, Cassius making sure to take Asp from the side of his bed, and I left to find Adronicus, giving Cassius some time to say a proper goodbye to Ellie.

Arriving at the weapon master's building I found him sharpening a cavalry sabre. The wider tip and heavier weight made for devastating cuts that could power through weak blocks put up by opponents.

He looked up as I walked in and gave me a sharp smile. "Welcome Calidan," he said, voice gruff. "I took the liberty of preparing this for you. Your strength should allow you to wield it as easily as any other weapon and I know that you prefer sabres." He proffered the blade hilt first.

I took the weapon and inspected it, testing the edge with my thumb. He had done a fine job, the blade drawing a thin line of blood where it pressed lightly against my skin.

"This will do nicely Adronicus, thank you," I replied. He grunted in response and stood, grabbing two packs.

"For you and Cassius," he said, passing them over. "Food and supplies for three weeks if you ration it carefully." He handed over a scabbard and I carefully slid the oversized cavalry sabre into it before attaching it to my waist. Adronicus then passed over a black leather jacket, its fabric heavy in my arms.

"Not quite an Imperator jacket," he murmured as he passed it over. "But it will protect you from minor slashes. Not that I would make a habit of letting anyone hit you though."

I snorted and slipped into the jacket, feeling it hang comfortably across my shoulders before spilling down to stop just around my ankles. The leather was thick and comfortable, the inside of the jacket filled with deep pockets that could hide a wide array of tools and weaponry. Fully fledged Imperators had full length jackets that had extra linings of some clever material sewn into the inside that offered decent protection against most cuts and even some protection against thrusts. It wouldn't dissipate the power behind the blows, still resulting in broken limbs and ribs, but it could turn a mortal blow into something more manageable. This leather jacket was a pale comparison to those exquisite pieces of workmanship, but still provided more protection than my normal Academy clothes would offer. Furthermore it was more of a hallmark of *status*. Imperators were rarely seen within the Empire and usually only by people that they were hunting, but stories abounded of those who travelled with their black coats.

Those stories may have even travelled as far as the Sunfa clan, potentially providing me with some element of value in their eyes.

Adronicus eyed me with a sceptical eye before nodding begrudgingly. "Fits you well," he said gruffly. "Wear it with pride and remember to take good care of it. The better you treat her the better she will treat you. Good rule for life, that."

The door opened behind us and Cassius slipped inside. Asp was clasped in a long sheath by his side, and a small pack of belongings hung over his shoulder. Adronicus grunted at him and threw the second jacket which Cassius caught deftly, grimacing slightly at the weight. Like mine it was perfectly tailored, close fitting but allowing for easy mobility. Whoever the Imperator Academy had tailoring their clothes was they had an incredible eye - I couldn't remember having been measured for clothing during my time here and yet this felt like it had been personally tailored.

"You're taking Asp I see," Adronicus rumbled, flicking his head towards Cassius's sword. "A good choice. Though I recommend keeping a sword of that quality hidden until the time comes that you need to draw it."

"You got it boss," Cassius replied, a broad smile on his face. His relationship with the weapon master was much more friendly than everyone else, his skill with swords and attitude to training having long endeared him to the huge man. He was one of the few people who could be so flippant and jovial with the giant.

Adronicus handed us each a harness to go under the leather coat. Made of tough yet thin leather it hosted a number of sheathes for the small armoury of blades that he revealed.

"One can never have enough knives," he said solemnly as he handed out the arsenal. "I recommend you keep these harnesses on when travelling. You all know how effective knives can be in combat, but I can tell you from experience that you can be much better received when entering new environments such as an inn if you do not have a sword at your side.

Whether you take that risk or not however is up to you." He eyed the sheathed blade at Cassius's side and spoke again, "Indeed I wouldn't let something that has the value of Asp out of your sight. It would be all too easy for a light-fingered person to steal when packed on your saddle."

He gave us a moment to affix the harness over our attire, the bulges for knives hidden by the flowing jackets. With a critical eye he double checked our packs and our blades and then with a grave nod he beckoned us to follow him. Despite the weight of the packs that we bore our steps were light, keen to exit and explore. I couldn't help but compare myself to Anatha, even with the relative freedoms that the Imps had within the walls of the Academy here I was joyous at the thought of heading out into the unknown. *What would it be like,* I wondered, *to stay within that citadel, only able to leave when ordered?*

Before long we arrived at the main gate. Grazing nearby were two horses, both already saddled. Adronicus helped secure our packs, his movements swift and practiced, and then stepped out of the way as we jumped up.

"You have a map, a compass, money, food and a location," he said as he unbarred the gate. "That's everything an Imperator needs. Stay safe and watch each other's backs, particularly when in towns and cities. I know that you both know the wild but the depths of any town can harbour more wildness and danger than you might expect." A glimmer entered his eye as he spoke and he gave a sly grin. "That goes triple for Port Cambal. One wrong turn there and you'll awaken more vipers than you can shake a stick at." He winked. "Lucky for you, your sticks have sharp edges. Try not to get into trouble but defend yourselves accordingly if you do. No one impedes an Imperator." His steely eyes found ours again. "No one."

With that he led our horses out the main gate, handed over the reins and with a grunt and a nod he walked back inside, a casual wave of his hand his final parting message. As the gate boomed shut behind us Cassius and I shared a look and kicked our horses into a trot, our smiles broad. The difference between our past missions and this felt like night and day. This wasn't a test or a trial of survival, nor was it a mission complete with chaperones. This was the Academy starting to trust us as individuals. The first taste of how life would be as actual Imperators. And it felt good.

Seya followed at a discreet distance, shadowing us but not so close as to spook the horses. I had relayed our mission and she had jumped at the chance to explore, though as to how we were to get her across on the ferry I didn't know - I could only hope that our contact would have a plan.

We descended into Anderal, the capital city of the Empire with its concentric road system that lived under the shadow of the citadel that was the Emperor's home. Despite its relative closeness to the Academy it wasn't a city that either Cassius or myself knew particularly well. Our reasons for going into the city were few and whilst it wasn't banned for higher year Imps to head into the city in their spare time it was a fair walk without a carriage or horse, which made visits either a mad rush or just not worth the effort.

To say the city was huge would be an understatement. To a bird flying overhead it would probably look something like an eye; a large central park the pupil and row after row of concentric roads the iris and bloodshot veins. Each primary ring was a large thoroughfare, allowing horses, carts and the masses of humanity easy access to the rest of the city. Four primary roads extended out from the innermost circle in compass point directions, effectively subdividing the city into sectors. Allegedly it made the city extremely simple to navigate, but at five times the size of Forgoth its sheer size made me unable to grasp its simplicity.

We traversed the city without problem and in good time. The roadways were full to brimming with traffic and yet it flowed at a reasonable pace. We garnered a few looks here and there, the outfits marking us as either terrible dressers or Imperator agents, but for the most part were studiously ignored in that way that only city folk can.

Unlike Forgoth where traffic outside the city was light with generally just farmers and the odd merchant leaving the gates, the flow of humanity barely dimmed as we left through the southern gate of Anderal. The Imperial highroad was the primary method for the transportation of goods throughout the Andurran empire and so instead of citizens going around their everyday business we were instead joined by cart after cart of goods. The benefit of this was that the Imperial highroad was one of the safest roads within the empire and potentially within the world. Aside from patrols that regularly ran up and down the main arterial routes outside of each major city the majority of merchants hired mercenaries, ex-soldiers and guards to protect their investments. It was often joked that if the empire was invaded the second line of defence would be the highroad due to the amount of military might that ran up and down it each day.

Five copper pieces gave us a private room within a way-station, some forty miles south of the capital. The beds were bare frames but we were comfortable enough with our jackets and a makeshift pillow of our packs. The next day we rose with the sun and pushed hard, reaching the Anafor ferry in the late afternoon. Anafor itself was a small fortified town. It guarded the mouth of the Arunavae river, tributaries of which stretched for nearly two hundred miles into the empire, as well as provided transportation over to the nearby Port Cambal, a journey of less than a day. Port Cambal was an Andurran owned strip of land that faced the Sun'ari sea and connected to the continent via manmade bridges at two points. It had been forcibly claimed by the Andurran empire nearly two centuries before and now it served as the primary port for the southern region, its deep waters allowing for ships of all sizes to dock there and the result was a thriving, vibrant mix of cultures competing to outdrink each other and the marine contingents that used it for shore leave. It sounded gloriously stupid and I couldn't wait to experience it for myself.

Our contact wasn't due to meet us until the next day and

so we hired a room at the Sinking Ship, a somewhat ironic-
ally named inn built on the decking nearest to the ferry. Over
time the wood that served as its base had warped, giving the
building the suggestion that it was due to fall over any moment. The inn itself was fairly pleasant; enough customers
within to give it a sense of hustle and bustle yet not enough
that you had to shout to be heard. The bartender was a short
but stocky man, his head balding and arms bulging with thick
corded muscle. Naval tattoos marked him as an ex-sailor and
his attitude was initially stiff when we approached, his eyes
quickly taking in our attire and the sword that Cassius carried
at his side. He relaxed when he saw the colour of our coin and
the charming smile Cassius gave him, releasing his grip on the
cudgel that he had hidden behind the bar and instead serving
us warm beer and a bowl of thick stew that he had on constant
simmer over the fireplace. By rights it should have been disgusting but the slow cooked vegetables and whatever type of
meat he had in there hit all the right spots, its flavour working surprisingly well with the beer. A few more coins and we
had ourselves a room, the cracks in the wood work serving as
windows into the outside world. With full bellies and content
smiles we wrapped ourselves in our jackets and dropped into
exhausted sleep.

I awoke in the early hours of the morning, sensing that something was off. Cassius continued snoring merrily away, bliss-
fully unaware of anything amiss, but I knew that something
had changed. The moonlit shadows that filtered through the
cracks in the wall flickered and I sat up, reaching out to my
nearby harness for a knife. Another flicker and then the whole
ceiling *creaked* as though something had just put its whole
weight onto it. Cassius was awake now, Asp half bared on his
lap. I held up a hand to stall him and breathed in, putting my
senses to work. After a moment I relaxed, giving a smile towards the biggest crack in the wall.

"Hello Borza," I said calmly. "Where have you been?"

An orange eye the size of my palm pressed itself into the

crack and fixed me in its sights. A shudder and then the piece of wood came free with the low crumble of rotted wood. In the gap was the mighty orangutan, a mischievous smile on its face. It collated all the wisdom of its years, all the ancient knowledge, secrets and comprehension and delivered it in one short sentence.

"Oook."

# PRESENT DAY

It was interesting that the further we pushed north the safer we seemed to be. Nothing lived out here. It was as if life had been extinguished with no evidence of birds or insects and surprisingly little in the way of vegetation. Whether the thyrkan had consumed everything as their armies had marched or there was some unnatural force keeping nature at bay I wasn't sure, but it meant that there was a complete lack of thyrkan forces to contend with.

The walking became almost pleasurable in a strange and weird way. There was no sound aside from the wind, resulting in an eerie but relaxing experience as Cassius and I toured the deep of the north. At one time we thought we spotted a couple of skyren roaming the grounds but they were gone in a flash and didn't come back so we kept on moving. Torrential rain and roaring winds kept us in a small hollow for three days, eating up our limited food supply and removing all potential tracks in the immediate area - potentially both a blessing and a curse if the skyren were on our scent. They don't tell you this when you sign up for the Academy, but rather than spending most of your time fighting monsters or people as an Imperator, each mission inevitably ends up more about fighting the weather. And that fight is always very one sided.

Nature's a bitch.

About a week after we left the Scourge team to their victory Cassius began acting strangely, or, more accurately, more strangely than usual. His face took on a paler hue which was worrying enough for a mountain born and his veins appeared to have a black tinge showing through his skin. He began to walk to the north west and only stopped for sleep, each step seemingly more of a struggle, his eyes and veins getting darker step by step and mile by mile. I had never seen such a thing and could only guess that it was to do with a concentration of black seraph in the area somehow calling to his own. It was a more comforting theory than wondering if he had been controlled by the Enemy. The gold-plated prick of an Emperor had promised that couldn't be done, but he had said many things over the years and I had long since stopped trusting anything that came out of his mouth.

Either way, Cassius was far too big and strong for me to stop and it seemed like as good a direction as any. We strode on and Cassius looked less like a man and more like some kind of demonic shadow wraith every day. The iris of his eyes became a swirl of black interlaced with gold and were somewhat terrifying to wake up to when he loomed over me in the morning.

Two days later he stopped on the rise of a large hill. It was a good vantage point and so I thought some part of him might have been taking the lay of the land but he was looking straight down as though he could see into the rock below. Intrigued, I walked to the crest and realised that the hill wasn't rounded, the far side of it ended in a sharp drop off. Much more interestingly was that when looking over the cliff I could see tracks on the floor emerging from the side of the cliff, and not just sets of one or two. Hundreds. Maybe thousands. The floor was so heavily pitted with the marks of boots and wagons that no amount of bad weather was going to erase it. I cast out my senses, trying to penetrate inside the mound but I didn't get anything back. Getting down to the tracks was easy enough and there didn't seem to be anything remotely fresh that would indicate that the inside was occupied, but I knew better than to trust my luck. With a hand on my sword I stepped forward and entered the gloom of the cave.

Immediately it became clear that it wasn't a natural cave. In fact I quickly became certain that the entire hill was man made. A gigantic set of metallic doors were just inside the cave and I fully expected our journey to stop there but Cassius just strode forward and the doors silently slid apart. Inside was a vast chamber filled with equipment that reminded me far too closely of that within Ash's complex. Row upon row of vats filled the room, each one empty and open. A set of stairs down and another row of vats. Another set of stairs and another. And another. There were thousands of the things, each of them empty. Each of them open. And I had a sneaking suspicion of where and what their occupants were.

Thyrkan.

I couldn't confirm it, but the thyrkan had come out of no-where like a wave of death. The Academy hadn't heard of any-thing remotely resembling a thyrkan before their sudden ap-pearance. Perhaps they had been created and grown in places like this?

Before I lost myself in thought I realised that Cassius hadn't stopped moving and was continuing to descend, heading fur-ther and further into the deep. I hurried to catch him and to-gether we made our way to the very bottom of the complex, guarded by another set of thick metal doors. Once again Cas-sius stepped forward and once again the doors opened, sliding apart to reveal a sight that left me simultaneously ecstatic and horrified.

Cassius looked almost as stupefied as I felt. Strapped to a large table and only able to weakly move its head to glare in our direction due to the sheer number of tubes extending from its body was a scene from a nightmare.

My nightmare in fact. The one I relieved every night where my entire village was slaughtered to feed a hungry demon.

On the table was the red eyed skyren.

# CHAPTER 29

## *Shenanigans*

Anatha sat in the dewy morning sun, wrapped in a thick cloak and inhaling a pungent cigar as though it was the last thing she would ever do.

"One of life's finer pleasures," she coughed as we walked over, the map given us by Borza's night-time misdemeanour a crude replica of Anafor complete with a big cross marking where we were to meet. "I'm glad you managed to find this location. I wasn't sure if you would manage it, what with your puny brain and all."

I held up the map and read off the other side, "A map of Anafor for the idiots in the Sinking Ship. Dawn. Don't be late. Idiot." I grinned and gave her a mocking bow. "Glad to know that you think so much of me."

A snort. "Don't give yourself airs boy; you know I don't think much of anyone!" She cocked an eye at Cassius who was demurely standing to the side with his arms folded. "Including you, young Cassius. Yes that's right, I know who you are, don't get your panties in a twist about it."

Cassius stared at the old crone; his expression perplexed enough for me to laugh in delight. "This is just the way she is," I chuckled softly. "She's a bullish, annoying egotist with a complete lack of manners and even bigger lack of ability to care." I could see a small grin starting to form on Anatha's craggy face and pushed on. "But for all her flaws - and they are many - once you get past her hard exterior you realise that," I eyed Anatha with a wicked grin, "there is a soft and loving centre deep within."

Anatha's expression was one of pure shock. "Soft and loving?" she barked. "Where on earth did you get that impression?"

I shrugged and indicated Cassius who was nodding as though he understood the deeper meaning of my words. Anatha turned pale as he stepped forward and turned his hand out for a shake.

"I'm Cassius," he said sweetly, "it's an absolute pleasure to meet you...?"

A pregnant pause.

"...Anatha," she finished somewhat disheartened as her eyes did their best to inflict the fear of god into him. Cassius took no notice, his chivalrous nature ensuring that he would disregard all attempts at driving him away in a vain effort to get Anatha to reveal her true self. Of course, he had no idea that there was no real soft centre to Anatha - she was granite through and through - but one has to have their little victories every now and again, even if Anatha's eyes promised retribution.

Once I judged her sufficiently annoyed by Cassius's heartwarming attempts to get to know her I stepped in again. "Sorry to interrupt you two but we have a mission to get done. Anatha, what do you know?"

If looks could melt I would have been a puddle on the floor.

"The Sunfa clan are a tribe that few know even exist," Anatha began in a bored voice. "They have lived in the Ellendar swamps for aeons and the swamps are inhospitable enough that only those who have reason to go there would do so. And unless that reason is to hunt swamp turtle then it's safe to say that not many have been. Fortunately for you idiots, I have."

"So you hunted swamp turtle?"

"Yes actually," she mused. "Surprisingly tasty. But not the

reason I went in the first place. The Ellendar swamps are a strange place. The land there is *broken*. Within and around it are remnants of some great war. Withered husks of metallic objects that the Sunfa use as shelter. When you arrive you will find that the ground is deceptive - what looks like sturdy grass will inevitably be a bog that will attempt to drag you down to your doom. The trees are the most useful way of getting about, they are strong and sturdy enough to take the weight of most creatures and are the primary method of transportation that the Sunfa use."

Her eyes narrowed in recollection. "The closer you get to the clan, the more that the overgrown, vine encrusted things you will be climbing on will actually be metallic. They have a habit for collecting them, you see; anything metal is of value to the Sunfa."

"So these old objects," I said slowly, organising my thoughts, "are we safe to think that they are from before the Cataclysm? That they might have some kind of active power device that can be used for the seraph detectors?"

Anatha nodded her head, her expression suggesting she was stunned at how slowly my brain had collated this all together. "That is the theory, yes. When I was there they had a number of cube like devices, some of which faintly vibrated when touched. The Sunfa didn't use them - not that I think much of anything that has been exposed to the humidity and toxicity of the swamp for that long would work anymore - but they collected them as they do all things of unknown origin. The Emperor believes that those cubes are a power source; one that can be used for any number of things but that yes, Calidan, can be used to power the seraph detectors."

"Seraph detectors?" Cassius asked.

Anatha gave me an approving look. "Seems like you can keep secrets closer to your chest than I had thought boy. Good. Imperators should guard their tongues; even to their closest friends."

"You gave me fairly good reason not to talk," I replied drily, trying not to see the hurt in Cassius's eyes and failing miserably.

Cassius looked at Anatha with renewed interest. "Who are you?" he asked, his expression intent.

I looked at Anatha and she gave me a tiny nod. "Anatha is… one of the Emperor's Great Heart bonded," I said quietly. "She has been training Seya and myself to become better partners." I could see that he had a host of questions and held up my hand to stop him. "I'll explain everything properly later, but know that she is second to practically only the Emperor himself. In short there is a potential threat at the Academy. One that involves black seraph."

Cassius visibly paled at those words.

"Anatha thinks that someone higher up at the Academy is being controlled. Apparently the citadel has a seraph detector, much like what Ash used to determine what types of seraph we each had, but it has ceased functioning. Hence the hunt for this power source."

Cassius looked like he had been on the receiving end of a boxing round with Adronicus; his eyes wide and distant. After a moment he shook his head, as though trying to dislodge cobwebs, and refocused on us.

"Got it," he said simply.

"Got it?" I replied, surprise evident in my voice.

"Yep, got it," he answered again. "We're most definitely going to be talking about this further, but for the time being the short version makes sense. So," he turned his attention to Anatha who regarded him curiously, "how are we getting to Port Cambal with Seya?"

"The same way Borza and I went last time," Anatha replied, eyes twinkling. "Bribery."

✳ ✳ ✳

It turned out that the Imperator Academy had a number of sea captains in their payroll. Captains that ranged from those who were passionate about the Andurran empire to those with unscrupulous morals who wanted an extra pay check. Of course there were Imperator owned ships as well, however these were kept aside for missions of more import, such as war. Of course, the Academy had to know that the captain for each mission was trustworthy and so each was carefully vetted before being put on the payroll. This meant that the captain of the Twisted Sister, the ship that transported us to Port Cambal, was paid handsomely for his troubles and would swear blind that no large crate had ever passed through his hold that at times sounded like there was a giant cat inside.

Anatha had mentioned bribery as the primary motivator, and I'm sure that a large part of it was, however I also know how the Academy works and examples must have been made of captains in the past who didn't respect the secrecy of their Imperator cargo.

Thankfully the trip was short. Seya made it well known how much she disliked the sea, her crate and life in general for the six hours we spent under sail. I was too busy throwing up over the side to agree. For a mountain boy from the arse end of nowhere I had at this point in my life seen a surprising number of things both amazing and terrifying, but the ocean was on a whole other level. It just went on and on, succeeding in making us feel infinitesimally small and insignificant. Powerless to do anything but cower in the face of its majesty and vomit up lunch, then breakfast, and then from the feel of it, my lower intestines.

Suffice to say none of us were happy. Well, except for Anatha. Surprisingly she said that she would be joining us on the trip, that she had been given the orders to do so by the Emperor in an effort to continue my training and evaluate my skill. The vision of her wrinkled face flapping in the wind as she hung in the crow's nest was something that I do not believe I or any of the dumbfounded crew will ever forget. Sadly Borza didn't get to experience the same joy and instead spent the trip in a crate next to Seya's.

By the time we reached Port Cambal, Cassius and I were swearing off the sea forever; much to the amusement of the crew. We stumbled off the ship, waited for the crates to be delivered to a non-descript individual who Anatha seemed to know and then walked into the seediest, most disgusting and most brilliant city I have ever known.

Port Cambal is a place of culture. Not refinement; its denizens would laugh in your face if you told them that, but wild and varied culture. I have often found that ports are natural melting pots of humanity, places where people from all over the world meet to trade, find work, eat, drink and be merry. Port Cambal is not the biggest port in the world but it is one of the most populated and as a consequence in a short walk through the cobbled roads Cassius and I encountered more cultures, languages and food types than we had the entirety of our lives to that point. To say it was eye opening would be an understatement.

Strangely, having Anatha with us didn't detract from our experience whatsoever. Perhaps surprisingly to those watching the ancient grandma, she seemed eager to live life to the fullest and revelled in haggling with market stall owners, holding sordid and lascivious conversations with prostitutes and giving cackling tirades with enough colourful language to quite figuratively make sailors blush. Like a tiny tornado of activities she pushed us forwards, encouraging us to try new foods, new drinks and to get into as much trouble as possible. One might think it strange that someone so close to the Emperor should be so keen to enjoy a place like Port Cambal, but looking back it is easy to see that she was closed off within the citadel - something she had repeatedly complained about - and was thoroughly enjoying the opportunities at her disposal. Which is why after four bars, three kisses, two brawls and a fight with a peacock I found myself stabbed.

Only minorly stabbed mind you, but the bastard had promised me that he had never failed at Five Finger Fillet. Considering that the bastard was Cassius I couldn't complain too much. His lack of a Great Heart bonded meant that alcohol hit him much harder than it did for me or Anatha (not that it stopped us from trying), but he had promised me, *promised,* that he could do it.

I might still be a little salty about it.

Thankfully I healed quickly so the knife wound that stuck my middle finger to the table beneath didn't stay around for too long. It didn't help that Anatha goaded Cassius into doing it again however, her expression one of pure joy as he drunkenly skittered his knife around, across and through my hand.

Definitely still salty.

It turned out that whilst Anatha had a passion for life that I have yet to be seen rivalled, she had a burning fire for gambling. Her need to roll the dice, show the cards, flip the bones and make inane wagers on practically anything put Rikol to shame. It was the games of pure chance that brought her the most joy. I think it was due to that frightening brain of hers. She could outplay anyone - and I mean anyone - in the five gambling dens we visited in our one night in Port Cambal. Whatever the game, even if she had allegedly never played it before, if it involved strategy more than luck she wouldn't lose. And she used all the winnings that she gathered through those games to fund our drinking and blow it on wild games of chance where the sheer anticipation and delight in her eyes made every loss worth it.

I woke up the next morning in a plush silk bed with a bandaged hand and a throbbing headache. The room was draped in coloured hangings, a blinding kaleidoscope of colours for my jaded eyes.

*The mewling cub is awake I see.*

It took me a few moments to gather my thoughts. *Morning Seya,* I groaned eventually. *Where are you?*

*Anatha's agent dropped Borza and myself off at a small copse of trees on the mainland and told us to wait there.*

I pursed my lips. *And so where are you?*

A paw batted the window open and she flowed in like liquid. *Enjoying the sights and smells of this place. Obviously.*

*You know that if someone sees you then they'll-*

*-be happy to have seen the majesty of a creature like me,* Seya finished with an air of finality. *Besides, it isn't like I came alone. And in a place like this who is going to believe rumours of giant animals and actually believe them? Practically every sailor comes ashore and starts drunkenly spouting stories of kraken and giant turtles.*

*Giant turtles?*

*I'm not saying they don't exist. Quite possible that they do. But my point stands.*

*True enough,* I yawned. *Did you have fun?*

*Of course,* she purred as she sandpapered my face with her tongue. *Anatha had a great time leading you two around the city. Borza and I had fun exploring and scaring the drunks. For a primitive ape he can move surprisingly swiftly.*

I coughed in shock as I heard the grudging admiration. *Not as swift as you though, obviously,* I replied after a moment.

Seya licked her paw. *Obviously.*

*Where is Borza now?*

*With Anatha. She has been up for some time organising the journey.*

*What?*

*Apparently not all of last night's activities were just for fun. She won seven horses and has traded four for supplies. She has visited where they are stabled and seen to it that they will be ready for noon. She is now eating breakfast in the room next door and invites you to join her when ready.*

*Cassius?*

Her eyes twitched in amusement. *Alcohol must really dull your senses,* she replied before swinging her head over to the side of the bed. Confused, I dragged myself over to the side of the bed and discovered Cassius asleep on the floor. He was sleeping the kind of sleep that only a drunk person can accomplish, one that makes you wonder if the person is still breathing.

"Cassius?" I said gently, trying to wake him up softly. "Cassius, wake up."

He snorted and rolled slightly under the bed. "Cassius," I said more loudly, reaching out and poking him in the shoulder. "Wake up!"

Still nothing. With a heavy groan I swivelled my feet off the bed and walked to the basin on the far side of the room. A swift dunk of my head and I felt a million times better. Briefly I considered throwing the basin over Cassius but then my eyes landed on Seya and a better plan came to mind.

*Seya, would you mind terribly giving Cassius a bath?*

She purred in delight and rose to her feet, stalking over to the sleeping Imp.

I dunked my head again, ignoring the screaming, shouting and desperate pleas that emanated from the corner of the room as Seya held Cassius down with one gigantic paw and unleashed the full might of her tongue. Finally, I walked over and looked down at my disgruntled friend.

"Sleep well?" I asked.

"I hate you both," he replied acidly.

Leaving Cassius to recuperate, I found Anatha in the next room. I had thought my room palatial but hers was gigantic, featuring a number of rooms and, most importantly, a heavily laden breakfast table.

"Come in boy," she murmured as I stepped inside. "And close the door. Cassius can join us when ready."

"Impressive rooms," I said appreciatively as I sat down. "Where are we?"

"The Dulcet Feather," she replied in between bites of toast. At the blank expression on my face she continued, "Word of advice boy, if you have the coin and want a good night's sleep then spend the extra on a top-class brothel. The best ones are like palaces inside and they are always a great place to pick up a little extra information."

I took a bite of sweet bread just in time for her words to make sense in my brain. Anatha calmly wiped the pieces of bread off her chest with a newspaper before fixing me with a bemused glare.

"A brothel?" I asked in surprise. "This place is a brothel?!"

"Of course," she replied. "Slightly more expensive than a quality hotel but with many more additional benefits." Her eyebrow raised at the look on my face. "Not necessarily *those* benefits Calidan, although they are certainly there for the offering. But the benefits of pleasant rooms, plump pillows and more importantly of all, information." She looked at me drily. "Do you really think that the Emperor would send me off on this trip with you if there wasn't an ulterior motive? Yes, I'm here to help train you and attempt to make sure that your tiny brain doesn't get you killed, but at the end of the day information is what really makes the empire so respected and feared. Information lets the sailor know the bribed Iffian captain to contact to slip the blockade, it lets the merchants buy and sell at the best price possible." She snorted. "It even lets the Emperor send a bunch of barely pubescent teens out to support tribes in a frozen wasteland." She eyed me frankly. "Everything has to have a use, boy. When you're sent on a mission there are likely a whole host of reasons why you are there and not just the one that you are going to be told. The Emperor is not one for keeping around baggage. You're known to him now. Keep being useful. Go above and beyond. Otherwise..." she drifted off; her visage troubled.

"Otherwise what?" I asked tentatively.

"Otherwise..." she sighed and shook her head. "Just stay useful Calidan. Besides using brothels as hotels it's the best bit of advice I'll give you today."

"Okay," I said, sensing her need to change the subject, "what did you learn from this brothel and who did you learn it from?"

"A good question." She paused for a moment to savour a sip of coffee. "I learnt many things. Like how many people it takes to carry a completely limp Cassius up a flight of stairs, how many drinks it takes to get someone bonded to Seylantha drunk and how quick that person's recovery time." She gave me a wink and whispered slyly, "It's always good to know what you can about the people you work with."

"Very funny," I replied with a tinge of annoyance. "Anything particular from the brothel itself?"

She shrugged. "The usual; which ships smuggle cargo, the latest black-market goods, that kind of thing. Oh and the governor of Serenia is gearing for war."

"War with who?"

Her eyes twinkled. "And now you see the benefit of information. If we knew that then we would be in a position of power to take advantage of it. As it stands the rumour is that he intends to march on Effifea, which might make sense as it is a small country that has a number of natural resources that Serenia would love to make use of, but that could be a counter rumour to hide the true target. Who knows?"

"Impressive," I replied as the door opened and Cassius staggered in. "What happens next?"

"Next we let Cassius eat as much as he possibly can and then we can set about getting ourselves our horses," Anatha replied. "Another rule young ones, always guard your tongues regardless of how safe you think you are. You never know who might be listening."

Cassius took Anatha up on her offer with gusto, falling onto the food with a ravenous hunger and turning the carefully laid table into a battlefield.

"What about the others," I asked softly.

"Others?"

"Our two...companions."

"Ah. They will find their way after us when it gets dark. Both of them will be happy enough here and the staff have been advised not to enter the rooms until tomorrow. They will be respectful of our wishes. Madam Selene will see to that."

"And if they choose not to stay here?" I asked carefully.

Anatha gave a craggy smile. "I'm very old Calidan and yet I am but a babe compared to our two friends. They will do what they think best and they both know the consequences if they are seen. That will have to suffice."

✳  ✳  ✳

### Seya

Seya curled up in the bed that Calidan had vacated, the wood groaning under her weight but deciding that it would be in its best interests to stay upright. She flicked an ear as Calidan and Cassius walked in to collect their gear but decided that ignoring them in favour of sleep was a much-preferred plan. When they were long gone and the sun was starting to go down she uncurled and stepped delicately off the bed and looked out of the window at the sights of Port Cambal.

*What to do?*

*So many options.*

In the end it was a simple thing. She could hear the big ape on the rooftop still snoring uproariously. The humans nearby must have thought that there was a localised thunderstorm on the rooftop. With a grin she teased open the window with a single, sublime claw and flowed her way out, twisting her torso through the tiny gap until she was facing up the building. Extending her claws she found purchase, pulled and began to climb.

Borza lay where he had been the entire day, sprawled on the top of the roof with a newspaper over his head. He still snored, the newspaper rustling in the wind of his breath, and Seya was careful to pick her way over to him, splaying her paws out wide and missing the patches of rooftop that looked like they would creak. Step by delicate step she made her way over to her target, freezing every time the snoring stuttered, until she was within easy pouncing distance. For a moment longer she watched her target and wondered if she should awaken someone so deeply asleep before deciding that if she was awake then he should be too.

After all...she was a queen.

Unleashing the powerful muscles of her body Seya sailed through the air and landed both front paws directly onto Borza's face. He stiffened and then a large orange furred arm shifted to tug on the paper that was under Seya's paws. Slowly it slid out from under her feet until they were eye to eye.

"Ooook?"

Seya gave a little playful snarl and bounced on Borza's stomach before dancing back to his face again. He tried to pull the newspaper back over his head but eventually gave up when she took the opportunity to try and squeeze herself onto the tiny square of paper, conveniently ignoring that Borza's face was beneath it. With a snort the massive orangutan shifted, his arms coming up to lift the cat away from his face and shifting her over to the roof next to him, showing almost no hint of strain at her weight as he did so.

Seya chuckled to herself as Borza slowly sat up. His eyes held mild curiosity at her antics, as though he couldn't work out why she would be deigning to bother him when sleep was available.

With a nudge of her head Seya indicated the city that sprawled out beneath them. Port Cambal in all its disgusting and entertaining glory. There had to be some fun out there for two Great Hearts, didn't there?

There was a scream of pain as the man slapped the woman he had pressed against the wall. Her sobs going unheard as his hired muscle made any would be saviour move on. The pimp struck again, earning another wail of pain. Shadows shifted at the end of the alley and if he had been listening the man might have wondered at the strange diminishment of the usual sounds of the night such as those of the rats that usually scurried everywhere. He raised his hand again and a low rumble broke the night to stay his blow. Turning towards the rear of the alley he took a half step back.

"Did you-" he began to the woman, breaking off when he saw what stepped out of the shadows. Teeth the length of his forearm reflected the weak light and with a scream he turned and ran, fleeing down the alley to the rest of his goons. He made it perhaps five steps before a huge hand came down from above and plucked him into the sky, leaving a trailing scream in its wake.

"Boss?" hissed one of the guards, as he slowly made his way into the mouth of the alley. "Boss, where are you?"

A scream grew in volume as an object descended from the roof at speed. The pimp struck the floor and instantly howled as a shin snapped. The guard took one look at his boss and at the approaching orbs that he was rapidly realising were gigantic eyes before turning and fleeing as fast as his feet could take him.

Seya brushed up against the now frozen woman, trying to give her a sense of safety, but with a repressed gasp she fainted, terrified beyond reason at the sight of such a large cat.

*Or awed into unconsciousness,* Seya reasoned. *Much more likely.*

Stalking her way to the screaming man she lowered her head and then slowly opened her mouth, revealing all of her gleaming teeth in all of their savage glory. A rumbling growl that shook the man's chest so hard he thought that his heart might explode and then the cat moved back into the darkness, disappearing as though she had never been.

The two chuckling creatures disappeared into the night as a crowd began to gather around the wounded pimp and terrified woman, eager to find more avenues for adventure. In the small hours of the night they stopped three more muggings, mistakenly terrified a couple who were rather physically enjoying each other's company and threw a murderer into the sea. On the way back from the docks, Borza, with much encouragement from Seya, pilfered a barrel of rum from the loading bay of a Raledian freighter. Losing themselves once more on the plentiful rooftops of Port Cambal they cracked open the barrel and drank deeply.

The burning sunlight attacked Seya's eyes with vicious abandon and the giant cat squirmed restlessly before blearily opening one eye. *Urrrgh,* she thought as a wave of nausea hit her, *why do humans do this to themselves? Never again.* Slowly she began to move before freezing in place.

Something was next to her.

*No,* she snarled in complete denial. *No, no, please no!*

Slowly she looked down at the orange furred arm that was wrapped around her and with a yowl of discontent she shot to her feet and stumbled her way out of the sleeping grasp of Borza.

*You will tell no one of this!* she growled at the unmoving orang-utan, her canines out and bared. *This never happened. I do not...* she shuddered in horror.

*I do not cuddle!*

# CHAPTER 30

## *Swamps*

The horses that Anatha had obtained were impressive specimens. I'm not much of a horse person but even I could admire their gleaming coats and muscular physiques. Whoever she had won them from must have been sorely cursing their bad luck and I couldn't help but wonder if Anatha had come to Port Cambal already knowing her target or if she had spent the exuberant night filling drinks and collecting stories until she learnt of the most likely person who would be willing to bet their horses. Knowing her she probably had a back-up plan in place and five more in case that didn't pan out either.

The journey out from Port Cambal was relatively uneventful. The first day was hard work as Cassius and I readjusted to being back in the saddle; both of us nursing our aching thighs (and Cassius his aching head) every time we stopped. Seya and Borza joined us in the early hours of the first night, both of them strangely reluctant to discuss what they had got up to in our absence. I could only imagine that it was nothing good.

At the end of the fourth day of riding we arrived at the border of Mustovar. A bored, uniformed border control soldier waved us through without giving us a second glance as Borza and Seya took a more circumspect route. Less than a day later we were standing on the ridge of a large valley, overlooking a dank, dense mass of foliage that steamed gently in the air.

"That looks...wet," murmured Cassius.

I turned to look at my friend, eyebrow raised. "Really?" I waved my hand towards the humid valley, "What gave it away? The humid air, thick foliage or the fact that it's called a swamp?"

He gave me a grin and finished off taking his bags from the back of his horse. Anatha was adamant that if we took the horses down into the swamp below then they wouldn't be coming back and so we had to progress down on foot. Anatha was already picking her way down the ridge, having barely spared the view of the valley a moment's glance. Borza and Seya were lurking nearby waiting for the light to fade before they would slip down to join us in case of any observant eyes within the trees. Leaving the horses on long tethers we began the treacherous walk down, scattering loose rock and shale with every step. Anatha maintained that this was the same path that she had taken when she first went into the swamps but it certainly wasn't a major thoroughfare, reinforcing the suggestion that the visitors in or out of the valley were rare.

At the base of the valley the rock and grass began to give way to clumps of reeds, bog and clouds of insects. As much as Cassius had been stating the obvious he wasn't wrong; it was *wet.* Not just because of the floor underneath that was quickly becoming more of a lake but an intense humidity that had sweat pouring off us in seconds. It rapidly became clear that the Empire by and large resided in a temperate climate and whilst I am sure that fully fledged Imperators had a choice of clothing that best fit the climate they were visiting; our jackets did little but act as ovens; quickly getting removed to be packed away and trading protection for comfort.

Soon enough Anatha swung into the low limbed trees that hung with swooping bows over the murky swamp water. She moved much like Borza, utilising efficient loping swings that had Cassius open mouthed in awe at the sight of the ancient woman flitting through the trees like a monkey. I could see why Anatha had mentioned the trees when we first talked about the swamp. Without them we would have had to build boats to navigate the brackish water, and considering the size of some of the creatures that I half saw in there I wouldn't fancy my chances when on the water line, whether in a boat or not. Unseen creatures created ripples and waves within the waters and trees rocked in their passing. Whatever happened none of us wanted to end up in there - survival certainly wouldn't be assured.

For half a day we fought our way through the dense under-growth, hopping from tree to tree and doing our utmost to avoid descending too close to the water. Our hands were rubbed raw from clasping onto the sharp bark of the trees - well, Cassius and my hands that is, aside from the heat Anatha looked completely at home in the canopy. As night began to fall Anatha called a halt and we took refuge in the most com-fortable trees that we could find and made ourselves as secure as we could. Whilst my eyes allowed me to see with perfect clarity in the dark both Anatha and Cassius didn't have those same benefits and the risk was too great of an accident. If we had thought the swamp problematic during the day then it was much, much worse during the night. According to Ana-tha the resident inhabitants of the water below were much more active during the night hours, and she wasn't wrong. I lost count of the number of roars, howls and screeches that plagued us through the small hours, of the scorpions that I carefully dislodged from the bark and of the silvery shapes that sailed, trudged and swam through the moonlight, some of which put Seya's size to shame.

Thankfully, we survived the night.

The next morning found a tired, grumpy and altogether dis-pleased trio as well as two Great Hearts in the surrounding trees. Whilst the rising of the sun made for a reduction in the activity of the creatures beneath us another hostile threat quickly made itself known. A creature that I thankfully hadn't had too much close contact with up to this point.

Mosquitos.

So many mosquitos.

Seya and Borza sat comfortably as we slapped, scratched and cursed our way through a bleak breakfast where we doubtless ingested as many mosquitos as we did our food. Clouds of them swept the swamp, hunting down any warm-blooded creature that dared rise its head above the surface. I quickly began to believe that the predators in the waters below were nocturnal by choice in order to avoid the incessant swarms.

The climb through the swamp continued to be unpleasant, but moving was far better than being a stationary target for the bloodsuckers and so we attacked it with aplomb, sprinting through the boughs at a pace that belittled the previous day's endeavours. As we forged further into the swamp trees began to be replaced by metal wonders, albeit wonders covered in thick layers of vines and mud. Some had wheels, some had legs, some big, some gigantic; the only things they had in common was that they were all made of metal and thankfully non-moving - I had far too many dark thoughts of friends of Ash's scorpion defender hunting us through the swamp and a glance at Cassius's worried face showed he was thinking the same.

Fortunately none of the metal machines woke up and we were soon just as comfortable using them as methods of transportation as we were with the trees, just replacing the creak of boughs with the groan of metal.

Some half day after we began we encountered our first sight of civilization. Wooden platforms began to adorn the trees and swamp waters below. To describe them as 'tree-houses' in the same context as children within the empire play with would be doing the Sunfa clan an injustice. The further we went into their territory the more it became clear that it was an expansive construction that spread over a large area. Walkways attached each platform, removing the need to travel through the trees themselves. The largest platforms surrounded the

giant metal constructs that towered out of the centre of
the swamp, some of the central constructs hosting multiple
levels until they rivalled some of the towers in Anderal and
dwarfed those in Forgoth. Seya and Borza held back, drifting into the shadow of the swamp whilst Anatha led the way
confidently forwards, hopping onto one of the walkways and
strolling along the swaying platforms as though she had every
right to be there. Cassius and I followed behind, ignoring the
growing group of people who gathered around us; the majority of them looking lean but with the wiry muscles gained
from hard living. Anatha walked to the largest platform, the
base of the tallest tower in the central ring where hundreds of
Sunfa had gathered to greet us with an excited murmur.

Anatha strode forward and stood in the middle of the platform with an imperious look on her face. With sharp, guttural
sounds she spoke to the crowd and looked satisfied when a vo-
luptuous woman strode forward. A short, expressive conversation began that neither Cassius or I could understand that
was punctuated with what sounded like argumentative tones,
but each woman's eyes held nothing but intense satisfaction
at what was presumably a very intriguing conversation. Some
five minutes of intense conversation later the two women
nodded and with a gesture from the Sunfa leader we were
guided to a nearby building that contained a number of bunks.

"So..." Cassius said slowly, looking outside at the crowd of
Sunfa who were seemingly having great fun watching us,
"what happened there?"

"Erin'ea is a feisty conversationalist," Anatha said from the
nearby bunk. "The Sunfa love a good debate. They don't get
many visitors but thoroughly enjoy talking with those they
do receive. Unfortunately much of the body language comes
across as hostile and combined with there being probably five
people in the world, myself included, who speak their language, anyone who somehow stumbles in here might get the
impression that they are an angry and inhospitable tribe. As
it is they are generally most abiding and in this instance will

give us a vibrating cube."

"Excellent!" said Cassius with an exultant grin. "I'm glad that you're with us Anatha. Attempting to do this without you would have been-"

"-impossible," she cut in. "Another reason why I was asked to join you."

I studied the old woman closely. After a moment she noticed my regard and cocked an eye. "Yes?"

"What's the catch?"

She gave a craggy smile. "Nothing much. You just have to hunt the Sunfa'shak."

Cassius's laughing face turned to stone. "The what?"

She coughed. "Loosely translated, Sunfa's bane."

The old woman didn't even have the decency to look abashed. "And what precisely is Sunfa's bane?" I asked through gritted teeth.

"I'm glad you asked, Calidan," she replied, a wide smile on her face. "As far as I can tell, the bane of the Sunfa clan is an eel."

"An eel?" replied Cassius dubiously.

"An eel big enough to swallow a full-grown man whole and has apparently taken a particular interest in human flesh. Apparently it likes to lurk around the waterside walkways and attempt to knock people off the pontoons. Most of the immediate waterways are heavily staked to prevent creatures getting through but as you know, eels are slippery. The Sunfa have attempted to hunt it themselves but so far they haven't had any luck. And for reference, the title of Sunfa'shak is awarded for any creature that has killed more than five members of the clan. As you might have guessed and considering the denizens of the swamp that we have seen so far, that title has been awarded to creatures on numerous occasions. Apparently humans can be quite a tasty treat in these parts."

I sat down on the bunk. "An eel?" I said weakly, thinking of falling into those dark waters. "That doesn't exactly sound like something we have trained for...you couldn't have bargained for the cube?"

Anatha gave me a look of blistering scorn. "Do you see much in the way of gold or trade around here? If I offered the Sunfa gold they would look at me with questioning eyes and probably throw it in the swamp - it has no value here as it is of no practical use. The cube is one of their key treasures; as you know they have a burning fascination with all things from before the Cataclysm. As such the trade offer had to be of an item that had equal value - hunting and killing a threat to their tribe was one of the few options available that could be done in a quick time frame. So deal with it."

I tried to ease my frown; she spoke an annoying amount of sense.

"Okay," Cassius breathed to himself. "So we have to kill an eel. Won't be the first big and scary creature we've had to kill eh Calidan?"

"And it will definitely not be your last," smirked Anatha. "This isn't one that you can go in on relying on brute force, you're going to need to understand your foe and use skill to kill it...or else you'll find yourselves the prey."

Sitting down heavily on a near bunk I let out a long, slow groan whilst pressing my temples with my fingers. "It's never easy is it? 'Go into a spider cave', 'meet some trolls', 'fight a skyren', 'kill an eel'. Just once it would be nice to have a fight against something we have trained for," I complained.

"It's a rare day that a Great Heart bonded gets sent for a 'normal' mission," Anatha replied drily. "Not that many missions that Imperators are involved in can be considered normal. Monster hunting is a key consideration when you have your own monster to assist, so you might want to get used to it."

"Fun times," I answered.

She ignored my sarcasm. "And you have been training against myself and Borza for the last few months so don't act like you have no experience fighting dangerous creatures."

Point to her.

"Fair enough," I replied finally. "Any advice on fighting an eel?"

"Don't fight it," she retorted. "You're thinking about this like it is going to be a battle. It is most likely not a Great Heart so it isn't going to be particularly intelligent. Hunt and trap it. Force it into an area of your choosing rather than the other way round."

Cassius nodded knowingly at her words. "She's right Calidan," he said. "If we can get it somewhere small and difficult for it to manoeuvre then Asp should be able to take care of it with a clean hit. We just have to herd it somewhere."

"You both make it sound so simple," I muttered, laying back on the cot and closing my eyes. "We just need to herd a swamp dwelling eel, a creature that is known for being incredibly wiggly and hard to catch at the best of times, to somewhere slightly less swampy...whilst being in the centre of a swamp."

"Who said anything about it being any less swampy?" Anatha retorted. "We're in a swamp, that's going to be hard to do. Why not just trap it? Use the Sunfa to help you build stakes and traps, get them to lower them down around the eel or get it to go into a cage. Cassius only said he needed a clean shot. If it is trapped in a cage half submerged in a swamp then I'm sure that what he can conjure with Asp can do the job. Isn't that right boy?"

Cassius nodded. "I'm certain that Asp will cut through the cage, water and occupant. If we can get it to that stage then the job will be done."

I miss Cassius being that confident. To be fair, I miss Cassius being anything other than completely insane. I couldn't help it though, his stalwart belief in himself and his ability to complete any task put in front of him was infectious. Suddenly fighting a killer eel in its own territory didn't seem quite so bad.

"Will the Sunfa help us do you think?" I asked, directing my question at Anatha.

"Of course. They want this creature removed and will support any decent idea as to how to do it. The actual killing of it is down to you though."

"And will you help?" I asked again, raising an eyebrow at the ancient Imperator.

"If it looks like you will die then I might step in. Emphasis on the might. This is your mission."

"The Academy trains us to use all tools at our disposal," I quipped, a small smile on my face, "I like to think that in this instance you're a tool," I placed heavy emphasis on the last word.

She stared at me for a long moment and I began to wonder if I had gone too far then a gleeful cackle began to shake her frame. "Best one yet boy, well done!" She gave another chuckle and shook her head in amusement. "The reason I am here is foremost to help this mission succeed, the secondary reason is to oversee your bond with Seya and how you work together. I will not step in unless there is mortal danger, but if it does look like one of you is going to die then I will do my best to stop that from happening. Happy?"

*Better than the fourth-year exam then,* I mused before nodding. "Happy."

"Good, then get your planning hats on and figure out the best way to do this."

∗ ∗ ∗

On the eve of the third day since we met the Sunfa tribe I found myself perched in a low-slung tree holding a long piece of rope that dangled into the water. Cassius and Anatha were nearby and both Seya and Borza were still maintaining their distance from the Sunfa but positioned as close as they dared without being seen in order to assist if needed. We were located within the Sunfa central area and so within the series of stakes and walls that the Sunfa had arrayed to protect their town as much as possible. The hope was that if the eel was inside the area then it would be the one to come to investigate the bloody slab of meat that was attached to the rope, rather than a whole host of other swamp denizens if we were to do this further out. We had built a cage with the help of the Sunfa and reinforced it with as much wood and vine as they could spare. It was big enough for Cassius and I to lie side by side in and so we hoped it would be large enough for the eel to enter. Once it did then Anatha would drop the rear gate and Cassius would unleash Asp upon the inhabitant.

Fool proof. Obviously.

Three hours of holding that rope; anticipation slowly giving way to boredom. Some fish came to investigate but nothing larger than a carp. Once I thought I sensed something larger moving towards the cage but it must have decided against investigating further. Either the Sunfa'shak had moved on or it wasn't interested in what we had to offer.

*Or...* I grabbed my knife; *it isn't interested in what's on the menu.* With a quick cut I sliced the meat of my forearm and let a small stream of blood trickle into the swamp water below. Barely a minute later I sensed something fighting its way through some thick rushes in the distance and not long after that the cage shook violently as something long and sinuous churned the swamp water. Instantly Anatha dropped the rear wall and Cassius unsheathed Asp. With intense focus on his face he raised the blade high and a shimmer of energy gathered around the razor-sharp edge. With a bark of effort he cut downwards and the air *shattered* as energy sheared out from Asp, slicing through the air at blinding speed and dissecting the cage in two. Frantic thrashing grew more frenzied as a pool of blood spilled out into the surrounding water and then the murky liquid stilled.

Shouts of joy, celebration and awe began to erupt from the onlooking Sunfa. They had told Anatha of how they had tried to hunt the eel with bow and spear but the scaled creature had shrugged off the majority of the blows they had landed. To see Cassius sever it in two with one blow must have been mighty indeed.

Cassius swung down lightly and perched on the broken cage. He stared intently into the water for a long moment before stabbing down with an impassioned thrust.

"It's dead," he voiced calmly, flicking the blood and water off Asp and sheathing it. The Sunfa cheered even more loudly, exuberant in Cassius's victory. Even Anatha allowed herself a small smile at a job well done.

I was moving before I even knew I had sensed it. I'm not sure what gave it away; a current that seemed out of place or the brush of a reed on the water's edge, but one second I was basking in a job well done and the next I was airborne.

It turned out that the Sunfa'shak was either a cannier predator than we had imagined or it was actually more than one creature. If so then the beast that Cassius had killed was probably half the size of the one that followed. It had closed in quietly, biding its time - or maybe it had always been there, who knew? The last ripple of movement gave it away as it propelled itself out of the water, its serpentine bulk winnowing through the air in a twisting torsion of coiled power. Its jaws hung wide in that creepy manner that eels can do and I had no doubt that it could easily swallow me whole. Perhaps that would have been more pleasant than what followed, for as my desperate tackle knocked Cassius off the cage and sent him sprawling into the water the gaping maw closed around my side and in an instant I was gone.

# CHAPTER 31

## *Sunfa'shak*

The world rushed past in a horror of blinding water, mud and brief, desperate clutches of air. Jaws clamped like steel around my belly and hip; teeth grinding against bone. I could taste blood in my mouth and by the furious vigour of the creature that carried me, it could too. I tried to reach for a knife, any knife, but my right arm was pinned against my torso inside its mouth whilst my left arm flailed uselessly outside. Rocks, branches and who knows what else battered every part of me that was outside the eel's mouth as it threaded its way into the swamp. Calls of horror and dismay came to me in drops of sounds in those brief moments where my head was above water. I tried to scream but the pain and fear rendered me incapable.

After a few eternal moments my brain switched from blind panic into pure survival. It recognised that I wasn't immediately dead and decided that it wanted to keep me that way. I began fighting back, hitting with my free hand where I could but unable to cause much damage. I managed to reach into my boot and grab my spare knife but lost it when my shoulder collided with something hard enough to drive all of the air out of my lungs. Out of weapons, I turned back to striking the creature but it was only when I shattered a tooth and began using it to stab into the surrounding soft tissue that I noticed any semblance of pain in the beast, and that was when it decided to get nasty.

Something I did not know about eels. Certain ones have two types of jaw. The outer jaw holds its prey and once it is secure the second jaw comes forwards and drags the prey into the depths of its belly. Not knowing this at the time, feeling something else rip into my arm from inside the eel was beyond terrifying. Thankfully I had enough of my body outside of its mouth to avoid being dragged into its stomach and continued delivering micro cuts that did nothing but piss it off.

My foot hit a patch of solid ground and suddenly I had purchase! Instinctively drawing on Seya's power I bucked my hips and *heaved.* The eel found itself raised out of the water and slammed onto the tree root that my foot had found. I had hoped it would take the hint and let go, but the eel was nothing if not tenacious and its mouth didn't remotely budge. It bundled up its coils and hit forwards like a piston, upending my footing and driving me into the mud and water.

I fought and fought and fought, but its writhing coils trapped my legs and stopped me from getting purchase again. As my vision began to darken an earth-shattering roar split the night and I found myself raised out of the water by the eel's teeth as Seya bit down on its neck, crunching through flesh and bone with ease. I could feel her fury in the vibrations that carried through the creature's body and thrummed through mine. With a savage *crunch* her teeth tore through the back of its neck and the eel's thrashing began to still. A moment later two simian hands grasped either side of its jaw and almost effortlessly the eel's jaws were forced apart, wider and wider until the top jaw sheared off entirely in a gout of blood and gore.

The last thing I remember was looking into the horrific visage of Anatha's craggy face and then everything went black.

* * *

I awoke to the sound of celebration. It is a pleasant thing to be awoken by people having a combined good time. Not just a bunch of drunks in the early hours of the morning - that is nothing but an annoyance - but waking up to a tribe wide party? Not bad.

Not that I could take part in it mind. I was bandaged almost head to foot and judging from the tender feeling in my shoulder, chest, hip and upper thigh, my wounds were still very much healing. Seya sat in the corner of the room with her eyes shut and body still. I could feel the power she was forcing through the bond between us; sending my body's natural repair methods into overdrive.

*Hello Calidan,* she voiced, eyes still shut. *Do not move, you need to rest.*

*Hi Seya,* I thought back, too tired to talk. *Did we win?*

*If you mean did you act as a natural chew toy until I got there to win for you, then yes, we won.*

*It wasn't intentional,* I grumbled. She twitched an ear in response.

*The Sunfa are very impressed at your...resilience. They're obviously much more impressed with me and Borza but hold you in high regard too. Apparently nothing has escaped the clutches of that eel before.*

I tenderly probed the wounds around my torso and winced at the pain. *I can understand why; I don't think eels like to release their prey. I doubt I could have got out without Borza removing its head; its jaws were clamping down like a vice.*

*If you had been stuck in my jaws as prey then you wouldn't have had time to think about it,* Seya mused wryly.

*Having been in your jaws many times over the years I can safely agree that I would not like you to have treated me as prey oh majestic queen of cats,* I replied.

*Flattery will get you far Calidan,* Seya replied, *I'm glad you're finally recognising that. Keep it up!*

I laughed out loud and then groaned as pain wracked my ribs. *Don't make me laugh. It hurts!*

*Nothing I said was a joke,* Seya returned swiftly, amusement tingeing her voice. *And it's your own fault that you're hurt, so suck it up.*

*If I hadn't got in the way then Cassius would have been taken in my plac-*

*-I'm not arguing that you saved Cassius's life,* Seya cut in. *It was a gallant act and bravely done. I'm calling you an idiot because of the way you did it. Next time try and do something a little more clever than just replacing the meat in the beast's jaws please...do you think Anatha would have done something like that?*

*Disregarding the fact that Anatha wouldn't jump in to save some-one in the first place...no,* I replied sullenly. *She no doubt would have dreamt up and enacted five responses in the time it took me to travel the distance to Cassius. But she does have some advantages there.*

*And you have others,* retorted Seya, fixing me with an intense gaze. *Just because the abilities you get from me mean that you can't enhance your thinking in quite the same way as Anatha does with Borza doesn't mean that you are lesser. You already know that your speed and reflexes are higher than hers. As Anatha intuited that you are likely to be facing large monsters in the future then you might want to train your reactions so that next time you lead with your sword rather than your face.* She finished the last thought by rising to her feet and giving me a raspy lick. *Your face is fool-ishly not made for fighting, so stop trying to put it in danger.*

I tried in vain not to laugh but failed miserably. *A good point,* I conceded, *next time I'll stab first and ask questions later.*

*Next time try not to get outsmarted by an eel,* she fired back. *They are about as dumb as things get. Seriously.*

*Yes Ma'am!*

Seya flicked an ear at me. *Do you want to get licked again?*

I was about to answer in a way that would undoubtedly have

resulted in a rough sandpapering when I was saved by Cassius walking through the door. He had Asp on his belt and a wooden bowl that was filled with the most heavenly smell. He grinned as my stomach made itself known and set down the bowl next to me.

"Don't move," he said as I started to sit up. Seya prevented my stupidity by reaching up a large paw and placing it on my head; instantly flattening me to the bed.

"Couldn't if I wanted to apparently," I replied.

*You'll thank me later.*

"You'll thank her later I'm sure," Cassius said as he placed Asp to one side and drew up a chair.

*See? Cassius gets me.*

"What's for dinner?" I asked, studiously ignoring Seya and trying to act as though having a panther paw on my head was completely normal. That said, it was about as normal as the two of us were ever going to get.

"'Victory stew', Anatha says the Sunfa call it," he answered. "In this case it seems to consist of vegetables, rice and eel."

"...the eel that tried to eat me and succeeded in eating a number of others?"

"The Sunfa don't like to let things go to waste," he replied. "And it's pretty good to be honest. And there is nothing else so shut up and let me feed you."

I grumbled and grimaced but in the end he got his way. Seya and Cassius, between the two of them I could never win. As he fed me Cassius updated me with the goings-on of the clan. Apparently the leader, Erin'ea, had already fulfilled her side of the bargain and provided a seemingly charged power cube to Anatha's safe keeping. They had offered us use of their hospitality as long as we wanted and invited us to hunt with them whenever we were nearby. They had also apparently offered their biggest metal contraption in return for Seya and Borza, both of whom were the largest and apparently most well-trained animals they had ever seen. I think that if they had known just what they both were rather than assuming that they were the same as the large creatures that they were used to seeing in the swamp then we would have been offered their entire village.

Once he finished feeding me Cassius put the bowl aside and sat back with his feet on the bed. He fixed me with a serious gaze and I knew I was in for a moving heart to heart.

"Thanks," he said simply.

I raised an eyebrow. "That's it? No big speech?"

He winked. "Oh I have one prepared if you want it but I figured that considering the lives we lead if I keep doing a long speech then we're probably going to be losing a fair amount of time to my voice over the years. So 'thanks'."

I barked a laugh then groaned again as my chest ached. "Don't make me laugh you bastard," I grunted. "And you're welcome."

"Next time, perhaps try saving me without getting eaten in turn?"

*Yes Cassius!*

I ignored Seya's exultation. "Next time how about you try not nearly getting eaten in the first place?"

He grinned ruefully and patted my foot. "Deal."

We stayed like that for some time, chatting and joking until fatigue took hold and I drifted off to sleep. My dreams were simultaneously hazy and vivid. Those dreams that you swear to yourself you are going to remember whilst in them and then promptly forget all about on waking. I would say fever dreams and they likely were - the combination of murky swamp water and the inside of an eel's mouth doubtless made for a pleasant combination but the amount of green seraph that Seya was pumping into me through our bond probably made it the shortest fever ever. I dreamt of the cave that we lived in for months, of glowing red eyes and demonic claws, riding a serpent through crystalline waters and colours, swirls and shadow. At one point I thought I saw Anatha talking to Seya with an intent yet sorrowful expression on her face but the next instant I was drowning underwater so I have no idea if anything I experienced that night was real.

I woke in the late morning in a bed damp with sweat but no pain in the cuts that surrounded my torso. Gingerly reaching beneath the plethora of bandages that swaddled me I felt around and braced for the pain. When nothing happened I probed a little further and eventually pulled the bandage off. Where the jagged wounds from the eel's teeth had been there was nothing but silvery scars. Fast healing - yet another perk of being bonded to Seya and one that I have relied on many times in my short but impactful career. Without her the punishment that I have put my body through over the years would have killed me many times over.

I gingerly stood up and felt the freshly repaired skin pull slightly at the edges of my wounds but other than that I had no lingering aches or pains to speak of. *Thanks Seya,* I thought at my partner where she lay on the floor. She twitched an ear in response and went back to reclining in the rays of sun that were speckling through the doorway. I ventured outside and every member of the Sunfa who I passed nodded at me as though I was a well-known figure - which I suppose I was, it probably wasn't every day that someone survived being in the jaws of such a large creature.

Members of the Sunfa directed me to Cassius and Anatha and I found both of them in a large hall on the largest strut of the ginormous dead machine that formed the centre of the town. Inside the hall were dozens of skulls and skeletons that decorated the walls and at times formed benches and chairs.

"Ah, you're finally awake," creaked Anatha. "Glad you could deign to join us." I smirked back and she cracked a grin. "Good to see you in one-piece boy. Try and stay that way next time."

"It's certainly not an experience I would like to repeat," I replied, "the smell lasts for ages."

She snorted and turned away, waving a hand at the hall. "I figured that you might want to see what your gallant stupidity has wrought. Welcome to the town hall. The bones of each Sunfa'shak have been memorialised here as reminders. The latest is just over here."

She walked over to a skull that looked a fair bit smaller than I felt that the skull should be, having been in its mouth.

She looked over, saw the scowl on my face and cackled. "They always look smaller when they're no longer trying to kill you don't they?"

Cassius and I looked at each and laughed. At Anatha's confused look Cassius explained, "This would register on the smaller side of the creatures that we have faced so far," he said with a shrug. "I'm pretty sure that the skeleton of the skyren we left down in the desert would not fit through the door!"

"You really don't want to compare kills boy," Anatha replied with a cocky grin. "I have a good century on you and a great many of those have been spent in the pursuit of monsters. And as you found with the spider queen you met in the ice caves, skyren are not necessarily the biggest creatures in the world though they are the most dangerous by far. Anyway, what I meant is that this is a learning opportunity. Tell me truthfully boys, does this look as big as what you faced in the swamp?"

We both shook our heads. "Of course it doesn't!" she exclaimed. "And that is because it isn't. Obviously it is missing the layers of flesh that cover the bones. But fear and adrenaline makes enemies and foes seem larger than they are, they can fill your vision and block out anything else around you. You might swear blind that the creature was twenty feet tall only to find out later than it was a mere twelve. Any you might think that it doesn't matter but as I have already explained in the mission, information gathering is vital."

She took a look at our stumped faces and sighed before waving a hand at the walls around us. "Look at all this. Look at it! Do you think there are this many oversized creatures in the Andurran empire?"

"I think that there are probably a lot more than we are aware of," I said slowly, picking my words with care.

"And you would be correct!" Anatha replied. "Which is one reason why Imperators exist. But creatures generally need a reason to get so big and they need an appropriate food source to sustain them. This is why it is uncommon to see multiple predators over a certain size in the same region. Some, like trolls, can sustain themselves on surprisingly little, but unless the creature is a Great Heart or otherwise created creature then they generally have to abide by the natural laws."

"So why is the swamp producing so many large creatures?" Cassius murmured, more to himself than anyone else but Anatha pointed a finger at him excitedly.

"Exactly," she said fiercely. "Why is the swamp producing so many large creatures? Can it support the quantity of large animals that are found here? Is it something to do with what caused the surrounding valley and the swamp in the first place? Is there a high density of seraph here? Can the Empire take advantage of it in some way? These are the kind of questions that an Imperator needs to be asking when they come across something interesting. Remember that and you will do well."

"What do you think?" I asked.

"About the swamp?" I nodded in confirmation and she continued, "I think that whatever caused the crater that formed this valley and swamp left a mark, and that mark - whether it is seraph or power from the machines left to rot here - causes aberrations in the surrounding fauna. My best guess is that their growth is stimulated and they become much larger than normal, but that this results in an increased need to feed and consequently why the Sunfa have so many Sunfa'shak - eventually the creatures turn to preying on the humans here." She smiled wanly. "It is only a guess mind, but based on the information I have it is the best guess I can make."

"Seems like a reasonable enough guess to me," voiced Cassius, giving a warm smile at the ancient being who returned a look that could have curdled milk.

"Don't coddle me boy. Flattery will get you nowhere."

*She has a different approach to you,* I mused to Seya as Anatha unleashed a verbal tirade upon a bemused Cassius.

*Each queen to their own,* Seya replied warmly. *Everyone has a best method of approach.*

*Including flagrant flattery in your case.*

*Of course,* she shot back, no trace of humility in her voice. *But it is only natural for you humans to need to flatter me. I am far above you after all.*

I snorted and directed my attention back to Anatha who was breathing heavily in the face of a wind-swept Cassius. "What do we do now Anatha? Got the cube?"

She reached into a satchel at her side and pulled out a silvery cube. "Here it is," she said softly with eyes full of wonder.

"That's it?" I asked, somewhat surprised. "It seems so...nondescript."

Anatha gave a huff. "Sometimes the more nondescript something or someone looks the more it will surprise you. This is made of a metal that our blacksmiths do not know how to make, as is most of the pre-Cataclysm equipment that you see lying around us. Furthermore it does this, catch," and tossed the cube at me.

As I caught the cube I felt a *thrum* through my hand and arm. Strong at first and then softer until I could almost imagine it wasn't there. "That's...interesting," I said slowly. "Why does it do that?"

Anatha let out another indelicate snort. "Why does anything pre-Cataclysm do anything? Who knows? Maybe it is meant to be an indicator of how much power it has left? Maybe it isn't meant to do that at all and is leaking energy into the world and holding it in your hand is right now killing you." She grinned evilly as I threw the cube back. "This isn't something that we understand. Well...the Emperor might but he has a tendency to understand everything that gets put in front of him." She tucked the cube back into her satchel. "At the end of the day, as much as I would like to understand it, we don't *have* to. We've done our mission, retrieved the cube, removed a threat and only one person got mildly chewed - a pretty good outcome for any Imperator."

I gave her my best glare and she responded with a wink. "As for what we do next, we head home. The job is done. So enjoy your last day with the Sunfa, we leave at first light."

# CHAPTER 32

## *Plans*

The journey back was largely uneventful. The Sunfa were sad to see us go but sent us off with many suggestions to return - an added bonus according to Anatha as it opened up potential trading opportunities. Two large creatures that looked like scaled reptiles with large mouths had a battle in the water beneath our chosen evening tree and came very close to battering our tree into pieces, but thankfully none of us were hurt. A weary climb out of the valley and then a slower five days on horseback to Port Cambal where Anatha sold the impressive and rested beasts to a gleaming eyed merchant for an undisclosed sum of money but more than enough to have us repeat our experience of the first night in port, quarters in the finest brothel available and passage back on the same Twisted Sister that we had hated travelling out on in the first place. Within seven days from leaving the Sunfa we were back in Anafor where Anatha left us, and two days after that we were back in the Academy, travel-stained, saddle sore, stinking and standing in Kane's office.

To his credit he didn't bat an eye at our appearance or wrinkle his nose at the smell. I very much doubted that we were the first travel weary members of the Academy to come before him without showering.

"So," he began after offering us both a whisky, "you made it back in one piece. That's a good start. Report."

Between the two of us we gave Kane the key content of our journey, describing the Sunfa settlement in detail, the defeat of the Sunfa'shak and the cube that Anatha had taken directly to the Emperor's citadel. When we finished he gave a thoughtful grunt and took a long sip of whisky.

"You've done a difficult task and it sounds like you've done it admirably," he said after a moment. "The Emperor has already given me notice that the cube is in his possession and to congratulate you both on a job well done. He has asked that you join him at the citadel tomorrow morning to break your fast," he paused to give us a grave look, "and reminds you to speak of the findings of your mission to no-one. Not me, not Adronicus, not your friends. Understood?"

"Yes Instructor," Cassius and I both intoned. It sounded like a harsh order but the plan that Anatha and I had in mind required complete silence in order to work so that everyone would walk through the citadel's seraph detectors without question.

Kane gave a nod. "Excellent. And Calidan," he said, fixing me with a look, "Anatha says you managed to find yourself in the jaws of a large beast. She asked me to remind you that most Imperators try and get the mission done without getting hurt, and definitely without getting eaten. I, for one, agree with her." He gave me a wry grin. "Whilst the inside of a mouth might look comfortable I ask that you go against your natural instincts going forwards and use your brain to complement your impressive reactions." His grin got wider as my scowl deepened and he finally chuckled and gave me a wink.

"But she also pointed out that you saved Cassius in an impressive show of gallantry. I personally commend you for that and in doing so I will choose to ignore the rest of Anatha's message where she highlights that Imperators are not knights and win no accolades for heroic feats."

I snorted and shook my head. Anatha was incorrigible.

Kane finished his drink and nodded his head in the direction of the door. "You've both done well. Cassius, Adronicus is eager to hear how Asp performed. Please indulge him when you've had a chance to clean up. Both of you should take the day to yourselves, you're excused from training and classes today and tomorrow. Clean up, eat and see your friends. Oh, and make sure to be at the citadel in good time tomorrow. I believe the Emperor breaks his fast at eight o'clock. Enjoy."

With thanks to Kane we both walked out and headed to the dorms. The others were in class and so we dumped our gear before heading to the baths. Two hours and three separate baths later we finally felt clean. The bath attendant had taken one look at the black muck streaking off us and immediately called for more water. It might have been embarrassing, but the Academy baths were designed to receive Imps who were coated in mud, sweat and no short amount of tears and the attendants had presumably long since lost their sense of smell.

Wearing freshly laundered clothes for the first time in a month was a singularly splendid feeling. Travelling with limited clothing is an interesting process. You start off changing regularly but after you have cycled through all your available clothes and not found anywhere suitable to wash and dry them whilst on the journey you begin the cycle of re-use. At first this feels wrong and disgusting but within a day you've forgotten all about it - humans are nothing if not adaptable. It becomes so commonplace to be wearing dirt-encrusted leather, mud-caked boots and having a sheen of grime across every aspect of your skin that it is only when presented with an opportunity to bathe that your brain resets and the disgust begins anew. All I can say is that stepping into that water was pure, unadulterated *bliss*.

After the baths, Cassius split off to find Adronicus whilst I went to check in on Seya and made sure to give her a well-deserved grooming. The others found me sleeping soundly in Seya's paws later that afternoon and the celebrations, hugs and story sharing began in earnest. The biggest concern to me was that seraph training had continued unabated whilst we were away and I had an intense fear that we would not catch up. Rikol put on a dazzling light show, highlighting just how far he had come and how far I had yet to go in that particular area. Scythe, Ella and Sophia regaled us with the latest news, incidents and goings on of the Academy and in return Cassius and I told tales of mosquito infested swamps and how an eel tried its best to eat me...all in all I think that they had the more pleasant month.

A night of eating and drinking later and Cassius and I stood in front of the citadel's imposing gates, having our identities checked by four equally imposing guards. After a few minutes we were guided into the grounds and led through the circular walkways until we reached an arching entranceway, full of grand, intricately detailed stone. The Emperor stood inside the vast hallway that lay within, idly fingering the frilled edge of a tapestry.

Our guide stopped at the entrance and waved us in. "Your guests, your majesty," he said with a bow.

"Thank you Sirin," rumbled the Emperor as he turned towards us with a beaming smile. "You are excused. Cassius and Calidan, welcome, come in and join me."

We walked into the grand hall, gasping at the many paintings, sculptures and statues that adorned the walls. The Emperor met us with a wide smile and an extended hand. After clasping each of our hands in one that dwarfed our own he led us on a brief tour of the hall, proudly describing each piece that caught his eye.

We followed, listening, nodding and gasping when we felt that it was expected. Cassius and I knew absolutely nothing about art. For two orphaned mountain folk we had exceedingly good educations - brother Gelman and the Academy had done us a great service there - but art wasn't a topic that was often covered and we just hadn't had much opportunity to be exposed to it.

The Emperor must have seen that we were getting glassy-eyed

for he chuckled to himself and led the way to a small side door. "I can see that the art of my hall does little for you and I can understand that for it does little for me too," he said as quietly as a fading avalanche. "But art is a useful thing to have as talking points for breaking the ice with foreign dignitaries. For some reason one man's collection of art is seen as a more avid sign of wealth and power than the success of his cities and country. Strange really. But anyway," he led the way into a small side corridor and into a small and imposing study made of the same obsidian stone that formed the citadel that he unlocked with a wave of his hand, "here we are. I took the liberty of ordering breakfast here. It should be along in just a moment. Once it arrives we can talk freely."

Barely seconds later a knock sounded at the door and a number of black clad staff walked in bearing heavily laden plates that they set up on portable tables. They were gone almost as quickly as they arrived, shutting the door behind them and leaving behind a mouth-watering array of food that looked quite literally fit for a king - or in this case, Emperor.

Once the door shut behind them the Emperor flicked his hand in its direction and there was the click of a lock sliding shut.

"There," he reverberated. "Now we can talk in perfect confidence. This room is completely soundproof and the only people in here are you, me and..." the obsidian wall slid back and a crinkled old bat stepped in, "Anatha." He turned to her and raised a questioning eyebrow to which she nodded.

"It works," she said in answer to his unspoken question. "It detected everyone's seraph levels who stepped through the door to the Great Hall. Type, quantity; everything looked to be in order."

"Excellent," he rumbled, "though I expected nothing less. Well done." He turned back and fixed us both with piercing eyes. "Come, eat," he rumbled, gesturing at the food. "Eat and we shall discuss what must be done. The Academy must be cleansed; the traitors rooted out. I will not allow the Enemy to have a foothold any longer than he already has." His voice grew thick with anger as he spoke and his eyes clouded like a storm. Tension grew more and more thick until it was like a physical pressure that rooted Cassius and myself to our seats. Just when I thought he was going to erupt; a pancake enveloped his face then slowly flopped to the floor.

"Sorry," cackled Anatha, "looks like I missed my plate!"

I braced myself for the explosion of anger but gone was the intensity of the moment before, now the Emperor had a look of pure bemusement as he touched his face.

"Ah!" he complained. "You coated it in syrup too? That's harsh Anatha."

"Well you were looking all murdery over there so I had to add a little extra to make sure to get your mind off it," the old woman replied with a mouth full of muffin. "What's done is done, you'll have your chance at revenge I'm sure. So stop moping about."

"Boys, take this to heart, no matter how old you are - and I am *old* - at some unknown point in life certain people somehow obtain the ability to preach, boss and push you around and they manage to do it without a care in the world. If you go and speak to any of my soldiers or probably the majority of citizens within my empire they would likely pale and wet themselves at the thought of a pancake being thrown at my face and yet here she sits, happily munching away and totally uncaring. I do not understand it but I do applaud it. It makes for a welcome change...at times," he finished with a slight narrowing of his eyes at the ancient woman.

"Bah!" Anatha replied vehemently, "you just love it when people do something unexpected. You're not even annoyed at the fact that the Enemy has infiltrated the Academy. You're frustrated at yourself for not seeing it coming. You probably respect Him even more now because He has managed to surprise you once again."

Silence and then a wry smile spread across the Emperor's face.

"For such a child you sometimes do see to the heart of things. My thanks Anatha. I shall attempt to not allow my emotions to get the better of me."

Anatha gave him a wink and went back to slurping a coffee.

I realised that Cassius had his hand in the air at the same time that the Emperor did. He looked momentarily taken aback before giving him a beatific grin. "Whilst I appreciate the courtesy Cassius, in this location please feel free to talk as normal. What can I do for you?"

Cassius blushed slightly and fidgeted uncomfortably before blurting out, "How old are you?"

The Emperor burst out laughing, heaving great thunderous peals of laughter than echoed around the room. Wiping an eye he finally stopped and gathered himself. "How old am I?" he murmured more to himself than anyone else. "A very good question. I can honestly say that I have no idea how old I am, just know that I am *old*." He heavily emphasised the last word. "As to the how and why of that I will let you guess." He gave Cassius a wink and clapped him on the shoulder before going to sit behind the beautifully carved mahogany desk that took centre stage in the room. Taking a bite out of a croissant and a slurp of coffee he put his feet up on the edge of the table with a thoughtful look on his face.

"So..." he began, "we're throwing a party."

"Calidan's idea," Anatha coughed around more muffin.

"And not a bad one," he replied. "The biggest question is what reason can we give to get the entirety of the Academy and every Imperator into the citadel. Such a thing has not happened since the Academy's founding. There are always too many missions to ensure that everyone is in the same place."

"With respect Sir," Cassius broke in, "why not just get everyone you can and then invite those left over to the citadel when back from missions?"

The Emperor rubbed his chin thoughtfully. "It could work, but if something goes sour at the event then any shadow-tainted individuals who were on missions would undoubtedly be made aware that I was on the hunt."

"And so would likely make a number of convenient excuses

not to come to the citadel," Anatha replied quietly. "You could make it a regular event. Purging the tainted now does not necessitate that more won't become controlled later. Make a recurring event, once every six months or so, that requires Imperators to come to the citadel and pass through the seraph scanners. The Imperators get some kind of celebration and excuse to meet with you, any that have high levels of black seraph within them are quietly removed, and those who can't make the party are more carefully watched. If those individuals can't attend a couple of other invitations or events then they are treated as suspect."

"I like it," rumbled the Emperor. "Efficient and gives both the Imperators a chance to unwind as well as an opportunity to discern any of those controlled. Two birds with one stone." He looked carefully at each of us with an intense gaze. "You've all been through the seraph detectors and Cassius, whilst you have an abundance of black seraph within you, I myself purged you of that corruption so I have no concerns regarding your loyalty. I ask that you give nothing less than your all to support me in the coming weeks. I hope that the corrupted can be rooted out swiftly, easily and without loss. However the Enemy is a cunning and pernicious foe and He could well have planned for this eventuality. Only time, as always, will reveal the truth.

"I will organise events here with Anatha. We will move quickly so expect invitations to the constituents of the entire Academy to be sent shortly. I would like you both to arrive on the early side of proper. Cassius, make sure to bring Asp. Calidan I want you to keep Seya hidden and siphon as much strength and speed as possible from her. Anatha has taught you how to do this, no?"

I nodded in affirmation and he continued, "If anything happens I will need you to respond as you see fit. My guards will be in attendance, as will I, and all will be equipped to deal with... difficult enemies. Support my people where needed and take down anyone who is revealed to be acting against the empire.

Understood?"

Cassius raised a pale hand and the Emperor nodded. "What if I know the person Sir? I'm not sure that I can..."

The Emperor held his gaze for a long moment before giving a soft sigh. "Sometimes I forget just how young and inexperienced you all are. That will change, and rapidly I'm afraid. Everything that you have experienced in the Academy up to now is to build you up to a certain standard, to improve you physically and mentally to the point where the next phase of training will not crush you completely. Believe me when I say that the fifth year of your training will make the rest look like a fun holiday."

Out of the corner of my eye I noticed a faint trembling of Anatha's hand, quickly stilled. It looked like the Emperor's words were bringing up bad memories.

"Imperators like Kane, Simone and Merowyn are all experienced and more importantly they are *prepared*. They know just how insidious the Enemy is. Indeed, you have both experienced the nature of that Enemy first hand. What separates them is that they are prepared to do what is necessary in order to win. Whilst you may not understand that at this point, you will. For now do what you can and what you think is right. However," he turned the full intensity of his gaze on the two of us, "do not interfere with the actions of the guards, Anatha or myself. Whilst I usually have restraint, my guards will not, and even with your skill sets you would find yourselves very hard pressed if you chose to stand in their way. Clear?"

Cassius and I both swallowed heavily and nodded. For all his charm and wonder the Emperor could be downright frightening when he wanted.

At that point in my life I had no idea just how terrifying he could be.

# CHAPTER 33

## *Celebrations*

L ess than five days after our attendance at the citadel the
Academy received notice that a ball was to be held at
the Emperor's citadel in recognition of their services
to the empire. The event was to be held twice a year and was
intended to be a moment that the Imps and Imperators could
look forward to and thus revitalise them for the remainder of
the year. Or at least that is what the notice said, obviously Cassius and I knew better. This ball had every possibility of turning bloody.

Ten days following our return from the citadel and we were
attending the ball. Ten days of relative normality, to immerse ourselves in the difficult training, exercise and learning provided by the Academy and centre ourselves again. It
was strange how the bone-crushingly hard exercise that Imps
did day in and day out could become something reassuring, but regardless of who you were and what you had just
been through it offered a sense of normality, a place of focus
in which to momentarily forget the pressures of the outside
world, and considering the number of Imperators who woke
at the same time and exercised and practiced just as hard as us
even without Adronicus or Kane bellowing down their ears I
imagined that it only became more and more compounded as

a method of meditation.

Ten days of training, of talking with teachers, of catching up with the dorm and friends and attempting to learn as much missed seraph content as possible. The growing buzz of anticipation surrounding the ball became a strange mixture of excitement and lead weight for Cassius and myself. We longed to be lost in the excitement of being invited to the Emperor's citadel, as we once were when younger, and to fully embrace the wonder and magic of attending a ball in such a place. Unfortunately the closer we got to the date of the event the more dread built in my chest. Cassius too had the same anguished look on his face when no others were looking. After all, it was quite possible that people we knew - friends even - might be removed by the Emperor during the event. Consequently, when I stepped out of the carriage dressed in my Imp finery - black clad formal wear with silver buckles and on loan to the Academy - the look on my face was one close to despair. Guards intercepted us as we stepped from the carriage, briefly checked our invitations and our bodies for ranged weapons but allowed us to keep our blades. Whether that was an order from the Emperor or a normal case I did not know but it wouldn't surprise me to learn that the Emperor had little fear of swords.

Striding forwards we stepped into the hallway and were greeted by a swarm of servants who brought champagne and hors d'oeuvres before directing us along the seemingly firefly lit corridor towards the Great Hall. Even though we had been there before, on seeing what the Emperor's staff had done to the magnificent room drew involuntary gasps from Cassius and myself. The room was festooned with the Academy colours of black and silver punctuated by blooms of colourful flowers that adorned each table. The centre of the hall had been cleared to make space for dancing, exposing a pristine and presumably ancient wooden floor that I imagined many of the nobility would kill to own. As per the Emperor's request we were here early, having arrived as one of the first carriages.

The ball itself was set to start at the seventh bell, and we had arrived some 15 minutes prior to that time, making us unfashionably early but from the look on the Emperor's face as he strode to meet us we were anything but an inconvenience.

He was clad in plate armour. It might seem like an odd choice of attire for a ball however the armour he was wearing looked surprisingly in keeping with the surrounding environment. The armour itself was seemingly comprised of obsidian or some other devilishly dark metal and highlighted with silver inlays. It made for an imposing and inspiring spectacle. I had absolutely no doubt in my mind that the armour would be completely functional and yet I doubted that the Emperor even needed armour - or at least anything visible anyway. His metal clad strides shook the room and aides hurried to protect vases of flowers from falling over in the wake of his passing. The Emperor was always larger-than-life and we knew that he was no ordinary man, but in this setting it really hit home just how different and extraordinary he was.

Here was a man to be admired, respected, and feared.

"Cassius, Calidan and friends," he boomed, "you are most welcome! Please take advantage of the hospitality of my hall. My servants will attend to your every need, you need but ask. Drinks and refreshments are available and the finest dinner you will ever enjoy will be served at the eighth bell. I ask that you celebrate and be merry for this party is in the Academy's honour."

Rikol, Scythe, Sophia and Ella murmured awestruck thanks at the godlike figure in front of them. He chuckled and waved us on before stopping Cassius and myself. "If it pleases you both I received some new information on the art we discussed last week, if you would like to come with me I will briefly show you."

He led us in the direction of the study and soon we were in the bolted and magically shut room. "Welcome both," he rumbled. Again the panel door slid open and Anatha stepped out. She shook her head at his questioning stare.

"Everyone in the hall already, aside from Cassius, has zero or minuscule levels of black seraph within them," she said softly. Cassius and I breathed audible sighs of relief which the Emperor noticed with an amused glance. "You're glad that your friends aren't tainted?" he murmured. "You should be, and I'm very glad that they are not. They are fine additions to the Academy and I would not wish to lose them." He gave us both an intense look. "Everyone who was in that hall when you arrived can presumably be trusted. I will not bring you in here again if I can help it. Word will reach your ears of suspect individuals if needed. If anything happens, save who you can and put down those putting up resistance."

"Kill them, sir?" Cassius asked, a pained look on his face. "Can't you purge them like you did with me?"

The Emperor sighed heavily. "You were not fully in the control of black seraph when I got to you Cassius and even then it was hard going. Those who have been in the grip of the shadow can have powers which you will not have seen in your seraph classes. Do you think Rya was taught any of what she nearly killed you with? I fear that if I tried to purge one then if there is another in the audience he or she will wreak untold havoc. So no, I intend for them to be put down, and swiftly. Do what you can and make me proud."

He gave us both a nod and then ushered us out of the room as Anatha slipped back into the hidden side panel. On our return to the main hall he gripped our shoulders tightly, nodded in a genial fashion and then moved on to mingle. With a dour look at each other Cassius and I did the same.

It's a strange feeling trying to enjoy a ball whilst keeping your awareness on edge and looking for anything out of the ordinary. People try and get you drunk, bringing drinks and food, and you take it as you don't want to raise suspicion - after all the Emperor had thrown this event purely for the Academy so why wouldn't I be getting rip-roaringly drunk? Thankfully there were so many people pouring into the hall at this point that it was easy enough to distance myself from those who knew I was acting oddly and introduce myself to others. Cassius and I spent the majority of the evening near the entrance hall and saw nothing untoward for the first couple of hours. We didn't see Anatha in our time there, didn't receive any secretive notes or warnings and there was no suggestion from the Emperor's smiling face and vocal attitude that anything was amiss.

I spent a pleasant half hour catching up with Simone and Merowyn, the two of them as inseparable as ever. Merowyn had more of a wild glint in her eyes than the last time I saw her and Simone a few more streaks of grey in his hair but other than that they were mostly the same. Both had been on missions around the globe that they largely refrained from talking about, only offering that some had been 'difficult'. I could only imagine what 'difficult' might mean in the context of two Imperators who were that highly trained but I didn't probe and neither did they regarding the fourth-year exam - just offering congratulations on passing and leaving it at that. Eventually the call for dinner rang and we made our goodbyes to join our respective friends.

The Emperor certainly hadn't been underselling the promise of the meal. Each time I went to the citadel I was blown away by the quality of the cuisine, I guess it was to be expected when dining with the most powerful man in the world. For starters we had delicate cuts of beef that had been marinated in some kind of spicy sauce. For a cold dish it gave an impressive kick that set the senses aflame and perfectly prepared the taste buds for the next seven courses. Each one was exquisite in flavour and, judging from the noises of approval coming from the ever-hungry Imps, perfectly cooked. Wine was constantly on hand and glasses were never allowed to go empty, each rapidly filled by eagle-eyed servants. Imps and Imperators drank and ate their fill; cheeks becoming red and eyes glassy. The Emperor was matching the Imperators drink for drink, challenging those he obviously knew well to game after game and leaving an array of passed out Imperators in his wake. Whether it was his size or some other quirk of his mysterious abilities he was barely swaying as he demolished each challenger one after the other, each victory only spurring on others as the hope began afresh that they would be the one to bring him down.

For the happily unconscious members that the Emperor left behind in his wake, servants came forward to help them out towards carriages that stood waiting outside to transport anyone that wanted to go back to the Academy. Or at least that's what I thought they were doing but as I extended my senses at least one pair of servants deviated from the course, taking a drunk Imperator who I had not met before on a different route. A number of people carrying blades and wearing armour closed in on the servants and quickly moved the Imperator down into the bowels of the citadel where my senses lost them.

*Clever. He must have a high amount of black seraph and the Emperor has used a drinking game to remove him from the board.*

It didn't look like I was the only one to notice. At least two Imperators and three Imps were showing signs of stress with increased heart rates and body temperature. They either really didn't enjoy drinking or had another reason for not wanting to join the group of stupefied Imperators in the Emperor's wake. One of the Imps was a third year and the other two were fifth years and the panic on their faces as the Emperor approached was a hard thing to stomach. I had a good idea of what the Emperor would do if they chose to fight - though if they were truly corrupted by black seraph then I doubted that they had much choice in the matter at all. Thoughts of Rya and her all too fleeting moments of sanity where she had broken free of control ricocheted through my mind and my hand tightened on the glass I was holding subconsciously until it shattered with a loud crack, causing a number of heads to turn and the three nervous Imps to jump before offering me intense glares. "Sorry," I murmured sheepishly as servants came forward to clean up the broken glass. "My hand slipped."

"Effan, running away so soon?" a voice like thunder rumbled and caused every head in the room to turn. I realised that one of the Imperators had used the distraction of my glass shattering to get up from the table and begin making his way towards the exit.

The Imperator stiffened and stopped in his tracks before slowly turning around. "My apologies my Lord but my stomach does not sit well with me today. I would like to return to the Academy to rest if it pleases you?"

"No need to apologise Effan, I am sorry to hear of your ailment. The best doctors in the empire are at your disposal, my men will escort you to them," with a wave of his hand a number of servants swept forward, "please do not worry, you will be taken care of with the best care."

Effan paled and I could have sworn that his heart must have been audible to everyone and not just me. His hand flexed and closed, as though itching to clutch the hilt of his sword. "That is not necessary my Lord, please do not worry yourself."

"Nonsense," the Emperor boomed. "Whenever one of my valued Imperators is *afflicted*," he ground out the word in a voice like crumbling rocks, "then it is my duty to free them from that malady. I won't take no for an answer - my staff will see to your needs."

One of the servants stepped forward and bowed before holding out a hand to the entrance way. Effan tensed, his eyes darting around the room as though looking for a solution before locking onto the Emperor's implacable stare. The Emperor made a gentle hand motion and Effan visibly swallowed before bowing and leaving in the direction that the servants indicated. Once again the servants directed him to the right where another squad of armed and armoured men intercepted him. There was a brief struggle and then Effan was limp in their arms, though whether dead or alive I couldn't tell before he disappeared into the underground.

This time it was almost like the remaining Imps and Imperator received a slap across the face at the same moment.

Eyes twitched and their bodies flared in my senses as though everything within their systems was on fire. As the rest of the guests returned to their drinks the Imps and remaining Imperator stood as one. Black veins throbbed to the surface and I watched in curious horror as their eyes filled with swirling black until it was like looking into an abyss and in this instance I was very sure that the abyss would be staring right back.

A thunderous clap shook the air and the four controlled Academy members were flung across the room and into the wall with a splintering crunch. A cacophony of alarm rang throughout the hall as Imperators saw what was going on, many of the Imps panicking whilst the majority of the Imperators drew blades and drunkenly stumbled to guard the Emperor.

"It has gone far enough," rumbled the Emperor, his gaze locked on the eyes of the lead Imperator. "Leave them and try again another time." It was clear that his meaning was to whatever or whoever was controlling the four and not the unfortunate souls who had been taken.

There was a stamping of feet and a squad of guards rushed into the hall, each complete in gleaming obsidian armour. "Clear the room," came a barked order from the lead guard.

Not a single Imperator moved.

"Imps below fourth year leave now," thundered the Emperor, his face showing no strain at holding the four. "Take those too drunk to stand with you. Kane, Acana, Adronicus, escort them out and keep them safe."

It showed the level of loyalty that the Imperators had to the Emperor as the three didn't utter a single word of the protest that I could see on their faces. Not even Acana Wyckan, the High Imperator.

A harsh croaking sound splintered the silence as the Imps began to be herded out of the room. A sibilant voice began to be uttered in disturbing fashion from all four individuals at the same time. "So you finally caught on, congratulations."

"It was inevitable," rumbled the Emperor. "Just like your

eventual defeat at my hands."

The resulting cackle sent shivers down my spine. "How eventual, old friend?" the voice queried. "I have never been stronger and you still play empire builder. Have you got bored with this one yet?"

"Do not listen to his lies children," the Emperor ground out between clenched teeth. "He is the Great Deceiver. And I am done listening."

"You never were good at it," sibilated the voice. "As predictable as ever. Enjoy this. I know I will."

As the voice finished all four individuals squirmed and roared, black veins flaring throughout their bodies and black flames rushed out from their limbs. The wall splintered as the Emperor brought more weight to bear on those he had trapped.

"Children," he said in a voice tinged with sorrow. "Three of you I wish I had known. Penye, you have been a faithful servant and if you are in there I want you to know that I appreciate all you have done for the empire." He nodded at the guards who were waiting with weapons bared. "Do it."

The four guards approached warily, each moving with the lithe grace of a dedicated weapon practitioner. I had no doubt that each knew Kaschan and that the armour they were wearing was likely custom tailored and a replica of the set that the Emperor wore so nonchalantly. If Tyrgan's insight into the bodyguards was still accurate then each would be a force to be reckoned with; together they would be practically unstoppable.

The first guard reached the nearest Imp and without breaking stride thrust his blade through the poor Imp's heart. Black eyes flickered and for a second I'm positive we saw the Imp's fear-filled eyes shine through before the black flames roared and burst forward, consuming the Imp's body and leaping towards the guardsman where it stopped dead as the Emperor raised his hand.

"Did you not think that I would anticipate the sacrifice of your pawns?" he asked, the scorn in his voice palpable.

"Absolutely," answered the voice. "In fact I counted on it."

The Emperor's face held a look of complete shock as a burning fist erupted through his sternum. His scream of pain became a roar of anger and Erethea, our fourth-year seraph instructor, flew through the room along with everyone within twenty feet of the Emperor to crash upon the walls. A moment of stunned silence and then the Emperor collapsed to his knees, blood trickling from his mouth. His hand reached to touch the hole in his chest and he slowly tilted over to the side to collapse on the floor in a crunch of armour.

As he collapsed, the pressure that held the corrupted individuals released. Instantly all hell broke loose.

The two remaining Imps leapt forward and immediately launched an onslaught against the guards. The calibre of the Emperor's elite was immediately noticeable as they drove off the horror of the last few moments and ducked into the fight. The two Imps were decent enough fighters but the only reason that they weren't immediately brought down was that every time they got close to one of the guards black flame gushed forward. Fortunately, the obsidian armour looked to provide some protection against the fire but it spread onto everything else that it touched. Soon the inside of the hall was a nightmarish inferno with living flame that actively leapt at anyone foolish enough to be in range.

I firmly believed that those who were corrupted and held in thrall could learn new skills under the tutelage of whoever controlled the black seraph, Rya was a perfect example. She had possessed skills that would not have been taught at the Academy. Which is why the two Imps must have been fairly recently turned as beyond the flames they didn't exhibit anything particularly impressive. And if the fight had just been the two Imps then things would likely have been over quickly.

As a normal Imperator, Penye must have been skilled.

As a corrupted Imperator he was a demon.

Twin whips of black flame lashed about him as he engaged the nearest two guards in a whirlwind of motion. The whips punished the guards, their armour allowing them to resist the fire but the impacts still sent them sprawling, and then he was amongst us. Screams of pain and horror erupted as the whips flicked along the Academy members. Some managed to get seraph shields up in time. Many others did not. The fire latched on to flesh and spread; turning people into tinder-boxes. The air grew thick with acrid smoke, burning lungs and blocking sight. Penye didn't seem to have any of those problems and took full advantage of all the inconveniences that we were suffering from to wreak untold havoc.

Even though the Emperor had told me to be wary I was still caught off guard at the sheer speed and brutality of our foes, not to mention the Emperor's death - that shook me to my core. Thankfully I had done as the Emperor had asked and drawn as much strength and speed from Seya as I could currently hold. I'm certain that it was the only thing that saved me. A whip hurtled out of the smoke and if I had reacted any slower I would have been consumed in black flame. As it was I managed to dance aside, draw my sword and then rush towards Penye. I say rush, in reality it was more akin to a complex dance. The bewildering speed and fluidity of Penye's weapon of choice was extraordinarily difficult to counter, and the whips themselves couldn't be touched as they were composed entirely of pure flame. This meant that deflecting any blows was completely impossible unless you had armour like the guards or impressive control of seraph.

Looking back, I probably should have left tackling Penye to the Imperators. Simone and Merowyn were not far behind me and had much more experience of utilising seraph in such a manner, I essentially just had to rely on overwhelming speed. It sufficed until Penye saw me coming. If I'd thought his attacks were fast beforehand, when he knew that a threat was closing in they became a barely visible blur; any one hit of which would have ended me right there and then. Fortunately, and as I have thought many times in my life, I had Cassius. And Cassius? He had Asp.

As I ducked, weaved, flipped and twisted my way through the string of attacks, Cassius concentrated on the weapon at his side. He drew from his pool and channelled energy into the blade until it was thrumming with power. With a bark of effort he drew the blade from the sheath and as he did so sent a slice of energy whistling through the air to shear through one flame whip that had been about to send me to an ashen grave. As soon as the whip was cut any part of it not connected to the Imperator's body flashed out of existence, giving me a much-needed momentary reprieve which I used to close the gap and deliver a sweeping cut from torso to neck. Or at least, that was the plan. I kept forgetting that his control of seraph was far, far beyond my own. My blade ricocheted off some kind of shield and shattered, the power behind the blow generating far too much stress for its nature to handle. For a moment I thought that was it - I could see the sneer on Penye's face, a look of amusement at someone having come so close only to fail at the last hurdle. But thankfully that was when Simone burst onto the scene, echoing Cassius by sending a beam of blue light that forced the corrupted Imperator to turn from me and re-inforce his seraph shield.

Without a blade I was worse than useless; unable to get in close to deliver any blows with my limbs due to the black fire that was running up and down the man's frame. My seraph knowledge had not remotely gotten to the point where I would be able to generate magical attacks like Penye or Simone and so I ducked under a whirling whip, waited for Penye to focus on Simone and then attempted to drive the nub of broken blade into his armpit.

I hit him; of that I was sure. But if he felt any pain he certainly didn't show it. Instead he flicked an arm at me and I was forced to dive out of the way to avoid being chargrilled. Another flick and another roll, the flame whip striking the wooden floor and adding to the conflagration that was building. He went for a third and then howled in agony as something thumped to the floor. Cassius had managed to send another blade of energy hurtling through the air and with barely any effort it had carved its way through the meat of Penye's arm before hammering into the far wall.

You would think that would be it, that a one-armed man fighting an army of Imperators would lose in an instant, but the loss of his arm barely seemed to slow him down. Instead of his hand holding a whip, a torrent of black fire burst out of his arm, as though without his hand there as a channelling point he had lost the ability to focus it into a refined form. In a building filled with flammable objects - including its denizens - it proved an effective tool, setting everything within reach aflame with wild abandon.

As I desperately made my way out of the grasping flames I saw the two Imps fall. The guardsmen abandoning all attempts to stay out of the flames and relying on their amour to see them through safely. It worked. With the threat of the flame gone the two Imps were not remotely a match for the four bodyguards and within seconds both their heads rolled onto the floor. There was a moment's pause and then the corpses exploded in a torrent of black fire, engulfing at least three of the fighters that had just a second before stood triumphant.

I looked back in time to see Penye's shield take three blasts of energy from different Imperators and then crumble as a gasping Cassius sent one last burst of power through the blade. The cutting edge of Asp's attack was nullified by the shield but still hit him hard enough to cause bones to break. I saw movement in the entrance hall - another obsidian clad soldier - and then she was there, her blade jutting from Penye's jugular. Even with all the speed I could borrow from Seya I could never move that fast; it was as though she had blinked in and out of existence. She blurred and then stood in front of us all, raising a hand to ward us off. Penye gurgled, his eyes rolling towards the Emperor who lay in a pool of blood and a bloody smile filled his face before flame rolled up and out in a billowing wave; consuming everything that was in its path.

Imperators flung shields up in a shimmering haze, roaring

with pain and effort as they battled the encroaching wave of black fire. I saw Rikol lend his talents amongst a number of the remaining Imps, his shield far smaller and less defined than those of the Imperators but more than I could produce nonetheless. The heat grew and the smoke burned lungs, causing Imperator after Imperator to collapse, weakening the shield even further. The black wave built, growing ever taller and more powerful whilst the Imperators struggled to survive. Dimly, in the flame filled haze I saw Simone and Merowyn side by side each fighting to contain the blaze, Scythe, Cassius and Ella unconscious on the floor and Sophia attempting to drag them outside but flame was beginning to block the way. I saw Erethea not even attempt to rise as Thosalt, one of the senior Instructors at the Academy, raised a blade high above her. As my vision began to dim I even thought I saw something that should have been impossible.

**"Enough."**

The voice was a clap of sound. It cut through the air as a physical force, staggering everyone still standing and a foreboding pressure enveloped everyone conscious enough to feel it, building more and more until it felt like a lead weight around my shoulders. Shields winked out against the force of the voice and the black flame roared forwards only to vanish out of existence in the next moment, leaving no trace behind. As the smoke began to rise all heads turned to the source of the voice and disbelieving eyes watched as the Emperor stood tall, the once gaping wound in his chest gone without a trace. His face like stone, he scanned the room before turning to where Thosalt struggled to regain his feet.

**"Leave her."**

Thosalt turned and bowed, moving away from the wide eyed Erethea who was scrabbling to try and stand up.

"How?" she gasped as the Emperor walked closer, his stride shaking the room, each footfall somehow showcasing his displeasure through sound.

He stopped in front of her and the foreboding visage relaxed.

Pressure lifted from the room and I found that I could breathe normally again. He crouched down in front of her face and locked his eyes on hers. One set calm and intense, the other panic stricken.

"Because I willed it so," he replied softly. "You disappoint me Erethea. The others I can forgive but you? You don't contain any black seraph...which means you serve Him willingly."

She started to speak but he held up a finger to her lips. "Quiet. You and I are going to have a long conversation later. The first of many." As he finished speaking Erethea stiffened like she had been struck by lightning, her eyes rolling into the back of her head before collapsing onto the floor.

Standing once more, the Emperor turned to look at what remained of his room, his Imperators and his Academy. With a wave of his hand the smoke swirled out of the room in a funnel and dissipated, allowing those of us still able to draw breath freely. The female guard who had killed Penye approached and knelt before him, quickly joined by another who walked in from the entrance way.

"Geryna," the Emperor said, acknowledging the woman in front of him. "Excellent work with Penye."

*Geryna, where do I know that name from?* I pondered. As the tall man came and lowered his spear to the floor in order to bow it hit me. *These are the twins! Andros and Geryna, the ones Tyrgan said were the Emperor's best!*

"Apologies for our tardiness," Andros said softly. "One of our other...guests did not want to go quietly."

"You arrived at the perfect moment," the Emperor replied, inviting them both to stand up. "Or more accurately I should say that Geryna did. But then again," he gave her a wink, "you always do."

As she stood, Geryna sheathed the twin sabres that she was carrying. One of them looked to have a number of stones encrusted in the hilt. *The way she moved...I'll bet anything that is a tyrant blade,* I thought whilst coughing up the black smoke out of my lungs. *But it has to be something more than just increased speed. Tyrgan had that and I was able to outmatch him. So what is it?*

A mystery for another day.

Of the four guards who had assaulted the Imps, two were standing. Of the two on the floor one was definitely a corpse - from the scent in my nostrils the flame had managed to get inside his armour. The other was wheezing through burnt lungs. The Emperor walked amongst them speaking softly and knelt beside the wounded man, peeling aside his armour with minimal effort and placing a glowing green hand on his chest. Moments later the man's wheezing eased and I could sense that the workings of his body were starting to get back to normal. He wasn't fully healed - being able to heal back to full health in moments was meant to be a myth. One that Erethea had informed us over and over again. Even with my affinity for green seraph, forcing my body to heal at such a pace was meant to be inherently dangerous, something that Seya agreed with.

But apparently not the Emperor.

*How did he do it?* I wondered as he made his way over towards me, smiling his beatific smile. *I'm sure she had him. How did he heal if unconscious? And that quickly?* With a start I realised that the Emperor had been talking to me and I had missed it.

"Calidan," the Emperor said again. "How are you feeling?"

"Better than my friends sir," I replied, indicating the others who were still struggling to cast off the effects of the smoke in their lungs. My green seraph and Seya's healing were making it easier and easier to breathe with every passing second. "And good to see you on your feet," I added.

His eye twitched, though whether with amusement or memory of a near mortal wound I didn't care to guess. "Good to be on them," he replied drily. Raising his voice he spoke again, "Doctors will be here momentarily. I'm afraid that not even I have enough seraph to treat this many wounded."

A lie, as it turned out. Though I can sympathise with wanting to keep his seraph ready in case Erethea wasn't working alone. In an assassination it is always useful to have a backup for the backup plan.

Before long a rush of feet echoed in the hallways and squads of the Emperor's elite soldiers and white robed doctors flooded into the room, the doctors barely stopping to take in the smouldering view before heading to the nearest wounded, quickly identifying the most seriously injured from the dead and organising stretchers to take them to the infirmary. Scythe, Cassius and the others were taken to be treated for smoke inhalation but I waved the doctors off, knowing that my wounds would heal fast enough on their own.

# CHAPTER 34

## *Rewards*

"So, how do you think that went?" the Emperor asked, pouring three cups of water and sliding two to Anatha and myself.

"About as well as it looked," replied Anatha drily. "So terribly."

"He got me good, I'll give Him that," the Emperor mused. "But I wouldn't say it went terribly."

Anatha's eyes narrowed. "Three Imperators and eight Imps dead, another fifteen so wounded that they aren't likely to recover to any semblance of normality and two of your guards killed. Oh, and you nearly died. So would you like to tell me how that isn't terrible?"

"Because I am still here," he replied simply. "Not to mention that we've uncovered that the Enemy doesn't just rely on control via black seraph - he must have known that at some point I would root out those who were corrupted - and removed at least one major player within the Academy. For that, I would say that the cost was worth it."

"She had the drop on you," insisted Anatha. "If her attack had been any more powerful then you could have-"

"-I assure you that her attack was powerful enough," the Emperor replied, rubbing a hand over his chest. He had taken off the broken armour and now wore a silk shirt in its place. He had changed in front of us in the study, as though to prove that he was unhurt, and all that remained of what should have been a gaping hole in his chest was a tiny scar. "I just have more tricks up my sleeve than she could account for."

Her voice turning more hostile than I could account for Anatha spoke again, "I know full well the *cost* of what happened here today Melius, it isn't something that you should be taking lightly."

The Emperor fixed her with an outwardly pleasant gaze that held steel undertones. "I allow you many liberties, Anatha but you presume too much. What is done is done. Instead of arguing as to how it was achieved you should better spend your time looking to the future." The warning in his voice was unmistakable and the temperature seemed to plummet as Anatha fought to hold his gaze. After what seemed like a lifetime she broke and looked away, grief evident in her features.

I held my breath, not wanting to be the focus of the Emperor's ire. Anatha's reaction seemed overblown to me - yes the Emperor had been delivered a seemingly mortal wound but he was here and seemingly fine, surely Anatha should be happy rather than distraught? These days I know full well the cause of her grief and I share in her sorrow.

Thankfully when the Emperor turned to me his eyes no longer held any of the ice that they had when speaking with Anatha. Instead he gave me a warm smile and an approving nod.

"Well done Calidan," he reverberated. "That was a difficult mission but you and Cassius performed admirably."

"We didn't really do much," I muttered, abashed.

"Nonsense," he replied, "you held off Penye and did it without receiving significant injuries. That allowed my guards to close and remove him from the equation. Without you and Cassius stepping in it is likely that there would have been much more death."

I coloured slightly at his words, praise from the Emperor was a high thing indeed. "Cassius deserves the praise, his use of Asp kept me alive. All I managed to do was succeed in shattering my sword," I said, tapping the broken hilt that lay in my sheath forlornly.

"Yes, his ability to wield Asp is very impressive, he certainly saved many lives with what he has learnt - I'm sure Adronicus will be proud," he replied. "As for your sword, I'm sure that something can be arranged, courtesy of myself of course."

I started to fluster, unused to gifts and he held up his hand to stop me. "I reward those who serve me well Calidan, you broke your sword going up against someone that by rights you should not have survived against. Particularly with the powers that the black seraph had provided Penye. Your knowledge of seraph is not remotely good enough to break through a master's shield, even with your prestigious strength, so it was unsurprising that your blade failed. I am just glad that you did not."

"What about the others?" I asked suddenly.

"Others?"

I gestured wildly. "The other Imps and Imperators! Those that were hurt during this. What will you tell them?"

"It's safe to say that the Academy will be under even more scrutiny from this day forward," the Emperor replied after a moment's thought. "Complacency is what allowed someone like Erethea to get into the position that she was in. Any budding Imp brought in will have to be thoroughly questioned until all senior authority members are satisfied. Imperators will ever be the trickier proposition however." He rubbed his chin in thought. "I assumed that my Imperators would never turn against me due to the loyalty that I believed I instilled. I wholeheartedly believed that the only way that they could be turned would be through use of black seraph." He chuckled softly to himself. "That overconfidence nearly got me killed today."

Turning back to me he gave a wink. "Just goes to show Calidan, that you're never too old to learn something new. I thought I was untouchable in my citadel and dared Him to prove otherwise. He managed it and through a method I had thought impossible; brilliantly done really, though He did lose a particularly well-placed tool in today's attempt."

I couldn't hold it any longer. With a voice trembling in a mixture of frustration and excitement I blurted out, "Who is this enemy? You act as if you know him. What is he to you?"

The Emperor looked at me in mild surprise, as though I had asked something that he hadn't even considered. He considered me for some time, pursing his lips in thought before shaking his head. "No, not yet Calidan. You know many secrets and many things, but this is not one that should be divulged just yet. Just know that there is one foe above all others that is a threat to this Empire. He - for the threat is a man, although more than a man in truth - has been known to me for a long time. Longer than anyone in fact. When you know someone for that long, even as an enemy, you begin to understand them; they become dear to you in some strange fashion." He gave a wry grin and shook his head again. "No, no more on that subject for the time being. When you're an Imperator then we can consider talking further about this. Not until then."

I nodded and sat back, taking a long drink of water. It tasted delicious through my smoke-caked throat. "So what now?"

"Now?" he rumbled. "Now you go back to the Academy and continue your training. I'm going to need you to train hard and learn fast Calidan, I need you now more than ever before."

Anatha coughed into her cup at that and looked at the Emperor sharply but he ignored her, continuing unabated, "Rest assured that changes will be made to mitigate the threat of the Enemy. Some of these changes you will see, others will be enacted in secret and only known to those that need to know." His gaze became more grave as he continued, "The Academy will need to become more secretive than ever. Those that train there will have to be under constant watch. If you notice anything different about your fellow Imps and in due course Imperators you will need to let it be known without raising suspicion. Understood?"

I nodded, mind filling with dark thoughts. *I didn't notice any-*

*thing untoward about Erethea so how would I know? Anyone could*
*be working for the Enemy.*

The Emperor must have noticed the discomfort on my face for
he stood and nodded towards the door. "Come," he reverberated. "Let's go get you something to fit your scabbard and then
get you back to the Academy. I'm sure that you are eager to
check on your friends."

Nodding, I joined him and together we left a scowling Anatha
in the study. As soon as we left the room four guards fell into
place around the Emperor - and by extension, me - and we
walked around the circumference of the citadel before coming to a stop before a thick metal door. The two guards on either side of the armoury saluted and quickly moved to open
the door, its well-oiled hinges allowing it to swing silently
open. The guards checked the room and then filed out to stand
aside, protecting the Emperor from all external threats. The
Emperor gestured for me to enter and I gasped in awe as I
stepped inside.

Row after row of weapons were stacked throughout the room.
Weapons of every different type imaginable and of such quality as to make Adronicus explode with delight.

"Welcome," the Emperor said jovially as my head span, "to my
personal collection."

"This...this isn't the main armoury?" I gasped, trying to take it
all in.

"For the citadel?" he scoffed. "Of course not. That armoury is
next to the barracks. It would be a foolish move to keep your
guards separated from their weapons. This is just my personal
collection of items that I have collected over the years. Nothing too outlandish mind, all those weapons like Asp and the
tyrant blades that I know you have become familiar with are
kept in a more secure location."

*The armoury in the Emperor's citadel isn't secure?* I wondered
idly as my gaze scanned the room. A series of great axes caught
my eye; my experiences with the Meredothians having given
me a taste of what I could accomplish with one.

The Emperor caught my gaze and nodded approvingly, moving to run his hand along the long rack of double-bladed weapons. "*Tasul, Seren, Afun, Illioth, Aeona*," he murmured as he touched the blades. Glancing up he gave a small smile. "Each of these are named blades and would serve you as well as they have served me."

"S-served you?" I stuttered, shocked. "What do you mean?"

He looked bemused. "I did say that they were my personal collection. Each item in here I have used and put to rest. I tend to find that my fighting styles change over the years. I go through phases of using bladed weapons and then a generation later I pick up a bow and master that instead. Over time this collection amassed itself."

Nothing. Nothing else that I had seen or experienced up to that point had remotely made me understand that the Emperor was no mere mortal more than that moment. There were easily a thousand weapons in that room alone and from the sound of it that number didn't comprise the Emperor's entire collection. If the Emperor was speaking the truth and had used and mastered each one of these tools rather than having bought them for the sake of collection then he wasn't just old. He was positively *ancient*.

He must have seen the look in my eyes for he gave a small grin and patted me on the shoulder. "Try not to think about it too much Calidan, knowing you, your head will explode from trying to do the maths." Stepping back he appraised me thoughtfully. "Hmmm, you're tall and getting taller. A long blade will always be a useful addition to further that advantage. Your strength is nothing to be sniffed at either but with Seylantha as your Great Heart bonded, speed and ferocity will always be your primary tools..." he murmured his way along the walls of the armoury, touching a weapon here and there, hesitating at some before moving on with a shake of his head.

"Ahhh," he exclaimed as he lifted a blade from the wall. "My old sun'wala." He flipped the blade over and presented the handle to me, "try her. I have a feeling that you two will go to-

gether well."
The hilt was plain, with black wrappings protected by a plain steel hand guard. The blade itself was a silvery colour that shimmered in the light as I took the sword's weight. It was light. Surprisingly so, considering that the curved edge of the blade was longer than that of a traditional sabre by nearly a third again. The width of the blade at the tip was wider too, giving it a savage heft as I swung it experimentally. I looked at the blade with profound curiosity. I would have to practice to become comfortable with the extra distance of its reach so as not to overcommit where I didn't need to, but if I did then the extra length and power would complement my preferred fighting style brilliantly.

"She's beautiful," I whispered reverently. "What is she?"
The Emperor positively beamed. "She is something I created many years ago. I call her type of blade a sun'wala. As you can tell it is a longer version of a sabre with a flared tip similar to that of a cavalry sabre. For most people it would be too long and possibly too heavy to wield with the same speed that a normal sabre could be, but for someone like you or I then the drawbacks are minimal and the benefit of the extra reach and power is not to be sniffed at." He patted the blade fondly. "Vona here, served me well through many a battle."
"Vona?"
The Emperor grasped the hilt and then with a sudden burst of motion swept the blade in an arc. A piercing sound cut the air, like the sound of wind howling through a small aperture. Handing it back he shrugged.
"Vona means sing in an old, dead language. She whistles when you put enough power into your strikes to cleave the air. Not particularly useful for stealth missions for obvious reasons, but the sound became synonymous with death and my enemies trembled when they heard it," his voice took on a note of fierce pride as he spoke, his eyes lost in memory. After a moment he shook his head and focused on me. "Imperators are often feared. It's an image that has been carefully cultivated.

A terrified individual is more likely to make mistakes. People want to help you to stay out of your bad books. Did you ever wonder why so many people know, deep down in their bones, what an Imperator looks like when they are truthfully rarely seen?"

I shook my head and he shrugged. "We share the information, a word here and there. Now when some cancer upon my empire is removed by the Academy then even if it was done with no witnesses people will talk about how the swish of long coats was heard down the street. Image, Calidan, is a powerful thing. And so with this sword I have no doubt that people will soon swear that the whistling wind is the sound of your blade. It gives you power, of a sort. Use it well."

"I can't thank you enough for this," I whispered, staring at the blade in awe. It truly was a thing of beauty.

The Emperor shrugged again. "I told you, I take care of my own. She is a wonderful blade and will serve you well, but she is just a normal tool. Keep serving me well and one day I will upgrade you with something that will make Asp look normal." He gave me a wink and nodded his head in the direction of the infirmary. "If you're happy with that blade then let's go and see your friends shall we? I'm sure that they are just as anxious to see you after all this."

I nodded, lost for words at the richness of the gift he had given me and followed him out into the hallway to find my friends. It's funny how in hindsight just how blatantly obvious his buying of my loyalty was, but to my young and naive mind I was lost in awe and didn't question any further. If I had known what I know now I would have taken that blade and stabbed it in his throat. It wouldn't have done much...but at least it would have been something.

✷ ✷ ✷

*The Emperor*

*The Emperor swept into the room, dismissing the watching guards with a nod of his head. Ex-Imperator Erethea Laniel stood fastened to the wall, her arms manacled with engraved chains that glowed softly with purple light. She looked beaten and battered, the guards obviously having shown their dislike for her attempt on the Emperor's life.*

*She watched him through lidded and swollen eyes but said nothing in the face of the Emperor's piercing stare.*

*Eventually he sighed and sat down, the very air itself compressing to hold his form. "Why?" he asked simply. "Why did you do it? Were you not treated well?"*

*Erethea spat out a bloody ball of phlegm and tilted her eyes in his direction. "You like to think of yourself as some hero that comes to protect and to save," she ground out hoarsely, "reasoning your actions in terms of acceptable losses and collateral damage as though weighing them up on some invisible abacus. But sometimes those losses aren't acceptable." A tear tracked through the dried blood that caked her face. "I still remember your Imperators purging my home. The indiscriminate violence. The lack of empathy or humanity as they took life after life in fear of a threat that none of us had heard of, let alone seen." She locked him with a steely gaze. "I stood there in the remains and swore to have my revenge. And He... He was there to help me do it."*

*"He is a monster," the Emperor rumbled.*

*"You are both monsters!" Erethea spat. "I wish that you would both do the world a favour and die, but you're both too cowardly to face each other properly. Instead you plot and you puppeteer and I am just one such puppet."*

*"And you do this knowingly?" he mused; surprise evident on his face.*

*"We're all puppets at the end of the day, dancing on the strings of those more powerful. For me, Charles gave me training and the opportunity to one day put an end to you. For what you did to my family I would happily stain my soul all over again."*

*The Emperor stood; his curiosity apparently satisfied. "For what it's worth, I am sorry for your family," he murmured as he made to leave.*

*Erethea barked a laugh. "No you're not. I don't think you even understand the concept of empathy. Whilst Charles is a monster through and through, you're a wolf in sheep's clothing, pretending to care when the reality couldn't be further from the truth."*

*The Emperor paused with his hand on the door before turning back, his expression amused. "You're right," he chuckled. "You literally mean nothing to me. Just like you meant nothing to Charles. You are mayflies, your sparks sputtering in and out of existence so rapidly that I can barely keep track. You should be thankful that I remember your name." He shrugged and turned away. "Or not, for as you said, I do not remotely care."*

*He opened the door and waved a hand, binding her mouth with seraph as she tried to scream after him.*

*"Enjoy your stay Erethea."*

# PRESENT DAY

The demonic figure lay helpless, its muscles wasted to a fraction of the intimidating strength that I so vividly remembered. Thick metal clamps that had presumably had to contend with the might of a skyren at its prime now easily held the beast in place as it half-heartedly bucked, doubtless eager to try and finish the job that it had started so long ago.

I took a step closer and the thing on the table gave a croaking growl through a throat long disused. Its body was festooned with a variety of tubes of different sizes that led into a number of machines dotted around the room. Even though the building looked to have been abandoned a long time ago it appeared as though the skyren's body was still slowly being harvested, with a small trickle of ichor slowly making its way down a see-through tube before my eyes.

I honestly didn't know how to feel. Before me was the enemy. Not the Enemy, as the Emperor would have us fight, but my enemy, my foe.

My nemesis.

And whilst I revelled in the sight of it brought so low I couldn't help but feel strangely bad for it - did anything deserve such a fate?

The familiar image of the trapped beast put me too much in mind of Seya and my thoughts darkened instantly. In a flash I was at the side of the skyren, Asp out at its throat.

"Do you remember me?" I snarled, half wanting to kill it out of a desperate, burning *need* for vengeance and the other half wanting to kill it to end its torment.

A muffled grunt from Cassius and I saw that he was by my side, Oathbreaker out and ready to use. His swirling eyes were unreadable, but I knew that he was just as ready as I to put an end to the cause of our misfortune.

The creature's eyes held no fear, just rage and perhaps an inkling of understanding. I knew what a skyren was capable of. They were intelligent creatures; their minds quick and sharp. It might not recognise or even understand us - some had the ability to speak but those that the Emperor had captured over the years had either possessed enough willpower not to talk despite his best efforts or lacked the function - but I bet it could remember its actions all those years ago.

"A village up on the Tordstein mountains," I barked, grinding my blade into the flesh of its shoulder and eliciting a pained growl. "You slaughtered everyone. My parents, my friends. Everyone, except for the two who escaped." I gestured to Cassius and myself and thought I saw a glimmer of recognition in its eyes.

"You deserve to die for what you did," I growled, twisting the blade and hoping to feel some satisfaction in the act, but nothing was forthcoming. Somehow I was being robbed of the satisfaction of my revenge and I hated it.

The lights flickered and I spun, my senses flaring. Behind us, standing as though he had been there the entire time, was a short man with wispy blonde hair and glasses.

"You'll find that Akzan won't be the most talkative of subjects I'm afraid," the man said softly. "I had no use for his tongue you see, so ensured that he wouldn't be using it ever again."

I stepped away from the writhing beast who was fixating hate filled eyes on the nondescript man and levelled Asp in his direction.

"Who are you?" I demanded. "What is this place?"

He laughed, the sound boyish and joyful. "Oh he prepared you well this time didn't he? You would have thought that an assassin of the Emperor would be more knowledgeable about his target."

I shook my head, perplexed. *What was a human doing all the way out here?* "You're not my target," I replied shortly, "the skyren on the table is. It slaughtered my village long ago."

The man chuckled. "Not just your village I'm afraid, Akzan had a right old time back then. Unfortunately he, Koranth and myself didn't quite see eye to eye in the end and Akzan attempted a little coup. We couldn't be having that so he ended up having a nice relaxing holiday here where he proved to be very useful."

*Koranth, why do I know that name?*

I stared at him, digging through my memories. Had I ever met this man before? I didn't think so.

"Who are you?" I repeated again, shifting my stance so that I was out of Cassius's way in case things turned ugly.

"Charles is the name," the man said brightly, doffing an imaginary cap. "A pleasure to finally meet you. Took you long enough to get here. I was beginning to wonder if my skills weren't what they used to be."

My brain sparked, sending me back to the desert all those years ago to when an artificial woman told us of a man who helped end the world. A man in thrall to a creature he had released from another world. A creature called Koranth.

"I can see that things are starting to click into place for you," Charles continued. "A little slow on the uptake aren't we?"

"You're the person Ash spoke of, the one who brought about the Cataclysm," I whispered, eyes wide as I tried to think of a way out of the situation. If he was who he said he was then going up against him would be practically suicide.

"I am indeed. I believe that your Emperor calls me something different. The "Enemy', if I'm not mistaken. An amusing enough title and somewhat accurate, if not very imaginative."

"Why are we here?" I knew this couldn't be a coincidence.

"You're here because I requested it and I imagine that your Emperor has some tricky plan up his sleeve to finally allow you to be here. The amount of black seraph I had to pump out to get your friend turned in this direction was quite surprising, but in the end it was enough. I've long been wanting to have a chat with him."

"What about?" I questioned, moving a half step closer.

The man snorted and shook his head. "As much as I like monologuing, why would I choose to reveal my intentions to you? You're nothing. Just pawns in a game of gods."

It was my turn to snort. "Gods? You're just men with more seraph than sense."

Charles's smile only broadened. "And what exactly is a god? Am I omnipotent? No. Not yet anyway. But do I have the power to alter the world as I see fit, to create or destroy with the blink of an eye? Yes I do. And humanity has fallen so far since the times of the seraphim that you're really all just a subspecies at this point so there is very little to challenge those few of us remaining. You're tools. That is all. Only fit to be ruled over. So to you, Calidan - and yes I know your name, I've known it for a long time - I am a god. So tread carefully. Now, move aside and let me see to your friend."

I stepped in front of Cassius protectively. "You'll have to go through me first."

Charles tsked, shaking his head. "Considering what I just said I would have thought you to have been more careful with your choice of words. Poor boy." A nod of his head and I cartwheeled across the room to smash into the wall hard enough to crack the rock. "Now stay there whilst I have a chat with your friend."

Cassius didn't take the sight of me being flung across the room lightly, with blinding speed he sent Oathbreaker screaming through the air only to stop dead at the merest look from Charles. Through the blood trickling across my eyes I could see the strain on Cassius's face as he tried to move, but his body was completely locked in place. Charles approached and put a hand delicately on Cassius's face. Instantly the big man's eyes rolled back into his head and he convulsed, his back arching like he was in agonising pain.

"Fascinating," Charles murmured. "He did some good work; I'll give him that. Hmmmm."

I could sense Cassius's heart racing faster and faster, his body going into overdrive. Focusing my will I moved my hand one inch, then another. When I was satisfied my hand was in the right position I focused and unleashed Asp's power at the figure tormenting my friend. The beam sliced through the air and upon reaching the Enemy it dissipated as though it had never been. Charles didn't even flinch and if he had noticed my attack he certainly didn't respond to it.

I tried lancing a seraph beam at him, funnelling my limited supply into a cutting edge. Again it disappeared, as though sucked into a vacuum. Cursing, I looked around for something, *anything.* My eyes locked onto the red eyed skyren and the direction of its hate filled gaze. *Better than death,* I thought grimly as I willed a finely controlled layer of seraph into place over its body, carefully slicing away the tubing and then the restraints. *Go and fucking kill each other.*

The skyren rose slowly, its emaciated form creaking and cracking as it stood on limbs that hadn't seemingly been used in years. Yet within that form was still a huge amount of raw power, never mind whatever skills this Akzan possessed.

Charles turned towards me and raised an eyebrow. "Releasing your mortal enemy is a bold move, I did wonder if you would."

"Is this all a game to you?" I ground out through gritted teeth.

He rolled his eyes in despair. "I thought that much was obvious. Everything is a game. Your lives, the building and destruction of towns and cities, the rise and fall of empires. Everything."

Akzan took a step forward, the thud of its foot vibrating the room and Charles tilted his head back in its direction. "When you're as old as I am, games are the only thing to alleviate the boredom."

Akzan let out a croaking roar and stomped forward, claws out and ready to rend. Charles raised a hand and the skyren stopped dead. Akzan growled and black energy swirled around its body, flaring against the unseen power that held it in place and it took another step. Charles smirked and stepped aside, twitching his hand as he did so and the skyren flew across the room to crash into the wall.

But I wasn't watching this crash of titans.

I was watching Cassius.

The gold in his eyes was shifting, swirling through the black and becoming blindingly vivid. His skin became almost translucent as light shone from within and a shimmering haze outlined his figure. As the light grew I could see his limbs begin to twitch, at first just fingers but in a matter of moments he was taking steps as though Charles's control wasn't there. He let out a piercing roar and Oathbreaker activated, flames rushing around the blade, but this time the fire was bright gold.

Charles swivelled and I could have sworn that a look of panic crossed his face at the sight of Cassius's descending blade. Instead of blocking, he dived out of the way and went straight into the tail of Akzan, sending him crunching into the floor in a spray of stone. Akzan rained blows down upon the prone figure, each hit sending him further into the ground.

A flash of black light and suddenly Charles was behind the skyren, his hand extended towards the back of the beast. A glowing foot connected with his torso and Charles shot across the room as though launched from a catapult. My eyes widened in amazement - not even in his current form had Cassius possessed that much power. It was almost like he was bonded with a Great Heart, but not even a Great Heart could provide that much overwhelming strength, not to mention the glowing side effects.

Cassius cut down with his blade, the glowing sword peeling apart metal like a hot knife through butter, leaving a flaming line in its wake. He spun and I realised that Charles had reappeared yet again on the other side of the room. Black lines covered his face and his eyes were of the purest black.

"**Enough.**" The word resonated and the world disappeared.

Utter darkness consumed the room.

Akzan howled, an agonising scream of terror and pain that rose in pitch with each passing second.

A glowing light slowly penetrated the blackness, each step bringing it closer towards me. For a moment I could have sworn that the figure was that of the Emperor but a second later and Cassius's face was before me.

"Time to go," he said calmly, raising a hand and placing it on my shoulder.

My mouth dropped open as golden light enveloped me. "Cassius, you're-"

Light flooded in and the Emperor stood at our side in his study in the citadel, a sheen of sweat on his face and his hand on Cassius's shoulder.

"-talking."

# CHAPTER 35

## *War*

Whilst the fight at the citadel might have been considered a victory for the Emperor in that he still lived, for the members of the Academy it was a terrible tragedy. The provision of the sword and being treated like a confidant by the Emperor himself had made me forget about it for a moment and perhaps I willed myself not to think about it for as long as I could.

But at some point we all have to face the music.

Anatha had been right, the tally of dead and grievously wounded was high. Too high. The Academy chose only the most talented, focused, broken or otherwise special individuals to become Imps and the recruitment process was sporadic and generally slow. Injuries and even deaths whilst training in the Academy were not uncommon - as we knew all too well - but to have so many at once, and of a level of Imp that was starting to resemble an Imperator? That was hard. It was a blow to the management of the Academy in a way that they hadn't experienced in some time.

What was much, much worse was that each and every Imp who had been in the citadel for that battle knew each one who had died. Considered them acquaintances, comrades or even friends. Needless to say; morale was low.

Funerals are not easy. Mass funerals are simultaneously easier and harder. They give you a sense of closure for the many people who died, a chance to grieve and to come to terms with what happened, but I feel that it numbs you to the grief, like your body can only handle so much pain and so shuts itself down. Damien's death had been terrible - a grief that we all still carried and would for many years to come - but the deaths of those fellow Imps, I feel like they each impacted us less due to that mass ceremony. Or maybe we were just getting hardened around the edges, becoming the hard diamonds that the Academy was compressing us to be.

Regardless, it was a suitably grand affair. The Emperor attended in person with a contingent of guards who kept a suitably dangerous look upon every attending member of the congregation. A number of Imperators made grand speeches about how they had died in the service of the empire and so had fulfilled their duty. Kane took a different approach.

"No one should die young," he said softly. "I grieve for Devan, Emur and Hol but they were fully fledged Imperators who had all the training and knew all the risks. Riln, Catalana, Emir, Ascin, Allando, Geland, Feyan and Jorna were Imps. Imps who were involved in a fight that was beyond them," his eyes glistened as he scanned the audience. "All of you here know that the Academy asks a lot of you and that the things we do whilst training hold inherent risk. The fourth-year exam is the tipping point where we try and balance risk against the learning experience, where sometimes we get it right but sometimes we get it wrong. But those Imps who attempt the exam are prepared for it to be hard, for it to be deadly. Imps do not expect life or death scenarios practically within the walls of the Academy and for that I say that we, the staff at the Academy, have failed you. We need to look after the next generation of Imperators and make sure that they at least have the chance to survive to become the heroes of the empire that they aim to be."

He took a steadying breath and continued, "Because of this

there are some things that you should know. There are forces at work against the Andurran empire. Some of you," his eyes briefly found mine, "had already encountered these forces. All of you now have. As you saw, this is not a game. The force arrayed against us is insidious and can corrupt those who are unwary. Imperator Erethea was one such individual and has trained many of you. Who amongst us can say that she was acting differently or odd?" He paused and scanned the room, nodding when he saw no-one raise a hand. "Exactly. No-one. And so whilst orders will be given that ask you to keep an eye on your fellow colleagues and to flag any potential changes, I - and I mean that personally - also ask that you trust your friends and colleagues. We work best as teams and without that trust we will be lost. Use your common sense but do not fear your friends. We all need to work together to survive and to win." With a deep breath he bowed his head to the fallen, nodded to the audience and then stepped back, allowing the thunderous steps of the Emperor to take his place.

"Children," the Emperor rumbled, "it is a sad day. What Imperator Kane said is correct; we are beset by an enemy that can whisper, plot and turn ourselves against each other. We must refuse this enemy at all costs!" His voice thundered as he said the last, echoes of his bellow rebounding through the Academy grounds.

"Remember your duty and remember your training and we will remove this foe from our midst, from our Empire and then from our world. We will not cease and we will not falter. You are Imperators, the hidden blades of the Empire, you will stand tall and protect all of us from enemies without...and from within. So yes, this is a sad day, but it is also a day to remember, a day of celebration, for We pushed back the Enemy, We defeated His minions and We. Are. Unbroken." Cheers resounded as his statement thundered through the air, his voice like a physical force.

Raising his hands for quiet he waited for calm before speaking again. "What happened should not have happened. This you and I know. Changes will have to be made, some you will see, others you will not. Further details will follow. But before we send these brave fallen to their final resting place I ask of you now; will you fall into the dark?"

"No!" shouted the crowd.

"Will you bow before the corrupt?"

"No!"

"Will you allow the Empire to fall?"

"No!" the crowd screamed, myself among them.

The Emperor grinned wolfishly; his gaze almost predatory. "Then my friends, it is time to embrace change. For the Academy...

...The Academy is going to war."

# EPILOGUE
Present day

I looked into Cassius's eyes, hoping to see the clever and witty eyes of my friend looking back at me. My heart sank. They were there but there was none of the intelligence that I had just seen. His eyes were unfocused as though he was daydreaming.

I turned my gaze upon the Emperor. "What just happened?" I asked, my tone cold.

"Success happened," the Emperor rumbled tiredly. "If not the total victory that I had wanted. But a successful field test certainly."

"A field test?" I murmured. "Of what?"

Deep down I already knew the answer.

The Emperor brightened. "Of Cassius of course! You just witnessed the first successful attempt of a human able to wield the power of a full-fledged seraphim."

"Those things you did to him," I replied, my gorge rising. "It wasn't just to make him stronger; it was to make him more like you, wasn't it?"

"Precisely," he replied, eyes twinkling. "Other test subjects have failed somewhat...shall we say, explosively, in the past. I needed to reinforce Cassius in order for his body and mind to be able to wield my power. Sadly the restructuring of his brain had some unintended side effects but overall I would say it was a resounding success."

I shifted and suddenly Asp was at the Emperor's throat. "You're a monster. You trained me to kill monsters."

The man didn't even twitch, his smile completely unfazed. "Now Calidan, we've been down this road before. You know full well how this goes. Even if you did manage to mortally wound me, you know exactly what will happen. I'll be back on my feet in moments and somewhere down below something very dear to you will not be."

He held my gaze and I knew that he would happily let me cut his throat just to teach me a lesson. Slowly I backed away and sheathed Asp. "You're as bad as Charles," I snarled. "Just using us for your own fun and games."

The Emperor let out a full-throated laugh, his body shaking with humour. "You act surprised. You are beneath him. You are beneath me. The surviving seraphim, Charles excluded, led humanity out of the darkness. You are only here because of us. This empire, the empire before that and the one before that, all of it is because of us. I can end it on a whim."

"If you're so powerful then why did you even need Cassius?" I asked, unable to keep the almost whine out of my voice.

The Emperor shook his head. "Taking on a seraphim on his home turf is a dangerous business. I needed to surprise him, to change the game if you will. Now I can use Cassius as an extension of my own self with very little risk to me, when the need is there of course."

I held out a hand to Cassius and turned my back on the Emperor. "So you're a coward. I see." The smile didn't even waver on his face. "I'm going to fix what you've done to Cassius," I promised him over my shoulder as I began to walk away. "I'm going to save Seya. And I'm going to end you for what you've done. End you all."

His laughter followed me down the hall of his citadel, reverberating the walls with its mirth. "Honestly my boy, I wish you the best of luck. It would be the most interesting surprise. Take care of Cassius for me on your travels; I'll be watching."

\* \* \*

Charles swept up the ashes of Akzan. Her levels of seraph had been far too low after her prolonged stay in his facility to remotely have been able to face his wrath. He lost himself in the simple action; his body content to move whilst his mind worked on overdrive.

The Emperor had adapted, using his own tactics against him and he had nearly been caught napping. His mouth twisted in a dark smile. Surprises were so hard to come by at this stage of his life, he had nearly forgotten how much fun they could be. Time to change the game again.

# AUTHOR'S NOTE

Well...this was a long time in coming! For anyone who has been waiting with bated breath for the next adventure of Calidan and Seya, I apologise. To paraphrase Jeff Goldblum in Jurassic Park, 'Life, uh, got in the way.'

Even with life getting in the way, progress on the third book is well underway and I've also written a much longer fantasy novel called Draconis which will also be released this year, so hopefully that is something for you to look forward to.

Thank you so much for reading this book (and presumably the one before it...I can't imagine anyone making heads or tails of what is going on if they jumped in at this point), your support means a huge amount to me.

If you can spare a moment to leave a rating or, even better a review, you will make my day. They are the lifeblood of indie authors and without ratings these books tend to disappear into the murky waters of Amazon algorithms and so, in this instance, every little truly does help!

Until next time.

Made in the USA
Middletown, DE
25 March 2021